THE CHILDREN'S HOUR

Marcia Willett

CORGI BOOKS

THE CHILDREN'S HOUR
A CORGI BOOK: 0 552 15062 2

Originally published in Great Britain by Bantam Press,
a division of Transworld Publishers

PRINTING HISTORY
Bantam Press edition published 2003
Corgi edition pubished 2004

1 3 5 7 9 10 8 6 4 2

Copyright © Marcia Willett 2003

Set in 11/13pt New Baskerville by
Falcon Oast Graphic Art Ltd.

Corgi Books are published by Transworld Publishers,
61–63 Uxbridge Road, London W5 5SA,
a division of The Random House Group Ltd,
in Australia by Random House Australia (Pty) Ltd,
20 Alfred Street, Milsons Point, NSW 2061, Australia,
in New Zealand by Random House New Zealand Ltd,
18 Poland Road, Glenfield, Auckland 10, New Zealand
and in South Africa by Random House (Pty) Ltd,
Endulini, 5a Jubilee Road, Parktown 2193, South Africa.

Printed and bound in Germany by
GGP Media, Pößneck.

Papers used by Transworld Publishers are natural, recyclable
products made from wood grown in sustainable forests. The
manufacturing processes conform to the environmental
regulations of the country of origin.

To Dinah

CHAPTER ONE

Early autumn sunshine slanted through the open doorway in golden powdery bands of light. It glossed over the ancient settle, dazzled upon the large copper plate that stood on the oak table, and touched with gentle luminosity the faded silk colours of the big, square tapestry hanging on the wall beneath the gallery. A pair of short-legged gumboots, carelessly kicked off, stood just outside on the granite paving-slab and, abandoned on the worn cushion of the settle, a willow trug waited with its cargo of string, a pair of secateurs, an old trowel and twists of paper containing precious seeds.

The tranquil stillness was emphasized by the subdued churring of the crickets, their song just audible above the murmur of the stream. Soon the sun would slip away beyond the high shoulder of the cliff, rolling down towards the sea, and long shadows would creep across the lawn. It was five o'clock: the children's hour.

The wheelchair moved out of the shadows, the rubber tyres rolling softly across the cracked mosaic floor, pausing outside the drawing-room. The occupant sat quite still, head lowered, listening to voices more than sixty years old, seeing chintzes scuffed and snagged by small feet and sandal buckles, an embroidery frame with its half-worked scene . . .

Hush! Someone is telling a story. The children group about their mother: two bigger girls share the sofa with the baby propped between them; another lies upon her stomach on the floor, one raised foot kicking in the air – the only sign of barely suppressed energy – as she works at a jigsaw puzzle. Yet another child sits on a stool, close to her mother's chair, eager for the pictures that embellish the story.

' "*I'll tell you a story,*" said the Story Spinner, "*but you mustn't rustle too much, or cough or blow your nose more than is necessary . . . and you mustn't pull any more curl-papers out of your hair. And when I've done you must go to sleep at once.*" '

Their mother's voice is as cool and musical as the stream, and just as bewitching, so that the children are lulled, familiar lands dislimning and fading as they are drawn into another world: the world of make-believe, of once upon a time.

In the hall, outside the door, Nest's eyes were closed, picturing the once-familiar scene, her ears straining to hear the long-silent words, her fingers gripping the arms of her wheelchair. The telephone bell fractured the silence, breaking the

8

spell, a door opened and footsteps hurried along the passage. She raised her head, listening until, hearing the clang of the receiver in its rest, she turned her chair slowly so that she was able to survey the gallery. Her sister Mina came out onto the landing and stared down at her.

'At least the bell didn't wake you,' she said with relief. 'Were you going out into the garden? I could bring some tea to the summerhouse. It's still quite warm outside.'

'Who was it?' Nest was not deflected by the prospect of tea. Some deep note of warning had echoed in the silence, a feather-touch of fear had brushed her cheek, making her shiver. 'On the telephone. Was it Lyddie?'

'No, not Lyddie.' Mina's voice was bracingly cheerful, knowing how Nest was inclined to worry about the family's youngest niece. 'No, it was Helena.'

Their eldest sister's daughter had sounded uncharacteristically urgent – Helena was generally in strict control of her life – and Mina was beginning to feel a rising anxiety.

She passed along the gallery and descended the stairs. Her navy tartan trews were tucked into thick socks and her pine-green jersey was pulled and flecked with twigs. Silvery white hair fluffed about her head like a halo but her grey-green eyes were still youthful, despite their cage of fine lines. Three small white dogs scampered in her wake, their claws clattering, anxious lest they might be left behind.

'I've been pruning in the shrubbery,' she told Nest, 'and I suddenly realized how late it was getting so I came in to put the kettle on. But I got distracted looking for something upstairs.'

'I should love a cup of tea,' Nest realized that she must follow Mina's lead, 'but I think it's too late for the summerhouse. The sun will be gone. Anyway, it's too much fuss, carrying it all out. Let's have it in the drawing-room.'

'Good idea.' Mina was clearly relieved. 'I shan't be two minutes. The kettle must be boiling its head off.'

She hurried away across the hall, her socks whispering over the patterned tiles, the Sealyhams now running ahead, and Nest turned her chair and wheeled slowly into the drawing-room. It was a long narrow room with a fireplace at one end and a deep bay window at the other.

'Such a silly shape,' says Ambrose to his young wife when she inherits the house just after the Great War. 'Hardly any room to get around the fire.'

'Room enough for the two of us,' answers Lydia, who loves Ottercombe House almost as much as she loves her new, handsome husband. 'We shall be able to come down for holidays. Oh, darling, what heaven to be able to get out of London.'

It was their daughter, Mina, who, forty years later, rearranged the room, giving it a summer end and a winter end. Now, comfortable arm-chairs and a small sofa made a semicircle around the fire whilst a second, much larger, sofa, its high back to the rest of the room, faced into the garden. Nest paused beside the french window looking out to the terrace with its stone urns, where a profusion of red and yellow nasturtiums sprang up between the paving slabs and tumbled down the grassy bank to the lawn below.

'We'll be making toast on the fire soon.' Mina was putting the tray on the low table before the sofa, watched by attentive dogs. 'No, Boyo, sit down. Right down. *Good* boy. There's some cake left and I've brought the shortbread.'

Nest manoeuvred her chair into the space beside the sofa, shook her head at the offer of cake and accepted her tea gratefully. 'So what did our dear niece want?'

Mina sank into the deep cushions of the sofa, unable to postpone the moment of truth any longer. She did not look at Nest in her chair but gazed out of the window, beyond the garden, to the wooded sides of the steep cleave. Two of the dogs had already settled on their beanbags in the bay window but the third jumped onto the sofa and curled into a ball beside her mistress. Mina's hand moved gently over the warm, white back.

'She wanted to talk about Georgie,' she said. 'Helena says that she can't be trusted to live alone any longer. She's burned out two kettles in the last week and yesterday she went off for a walk and then couldn't remember where she was. Someone got hold of Helena at the office and she had to drop everything to go and sort her out. Poor old Georgie was very upset.'

'By getting lost or at the sight of her daughter?' Nest asked the question lightly – but she watched Mina carefully, knowing that something important was happening.

Mina chuckled. 'Helena does rather have that effect on people,' she admitted. 'The thing is that she and Rupert have decided that Georgie will have to go into a residential nursing home. They've been talking about it for a while and have found a really good one fairly locally. They can drive to it quite easily, so Helena says.'

'And what does Georgie say about it?'

'Quite a lot, apparently. If she has to give up her flat she can't see why she can't live with them. After all, it's a big place and both the children are abroad now. She's fighting it, naturally.'

'Naturally,' agreed Nest. 'Although, personally, if it came to a choice between living with Rupert and Helena or in a residential home I know which I'd choose. But why is Helena telephoning us about it? She doesn't usually keep us informed about our sister's activities. Not that Georgie is much of a communicator either. Not unless she has a problem, anyway.'

'I think Helena has tried quite hard to keep Georgie independent, and not just because it makes it easier for her and Rupert,' Mina was trying to be fair, 'but if she needs supervision they can't just leave her at their place alone. Anyway, the reason for her telephone call is to say that the home can't take Georgie just now, and would we have her here for a short stay?'

12

Nest thought: Why do I feel so fearful? Georgie's my sister. She's getting old. What's the matter with me?

She swallowed some tea and set the mug back in its saucer, cradling it on her knee, trying not to ask: 'How long is a "short stay"?'

'What did you tell Helena?' she asked instead.

'I said we'd talk it over,' answered Mina. 'After all, this is your home as much as mine. Do you think we could cope with Georgie for a month or two?'

A month or two. Nest battled with her sense of panic. 'Since it would be you who would be doing most of the coping,' she answered evasively, 'how do *you* feel about it?'

'I expect I could manage. What I feel is,' Mina paused, took a deep breath, 'or, at least, what I *think* I feel is that we should give it a try.' She looked at her sister. 'But I suspect that you're not happy about it.' She hesitated. 'Or frightened of it? Something, anyway.' She didn't press the point but stroked Polly Garter's head instead, crumbling a little of her shortcake and feeding her a tiny piece. Nogood Boyo was up from his beanbag in a flash, standing beside her, tail wagging hopefully. She passed him a crumb and in a moment all three dogs were beside her on the sofa.

'You're hopeless.' Nest watched her affectionately as Mina murmured to her darlings. 'Utterly hopeless. But, yes, you're right. I've been feeling odd all day. Hearing voices, remembering things. I have this presentiment that something awful

13

might happen. A hollow sensation in my stomach.' She laughed a little. 'But this is probably just a coincidence. After all, I can't think why poor old Georgie should be cast as a figure of doom, can you?'

She leaned forward to place her mug and saucer on the tray and then glanced at Mina, surprised at her lack of response. Her sister was staring into the garden, preoccupied, frowning slightly. For a brief moment she looked all of her seventy-four years, and Nest's anxiety deepened.

'Your expression isn't particularly reassuring,' she said. 'Is there something I don't know about Georgie after all these years?'

'No, no.' Mina recovered her composure. 'Let's have some more tea, shall we? No, I'm simply wondering if I can cope with Georgie, that's all. I'm only a year younger. Rather like the halt leading the blind, wouldn't you say?'

'No, I wouldn't,' answered Nest sharply, not particularly comforted by Mina's reply. 'You don't burn out kettles or go for walks and forget where you are.'

'Just as well.' Mina began to laugh. 'There wouldn't be anyone to find me up on Trentishoe Down.' A pause. 'What made you think it was Lyddie?'

'Lyddie?' Nest looked at her quickly. 'How d'you mean?'

'The phone call. You asked if it were Lyddie. Has she been part of this presentiment you've had all day?'

'No.' Nest shook her head, grimacing as she tried to puzzle it out. 'It's difficult to explain. More like a very strong awareness of the past, remembering scenes, that kind of thing.' She hesitated. 'Sometimes I'm not certain if it's what I actually *do* remember or if it's what I've been told. You were always telling me stories, interpreting the world for me. Giving people names of characters in books. Well, you still do that, of course.'

Mina smiled. 'Such fun,' she said, 'although a little bit tricky when you called Enid Goodenough "Lady Sneerwell" to her face. Poor Mama was horrified. I was praying that Enid hadn't a clue what you were talking about. Still, it was a sticky moment.'

'It was fright,' Nest excused herself, laughing at the memory, 'coming upon her unexpectedly after everything you'd said about her.'

'Lady Sneerwell and Sir Benjamin Backbite. What a poisonous pair the Goodenoughs were.' Other memories were connected with this thought and Mina bent to stroke Nogood Boyo, her face momentarily grim.

'I was remembering the stories,' Nest was saying, 'earlier when I was crossing the hall. I was thinking of us all down the years. Sitting on the sofa listening to *Naughty Sophia* and *Hans Brinker*, or the *Silver Skates*. Do you remember?'

'And *A Christmas Carol* on Christmas Eve while we decorated the tree. How could I forget? So. Not Lyddie, then?'

'Not particularly. At least, I don't think so.'

'Good.' Mina fed Captain Cat the final piece of shortbread and dusted the crumbs from her knees. 'So what do we do about Georgie? Are we up to it? Perhaps we should ask Lyddie what she thinks about it?'

'Why not? Let's clear up first, though.'

'Good idea. By then she'll have finished work for the day and we won't be interrupting her.' Mina put the tea things onto the tray and, with the dogs at her heels, crossed the hall to the kitchen, Nest wheeling more slowly behind her.

CHAPTER TWO

Lyddie made a final note on the typescript, fastened the sheets of the chapter into a paperclip and leaned both arms on the desk, hunching her narrow shoulders. Black silky hair, layered into a shiny mop, curved and flicked around her small, sweet face: ivory-skinned with a delicately pointed chin. Dressed warmly in a cloudy-soft mohair tunic, which reached almost to the knees of her moleskin jeans, nevertheless she was chilly. Her tiny study, the back bedroom, was cold, the light dying away, and she was longing for exercise. The large dog, crammed into the space between her desk and the door, raised his head to look at her.

'Your moment just might have come,' she told him. 'You just *might* get a walk. A quick one.'

The Bosun – a Bernese Mountain dog – stood up, tail waving expectantly, and Lyddie inched round her desk and bent to kiss him on the nose. He had been named, after consultation with her

Aunt Mina, for Byron's favourite dog, Boatswain, whose inscription on the monument to him at Newstead – '*beauty without vanity, strength without insolence, courage without ferocity, and all the virtues of Man without his vices*' – was particularly apt for his namesake, at least so Lyddie believed.

'You are very beautiful,' she told him, 'and good. Come on, then, and careful on the stairs. You nearly had us both down yesterday.'

They descended together and he waited patiently whilst she collected a long, warm, wool jacket and thrust her feet into suede ankle boots. As they walked through the narrow alleys and streets that led into the lanes behind Truro, Lyddie's attention was concentrated on keeping the Bosun under restraint until, freed at last from the restrictions of the town, he was released from the lead. She watched him dash ahead, smiling to herself at his exuberance, remembering the adorable fluffy puppy that had been waiting downstairs for her on the morning of her first wedding anniversary: a present from Liam.

'You need company,' he'd said, watching her ecstatic reaction with amusement. 'Working away up there, alone all day while I'm at the wine bar.'

It was just over two years since she'd given up her job as an editor with a major publishing house in London, married Liam and moved to Truro, to live in his small terraced house not far from the wine bar that he ran with his partner, Joe Carey. It was a trendy bar, near the cathedral, not sufficiently prosperous to employ enough staff to enable her and Liam to spend many evenings alone together. Usually he was at home for what he called the 'graveyard watch' – the dead hours between three o'clock and seven – but this week one of the staff was away on holiday and Liam was taking his shift. It made a very long day.

'Come in as soon as you've finished,' he'd said, 'otherwise I'll see nothing of you. Sorry, love, but it can't be helped.'

Oddly, she didn't object to going to The Place; sitting at the table reserved for staff in the little snug, watching the clients and joking with Joe; eating some supper and snatching moments with Liam.

'No fertilizer like the farmer's boots,' Liam would say. 'We have to be around for most of the time. The punters like it and the staff know where they are. It's the secret of its success even if it means irregular hours.'

She never minded, though. After the silence and concentration of a day's copy-editing she found the buzz in The Place just what she needed. Liam's passionate courtship had come as a delightful, confidence-boosting shock after a three-year relationship with a man who'd suddenly decided that he simply couldn't commit to the extent of he and Lyddie buying a house together or having children, and certainly not to marriage. James had accepted the offer of a job in New York and Lyddie had continued to live alone for nearly a year, until she'd met Liam, after which

19

her life had begun to change very rapidly. She'd missed her job and her friends, and the move had been a frightening rupture from all that she'd known, but she loved Liam far too much to question her decision – and her darling old aunts were not much more than two hours away, over on Exmoor.

Aunt Mina's call had caught her within ten minutes of finishing work but she'd let her believe that she was all done for the day. They were such a pair of sweeties, Mina and Nest, and so very dear to her, especially since the terrible car accident: her own parents killed outright and Aunt Nest crippled. Even now, ten years later, Lyddie felt the wrench of pain. She'd just celebrated her twenty-first birthday and been offered her first job in publishing. Struggling to learn the work, rushing down to Oxford to see Aunt Nest in the Radcliffe, dealing with the agony of loss and misery: none of it would have been possible without Aunt Mina.

Lyddie hunched into her jacket, pulling the collar about her chin, remembering. At weekends she'd stayed at the family home in Iffley with her older brother, Roger; but she and Roger had never been particularly close and it had needed Aunt Mina to supply the healing adhesive mix of love, sympathy and strength that bound them all together. In her own grief, Lyddie had sometimes forgotten that Aunt Mina was suffering too: her sister Henrietta dead, another sister crippled. How heavily she and Roger had leaned upon her: sunk too deeply in their own sorrow to consider hers. The small, pretty house had been left to them jointly and it was agreed that Roger, an academic like his father, should continue to live there until he could afford to buy Lyddie out. Until she'd met Liam, Lyddie had used the house as a retreat but, when Roger married Teresa, it was agreed that between them they could afford to raise a mortgage which, once it was in place, would give Lyddie the sum of one hundred and fifty thousand pounds.

Running the wine bar meant that she and Liam rarely managed to visit Oxford but Roger and Teresa had been to Truro for a brief holiday and, for the rest of the time, the four of them maintained a reasonable level of communication. Nevertheless, Lyddie felt faintly guilty that she and Liam had more fun with Joe and his girlfriend, Rosie – who worked at The Place – than they did with her brother and his wife.

'It's all that brain,' Liam had said cheerfully. 'Far too serious, poor loves. Difficult to have a really good laugh with a couple who take size nine in headgear. Roger's not too bad but dear old Teresa isn't exactly overburdened with a sense of humour, is she?'

Lyddie had been obliged to agree that she wasn't but felt the need to defend her brother.

'Roger can be a bit insensitive,' she'd said. 'He's generally a serious person but there's nothing prissy about him. At least he's not patronizing about other people having a good time.' She'd added quickly, 'Not that I'm implying that

Teresa . . .' and then paused, frowning, trying to be truthful without criticizing her sister-in-law.

Liam had watched her appreciatively. 'Careful, love,' he'd warned. 'You might just have to say something really unkind if you're not careful.'

She'd been embarrassed by his implication but Joe had intervened. They'd been sitting together in the snug and Joe, seeing her confusion, had aimed a cuff at Liam's head.

'Leave her alone,' he'd said, 'and get the girl a drink. Just because you can't understand true nobility of spirit when you see it . . .' and Liam, still grinning, had stood up and gone off to the bar, leaving Lyddie and Joe alone together.

As she paused to lean on a five-bar gate, watching the lights of the city pricking into the deepening twilight, Lyddie attempted to analyse her feelings for Joe. He was always very chivalrous towards her, unlike Liam's rough-and-tumble way of carrying on, and his evident admiration boosted her confidence which, because of Liam's popularity, could be slightly fragile. She'd been taken aback by the hostility she'd encountered from some of Liam's ex-girlfriends and it was clear that a few of them did not consider his marriage to be particularly significant. Two or three women continued to behave as if he were still their property: they obviously had no intention of changing their proprietorial habits and treated Lyddie as an intruder. Liam tended to shrug it off and she quickly learned not to expect any particular public support from him: they were married and, having made this statement, he expected her to be able to deal with these women sensibly. This was not quite as easy as it sounded. Apart from the fact that her confidence had been seriously damaged by James's departure, her husband was extraordinarily attractive – hair nearly as black as her own silky mop, knowing brown eyes, lean and tough – and he knew it. Without his presence The Place was a little less exciting, the atmosphere less intimate. He had an indefinable magic that embraced both sexes, so that men called him a 'great guy' whilst their women flirted with him. There was a sense of triumph at a table if he spent longer than usual talking and joking: the male would have a faintly self-congratulatory air – Liam didn't waste too much time on dullards – and the woman would preen a little, a small, secret smile on her lips, conscious of the other females' envious stares.

Joe's quiet, appreciative glance, his protectiveness, helped Lyddie to deal with the competition and she rather liked to hear Liam protesting against Joe's attentions. Of course, there was Rosie to consider. Lyddie had hoped that she and Rosie might become more intimate but, although she was friendly, Rosie had a touchy disposition, and a searching, calculating gaze that held Lyddie at arm's length. There might be several reasons for this: perhaps Rosie felt less secure in her relationship with Joe because of Lyddie's married status; maybe she slightly resented the special treatment that Joe, Liam and the other members of staff accorded Lyddie. At The Place, Rosie was one of the waitresses and that was all. Lyddie was careful never to respond too flirtatiously to Joe when Rosie was around but it was often hard, when Liam was chatting up an attractive female punter, not to restore her own self-esteem by behaving in a similar manner with Joe.

Lyddie turned away from the gate, called to the Bosun – who gazed reproachfully at her, as he always did, amazed and aggrieved that his fun should be cut short – and headed back towards the town, thinking about the Aunts. It seemed rather unfair of Helena to ask Aunt Mina to cope with her older sister for so long.

'Two months?' she'd repeated anxiously. 'It's an awfully long time, Aunt Mina, especially if she's being a bit dotty. I wish I could help but I'm booked up for the next six weeks . . .'

She could hear that Aunt Mina was battling with several emotions and so she'd tried to be practical, pointing out the obvious problems of dealing with an elderly and strong-minded woman – who was probably in the grips of dementia or Alzheimer's – with no help except limited assistance from another sister who was confined to a wheel-chair. At the same time, Lyddie was able to identify with Aunt Mina's need to help Georgie.

'She is our sister,' she'd said – and once again, Lyddie had remembered how, ten years before, Mina had had the strength to bear the horror not only of Nest's injuries but also of the death of their sister Henrietta.

Lyddie had swallowed down an onrush of sadness.

'You must do what you think is right,' she'd said, 'but do tell me if it gets tricky. Perhaps we could all club together for you to have some help if Helena and Rupert don't suggest it themselves. Or I could work at Ottercombe if necessary, you know.'

'I'm sure you could, my darling,' Mina had answered warmly, 'but we'll probably manage and it will be a change for us. Now, tell me about you. Is everything all right . . . ?'

'I'm fine,' she'd answered, 'absolutely fine. And Liam too . . .'

By the time they'd finished talking she'd had the feeling that Aunt Mina had already made up her mind about Georgie, and suspected that the telephone call had actually been to make certain that all was well with her niece in Truro rather than to seek advice. Lyddie was filled with a warm affection for her aunts; there was a toughness, an invincibility about them both. Nevertheless, a trip to Exmoor would put her mind at rest. Lyddie put the Bosun on his lead as they made their way back through the narrow streets, thinking now of the evening ahead, her spirits rising at the contemplation of supper at The Place with Liam and Joe.

Later, in the scullery at Ottercombe, Mina was clearing up after supper. The routine was gener-ally the same each evening: Mina prepared to wash up whilst Nest, sitting beside the draining-board, would wait, cloth in hand. Once dried, each item would be placed on the trolley next to her chair and, when it was all done, Mina would push the trolley into the kitchen whilst Nest went away to prepare for the remainder of the evening's entertainment: a game of Scrabble or backgammon at the gate-legged table, a favourite television programme, or a video of one of Mina's much-loved musicals. She had never lost her talent for reading aloud and books were another mainstay of their amusement. Their simple diet included not only the well-loved classics – Austen, Dickens, Trollope – but also Byatt, Gardam, Keane and Godden and was interleaved with travelogues, a thriller or *The Wind in the Willows*, depending on their mood. Lyddie occasionally brought along a current best-seller or the latest Carol Ann Duffy volume to liven up their appetites.

Mina dried her hands on the roller towel behind the scullery door and wheeled the trolley into the kitchen whilst the dogs continued to lick at their empty, well-polished bowls.

'You've finished it all,' she told them. 'Every last scrap.'

Polly Garter and Captain Cat pattered after her into the kitchen but Nogood Boyo remained, quartering the floor, just in case some morsel had been mislaid.

As she put the plates back on the dresser and slid knives and forks into the drawer, Mina was making plans for Georgie's arrival. Although she'd known almost immediately that this visit couldn't be avoided – how could she deny her own sister? – nevertheless, she was deeply unsettled by the thought of it. Her own anxieties about whether she could cope had been overshadowed by Nest's formless premonitions. Or were they formless? Every family had skeletons of one shape or another – and Georgie had always loved secrets. She'd used them as weapons over her siblings, to shore up her position as eldest, to make herself important.

'I know a secret' – a little singsong chant. Mina could hear it quite clearly. Her heart speeded and her hands were clumsy as she arranged the after-supper tray, lifted the boiling kettle from the hotplate of the Esse, made the tea. Was it possible that Georgie knew Nest's secret?

'Don't be more of an old fool than you can help.' She spoke aloud, to reassure herself, and the dogs pricked their ears, heads tilted hopefully.

If Georgie had suspected anything she would have spoken up long since. And, if she'd kept silent for more than thirty years, why should she speak now? Mina shook her head, shrugging away her foolish forebodings. It was Nest's fear that had infected her, bringing the past into the present. There was no need for all this silly panic. Yet, as she refilled the kettle, her heart ached suddenly with a strange, poignant longing for the past and she thought she heard her mother's voice reading from *A Shropshire Lad*: Housman's 'blue remembered hills'.

Mina stood quite still, her head bowed, still holding the kettle. The land of lost content: those happy, laughter-filled years. The tears had come much later . . . Presently she placed the kettle on the back of the stove and bent to caress the dogs, murmuring love-words to them until the moment passed and she was in command again. Picking up the tray, willing herself into calm, Mina went to find Nest.

CHAPTER THREE

Despite the games of backgammon, Mina's thoughts strayed back to the past; to those long-ago years with Papa away in London for much of the time so that the children had Mama all to themselves, reading to them, taking them to the beach, for excursions on the moors; the rules belonging to the smart London house relaxed into permanent holiday.

Mina is eight years old when her mother, Lydia, is sent down to Ottercombe for a long rest. The youngest child, Josephine – for Timmie and Nest are not yet born – has just had her fourth birthday and in the last three years there have been two miscarriages. Ambrose believes that the sea air will do Lydia good, strengthening her, so that she will be able to give him the son for which he craves.

'All these women!' he cries – but she hears the irritation rasping beneath the geniality and feels the tiny tick of fear deep inside her. She has had twelve years in which to discover the seam of cruelty buried deep in Ambrose's bluff good temper. He is not physically cruel – no, not that – but he uses language to prick and goad so that Lydia learns that a voice can be both instrument and weapon.

Her own voice is an instrument: pure, sweet, controlled. She sings to her babies, lulling them with nursery rhymes, and reads to them.

'All these books,' says Ambrose. 'Oh, for a boy to play a decent game of cricket.'

Ambrose is an attractive man; not much above average height, with brown curling hair, which is cut very short. His eyes are a bright, sparkling blue and he has an easy, confident approach which makes people, at first, feel very comfortable with him. It is he who names the children: Georgiana, Wilhelmina, Henrietta, Josephine. Only later does Lydia understand that these lovely names are part of his strange humour, related to his frustration at being the father of girls. He is not the type of man to be interested in babies, and she thinks it is just a joke when he asks after George or Will, but, as they grow, the joke wears thin. She hates to hear her pretty daughters addressed as George, Will, Henry and Jo but he does not relent.

'Don't be so sensitive, darling,' he says, the blue eyes a little harder now, less sparkling, as they look at her; she tells herself that she must be careful not to irritate him, and that it's simply, like most men, he longs for a son. She feels inadequate, as if she is failing him, and hopes for another child to follow Josephine; a little boy, this time. After her first miscarriage Lydia begins to suffer asthma attacks and during the winter of 1932, so as to avoid the London fog, she is despatched to Ottercombe. She cannot quite believe her luck. Since a child, Exmoor has been her idea of paradise and, although Ambrose has consented to summer breaks in the old house at the head of the cleave, he does not like to leave her behind when he returns to London. He is a senior civil servant and his delightful wife is a great asset to him. Lydia is beautiful, popular – and useful. So she is deeply touched when he announces that he is prepared to manage without her for as long as is necessary. Her health, however, is not the only reason for Ambrose's unexpected attack of philanthropy. Ambrose has made a new friend, a wealthy widow whose robust appetites and tough ambition match his own, and he seizes this opportunity to know her better.

He is too clever, though, to rouse Lydia's suspicions, and he makes certain that – by the time the party is due to set out for the South-west – she feels too guilty at leaving him to think of her husband with anything but gratitude. He drives them himself, in his handsome, much-cherished Citroën, and settles them at Ottercombe. The young local couple, who are glad to earn extra money to caretake the house, are given instructions to shop and clean and care for Lydia and her children so that the following morning, when Ambrose drives away, his thoughts are all directed towards a certain house in St John's Wood.

As the sound of the engine dies in the distance, Lydia gives a great sigh of relief. Her children run shouting and laughing on the lawn and Wilhelmina tugs at her arm.

'May we go to the beach, Mama? If we wrap up warmly?'

Lydia bends to hug her. 'Of course we shall. After lunch. Afternoons are the best times for the beach, even in the winter.'

'And we'll come back and have tea by the fire, won't we? Will you read to us?'

'Yes, my darling, if that's what you'd all like. I'll read to you.'

So it begins.

In her bedroom, which had once been the morning-room, Nest was very nearly ready for bed. The room, adapted for her needs, was austere, simple and unadorned, no roads back to the past by way of photographs or knick-knacks; no idiosyncrasies by which to be interpreted; no possessions with which she might be defined. Only necessities stood on the small oak chest, although several books were piled upon the bedside table along with her Walkman. She was able to stand for short periods, to haul herself along using furniture and her stick as aids, but she tired quickly and the pain was always there, ready to remind her that she was severely limited. At first, in the dark months immediately following the accident, she hadn't wanted to move at all. Suffering was a penance for her guilt. She'd lie on her bed, staring at the ceiling above, reliving the appalling moment: Henrietta at the wheel, Connor beside her, head half-turned to Nest in the back seat. If only she hadn't spoken, hadn't cried out in frustration, maybe Henrietta wouldn't have been distracted for that brief, vital, tragic moment.

It was Mina who had propelled Nest back into life, both physically and emotionally; bullying her into her wheelchair so as to push her into the garden, manhandling Nest and her chair into the specially adapted motor caravan, forcing her to live.

'I can't,' she'd mumbled. 'Please, Mina. I don't want to see anyone. Try to understand. I have no right . . .'

'Not even the deaths of Henrietta and Connor give you an excuse to wall yourself up alive. Anyway, Lyddie needs you . . .'

'No!' she'd said, straining back in her chair, head turned aside from Mina's implacability. 'No! Don't you see? I *killed* them.'

'Lyddie and Roger know only that Henrietta misjudged the bend, not why. They need you.'

Lyddie's love and sympathy had been the hardest burden to bear.

'I think you'll find,' Mina had said much later, 'that living and loving will be just as cruel as self-imposed seclusion could ever be. You'll be punished quite enough – if that's what you want.'

So Nest had given herself up to life as best she

could, withholding nothing, accepting everything – nearly everything. She still refused to allow Mina to push her down to the sea. The sea was the symbol of freedom, of holiday; the reward after the long trek from London. Oh, the smell of it; its cool, silky embrace on hot hands and feet; its continuous movement, restless yet soothing.

Now, as she lay at last in bed, exhausted by the exertions of getting there, she could picture the path to the sea. Here, between Blackstone Point and Heddon's Mouth, the steep-sided cleave, thickly wooded with scrub oak, beech and larch, cuts a deep notch into the cliff. At the head of the cleave, a quarter of a mile from the sea, stands Ottercombe House, sheltered and remote in its wild, exotic garden. A rocky path, stepped with roots, runs beside the stream which rises on Exmoor, on Trentishoe Down. A tiny spring at first, it gathers speed, trickling from the heights, spilling down the rock-face in a little waterfall behind the house, welling through the culvert in the garden and pouring along the narrow valley until, finally, it plunges into the sea.

Her eyes closed, Nest could picture each bend in the path to the beach; she could see the rhododendrons flourishing, despite the shallow covering of soil over the rocks: those Morte Slates, which run in a narrow band from Morte Point, across Devon and into Somerset. In early May drifts of bluebells grow beneath the terraces of trees, a cerulean lake of falling, flowing colour. In August, when the heather is in flower, the shoulders of the moor, which hunches above even the highest trees, shimmers bluish-purple in the afternoon sun. The path itself holds tiny seasonal treasures: bright green ferns, a clump of snowdrops, yellow-backed snails. How the children dawdle, postponing that delicious moment when they can at last see the sea; the cleave widening out as if to embrace the crescent-shaped beach, the cliff walls descending steeply into the grey waters. The stream, which has been beside them all the way, tumbles into a deeply shelving, rocky pool and then travels on, carving a track across the shaly sand until it is lost in the cold waters of the Bristol Channel.

Nest and her brother, Timmie, learn to swim in the rock pool; they paddle there too, with shrimping nets and bright, shiny tin buckets, and share a passion for the wildlife on this rock-bound coast.

'We'll live here together when we grow up,' he tells her, his cold sandy hand clutching the handle of his bucket, which contains a crab and two minute shrimps.

'But who will look after us?' The youngest of the family, it is beyond Nest's experience that she might one day do this for herself.

'Mina will,' he answers confidently. Nine years older than he, Mina at fourteen seems already adult.

'Yes,' she agrees contentedly. 'Mina will look after us.'

Stirring restlessly, Nest recalled this prophecy. Mina had, indeed, looked after her – and now she must look after Georgie too. Panic fluttered just below Nest's ribs, her fears returning – bringing memories with them – and she groaned. Sleep would elude her now, and she would become prey to those night-time terrors that left her exhausted and ill – but there was a tried-and-tested remedy at hand. She hauled herself up against the pillow, switched on the bedside light and reached for Bruce Chatwin's *In Patagonia*.

In her bedroom upstairs, Mina was pottering happily. The dogs, curled ready for sleep in their baskets, watched her as she moved about, their ears cocked as she murmured to them, a quiet monotone – 'Good dogs, good little persons. There then, settle down now, and we shall have a lovely walk tomorrow, won't we? Who's my baby, then? Who's a good Boyo?' – and then that little exhalation, an explosion of air escaping from her lips in a descending scale, 'po-po-po', as she paused for a moment to brush her silky white hair.

This room, which had once been her mother's bedroom, was a complete antithesis to Nest's cell. Here, freed briefly from the necessary disciplines of nearly a lifetime of caring first for her mother and then for Nest, Mina allowed her passion for vivid, visual drama full rein and, glad to see her creating something of her own, various members of the family had contributed by bringing her presents: prints, silk cushions, ornaments, even small pieces of furniture. Mina received them with delight and made haste to find homes for them.

The walls were crammed with images – Klimt's *The Three Stages of Life* and *The Kiss* next to Paul Colin's *Là Revue Nègre* poster – whilst a set of prints depicting what Mina thought of as Jack Vettriano's gangster world hung beside Jackson Pollock's silk-screened *Summer Time*. A *chaise-longue*, draped with silky shawls and loaded with cushions, reposed beneath the window facing a Lombok tallboy, exquisitely painted with exotic birds, which stood against the opposite wall beside a bucket-shaped cane chair. Odd, fascinating objects jostled on every polished surface: photographs in a variety of pretty frames, a pair of Chinese *cloisonné* vases, a charming set of amusing papier mâché ducks. A puppet, long-limbed, was suspended from a hook, his clever magician's face lit by the gentle light of an elegant brass lamp with a tulip shade made of blue glass.

The room brimmed with colour. A velvet throw covered the deep, high double bed, its jewel colours – amethyst, sapphire and ruby – repeated in the long, heavy curtains, and three long shelves creaked with books, stacked and piled together, old-fashioned, elegant leather jackets residing happily alongside modern, cracked, paper spines. A thick, plain grey carpet was almost completely covered by beautiful, ancient rugs and a high, lacquered screen half-hid the alcove in the far corner.

After the glowing, extravagant display of textures and tints, the starkness of the small alcove was a shock to the unprepared. A simple shelf, containing a computer monitor with a keyboard and a printer, ran the length of the wall, a typist's swivel chair beside it. There was nothing here to distract from the simple, working atmosphere. Mina came around the screen, switched on the computer and sat down, humming beneath her breath. Connected to the world by means of the Internet, she settled happily, still humming, pulling her long fleecy robe more cosily around her knees whilst the screen scrolled and flickered. She typed in her password and waited, watching eagerly, her grey-green eyes focused and intent. She was rewarded at last: 'You have four unread messages.' The mouse moved busily, covering and clicking. With a sigh of pleasure Mina began to open her mail.

CHAPTER FOUR

When Lyddie woke, Liam was already up. She could hear him in the bathroom, whistling beneath his breath, as he ran hot water for his shave. Stretching out across the bed, pulling the pillows about her, she lay contentedly – half waking, half dreaming – until a gush of water in the wastepipe and a closing door announced Liam's presence.

'Not *still* asleep?' He sighed, shaking his head as he dragged on jeans and a sweatshirt. 'And me thinking that you'd be downstairs getting the coffee on. That poor dog will be crossing his legs, I should imagine.'

'You've let him out already. *And* had some coffee.' She was unmoved, too comfortable to feel guilty. 'What's the time?'

'Ten to eight. Of course, it's all very well for those of us who work at home . . .'

'Oh, shut up,' she said lazily. 'You'd hate to work at home. You can't go half an hour without needing to speak to someone.'

'Just as well in my job,' he answered cheerfully. He bent to peer at himself in the glass on the small pine chest, whistling again beneath his breath as he dragged a comb through his thick, dark hair.

'Who's opening up today?' she asked, hands behind her head, watching him appreciatively. 'Isn't it Joe's turn?'

'It is, indeed. A nice slow start for us, although I need to go to the bank.' He turned to look at her, catching her glance and smiling to himself. 'You look very beautiful, lying there.' He bent over her, kissing her lightly, and she put her arms about him, pulling him down, so that he was half kneeling, half lying. 'And to think,' he murmured in her ear, 'if it hadn't been for that damn dog of yours, I wouldn't be up at all. And you feeling sexy this morning. Isn't it just my luck?'

She chuckled, releasing him. 'You don't do too badly. A doting wife and all that adulation from your female customers.' She was learning that a light touch earned approval. 'Most men would kill for the amount of attention you get.'

'Ah, there's safety in numbers,' he told her, kneeling back on his heels. 'And what about you and Joe, if it comes to that, canoodling together in the snug while I'm working like a dog? What do you talk about, the two of you?'

'Joe's nice.' There was a sweetness in the knowledge that he'd noticed. 'He's great company. He talks about things that you find boring, like books and films. We discuss the plots and relationships, how they work and why, and he gets right into the characters so that it's like talking about real people. He's compassionate too: he doesn't mock at their weaknesses like you do.'

'Ah, that's just his way of chatting you up, cunning fellow that he is. You'll need to watch yourself, I can see that. But he doesn't make you laugh the way I can.'

'No,' she admitted, almost reluctantly, a tiny frown appearing, 'no, he doesn't, but then he doesn't flirt like you do, either . . .'

He kissed the rest of the sentence away – until she forgot Joe entirely and the frown was smoothed into delight – and then carefully, gently, detached himself. She clung briefly, though instinct warned her against any show of possessiveness, and sighing regretfully, she pushed back the duvet, running her hands through her black hair.

'Make me some coffee while I have a shower, would you, Liam? Tell the Bosun I'm on my way.'

'I'll do that.' He hesitated, watching her thoughtfully. 'If you were quick we could drive out to Malpas and give him a walk along the river. It's a fantastic morning. Would you like that?'

'Oh, I'd love it.' Her face was bright with anticipation. 'And so would he. Are you sure?'

He shrugged. 'Sure I'm sure. Joe can manage without me for an hour or so. It doesn't get really busy until around midday and we'll be back long before then.'

'I'll be five minutes,' she promised. 'Well, ten.'

She fled along the passage to the bathroom and Liam went downstairs, frowning a little, to tell the Bosun about the treat in store for him.

'It's a glorious morning.' Mina opened the kitchen door to let the dogs out into the freedom of the garden. 'How about a little trip in the camper?' She stood watching Nogood Boyo quartering the ground below the bird-table whilst Polly Garter sat down on a mossy flagstone to scratch vigorously at an ear. The little yard was full of morning sunshine, glinting on tiny ferns and the round-leaved pennywort growing in the cracks of the cliff, which rose sheer as a wall behind the house.

Nest, eating a Victoria plum from the orchard, turned her chair from the breakfast table and looked out.

'We could go to the Fuchsia Valley,' suggested Mina, 'and have some coffee. Or the Hunter's Inn. Or over the moor to Simonsbath.'

'Simonsbath,' said Nest, dropping the plum stone into her cereal bowl and licking her fingers appreciatively. 'It's just the morning for a drive across the moor.'

'We could take the whole day off,' offered Mina. 'Coffee at Simonsbath, on to Dunster and back over Countisbury. We might as well make the most of it.'

She didn't add 'before Georgie arrives' but it was implicit in the glance the sisters exchanged.

'Did you manage to get through to Helena just

now?' Nest asked, trying to sound casual, almost indifferent.

'Yes.' Mina was now peering out of the door. 'Yes, I did. She was very relieved. And grateful. They're bringing Georgie down on Saturday.'

'On *Saturday*?' Nest exclaimed. 'Good grief! They're not wasting any time.'

Mina turned to face her: she looked uncomfortable. 'It seems they have the opportunity to sell her flat, d'you see? They didn't want to miss the opportunity.'

'I don't believe it. My goodness, they don't hang about, do they?' Nest began to laugh. 'I hope Georgie has agreed. They've got it all worked out, by the sound of it.'

'They need the money from the flat, so Helena says, to fund the nursing home.' Mina, as usual, was trying to be fair. 'They want her to have the best.'

'Sure they do!' said Nest drily. 'And what if we couldn't have had her here?'

Mina shrugged. 'They'd have thought of something else, I expect.' She still looked unhappy. 'I suppose I shouldn't have been quite so available but, after all—'

'Don't be silly,' said Nest quickly. 'I'm sure we're doing the right thing. It just irks me that whenever Helena and Rupert dish the dirt they always come up smelling of roses. But that's because I'm a cow. There's nowhere else for her to go, poor old Georgie.'

Mina was silent for a moment. She knew that

Helena had also contacted her cousin Jack, their brother Timmie's son, asking if he and his wife, Hannah, could take Georgie in, if necessary. Mina knew that Nest would disapprove of this but she suspected that the truth would out before too long – Jack was very fond of his two aunts and in constant contact – and she decided that Nest might as well know at once.

'Actually, I had an e-mail from Jack last night saying that Helena had been in touch,' she admitted. 'If we'd refused she was going to ask him if he and Hannah could cope.'

'You must be joking?' Nest was incredulous. 'I should have thought that those two have quite enough on their plates already. They've just started a new term with a houseful of boys to organize, as well as two children of their own. I can just see Georgie in the middle of a boys' preparatory school. The mind boggles.'

'Jack would have done it,' said Mina, smiling a little.

'Jack would do anything for anyone. He's Timmie's son. And Hannah, bless her, would go along with it.'

'He was anxious about us managing. Goodness, I don't know what we'd do without that boy. Or without Hannah, for that matter. And then there's Lyddie, always in touch and worrying about us. How blessed we are.'

'It's odd, isn't it,' began Nest slowly, 'that we don't have that same sense of . . .' she hesitated, feeling for the right word, '*satisfaction* about

Lyddie and Liam that we have about Jack and Hannah.'

'Liam's great fun,' said Mina quickly, 'and terribly attractive . . .'

'But?' prompted Nest. 'There has to be a "but" after that.'

'But it's as if Lyddie feels that she needs to live up to him. Of course, she was knocked sideways when James left her and I sense that she's vulnerable with Liam, as if she's afraid that it might happen again if she's not careful. I feel a kind of wariness on Lyddie's side. There's no . . .' this time it was Mina searching for a word, 'no *serenity*. Not like there is between Jack and Hannah. I hope she doesn't do something silly.'

'What sort of thing?' Nest looked anxious.

'Oh, I'm being an old fool.' Mina tried to shrug away her imaginings. 'I was just remembering when we went to Truro and had lunch with them at The Place. I thought that she and Joe were very friendly together. She seems quite at ease with him, there's no tension and she can be herself, but I had the feeling that Liam didn't care for it.'

'Joe and Liam have been friends since school,' said Nest, trying to reassure herself as well as Mina. 'I can't believe that Joe—'

'No, of course not. I told you, I'm being foolish. We're both on edge at the prospect of coping with Georgie.'

'I've had a thought.' Nest was smiling. 'Why don't we invite Jack down whilst Georgie's here? He'll sort us all out.'

Mina began to chuckle. 'That's quite an idea. It's term-time, of course . . .'

'I know it is, but he and Hannah and the children could probably manage an exeat weekend or a visit during half-term.'

'Dear Jack. So like his father. Oh, poor old Timmie.' She gave a great sigh. '*How* I still miss him!'

'I never wanted him to be a soldier,' Nest said almost angrily. 'I remember pleading with Mama about it. She said, "He would be unhappy doing anything else," but then she never imagined what would happen in Northern Ireland.' Her face was bleak. 'I often imagine—' She broke off in distress. 'At least he can't have known anything about it.'

'He was such a tower of strength,' said Mina gently, 'although in a very quiet way. It can't have been easy being the only boy amongst five girls.'

'Papa must have been delighted,' said Nest, 'when Timmie turned up. And Mama too, of course. I must have been a bit of a disappointment coming after him. Another girl . . .' A tiny silence. 'Anyway, I'll go and get myself ready. Can you manage with the breakfast things?'

'Of course I can,' said Mina. 'This won't take a moment. Away you go. And of course you weren't a disappointment. Of *course* you weren't.'

She watched Nest wheel across the hall, thinking of the secrets kept for so many years – and Georgie's singsong chant: 'I know a secret. Can you guess? We've got a little brother. Do you think Papa will love us any more?'

Piling the plates beside the sink in the scullery, calling to the dogs, Mina found herself thinking of that year before Timmie was born, the year that Timothy Lestrange first arrived at Ottercombe House.

During that year of 1932, Lydia and the children spend only the school term-time in London. When Ambrose arrives early in August for the summer break he has a tall, fair-haired stranger with him.

'This is Timothy Lestrange, darling. One of my oldest friends. He was halfway up some un-pronounceable mountain when we got married and he's been abroad for most of the time since.'

Lydia, smiling at Timothy, taking his hand, senses at once that he is an ally. The apprehension she always feels when Ambrose is due at Ottercombe is dissipated by an inexplicable relief.

'Ambrose insisted that I would be welcome,' he says, holding her hand in his own warm brown one. 'I apologize for arriving unannounced.'

'He turned up last night,' says Ambrose, 'due for a long leave. We haven't seen each other for years. I couldn't just give him a drink and say goodbye, could I?'

'Of course you couldn't,' agrees Lydia.

'I explained that there's no telephone here so we weren't able to warn you.' Ambrose airs an old grievance. 'In fact there's not much here at all.'

'Not much?' Timothy's eyebrows are raised. 'Only glorious countryside, a lovely old house and your wife and children. Oh, no, not much.'

'Oh, well, if you put it like that . . . Where are the bandar-log, Lydia?'

Ambrose is a great Kipling fan and Lydia and Timothy exchange another smile.

'The children are down at the sea. They'll be home for tea quite soon. Would you like to bring your luggage in while I make the guest-room ready?'

She watches them go out into the sunshine, standing for a moment to relish this new strange joyfulness, and then hurries away upstairs.

The children immediately respond to Timothy's warmth; their father is less abrasive in his company, less critical, and instinctively they know that it is to Timothy that they owe this respite. He smooths away irritation and draws the sting from the genial brutality of Ambrose's remarks. It is Timothy who renames the children and so earns Lydia's gratitude.

'Here they are,' says Ambrose, as the children straggle up from the beach, 'here are the bandar-log. This is the eldest, George. Then Will and Henry. And this is the youngest, Jo.'

Timothy shakes hands gravely with each child. 'But why such names?' he asks, puzzled. 'Such pretty children and so like their mother. Why boys' names?'

'Next best thing to having sons,' says Ambrose bluffly – and Lydia turns her head away, biting her lip, shepherding the children into tea.

Timothy sees how she is hurt and gradually, as

he talks to the children and plays with them, he softens George into Georgie, renames Will as Mina, Jo becomes Josie – but Henry . . . 'is Henrietta', says Lydia, 'because nothing else quite works'.

'I like my proper name,' says five-year-old Henrietta firmly. 'It's a nice name.'

The others, meanwhile, are enchanted with their new names and, made bold by Timothy's championship, refuse to answer their father if he doesn't use them. Even Georgie, who craves her father's love and approval, is affected by Timothy's quiet charm.

'Mutiny,' says Ambrose, slapping Timothy on the back. 'Mutiny in my own home,' but he too accepts the change although he doesn't always remember without prompting.

'Timothy is nice, isn't he, Mama?' says Mina. 'He's like a very kind magician. Like Merlin.' Lydia is reading T. H. White's *The Once and Future King* to them after tea during the children's hour. 'He's put a spell on all of us, hasn't he?'

And Lydia, dreamy-eyed, answers, 'Yes, my love, I think he has.'

'Don't ask him what he does,' instructs Ambrose, as they change for dinner that first evening. 'It's all a bit hush-hush. He does all this exploring and so on but, in fact, he's attached to the army. He'll tell you a few yarns, I expect. Hell of a chap. Crazy, though. Won everything going at school but took it all in his stride.'

'He doesn't seem that kind of man,' says Lydia,

putting in her ear-rings, staring at herself critically in the glass. Her black hair, piled high, emphasizes the pale oval of her face and long creamy neck. Her eyes glow with a new, disturbing happiness. 'He's not at all the overgrown schoolboy, adventurer type.'

'Timothy was always a law unto himself,' answers Ambrose proudly – as if he has invented Timothy and is personally responsible for his unusual qualities. 'He was terrifically popular.'

'Yes,' says Lydia, smiling secretly at her reflection. 'Yes, I can believe that.'

As the weeks pass, Timothy becomes part of the family; yarning with Ambrose in his study; walking with Lydia in the woods; playing with the children on the beach. Lydia blossoms into radiant health, Ambrose loses his city pallor, growing bronzed and fit, and the children are happy and at ease.

'He should be called Kim,' says Mina – they have moved on to Kipling by now – 'not Tim. Kim, the Little Friend of all the World. Only he's a big friend.'

By the time the holidays are over, and Ambrose and Timothy return to London, Lydia is pregnant again.

CHAPTER FIVE

Mina wakened to a gripping, formless panic. The bedroom, which faced east and south, was already filled with early sunshine and she lay for some moments, breathing deeply, watching the shift of light and shade on the wall. Slowly, this nameless terror formed and shaped itself into very real problems. As she grew older her natural optimism was becoming prey to the fears of encroaching infirmity: for how much longer would she remain fit and strong enough to look after Nest? Resolutely, and with an enormous effort, she turned her thoughts into happier, more positive channels and presently the anxiety attack passed. She sat up, reaching for her dressing-gown, murmuring to the dogs, who stirred in their baskets, watching with bright eyes.

'Shall we go downstairs, my darlings? Shall we? A cup of tea for me and perhaps a biccy for you? Would you like that? Yes, you shall have one, Boyo. And you too, old lady. Come along, then.'

She passed along the galleried landing, humming to herself, the dogs at her heels; on down the wide, shallow stairs and into the kitchen. Like the drawing-room, the kitchen was long and narrow: the working half, with the Esse and white-painted shelves and cupboards, had a door to the scullery, but the other half was a cheerful, cosy area. The square pine table was set beneath the window and a wicker chair stood beside the glass-paned door, which opened into the little courtyard. There were bookshelves here, and photographs in assorted frames stood on the windowsill alongside a blue china pot of tiny cyclamen. The whole space had been arranged to accommodate Nest's wheelchair without sacrificing the comfortable, intimate atmosphere that Mina had created in the latter years of her mother's life.

'Just right for two, but for *three* . . . ?' wondered Mina anxiously – and then pulled herself together.

There was plenty of room for Georgie; it was simply that there hadn't been more than two people living in the house for more than forty years and, naturally, some adjustments would have to be made.

'And it's only for a short while,' she said aloud, opening the door so that the dogs might go outside. 'A little holiday. It'll be fun.'

The dogs disappeared into the wild, exciting garden beyond the courtyard and Mina filled the kettle and put it on the Esse, her remark hanging rather forlornly in the silence. With the tiny, explosive 'po-po-po' escaping her lips, after tying her dressing-gown more tightly round her spare frame, she took the scissors from a selection of utensils in an old Kilner jar and cut a few grapes from the bunch in the fruit bowl. She sliced them carefully into halves, collected together some pieces of bread and went outside to feed the birds. She crumbled the bread on to the bird-table and checked that the feeders were full of nuts and seed, but the pieces of grape she scattered carefully amongst the rocks of the alpine garden which, long ago, Lydia had made.

Captain Cat was the first back, hoping for his biscuit, and Mina took a handful from the box and carried them to the door. Nogood Boyo arrived as if by magic but Mina waited until old Polly Garter came pottering into the courtyard before she rationed the biscuits out: two each and a pat and a murmuring of love for the three of them.

She took her mug of tea, turned the wicker chair so that it stood in the sun and, sipping gratefully, watched for the blackbird. The dogs scrunched their biscuits, Nogood Boyo finishing first and watching hopefully in case the other two should leave a crumb. Captain Cat warned him off with a throaty rumble but Polly Garter, mother and grandmother, allowed him to edge in close for a neglected morsel.

Mina smiled as she watched them and murmured: 'You'd be a *good* Boyo, if anyone would let you!'

The blackbird came running amongst the rocks, dark as a shadow, with only his yellow beak to give him away. The dogs, grooming themselves in the sunshine, didn't see him find his breakfast amongst the parahebe's last pale blooms, sheltering beneath the branched stems and drooping red flowers of the zauschneria as he pecked the sweet, delicious fruit. It was his mate, hopping over the rocks, scattering sparkling, flashing drops of dew from the feathery blue leaves of the juniper, who chased him away.

The bird-table was alive with movement and colour: the flick of tiny wings, a rippling of gold and blue, smooth-feathered heads darting and pecking. Mina finished her tea but continued to watch, dreaming and remembering in the sun.

It is Timothy who encourages the building of the rock-garden. In the days long before tubs and pot-plants, the courtyard is a rather dreary place with its rock wall and mossy flagstones. Lydia likes to cook, to grow herbs beside the kitchen door, and Timothy shows how she could build a miniature garden full of colour to delight her as she works. Ambrose is smilingly tolerant of anything that Timothy suggests and waves them off to search for appropriate plants at nurseries in Ilfracombe and Barnstaple.

Georgie and Mina struggle through the garden carrying between them shapely rocks, and even Henrietta toils back from the beach with pretty stones in her bucket. The rock-garden becomes the main topic of conversation, the pinnacle of endeavour, whilst seed catalogues and reference books litter the morning-room table, varieties of plants ringed with circles of red ink. After tea, as Lydia sews, and Henrietta and Josie crayon busily and inaccurately in their colouring books, Timothy tells stories of travelling in the Pyrenees and the Alps, describing the flowers he has seen, and throwing in a few bandits for the sake of Mina, who listens round-eyed. Georgie sits ostentatiously on her father's knee whilst Ambrose continues to smile paternalistically upon the whole group.

Later, when Lydia and the children are alone again, strange packages arrive: rare and pretty plants from other countries, destined for the rock-garden. As the child grows within her, Lydia sings and plays with her daughters and waits for the spring when the white-bloomed hutchinsia will flower along with the yellow euryops daisy from South Africa. In the winter evenings, with the children tucked in bed, she takes the letters from her sewing-box: sheets of thin, flimsy paper, in blue-lined envelopes bearing exciting foreign stamps, covered with a looping, inky scrawl. A rosy glow from the oil lamp's glass bowl, the crackling of wood in the grate, some stems of winter jasmine in a green vase, these inform the moment of intimacy as she shares her lover's adventures, his fears, and the precious outpourings of love.

In the light early evenings of a cold sweet spring, the lazy broken fluting of the blackbird's song fills her with a poignant restlessness and, after the children's hour, to their delight, she wraps them in warm clothes and takes them down to the beach. The sea's surging song, as it sweeps across the ridged and buckled sand, calms her longing and quietens her need. She watches her children play but her thoughts are far away. Georgie and Mina have races, drawing the finishing line with a sharp stone, choosing a certain rock as an excellent starting post. The wet sand flies up under their hard little feet as they run, heads down, legs pumping.

'I won!' cries Georgie boastfully. 'Did you see me, Mama? I was first.'

Mina doubles up breathlessly, bundling her flying black hair into an elastic band, and Lydia waves to them, laughing, holding her hands high to clap lightly, as she keeps an eye on Josie scrambling beside the rock pool. She knows that Georgie cheats and so it is Mina whom she holds for an extra second or two when they come running across the beach for a hug. Henrietta shows them her basket of shells and stones and, as the moon rises, netted and held in the bare branches of the trees up on the steep cleave, they gather their belongings and set off for home in the gathering twilight. Moths flit beneath the trees as bats dart and swoop above their heads, causing Henrietta to scream.

'Don't be silly,' says Georgie, copying Papa's patronizing tone. 'They won't hurt you,' but Henrietta clings to Mama's hand. She rather enjoys screaming, it excites her, and she usually ignores Georgie's admonitions, resisting her oldest sister's self-assumed role as Papa's deputy, intuitively guessing that Mama doesn't approve of it. She screams again, just to make her point, and then jumps along cheerfully, still holding to Lydia's hand.

'Tired,' says Josie, sitting down suddenly amongst the ferns beside the stream. 'Carry.'

'Oh, darling,' says Lydia anxiously. 'Can you manage just a few more steps?' She is weary too, and Josie is heavy. Lydia is fearful of losing the child within her, which she has managed – so far – to carry so successfully. 'We're very nearly home. *Do* try, darling.'

'Tired,' whimpers Josie, beginning to grizzle, refusing to budge, and it is Mina who hauls her up into her arms and staggers along with her. Josie, good-humour fully restored, beams down triumphantly upon Henrietta, who puts out her tongue.

Soon, even the walk to the sea is too much for Lydia and she is confined to the garden and the house. Jenna, the young woman who helps to shop and clean, cycles over to Ottercombe most days to assist with the younger children whilst Georgie and Mina are at the local school. One morning, soon after the Easter holidays have begun, Lydia doesn't get up at all; messages are sent to London and the doctor calls in his small, black Ford.

'I know a secret.' Georgie sidles behind Mina,

an eye on Jenna, who is spreading a picnic lunch on the rocks. Henrietta helps her to weight down the cloth with stones whilst Josie peeps hungrily into the large wicker basket. The house has been in confusion for several days: their father is down from London, bringing a woman in nurse's uniform with him, and Mama remains in her bedroom. Georgie, who comes running down from the house to join the others on the beach, is breathless. Her skinny chest heaves beneath the Fair Isle jersey she has been told she must wear, for the late April weather, though sunny, is cold. She gasps and presses her hand to her side.

'I've got stitch,' she says.

'We were supposed to stay here until we were called,' says Mina, who has been helping her younger sisters build a sandcastle. It is a splendid edifice with a moat, and its towers are stuck about with small paper flags. 'Where have you been?'

Mina knows that Mama is to have a baby but she is frightened. She was too young, when Henrietta and Josie were born, to understand about babies – but now she can see the baby growing inside Mama and she wonders how it will emerge. Mama is so calm and happy that, clearly, the ordeal cannot be too terrible. 'It is a kind of miracle,' she tells Mina, 'but you are too young yet to understand. Later, when you are older, I shall explain it to you.'

A miracle. Perhaps it's like curing the man of the palsy or one of the other Gospel stories, and, after all, Mama has already had four babies . . .

'I know how babies come,' says Georgie importantly, 'but I can't tell you. It's a secret.' But Mina doesn't believe her.

'Is it Mama?' asks Mina now, fearfully, her heart heavy and sinking, her stomach curdling with terror.

'It's a secret.' Georgie still has an eye on the group by the rocks. 'Can you guess? I'll tell you if you promise to be surprised later on when Papa tells us.'

'I promise,' says Mina, shivering, her black hair whipping round her cheeks. 'Cross my heart and hope to die. Is Mama dead?'

'No,' answers Georgie scornfully. 'Of course she isn't dead, silly. We have a new baby brother.' A pause. A cloud covers the sun, shadows rippling over the sand, and the wind is chill on their bare legs. Mina is too weak with relief to feel the discomfort but Georgie stares at Mina, her pose forgotten, her eyes frightened. 'A brother. Do you think Papa will still love us?'

Lyddie closed the front door, paused to stroke the Bosun, who lay deeply asleep in the narrow hall, and carried the Jiffy bag up to her study. The bag contained the typescript for her next editing project – an historical saga by an author she'd copy-edited before – and she was looking forward to it. The editor, an old friend and a former employer, had already discussed certain points with Lyddie on the telephone.

'We've had to do quite a lot of revising so the

new material might not quite gel with the original,' she'd said. 'Look out for the timing, will you?'

She'd booked Lyddie for another project, for the first two weeks of December – a repeating author who wrote one thriller a year – had a gossip and hung up, but not before telling Lyddie how she envied her being able to work in Cornwall. Lyddie was not in the least deceived; most of her colleagues had been shocked at the idea of her giving up her job and working free-lance from Truro. She'd known that they were anxious for her. Her story of how she'd met Liam whilst she was on holiday in Cornwall, the speed at which the relationship had warmed from attraction into love, sounded too much like fiction. The fact that he'd asked her to marry him went some way to allaying their fears but it was a huge step. It sounded wonderful, they'd agreed cautiously, but wouldn't she miss London?

Lyddie, studying the calendar on her notice-board, marking in blue ink the date of the arrival of the typescript, smiled reminiscently. It had been difficult to describe her love for Liam or explain her readiness to quit London for the old cathedral city of Truro. Once they'd met Liam, of course, those colleagues had been more under-standing. Knowing that they could trust her, they were also very ready to offer her freelance work.

'I'd hate to give it up completely,' she'd told Liam, 'and the money will be useful.'

He couldn't deny it: the lease on The Place

hadn't come cheap and he'd insisted that the refurbishment must be classy; nothing tacky. Joe had agreed with him; Liam knew the market, knew just what was needed – and he'd been right. The Place was hauling in the punters, filling a particular well-heeled niche. The mortgage with the bank, however, was a large one.

As she noted in red ink the date on her calendar when the typescript was due back to the publisher, Lyddie wondered whether she should offer the money from what could be raised on the house in Iffley, once the deal was completed. Liam hadn't mentioned it and, oddly, she felt a certain restraint in raising the subject. Liam was deeply possessive about his business – it was his child, his world, and, although he encouraged her to come in for supper or lunch, he never made her feel truly a part of it. He and Joe were partners; The Place was theirs. Neither of them ever sought her advice or opinion but continued to treat her as though she were a valued, very special guest. In some ways she liked this: there were no pressures, no expectations. In the snug, after a day of copy-editing, she could simply relax, let her thoughts wander, chill out. She was never hurried from her cup of coffee, as Rosie was, should a customer be waiting at the bar, and her meals were presented with all the courtesy given to any of their clients. Yet her particular association *did* make her more special, which was rather fun. Did she want to change the balance? Would she be capable of putting a large sum of money into a business that didn't encompass her, without wanting to become involved in any way? Having invested her money in The Place, could she remain disinterested? And why should it make any difference if she had no control? After all, she was already dependent on the business: it was her livelihood, as well as Liam's and Joe's. The proceeds provided for her, paid the mortgage of the little terraced house – but not completely. She had her own work, the results of which shared their own personal financial load, and Liam was very proud of her. If he saw a review of one of the novels she'd copy-edited or heard one mentioned on the radio, he was filled with pride.

She was afraid to change the status quo, yet unhappy at the idea of not contributing more substantially if she had the means. Perhaps she would speak to the Aunts about it before she suggested it to Liam. Tomorrow was a day off and she'd planned a trip to Exmoor; Lyddie felt a little glow of expectation. Sitting down at her desk, pulling on a fleece jacket, she settled down to work.

CHAPTER SIX

The three dogs sat together at the end of the terrace, ears alert. Voices could be heard, rising and falling from inside the house, but the dogs' attention was fixed upon the Bosun, who stood uneasily, half in, half out of the french window. He was a handsome fellow, with his jet-black, silky coat, white chest and russet markings, but the Sealyhams were unmoved both by his good looks and his sweet nature, which was viewed contemptuously – by Captain Cat, at least – as weakness.

The Bosun took a few cautious steps, emerging very nearly onto the terrace, his tail waving gently in a faintly deferential way. Captain Cat growled, an ear cocked towards the drawing-room, and Nogood Boyo, who had been considering a more balanced approach, sat down again, his ears flattening. Polly Garter, too old to sustain more than a token display of territorial aggression, yawned widely, curled into a ball and settled herself to sleep in the sun. The Bosun, seeing an opening for negotiation, emerged fully onto the terrace. Once outside he lay down quickly, indicating that his approach was entirely friendly, lest the two dogs should set up a volley of barking in defence of their invaded space. The Bosun laid his head on his paws, though his ears were pricked warily, and his tail beat a feathery tattoo upon the warm stone.

Captain Cat stirred about, irritated. His plucky, fiery temperament demanded that he should fly out at this intruder, that this large alien should be assaulted and driven from their favourite, private place; yet he knew from long experience that this perfectly reasonable, natural response would bring shrieks and reproaches about his ears and, possibly, even the deprivation of certain treats. Stiff-legged, hackles up, he rumbled frustratedly, deep in his throat, staring insolently at his huge, handsome, gentle opponent, who could have had all three of them for lunch if he'd only had a mere pawful of decent pride.

Nogood Boyo whined a little. He enjoyed a good scrap as much as the next fellow – but his instinct was to approach the Bosun with friendly caution. Captain Cat could feel control slipping away from him but, before the situation became dangerous, the three women emerged into the sunshine, the balance of power shifted and the tension lifted.

The Bosun stood up, tail wagging wildly now, and hurried to sit beside Lyddie's chair; Nogood

Boyo, hostilities forgotten, examined the contents of the tray placed on the bamboo table; Captain Cat gave a few short barks, so that the Bosun should realize – and be suitably ashamed – that his skin had been saved by a pack of women, and settled beside Nest. Only Polly Garter continued to lie dreaming in the sun, beyond the prick of lust, whether for blood or love or even food; all passion spent.

Mina reached a hand to her warm white coat, smiling to herself, remembering other, earlier years, and then began to pour the coffee.

'We're all ready,' she told Lyddie cheerfully. 'Her room's looking very pretty – just the flowers to do. I hope she likes it. It's the one she and I shared when we were children during the war. You know, we haven't seen Georgie for ages. Oh, more than a year at least. It'll be fun, won't it, Nest?'

Nest's eyelid flicked as Lyddie looked at her and she smiled as she took her mug. 'I'm sure it will,' she answered. 'We'll make it a real holiday.'

Lyddie slipped her arm round the Bosun's neck as he sat, solid and comforting, beside her. 'But you would say, wouldn't you, if things got a bit . . . well, a bit out of hand?'

'Poor Georgie,' said Mina lightly. 'She's not some kind of lunatic, you know. Only getting rather old and forgetful. Well, aren't we all! I don't think we shall need physically to restrain her.'

'And if we do,' added Nest lightly, sipping her coffee, 'we'll knock her out with a treble dose of my tramadol hydrochloride and tie her to her bed.'

Lyddie chuckled, as Nest had intended she should. 'I wouldn't put it past you, either,' she replied. 'You're both very unscrupulous women.'

Mina raised her eyebrows. 'How exciting you make us sound. So how is Liam?'

The slight pause caused both women to glance at her although each steadfastly avoided the other's eyes. Lyddie stroked the Bosun's soft sun-warmed head and crumbled some shortcake with her free hand.

'He's fine,' she said at last. 'Great. Everything's fine. But, actually, I did want to talk to you about something.'

She hesitated again, whilst Mina and Nest strove to contain their nervous impatience.

'Nothing too serious?' suggested Mina at last, unable to bear the tension any longer. 'Nothing . . .' She was unable to formulate her fears and glanced helplessly at Nest, who shook her head warningly.

'No, no,' said Lyddie quickly. 'Of course not. It's simply what I ought to do with my money once Roger has got his mortgage sorted out. I should get a hundred and fifty thousand. Liam's never mentioned it but I know The Place has got a big mortgage. Do you think I should offer it to him to help pay it off?'

'No,' said Nest sharply and at once – and both Mina and Lyddie stared at her in surprise.

Lyddie gave a small embarrassed chuckle. 'Well,

that's honest, anyway,' she said – but she looked worried.

'Sorry,' said Nest quickly. 'That was rather a knee-jerk reaction but probably an honest one. Sorry . . .'

'I asked you,' said Lyddie quickly. 'Don't apologize. But why do you say that? After all, it's my livelihood too, isn't it? And Liam's my husband. Shouldn't the whole thing be a partnership? Financially as well as emotionally and . . .' She shrugged. 'Well, you see what I'm getting at.'

'The money could perhaps be invested,' began Mina carefully, 'against hard times. The Place is a huge success, anyone can see that, but things can go wrong and it might be wiser—'

'But it's not just that,' interrupted Nest. 'Sorry, Mina, but I think this should be said – given that Lyddie's asked us. My view is that The Place is very much Liam's show. Well, his and Joe's. It seems to me that you're not really included in any way. Would you say that's a fair observation?'

'Perfectly fair.' Lyddie sat upright, her silk-black hair gleaming in the sunshine.

Her small face looked sad, the wide, grey-green eyes thoughtful, and the two older women each experienced a clutch of fear. Mina longed to put her arms about her, as she had when Lyddie had been small, and Nest felt an unjustifiable surge of dislike for the absent Liam. Lyddie sighed a little and fed a corner of shortbread to the Bosun. Nogood Boyo nipped over to check it out and the large dog looked benignly upon the small opportunist who hoovered expertly round his large paws. Encouraged, Nogood Boyo wagged his tail and settled beneath the table, an eye on Captain Cat, who pointedly looked the other way.

'You've really put your finger on it,' Lyddie told Nest, after a moment or two. 'I'm not included in any aspect at all. He never discusses it with me. It's almost weird but I can understand it. Liam can be very possessive. Possibly it might be different if he didn't have a partner.'

'But that's the point, isn't it?' Nest was quick to pick this up. 'He does. You wouldn't only be backing Liam, you'd be backing Joe too.'

'There might be some legal way of splitting it into three. Or into shares,' Mina was determined that all aspects should be considered, 'so that if Joe were to leave or ask to be bought out . . .' She paused, frowning, not certain where her argument was leading.

'It's risky.' Nest was sticking with her gut reaction. 'And if Liam hasn't asked, why offer? He's a very independent man and he probably prefers to keep his business quite separate from his family life. It's a very wise decision. He and Joe can slug things out between them but two against one means trouble. I should think it would be almost impossible for you to put money into The Place and then manage to stay disinterested, especially should things begin to go wrong. At the moment it's Liam's problem, the decisions are his, and you can remain free of it. You don't have to question or argue or fall out over it. You might make it very difficult for him if you make him the offer.'

'I'm sure,' Mina agreed quickly, 'that if he were hoping for some financial assistance he would have mentioned it by now.'

'You could be right.' Lyddie was looking more cheerful. 'I'll think about it carefully but you've cleared my mind. Sorry to bring it up or worry you.'

'Don't be silly,' said Mina robustly. 'It's what we're here for. Have some more shortbread and eat some of it yourself this time. I made it specially – and not for the Bosun or for Nogood Boyo. There, take a nice big piece and tell us what you're working on at the moment. An Aga-saga, is it? Or a juicy thriller?'

Lyddie saw that the subject was closed, accepted the shortbread and settled back in her chair to talk about books.

Much later, once Nest was in bed, Mina seated herself at the computer. It was her nephew Jack, Timmie's son, who had introduced her to the world of the Internet just as once he'd introduced her to *Private Eye*. During the early months after the car accident, with Nest almost destroyed by pain and grief and guilt, Jack had shown Mina how to communicate with other people in a similar position to her own: those people who emptied themselves into a self-giving of warmth and humour and patient love.

'You need something of your own,' he'd told her, 'otherwise your whole investment will be in

69

Aunt Nest and that's dangerous. Surf the Net. Talk to other carers; there are so many people out there who are in the same boat. Exchange jokes and let off steam. Just don't sink yourself into becoming a slave like you did with Grandmama. Oh, I know you loved her, and that you were happy looking after her, but I've seen you doing your own thing for the last ten years: going off to the States to visit Aunt Josie and the boys, going to Oxford, buying puppies. I don't want you to disappear,' and he'd grinned at her and kissed her briefly on the lips.

It was odd that he should always do this – not a kiss on the cheek, or a hug, but a gentle salute on her withered lips. Afterwards, once he'd gone, she'd press them gently with her fingers, as if holding the kiss in place. Darling Jack! Tall and blond, just like his father, just like Timmie.

Ambrose, bursting with pride, insists that Timothy must be godfather to his new son and 'We'll call him Timothy' he says to Lydia. 'What do you say? I was thinking of naming him Ernest, after my father. But let's call him after old Timothy, shall we, darling?'

Lydia agrees gratefully, rocking her new baby boy, marvelling at his fairness after four black-haired girls. Ambrose returns to London in tearing spirits whilst Lydia and her daughters settle into a new pattern of living. Ambrose's delight has cast a mantle of happiness over his entire family; he is expansively generous, loving to all, and even Georgie, for now, feels no cause for jealousy. Timmie – 'Timothy' is quickly shortened by Josie – is a contented, cheerful baby, and his sisters vie for the responsibility of watching over him and showing him off to their few neighbours.

'How strange,' murmurs Enid Goodenough, hanging over the cradle. 'So blond. Not like his sisters at all, is he?'

She glances with bright, malicious eyes at her brother, Claude, who rocks to and fro, now on his heels, now on the balls of his feet, as he stands beside the french window fingering his moustache.

He titters a little, drooping an eyelid at Enid. 'Quite a little changeling.'

Lydia pours the tea calmly. 'He takes after my father,' she tells them. 'He was very fair and very tall.'

'How *very* convenient,' murmurs Enid Good-enough, so low that Lydia does not quite catch the words.

But Mina, who is never very far from her new brother, hears what she says and is puzzled.

'I don't like the Goodenoughs,' she tells Georgie, after they've gone. 'They're . . . tricky,' but Georgie is too busy being the eldest, 'a proper little mother' as some kinder neighbour has dubbed her, to care about Enid and Claude. She bustles away on some important errand and Mina is left to herself, trying to analyse the aura of disquiet that clings to the Goodenoughs, leaving edginess in its wake. Mama is restless after their visit, preoccupied as she lifts the baby from his cradle and holds him so that her cheek rests against his round blond head. Mina watches, longing to restore the harmony the Goodenoughs have destroyed.

'It's time for our story, Mama,' she says, knowing that the children's hour creates a special world of its own. 'Do you think Sophia will think of a new story to tell the robber Baron? I can't wait to hear what happens next. Shall I call the others?'

Mama smiles, touching Mina's hair, and nods, the anxious lines smoothing from her face, and Mina sighs an unconscious gasp of relief as she runs away to find her sisters. At nine years old, books are her chief delight, her greatest comfort. Their created worlds are her reality and she peoples the cleave and the beach with these characters who are so well known to her, whose words rise so readily to her own lips. *Naughty Sophia* especially lends itself to being re-enacted in Mina's environment and the children's hour is, for her, the most magic moment of the day. Soon they are ready: Georgie and Mina on the sofa, with Timmie supported carefully between them, Josie lying on the floor with her wooden jigsaw puzzle and Henrietta on the stool where she can see the pictures. The windows are open to the scents and birdsong of the summery garden and the scene is tranquil. Mina relaxes against the cushions, waiting for her mother's voice. The book is opened and Mama begins to read.

'"Chapter Seventeen. How the Robbers listened to a Ghost Story".'

Mina, humming to herself as she clicked and scrolled about the screen, was wondering just how much her life had been defined and influenced by books. Sometimes she feared that she'd never left the sheltering walls of make-believe, living most of her life in this beautiful and peaceful backwater; and then she'd remind herself of her own shattered love affair, those war years in London and her marriage, followed by her young husband's death in Jerusalem after the war. What contrasts she'd experienced! Those few years, with their unique atmosphere combining daily tragedy and fear with a fervent, greedy desire for living, had been followed by the quiet, routine-driven world that invalids inhabit. Her love of books had saved her from boredom and frustration and, back again at Ottercombe, she'd been able to steep herself in other worlds and other lives so that she often had difficulty in separating them from her own. It was because of her passion for literature that she'd met Elyot. His wife was disabled and he too used the Internet to keep in touch with the world beyond their small, restricted lives. He and Mina had visited a chatroom that was used as a literary forum and – both being enthusiastic about a particular book – had begun to exchange opinions and recommendations more directly. He was simply 'Elyot'. Gradually their correspondence had begun to deal with more than the contents of books as carefully, without disloyalty, they began to describe their frustrations and fears, each encouraging the other, sympathizing and boosting morale.

It was difficult not to allow themselves to become more intimate; certainly Mina longed to know more about this intelligent, witty man, although she was well aware that disappointment was bound to result if she were to probe too closely. Meanwhile, they enjoyed an intimacy of their own which related to fictional characters, certain phrases and gentle badinage. He was without siblings, and was fascinated by her stories about her family and especially about the prospective visit from Georgie. His last e-mail had been full of admiration.

From: Elyot
To: Mina

What a brave woman you are. I shall resist the temptation to use literary references which relate to three sisters but, seriously, I hope you won't be overwhelmed. I also hope you won't be too busy, my dear friend, to 'e' me.

Her heart had been foolishly warmed by that short phrase 'my dear friend' and, hoping to make him smile with her own passing reference to 'black and midnight hags', she'd assured him that she would stay in touch. Tonight, ready to distract herself from more pressing problems and Georgie's imminent arrival, Mina began to open her mail.

CHAPTER SEVEN

'Tea,' said Liam, putting the mug carefully amongst the papers on Lyddie's desk. 'How's it going?'

Lyddie, who was checking an anachronism in her copy of the *Oxford Twentieth-Century Words*, pushed the book aside and stretched her arms above her head, smiling at him.

'We've got a Jenny, a Janie and a Julie,' she said, 'which is very confusing. I'm afraid that the author is going to have to rechristen at least one of them, probably two.'

Liam looked approvingly at the workmanlike layout of her table, quite different from the muddle of his own desk. The typescript of the historical saga on which she was working was marked with pencilled corrections, queries were listed on a sheet of A4 beside it, and her ancient, beloved *Collins English Dictionary* was near at hand with other reference books. Lyddie was wrapped in a long, soft, knitted coat in a dark forest green. Liam glanced about him, frowning a little.

'Mother of God, it's cold in here!' he exclaimed. 'You'll be getting stiff, sitting there for hours on end with winter coming on.'

Lyddie shrugged, picking up her mug and holding it in both hands. 'It's lovely and cosy when the sun's shining,' she said. 'Anyway, the room's too small to have an electric fire with the Bosun in here. His coat would singe.'

Hearing his name the Bosun, who was stretched out across the only available floor space, opened one eye and his tail beat once or twice.

'Wouldn't you rather have a fire?' Liam poked the Bosun teasingly with his toe.

'No, I wouldn't,' answered Lyddie indignantly. 'He's company for me. That's why you got him in the first place. Remember?'

'Sure.' He leaned both hands on the desk and reached across to kiss her. 'Sure I remember. You look beautiful, have I told you that yet? Your eyes are green today, not grey at all. A dark, gorgeous green. Amazing!' He leaned back to look at her appreciatively, kissed her again and straightened up. 'And I have to be away into the town. I'll see you later. If I don't get back I'll expect you at The Place.'

'Oh.' She was disappointed. 'I'll be finishing in an hour or so and I was hoping we might have time for a walk, now that the rain seems to have stopped.'

He edged round the Bosun. 'Sorry, love. Not this afternoon. Maybe tomorrow.'

'Are you going to the cash and carry?' She felt foolishly forlorn, looking forward as she did to those few hours together when she finished at about five and he went to the wine bar at seven o'clock. Yet, as usual, instinct warned against making demands, expressing her need. 'Are you taking the car?'

'No.' He shook his head. 'I don't need it. You can have it if you want to get out into the country.'

'I'll see how I feel. With the nights drawing in, I think I'll have to give the Bosun his walk earlier. So where are you off to?'

'Oh, here and there. I want to see a guy about some advertising in a new local magazine. I have to pop into the bank.' The lifting of the shoulders, the gesture with his hands, mimed boring, necessary tasks. 'Just things. I'll see you.'

She heard him run lightly down the stairs and a few moments later the front door closed behind him. Lyddie sipped her tea; her concentration was shattered by his brief visit and his kiss had unsettled her. Liam had made several visits to the bank just lately, although he never discussed the outcome with her, and he was a trifle preoccupied. He was loving, affectionate towards her, and was as professional as always when he was on duty, yet she could feel a reservation that even Liam's experience couldn't disguise. His love-making had an urgent, needy edge that excited and delighted her, yet she hated to think that he could not confide in her. One of the things that had attracted her to him was that there was nothing of the boy about him. He was attractive, tough, self-contained, and his choosing her from such a wide field had been terrifically good for her ego.

Closing her eyes she recalled the moment at which he'd paused beside her table during that lunch-time at The Place, looking down at her with a flattering concentration.

'Are you happy?' he'd asked, as if he really wanted to know; really cared.

She'd burst out laughing at such an odd approach.

'Nearly,' she'd answered with a surprising insouciance – for she was usually rather shy with strangers – 'very nearly but not quite.'

His face had lit into a disarming smile and the new look that slid into his brown eyes had caused her heart to bang unevenly.

'Well, now, and what can we do to make the difference?' he'd asked. 'Some more coffee? A brandy? It's a terrible thing to be nearly happy but not quite. Better to be entirely miserable.'

She'd pretended to muse over her answer, longing to be witty and original but knowing quite certainly that she would fail. She'd watched him going the rounds, stopping at each table in turn, making the men laugh and the women bridle, and she wanted to be different, unpredictable.

'Oh, I don't think I agree with you,' she'd responded coolly. 'And I think, after such a delicious meal, that what I'd like most is a walk.'

Her smile had been very nearly dismissive,

although it was a tremendous effort to look away from him, to pick up her bag and casually glance into it for her purse.

'And I'd say that you were right.' He was watching her thoughtfully. 'I know exactly the place I'd go on a lovely afternoon and only a short way away. I was just going out myself, and I'd be delighted to show you. Afterwards, you might like to come back for a cup of coffee to set you on your way?'

It had been a moment of pure, magical madness. A hush had fallen on the tables as he'd raised a hand to Joe and they'd gone out together, to walk beside the river.

'Why do you call it The Place?' she'd asked him.

'Because it's the best place to be, the only place to be, the place to be seen, where it all happens, why else?' he'd answered, shrugging, and she'd laughed.

'And are you entirely happy now?' he'd asked later, as they'd paused for a moment in the shadow of the cathedral.

'Entirely,' she'd answered recklessly – and so it had begun.

'I've never seen old Liam like this,' Joe had told her. 'You've really knocked him sideways. Mind you, I can't say I blame him.'

His glance was approving, envious, and she'd felt as if another woman had slipped inside her skin: confident, brave, sexy, clever. Liam loved her and he wanted to marry her; oh yes, she was entirely happy. Later, watching him weaving among the tables, seeing the slack-limbed, almost vacant expressions of the women who desired him, she'd felt the weakening shiver of vulnerability, yet it seemed to her that the real driving force in Liam's life was The Place; separate from his love for her but absolutely necessary to him. He would work for it, fight for it; it was his *raison d'être*. Might it be possible that its future was threatened?

After her visit to the Aunts she'd decided that she would not offer to put her money into the business unless Liam asked for it. If he did, then she would have to reassess her own position. It was horrid, however, to think of him worrying about the loan if she were in a position to help him but, until Roger got his act together with remortgaging the house in Iffley, she didn't have the money anyway. The whole question was, for the moment, academic.

Lyddie finished her tea, picked up her pencil and plunged back into the eighteenth century.

Mina, clearing up the leaves on the lawn, heard the car approaching. It bumped slowly into sight, stopping on the gravel sweep to the side of the house, and she dropped the rake and hurried across the grass with the dogs running ahead. Georgie was in the passenger seat, Helena driving, and for a moment the two sisters stared at each other through the glass of the window whilst Helena switched off the engine and began to climb out. Georgie sat quite still, her expression stubborn, resentful, almost secretive. Dressed very tidily in a hand-knitted brown jersey with the white collar of her shirt showing at the neck, and a brown plaid kilt, she had the appearance of an elderly – and very cross – child.

Mina thought: She looks just like she did when we were at school in London. Our uniform was that colour, brown jerseys and kilts. Oh dear. She looks so *old*.

She was moved with love and pity at the sight of her older sister's vulnerability and she hastened to open the door.

'Georgie,' she said warmly. 'This is such fun. How nice to see you.'

Helena was hurrying round the back of the car, embracing Mina and bending to extend her arm, so as to assist her mother from her seat.

'There!' she exclaimed brightly. 'Isn't this nice? We've had *such* a lovely trip across the moor, Aunt Mina, haven't we, Mother?'

Georgie allowed herself to be helped from the car, her glance sliding slyly over Mina's face, watching for a reaction. Mina, who knew that Helena could be intolerably patronizing, grinned briefly at her sister, sending a tiny wink, and, for a moment, the years rolled back, uniting them in that inexplicable partisanship of siblings, of shared history. Georgie stood upright, shook off her daughter's arm and looked about.

'Where's Nest?' she asked.

Mina suppressed a smile: trust Georgie to require the full welcoming committee.

'She's probably asleep,' she answered. 'Poor Nest has bad nights, so she makes up for it by taking a nap after lunch.'

Georgie snorted contemptuously. 'I've never slept in the day in my life,' she said. 'Sign of old age and senility.'

'You haven't been crippled in a road accident,' retorted Mina sharply.

'If she didn't sleep all afternoon she'd probably sleep better at night.' Georgie ignored the dogs, who scuffled on the gravel for attention, and turned towards the house.

'It's pain Nest suffers from, not ordinary insomnia.' Mina's feeling of sympathy was rapidly disintegrating into irritation. 'Do try to use your imagination.'

'Now, now! No squabbling,' cried Helena gaily, hauling several cases from the car. 'Of course, Mother's stamina is quite extraordinary. She'll wear you out, you'll see.'

Georgie turned her head away sharply, and Mina glanced at her curiously. It was clear that Georgie was suffering from humiliation; old and helpless, she was being passed round like a parcel, and her prickly pride was being painfully squeezed into the new shape of dull acceptance. A chill struck deep into Mina's heart. How long before she and Nest would be unable to manage -- and who would care then?

'Come and have some tea,' she said.

She saw now that sympathy from her younger sister would be unendurable to Georgie's dignity

– such rags of it that remained – and she took pains to keep her voice quite unemotional. Georgie stumped ahead, refusing to accept the role of guest; determined to lay claim to equality.

'Nothing changes,' she said, looking around the hall with satisfaction. 'Where have you put me?'

'In our old room: the one we shared during the war.' Mina watched for a negative reaction. 'I thought you'd like to be back in it again.'

'Mmm.' Georgie was non-committal, withholding approval. 'I need the loo.'

She crossed the hall and disappeared upstairs, rejecting the downstairs cloakroom.

Mina looked at Helena, eyebrows raised. 'She seems on very good form?'

It was a question – and Helena responded defensively. 'She looks wonderful, I couldn't agree more. And she sounds perfectly lucid. But,' she shook her head portentously, chin drawn in, lips pursed, 'you wait. There will be a gradual change. Loss of memory, fumbling for a word, that kind of thing.'

'Really?' Mina sounded sceptical.

'Yes, really!' Helena, beginning to lose her patience, suddenly remembered that it would be foolish to overdramatize Georgie's problems.

Mina watched her, amused by her dilemma, and saw her niece struggling to control her irritation.

'Look, Aunt Mina, I promise you that we're doing our best for her, as we see it. And our GP agrees with us, if that's any comfort. The home is absolutely lovely and she'll be much happier there than stuck in an extension, with some kind of minder, and me and Rupert out all day. After all,' Helena's face was suddenly pathetically despondent, 'it's not as if she's ever liked Rupert . . .'

'I know.' Mina was moved by such genuine hurt to a sudden sympathy. 'I understand your difficulties.'

'It *is* difficult.' Helena looked as if she might suddenly burst into tears, her managing, confident exterior abruptly crumbling. 'To be honest, we spend a great deal of time with her, we rarely get a moment to ourselves, and she's *utterly* ungrateful. She's rude to Rupert and nothing I do is ever right. At the same time I feel dreadfully guilty, putting her into a home. I know what you're all thinking but I don't know what else to do. We'd never find anyone who'd put up with her full time and I don't see why I should give up my job when she never shows me the *least* affection . . .'

A door closed upstairs and Helena fell silent, biting her lips. Mina touched her niece lightly on the arm, shocked at such an outburst from the well-controlled Helena.

'I'm sure you're doing the right thing,' she said gently. 'We aren't judging you. Remember, I know Georgie better than any of you.'

Helena stared at her. 'Yes,' she said. 'Yes, of course you do. And it won't be for long, honestly.'

'Don't worry about it,' Mina said. 'We'll manage somehow.'

Georgie descended the stairs and rejoined them, a secret smile on her lips.

'It looks very nice,' she said to Mina. 'Very comfortable. So what was that about some tea?'

'A quick cup of tea would be wonderful,' said Helena, regaining her poise, 'and then I must be on my way. I've got a long drive ahead.'

'Well, we don't want to hold you up,' said Georgie sharply. 'Do you still have tea in the drawing-room, Mina?'

'We do,' replied Mina, 'but since Helena needs to get off we'll keep it simple and have it in the kitchen. You and I can have a proper tea when Nest gets up. That's what we usually do.'

Later, as the sisters waved Helena off, Mina felt panic fluttering under her ribs. Georgie was watching her, an odd expression on her face as the sound of the engine grew fainter, and Mina wondered what she should say to her older sister. Should she say: 'Welcome back?' or 'It's good to have you home again?' Instead, surprising herself, she said something quite different.

'Do you remember,' she asked, 'how we used to go to the top of the drive to wait for Papa or Timothy and ride down on the running-board?' In the silence, the sunlit garden was suddenly full of memories and she saw Georgie swallow, her face crumpling. 'Come on,' Mina said, taking her arm. 'Let's walk down to the sea.'

* * *

After Nest's birth, it is Timothy, rather than Ambrose, who is the most frequent visitor to the house on Exmoor.

'Another girl,' says Ambrose, almost indifferently. The novelty of having a son is wearing a little thin in the face of his growing affection for the widow in St John's Wood. Well born, well placed in society, she has no children to distract either of them from their needs, and she is clever at choosing the right company to amuse him and further his ambition. Lydia and the children are encouraged to spend more and more time at Ottercombe and Nest's birth gives Ambrose the perfect excuse to send Lydia out of London for the long summer holiday, insisting upon the necessity of peace and rest for her health.

'We'll call her Ernestina, after my father,' he says – and it is Timmie, not yet two years old, who cannot frame the long word and renames her Nest. Pale-skinned and black-haired like her sisters, Nest grows up as Timmie's shadow: the Tinies. Lydia is content to allow Mina to play a large part in the mothering of the two youngest whilst even six-year-old Josie considers herself grown up in contrast with Timmie and Nest.

Timothy visits, bringing strange toys and delicious sweets, treating the children with a tenderness they have never been shown by their father. These visits are awaited with impatience and, when they hear the familiar toot-tooting of his horn echoing from the high coastal road, the children toil up the drive to meet him. Clinging like monkeys to the doors, they balance on the running-boards, screaming with excitement as they bump down towards the house. He is dragged from the car, each child importunate in her – or his – demand to show the latest achievement or to hurry him down to the sea. The sea is the natural reward for anyone who has travelled to Ottercombe House and the children like to share in the joy and delight of the visitor who experiences it. But 'Mama first,' insists Timothy and they wait impatiently whilst he goes to greet Lydia in the morning-room. Timothy is instinctively accorded Papa's privileges and he sees her alone whilst the children squabble in the hall about which should be the first treat on his agenda.

They all know, however, that it will be exactly, reassuringly, as it always is: first the long, rambling walk to the sea and games on the beach, then home again for tea in the drawing-room, and finally the latest chapter of the current book. This is the time of quiet, the unravelling of the long day's cares; it is the children's hour.

CHAPTER EIGHT

'Hello. Sorry, who . . .? Oh, *Jack*! Sorry, I've just got in from a walk. How are you?' Clutching the telephone receiver, Lyddie dropped her coat on a kitchen chair and went through into the long room so as to perch on the end of the table. 'And how is my god-daughter?'

'Your god-daughter is a wild child,' answered her cousin, 'and if she wishes to live to see her second birthday she'll need to mend her ways. How are things in Truro?'

'Fine.' Lyddie chuckled. 'Poor Flora. What's she been up to now?'

'Poor *Flora*!' echoed Jack indignantly. 'What about us? Hannah and I are worn to a ravelling, Tobes is bullied and terrorized and you say "Poor Flora"! So when are you coming to see us?'

'Oh, Jack, I'd love to,' replied Lyddie longingly.

She visualized the old stone house in Dorset, set in the parklands of the school grounds, with the eight small boys who lived with Hannah and Jack for the first year of their prep-school life. Her cousin's wife was quick, capable, warm-hearted, a perfect foil for Jack's unflappable, rock-like strength, and the boys adored both of them equally. Four-year-old Toby had a ready-made family of elder brothers who spoiled Flora shockingly. A few days with Jack and Hannah was a tonic that restored Lyddie whenever she was low: a sanctuary where she could be herself.

'Half-term next week,' offered Jack temptingly. 'The boys will be gone – the Lord be praised – and your god-daughter would love to see you.'

'Oh, it would be heavenly.' Lyddie calculated rapidly. 'Perhaps just for one night. I'll check with Liam. It would be great to see you. It's sweet of you to offer when you're probably both knackered.'

'Well,' Jack's voice was teasing, 'to be honest, it's the Bosun we really want to see but we know that he can't come without you. Seriously, though, how are the Aunts? Have you seen them?'

'Not since Aunt Georgie arrived.' Lyddie decided to overlook the insult. 'We've had speaks and Aunt Mina seemed OK. It was obvious that she had an audience and couldn't say too much but she sounded quite jolly. I'm hoping to go over on Sunday for an hour or two.'

'We were wondering whether to dash down to see them during half-term.' He sounded cautious. 'Would they be up to it, d'you think?'

'I think they'd love it. Come on, Jack! You know they would. You and Han and the kids are their favourite people.'

'You underestimate yourself,' he answered gently, 'but thanks. Yes, I know that Mina and Nest are always pleased to see us but I'm not too certain about Aunt Georgie. If she's getting a bit . . . well, a few sandwiches short of a picnic, it could be a bit tricky. I don't want to make problems for Aunt Mina. Four extra people to entertain and Flora, bless her heart, is a real handful at the moment.'

'They'll manage,' promised Lyddie confidently. 'So when were you thinking of going?'

'Well, that's why I've phoned. If you can manage a visit we'll fit it round that. I know you have deadlines to keep.'

'Yes, I do,' said Lyddie gratefully. 'Look, I need to check with my calendar and with Liam and I'll get back to you this evening. Will that do?'

'Great,' he said. 'We'll wait to hear from you. Hannah will be really pleased at the thought of some female company apart from Flora.'

'Give them a hug from me,' said Lyddie, 'and thanks, Jack. I'd love it.'

'Speaks later, then,' he said – and hung up.

Lyddie replaced the receiver more slowly. It was odd – and very slightly worrying: that fleeting image of the old stone house and the releasing, tempting reminder that, there, she was able to be herself. It implied a lack of honesty, of strain, in her life here in Truro with Liam. She picked up her coat, her eyes thoughtful, allowing herself to admit the element of fear in her relationship with her husband. Oh, not a physical fear, no, but

91

a fear of losing him if she should confront him too openly with her own needs: the need to be part of his whole life and her growing longing for his child. Each tentative approach was cleverly fielded with a smile, a shrug, a caress, whilst she struggled to find a fingerhold or weakness in his smooth resistance to her cautious advances. Yet why should she be cautious? Why not speak out honestly? What should prevent her from expressing these reasonable, natural desires? She knew the answer even whilst she instinctively refused to face it: Liam did not require her to be part of his whole life, nor was starting a family on his agenda. His was the strength of those who withhold some vital part of themselves, who can withdraw love at will, and some atavistic instinct warned her against the risk of making demands.

Lyddie shivered at the thought of losing him, remembering how James had left her because he was unable to commit to a serious relationship. Liam, at least, had been very ready to marry her – the rest would surely follow. She must be patient a little longer.

Georgie's arrival had done very little to assuage Nest's fears; rather, her sister's presence only increased her anxiety. It was clear, after a few days, that Georgie was walking a narrow path between normality and instability. She refused the role of guest with a confidence that was almost offensive, behaving as if they were still all young together and she, as eldest, had the most authority. Meals were altered – 'Surely you eat more than cereal for breakfast?' – their quiet evenings disrupted – 'Time for my soap. Daren't miss an episode or I simply shan't know where I am. You don't mind if I switch the television on, do you?' – and the plans for each day were dictated by her particular needs.

'Barnstaple today,' she'd say at breakfast, spooning up her porridge and looking to see whether Mina was ready with the scrambled eggs. 'I need some wool and something new to read. Is the toast burning? You know I've always hated burned toast.'

'I shall kill her,' vowed Nest after a particularly trying day. Georgie had retired early with a headache and she and Mina were clearing up after supper. 'My sympathies, I have to say, are now utterly with Helena and Rupert. Mind you, I shouldn't think the home will keep her for more than a week. They'll probably expel her . . . *Can* you be expelled from a nursing home?'

'Not at those fees,' said Mina cynically. 'The higher the fees the greater the tolerance, that's my experience.'

'Then they'll need to be very high indeed,' said Nest grimly. 'Of course, she was always a bossy-boots, wasn't she? But even so . . .'

'She can't bear to lose face,' explained Mina. 'Think how humiliating it is for her to be bundled off to us whilst Helena sells up her flat and arranges for her to be shipped off to a home. The powerlessness, for someone as control-minded as Georgie, must be terrible.'

'Given that she's treating you rather like a servant I think you're very noble.' Nest was almost irritated by Mina's compassion. 'After all, this *is* your house. Mama left it to you. Georgie's behaving as if we've all slipped back fifty years.'

'I think that's exactly what she's done. I expect—'

The door opened, very slowly and silently, and Georgie stood looking at them. Her sisters stared at her, startled into immobility, each wondering how long she'd been there, trying to remember what they'd said. Even the dogs remained on their beds, ears cocked and alert. Georgie was the first to speak.

'I've come for a glass of water,' she said.

She frowned a little, as if trying to get her bearings, and came further into the kitchen. Her silvery white hair was rumpled into a fluffy crown and her eyes were vacant, staring sightlessly. The long dressing-gown and high-necked nightgown lent a strangely nightmare quality – there was nothing cosy about the scene – and Nest swallowed nervously.

'I thought I'd given you one.' Mina's voice was calm. 'Never mind. Go back to bed and I'll bring it up. Would you like a hot drink?'

Georgie's face crumpled a little, her eyes filled with tears and she looked quite unbearably sad but, before either of her sisters could speak, her expression changed again, smoothing into an odd, listening look, distant and unearthly, as if she could hear a conversation that neither of them could detect.

'Where's Mama?' she asked plaintively. Her glance strayed between the two of them, puzzled, and Mina took her arm.

'Not here,' she said. 'Not at the moment. You must go back to bed. I'll come with you.'

They went away together, Georgie allowing herself to be led as though she were a child. Nest remained quite still, shocked, almost frightened, until Mina returned and the dogs scampered to greet her.

'Is she OK?' Nest asked fearfully.

'I think so.' Mina looked shaken, stooping to caress her darlings as much for her own comfort as theirs. 'I think she's confused about exactly where she is. For a moment she thought that I was Mama.'

'You look like her,' said Nest. 'We all do, it's quite uncanny, but you most of all, I think. Oh, Mina, I wondered if she might be sleep-walking to begin with. She looked almost mad.'

Mina touched her arm comfortingly but looked preoccupied. 'Well, Helena warned me that she had these moments,' she said, 'but I didn't imagine them quite like that.'

'It was creepy.' Nest shivered. 'You don't think she might get up again and wander about?'

'I hope not,' answered Mina anxiously. 'I wouldn't dare to lock her in, even if I had a key. She could be perfectly normal five minutes from now and then think how embarrassing it would be.'

'Anyway, she might need to go to the loo.'

They stared at each other nervously, each quite suddenly on the point of hysterical laughter, and Mina took a deep breath.

'Get off to bed,' she said. 'I'll listen out for her while I undress. And don't lie awake worrying. Take a sleeping tablet. It's your physio day tomorrow and you need to be as relaxed as possible.'

'I might do that.'

They embraced and Nest wheeled herself away to her bedroom. Alone, preparing for bed, she found herself listening for movement, for voices; fear making her clumsy and slow. In bed, waiting for the tablet to take effect, dreams and memories merged into jumbled, confusing patterns until, at last, she slept.

'I know a secret,' says Georgie importantly. The afternoon is hot but tall beeches crowd about the lawn, giving shelter from gales and sun alike, and it is cool and shady in the corner where Timmie and Nest are giving a tea-party for their toys.

'Bet you don't.' Eleven-year-old Josie turns cartwheels across the mossy grass, the skirt of her cotton gingham frock falling over her ears.

The Tinies draw closer together, envious of Josie's indifference. Sometimes Georgie's secrets are frightening – and they remember how she showed them the bodies of three dead baby birds in a nest.

'It's a lesson,' Georgie told them, relishing their

horror, 'to teach you not to disturb the birds by climbing the trees in spring. Papa said so. But don't tell anyone and you won't get into trouble. It's a secret.'

Now, Timmie's lips tremble but he presses them firmly into a smile and holds Nest's hand – for she is youngest. The dolls, a knitted rabbit and two teddy bears, propped about the picnic table, are forgotten as they draw closer together, gazing at Georgie as she leans towards them.

'There's going to be a war,' she says.

They stare at her blankly, uncomprehending, almost relieved.

'What is war?' asks Timmie, who is six now. 'What does it mean?'

Before she can answer, Mina comes out of the house calling to the children to come in for tea.

'Don't say anything,' says Georgie to them quickly. 'It's a secret. Papa will be cross.'

But Timmie is beginning to learn that Georgie cheats, binding them by threats that are groundless, and he feels instinctively a need to protect Nest from horrors such as the ghastly corpses of the dead fledgelings.

'But what is it?' he asks in a louder voice, feeling brave now that Mina is in earshot. 'What is war?'

Georgie turns to face Mina, trying to appear nonchalant, hoping Mina has not heard Timmie's question, but Timmie's anxious childish treble is high and clear and it carries over the hushed garden. Mina is angry – which, oddly, frightens

Timmie even more – and she and Georgie glare at each other across the pathetic remains of the little tea-party.

'Mama told you not to tell them,' she says. 'She told all of us,' and her voice is low and furious.

Georgie shrugs, pretending indifference, but she looks uncomfortable. Nest, upset by Mina's uncharacteristic rage, begins to cry so that Mina is distracted and Georgie is able to slip quickly away.

'But what is war?' Timmie is genuinely frightened now, sensing something serious, much worse, perhaps, than the baby birds.

'It won't happen here.' Mina is comforting Nest, pretending to give the brown knitted rabbit some milk, distracting her. Nest's tears dry upon her cheeks as she laughs, taking the cup so as to feed the rabbit herself, and Mina looks up at Timmie. 'It's nothing to do with here. It's to do with countries fighting over something they both want. Their rulers are arguing about land, and then fighting starts and everyone takes sides, d'you see?'

'I think so.' He frowns. 'Like Josie and Henrietta and the tennis shoes. Both wanting them but not really knowing whose they were.'

Mina smiles at him. 'Just like that only bigger. But nothing will happen here except that we shan't see Papa so much. We shall stay here until we see how things go but Papa will have to stay in London. He's needed there. He won't be actually in danger but the thing about war is that lots of people become involved in it, even if they aren't doing the fighting.'

Timmie reflects on this for a moment. 'But we don't see Papa much, anyway,' he points out at last, quite cheerfully. Another thought strikes him. 'Shall we see Timothy? Will he have to do fighting?' he asks anxiously.

'I don't know. We'll have to wait and see. But you and Nest are quite safe. Now come and have some tea.' She hesitates. 'Perhaps it's best not to mention it, Timmie. Nest's quite happy now' – they look at Nest, who is redressing her teddy bear and singing to herself – 'and Mama is . . . tired.'

He nods, feeling a delicious sense of adult complicity, and they follow her across the lawn and in through the french windows whilst the toys remain ranged about the table, forgotten and forlorn, as the twilight deepens and shadows stretch across the lawn.

CHAPTER NINE

Mina had other memories as she settled the dogs, the bedroom door slightly ajar so that she could hear Georgie should she get up. The familiar, well-loved surroundings soothed her and by the time she was wrapped in her long fleece robe – a birthday present from Lyddie – she felt ready for her nightly session on the Net. She read an e-mail from Josie, full of questions about Georgie, and sent a carefully edited report back. There was no point in worrying Josie, who was too far away to be able to help and would simply feel frustrated. With Elyot, however, she was much more honest.

From: Elyot
To: Mina

How are things with you? A truly bad day today with Lavinia. She doesn't recognize me and cries out in fear if I go near her. She's had times when she's confused me with other people but this was

terribly distressing. She's in bed now but I shall sit
up for a while and hope to have a chat with you,
if you're around this evening.

The knowledge that he, too, was suffering anxiety
in a similar condition filled Mina with a kind of
grateful relief and she was far less cautious than
usual as she described the evening's events. He
was swift with his reply.

From: Elyot
To: Mina

It's the combination of helplessness and fear, isn't
it? I feel like this. Sometimes I simply want to
shout at her because it seems impossible that she
doesn't know me or could believe that I would
wish to harm her. I feel hurt and terribly, terribly
lonely.

Mina sat staring at these words, her heart aching
with a longing to comfort him, warmed by a sense
of comradeship.

From: Mina
To: Elyot

Dear Elyot, if only I could really be of help to you.
Do you have friends who could take the load
occasionally or does Lavinia find them threatening? I know you've described certain – shall we
say 'interesting' – scenes but you've made such

light of them that I've probably underestimated how difficult it really is. Georgie is nothing to this. We had a very chequered relationship throughout our childhood and we've seen very little of each other for the last forty years. You and Lavinia have lived together all that time and it must be appalling for you, not only to feel so outcast but to watch someone you love disintegrating. Having had one tiny experience of it tonight I can only be amazed at your courage.

His reply came quickly.

From: Elyot
To: Mina

Your experience has been a different one, dear old friend, but just as demanding. You've seen a beloved sister crippled, suffering the agonies of frustration and remorse. You were plunged into a shocking disaster to which you had instantly to adapt, not only dealing with Nest but also relied upon heavily by various other members of your family. There has been a violence to your whole experience which is missing in ours. I see now that we have been slowly advancing into a mist of muddle, 'Was I supposed to be back for lunch? Well, we all get things wrong sometime, never mind'; forgetfulness, 'I simply cannot remember why I've come into this shop'; confusion, 'I've forgotten what I was going to say. My mind's gone utterly blank', which, in themselves, are innocent enough until one realizes that the mist has deepened insidiously into a thick fog through which neither of us can find our bearings. I have to remain cheerful or she becomes anxious.

This last sentence filled Mina with a terrible pity and reminded her, with an almost physical shock, of Mama during the war years at Ottercombe. She sat for some time, trying to come to a decision, and at last typed one more message to Elyot.

From: Mina
To: Elyot

I've never known you have a holiday away from Lavinia in all the time we've been corresponding. Might it be sensible to have a break? Is there anyone to whom you could entrust Lavinia without feeling worried or guilty? Although it might, at present, sound like a busman's holiday you could always come here for a few days. Don't answer now. Think about it. We'll talk tomorrow. Goodnight, Elyot.

She closed down the computer, her heart knocking foolishly in her breast. Would he agree? Was it possible that she might, at last, meet the man who had been such a source of comfort to her?

'You're an old fool,' she muttered, listening one last time for a sound from Georgie's room before she closed her door. The dogs stirred, groaning a little, and Mina paused beside the rosewood table to look at the small objects that had been so familiar to her as a child. Towards the end of her life, these things had been kept on Mama's bedside table: a delicately carved wooden rosary; a pretty, flowered Wedgwood bowl for special treats; a tall, narrow, engraved vase for one or two delicate blooms and, lastly, the small silver case that held a green glass bottle.

Mina clipped open the silver top and held the bottle to her nose. Even now, twenty years after Mama's death, the faint scent of the smelling-salts had the power to carry Mina back to those last years of her mother's life, and beyond that, to the early years of the war.

'I want to go to London with Papa,' says Georgie, one July morning in 1940. 'I don't want to be stuck down here with a war going on. There must be something I could be doing and I can look after him until I decide what it is.'

Lydia slips the thin blue sheets of her letter into the envelope and looks at her eldest daughter. How pretty she is, with her silky black hair rolled into a pageboy bob and her clear white skin; how lovely – and how determined. 'You haven't finished school,' she answers patiently but firmly, 'and you're barely seventeen . . .'

The Tinies watch anxiously, spoons suspended, as another battle of wills is joined across the breakfast table.

'There's no *point* in school any more,' cries Georgie, exasperated by her mother's refusal to face the hard fact of war. 'If I wait another year I might have no choice in what I have to do. Papa says he can get me a job as a driver at the War Office.'

Lydia picks up her coffee cup – and sets it down again – her fingers nervously smoothing the letter folded beside her empty plate.

'In a year it might be over,' she tells her children.

'Oh, honestly!' Georgie rolls her eyes in disgust. 'That's what they said about the last one: "It'll be over by Christmas." But it wasn't, was it?'

Only Mina hears the almost pleading note in Mama's voice and sees her flinch at Georgie's reply. She watches her mother's restless fingers and notes the bistre shadows beneath her eyes.

'I think it would be a good idea for Georgie to go to London,' she says – and Georgie glances at her quickly, gratefully. 'She'll have to do something soon and it will be nice for Papa to have her with him. They can look after each other. I can understand that she wants to be useful. We all do . . .'

Lydia stares at her. 'Not you too?'

'No, not me too.' Mina smiles at her reassuringly. 'Not like that, anyway. I shall stay here and look after all of you. But Georgie's right. It's pointless going back to school and you can't cope with everything on your own, Mama. Not now, with Jean and Sarah and the babies as well as the Tinies.'

Lydia's two young cousins, with their children,

have evacuated to Ottercombe, which is part of Georgie's reason for wishing to be gone. She is not naturally maternal and having to share a bedroom with Mina irritates her. The two young mothers, with two babies and a toddler between them, take up a great deal of space and, with the younger children unable to go to school, a great deal of organization is required.

'How fortunate,' says Enid Goodenough, who still visits with her brother but less often due to petrol shortages, 'that you have enough family to fill the house –' by this time evacuees from Bristol and Croydon are arriving on Exmoor – 'so that you don't have to put up with strangers.'

'I suppose we are,' agrees Lydia sweetly, unaware as usual of any undercurrent, 'although nine children put a tremendous strain on the resources.'

'We've only got one lavatory,' twelve-year-old Henrietta tells them importantly, 'but lots of chamber pots, luckily. Although the babies—'

'And Ambrose?' asks Enid, quickly changing the subject; she is not interested in chamber pots and babies. 'How does he manage all alone?'

She manages to invest the last two words with a subtle inference that alerts Mina and causes even Lydia to frown.

'He's very capable,' she answers calmly, 'and Mrs Ponting goes in every day now that we have settled here for the duration. She's been looking after us for years and I feel quite sure that Ambrose has everything he needs.'

'Oh, I'm certain you can be confident about *that* . . .'

Now, remembering those words and the sneering smile that accompanied them, Lydia suddenly thinks that Georgie's idea is, perhaps, a good one.

'Very well,' she says. 'I will speak to Papa. I can quite see that it must be frustrating for you here, now that you're growing up. No parties or dances and no-one of your own age to meet, as well as being unable to contribute, even in a small way, to this terrible thing which is happening to our country. I'll speak to him, I promise.'

'Thanks,' says Georgie to Mina later, in their bedroom, just before lunch, 'for sticking up for me. It seems a bit mean, though, leaving you to all this.'

She riffles through their wardrobe, selecting and rejecting garments and watching herself in the long glass.

'Oh, I don't mind a bit,' answers Mina honestly. 'I shan't go back next term either. I shall teach Henrietta and Josie and the Tinies. It'll be good practice if I want to be a teacher after the war. And Mama can't possibly manage alone. Anyway, it'll be nice for Papa – if he agrees. You're not frightened about air raids?'

'Well, nothing's happening, is it?' Georgie shrugs as she turns away from the looking-glass and lies full length on her bed. 'It'll be fun. Sally Hunter says she's having a terrific time. Lots of handsome young officers and parties and things. She drives an old general about, that's what made me think of it. I might join the WRACs eventually.'

'And did Papa really say that he could get you a job driving?'

Georgie nods, hands behind head. 'If you ask me he's got a bit fed up with being on his own so much. He took me around a lot when I went up to London last time. Showing me off. You know? "And this is my eldest daughter, come to look after her old father", that kind of thing. I liked it, rather. He's still very good-looking, isn't he? Well-preserved. I hadn't realized how important he is and everyone was very nice to me. There was a woman who seemed to turn up everywhere we went who didn't seem to like it much. She was very offhand with me. Once I saw her crying and he was reasoning with her but he looked horribly uncomfortable.' Georgie frowns as she recalls her own reaction: distaste that her distinguished father should be obliged to look . . . well, shifty; undignified. 'It was a bit odd.'

The sisters exchange a glance, puzzled, slightly fearful; on the edge of exposing some adult secret. Instinctively, each retreats from discussing it further.

'Well then, perhaps it's a good thing you're going,' says Mina. 'You can tell me when the parties are on and I'll try to get up for one.'

'Of course I will.' Georgie is full of generous goodwill. 'But you'll need some decent clothes. What fun it will be.'

Mina watches as her elder sister swings herself off the bed, notices the silky pleated skirt clinging to her long white legs.

'Isn't that Mama's skirt?'

'Mmm.' Georgie twirls. 'It's a Fortuny. I found it in her wardrobe in London. She bought it in Venice ages ago and she simply never wears it so I asked to borrow it. After all, there's not a lot of use for it down here, is there? She's got loads of things she never wears now. Look at this jacket. It's vicuna.' Georgie twirls again, holding it against her. 'What d'you think?'

Mina, glancing down at her cotton frock, feels a twinge of pure envy. 'It's a bit mere,' she says casually.

Georgie shoots her sister a sharp glance. 'Mere' has been a favourite word ever since they rediscovered *The Young Visiters* on the bookshelf in the nursery. It is a code word between them that they apply secretly, to people, places, events, and can reduce them to fits of giggles. Quite suddenly, Georgie feels a huge surge of love for Mina, their differences forgotten in this unexpected experience of true sibling affection.

'You'll come to London, won't you?' she says. 'Sally's meeting simply loads of gorgeous men.'

'Course I shall,' says Mina. 'Anyway, you can write and tell me all about it. Hurry up and change, lunch will be ready soon.'

As she goes downstairs, she sees someone moving about in the drawing-room and crosses the hall, wondering if it is one of the Tinies; but it is Lydia who sits on her heels before her sewing-box, putting something away. She glances over her shoulder as Mina comes in and there is the sudden crackle of paper and the sharp little bang of a drawer closing.

'I thought it was Nest or Timmie,' Mina tells her. 'They have this game of hiding before lunch . . . Are you feeling unwell, Mama?'

Lydia straightens, holding on to the back of the sofa. 'No, no. Well, perhaps a little tired. The babies were crying again last night but it's not their fault, poor sweets.'

Her face is thin and there is so much pain in her eyes that Mina is shocked: this is more than sleepless nights and crying babies. She has never questioned Mama before but she senses a shift in their relationship that might allow a new kind of intimacy. 'Was your letter . . . ? I saw you reading it at breakfast. Did it have bad news?'

Mina's eyes are on a level with her own, her look is grave and compassionate, and Lydia longs quite desperately for the luxury of confession. She must trust someone and why not this, the dearest of her daughters?

'It was from Timothy,' she whispers. 'He is being sent on some secret mission. He can't speak of it . . . Only to let us know that he will be gone for some time.'

Her eyes blur with tears, her lips tremble, and Mina instinctively puts her arms about her mother as she might with Timmie or with Nest.

'Oh, poor Mama. We shall all miss him, shan't we? Will we be able to say goodbye to him?'

Her innocent acceptance soothes Lydia's guilt

and gives her courage. It is heaven merely to be able to speak his name aloud.

'No, no,' she says. 'He can't possibly get away but I'm glad to share it with you, Mina. I've been expecting it. He makes light of it, naturally, but it's dangerous, I know it is . . .' She hesitates, looking anxiously into those clear untroubled eyes. 'Perhaps we shouldn't mention it to the others?'

'Oh, no,' agrees Mina at once. 'They wouldn't understand and the Tinies might be frightened.'

'Yes,' says Lydia, weak with relief. 'That's what I thought. It's a secret between you and me, my dear child.'

Mina, feeling proud and very grown-up, kisses her mother lightly on the cheek. 'It's lunch-time,' she says. 'Go and make yourself pretty whilst I get the children organized.'

She hurries away, so as to intercept the children coming in from the garden, and Lydia goes upstairs, comforted.

CHAPTER TEN

In the terraced house in Truro something unusual was taking place. The Bosun lay at the foot of the stairs in the narrow hall, nose on paws, but he was far from sleep. His eyes watched anxiously as his two humans paced the long room, which stretched from the front of the house to the back, and he listened uneasily to their voices. Dog he might be but he knew very well that an important note was missing; a note that conveyed happiness and affirmed that all was well. Each time either approached the open doorway his tail beat humbly upon the floor, his ears pricking hope-fully; once or twice he sat up, in an attempt to deflect their attention, but neither noticed him. Their feet passed to and fro, marking angry tracks across the carpet, and the sour, unhappy scent filled him with misery. With a tiny whine he settled himself again, nose on paws, waiting, listening.

'OK, so it's I who am in the wrong entirely. I am at fault for taking exception to your opening a letter addressed to me. That's the way of it, is it?'

'Oh, for Heaven's *sake*.' Lyddie was trembling with anger and shock: Liam's reaction had been quite unexpectedly violent. 'It was a mistake. So I didn't look carefully at the address. So big deal. We *do* have a joint account at this bank, remember. Anyway, why all the secrecy? We're married, after all. Is it really so terrible that I should open one of your letters by mistake?'

He stopped pacing, so as to stare at her, and she was struck by the realization that he was utterly unfamiliar to her; the flow of chemistry that connected and fused them into a special, unique entity had been switched off. Lyddie felt an odd combination of fright and loneliness.

'So that's fine, then,' he said, 'except, you see, that I don't believe that it was a mistake.'

Lyddie swallowed, looking away from his wholly unfriendly, penetrating stare. Unfortunately his suspicion was all too true. Liam's increasing edginess had begun to worry her to the extent that, when the letter arrived with the flap not quite stuck down, she'd given way to a terrible need to see what was happening at the bank. She was deeply ashamed of herself but, even so, had been quite unprepared for the scorching blast of Liam's fury.

'The letter was *not* closed properly,' she answered evenly, sitting down at the table, crossing her arms beneath her breast, 'and I hadn't looked to see to which of us it was addressed – there was quite a lot of post – but, yes, OK, when

I realized that it was about The Place and not us, I looked anyway. I've been very worried about you and I thought you'd been trying to protect me from . . . whatever.'

He smiled, not a pleasant smile. 'Ah, so you were worrying about me. What a devoted wife it is, imagine.'

Lyddie bit her lip, her cheeks burning. 'It's very hard,' she told him, 'to keep myself completely cut off from the business you love so much and which supports us. It's . . . well, it's unnatural, can't you see that? You know all about *my* work and what I earn—'

'And you know all about The Place. Mother of God, you're in there every day and treated like the Queen of Sheba! How can you say you're completely cut off from it?'

She uncrossed her arms, pleating her fingers together, trying to sort out her thoughts. 'I'm treated like an honoured guest,' she agreed at last. 'I know that – and I admit that I like it. Everyone enjoys feeling special and I'm no exception but, at the same time, I know even less about it than . . . than Rosie does.'

'And what does Rosie know about anything?' he asked sharply.

She stared up at him, puzzled. 'You know what I mean. She's . . . *involved*. OK, it's at a superficial level but it's more than I've got.'

'I imagined that as my wife you wouldn't be concerned about what the barmaids think they know,' he answered stingingly.

'I'm not. It's not *like* that. I don't want to work behind the bar or— Oh, let's stop this, can we?'

He raised his eyebrows, watching her. 'I don't know. Can we?'

'Oh, Liam, I'm truly sorry.' She controlled her longing to move towards him: his whole body language warned her off. 'It was quite wrong to read your letter but you won't tell me anything. What would *you* do if you could tell something was worrying me but I wouldn't share it with you?'

'I'd imagine that you were adult enough to have the right to your privacy and honour it accordingly.'

He might just as well have slapped her.

'Yes,' she said on a deep, deep breath. 'Well, there's no answer to that.'

'And so now you know all about my problems how do you plan to lift the burden from my shoulders?'

She was silent, still smarting with embarrassment.

'You see,' he continued after a moment or two, 'it's not just me, is it? It's Joe. He might not like you knowing all his secrets too.'

'But this wasn't to Joe, was it?' she replied miserably but determined to keep the record straight. 'I imagine the company correspondence goes to The Place. This was to you, personally.'

'So it was. But you read it anyway.'

'Yes,' she said wearily. 'I read it anyway and I know that you're going to increase the mortgage on this house.'

Silence. She looked at him, dark, saturnine and

elegant, and was consumed with longing for him; it was utterly necessary to break down this barrier to their love.

'Why?' she pleaded. 'Why, Liam, when you know I can raise some money on the house in Iffley?' Her conversation with the Aunts and her subsequent resolution was so much dust and ashes now, in the face of his icy rejection. 'Why won't you let me help you?'

'I don't want to be "helped".' He spoke the word with distaste. 'I started this business and whether it stands or falls is up to me. Can you not understand that?'

'Yes, yes, I can understand it. But don't I come into this at all? This house is yours but we share it now. Suppose you put it at risk by increasing the mortgage on it? It's my home too.'

'So it is. But I shan't let you down. You'll have to learn to trust me.' A tiny pause; a light, very slight relaxation of his bunched muscles. 'Do you find that impossible?'

'No, of course not.' She felt too wretched to protest further; all she longed for was the old familiar harmony. 'It's clear that The Place is a terrific success . . .' She hesitated, afraid of endangering the faint, very faint, warming of the arctic atmosphere between them. 'I'm truly sorry, Liam . . .'

'And so am I.' It wasn't clear whether he was referring to her misdemeanour or tendering an apology, but he touched her lightly on the head before moving swiftly to the door. 'I've got an appointment in the town and I shall go straight on to The Place. See you later for supper, I expect.'

The door closed behind him: Lyddie sat quite still. It was terrible to be so much in love that almost nothing mattered except the beloved's kiss. She wrung her hands together, humiliated by the depth of her physical need for him, willing him to return, but only the Bosun appeared, padding gently, warily, to sit beside her, offering her the grateful, warming benefit of his love.

Later that afternoon, just as Jack and his family were assembling for tea, the telephone rang. With a resigned gesture he hurried away to his study whilst Hannah groaned with irritation. Her energetic vivacity kept her as slender at thirty-three as she'd been at twenty, and she was pretty and stylish in a sharp, up-to-the-minute way; it was as easy to imagine her in some smart city restaurant as it was to see how utterly content she was in the cluttered kitchen of this school house in the Dorsetshire countryside. Despite looking after Jack and their children, as well as eight small boys during term-time, she still managed to keep her own catering business in operation – although, at present, it consisted mainly of cooking for lunch parties and very special occasions. She was devoted to her children and adored Jack, who teased her, drove her mad with his refusal to be organized, but panicked privately lest anything should happen to his three very special people. Hannah knew all about this very real terror, and his desire to protect them from anything harmful, and tried to steer a sensible path that embraced reasonable caution and natural development.

When he came back into the kitchen he looked preoccupied but he smiled at Toby across the table and slid into the seat beside his daughter's high chair.

'Who was it?' demanded Hannah, 'and *why* does the telephone ring the moment we all sit down at the table together? There's a conspiracy out there.'

'Honey,' said Flora. '*Not* jam. No, no, no . . .'

'Is there some resonance about the word "no",' mused her father, moving the honey-pot with a practised thrust beyond Flora's sticky reach, 'which lends itself to the childish imagination? Why not "yes" or "please"? Wasn't "no" the first word our darling daughter uttered? Not "Mum-mum-mum" or "Dad-dad-dad", as I once understood was usually the case, but "No".'

'Actually,' answered Hannah, putting Marmite soldiers on Toby's plate, 'it was "Bog off!" courtesy of young Jackson.'

Toby made round eyes and mouthed 'Bog off!' at his father, who winked back at him.

'What a lovely boy he was,' he said, with a reminiscent sigh. 'We owed so much to him by the time he went.'

'Yes,' agreed Hannah grimly. 'Tobes's vocab-ulary was startlingly improved. OK, Flora, if you don't want it I shall give it to Caligula.'

Flora stared down at the enormous, predatory

tabby cat they'd inherited from the former history master, and sniffed pathetically, eyes wet with frustrated tears. Toby watched sympathetically, instinctively knowing that her enormous pride needed some kind of assuaging before she could back down.

'It's new jam,' he told her encouragingly. 'Not the old one. It's really, really nice.'

Flora's lower lip resumed its normal size and her arched limbs relaxed a little. She allowed, grudgingly, a tiny portion of bread and jam to be inserted into her mouth. When none of it re-appeared her parents breathed deeply and smiled at each other, as if some great object had been achieved.

'Tobes is destined for the Diplomatic Corps,' observed Jack, 'if we've still got one in twenty years' time.'

'Possibly,' agreed Hannah, 'but who was it on the phone?'

'Oh yes!' Remembering, Jack's face fell. 'It was Lyddie. She can't get over to see us after all.'

'Oh, no!' Hannah put down her mug of tea and stared at him in disappointment. 'Why on earth not?'

He hesitated. 'I'm not absolutely sure. She sounded really down but she insisted she was OK. Just said that everything was a bit on top of her and she couldn't get away.'

'Rats!' said Hannah crossly. 'I was really looking forward to it. We all were.'

'I wanted to show her how I could ride my

new bicycle,' said Toby sadly. 'And I'd done a picture.'

'And Flora wanted to show off her new word,' said Jack, trying to raise their spirits a little. 'Didn't you, my darling?'

Flora scowled at him, cheeks bulging, crammed with bread and jam, and he grinned back at her.

'What new word?' asked Toby, interested.

'Jack!' warned Hannah. 'That will do. It's not like Lyddie to stand us up. Are you sure she's OK?'

'Not really,' admitted Jack. 'I couldn't get anything out of her, though. The good news is that she's agreed to drive over to Ottercombe when we go on Saturday. She wants to see the Aunts and I've made her promise, otherwise I've said we'll set Flora on her.'

'Well, that's something,' said Hannah reluctantly. 'But we won't be able to have a really good gossip.'

'Will she bring the Bosun?' asked Toby eagerly. 'I do love him. And so does Flora, don't you, Flora? I wish *we* could have a dog.'

'I know you do,' said Hannah. 'You've told us before, actually. Just once or twice.'

'On the hour, every hour. But, yes, Lyddie is bringing the Bosun so you'll be able to take him down to the beach.'

'The sea.' Toby's face was lit with excitement. 'Flora! We're going to the sea.'

'Bistik,' demanded Flora threateningly, drumming on her tray. 'Bistik!'

'We'll take Flora swimming,' said Jack, his eyes brightening with fell intent. 'Isn't there some scientific discovery which proves that small children can't drown? Should we test it?'

'Don't tempt me,' said Hannah longingly, passing her younger child a small square of shortbread and starting to peel an apple. 'Just don't, that's all.' She passed a quarter to her son. 'Get on with it, Tobes, and then we'll all go for a walk. *All*,' she repeated firmly, as Jack swallowed the remains of his tea hastily and glanced purposefully at his watch. 'It'll do us all good.'

Jack made a series of faces, which sent Toby into fits of laughter, and even Hannah grinned unwillingly.

'Hopeless,' she said. 'Eight-year-old boys are a better example than you are. No, Flora, that's enough biscuit. Apple, now. Eat up and we'll walk down to the river. You can ride your bike, Tobes, and Daddy will give you a piggy-back, Flora. You like that, don't you?'

Flora, who did indeed feel that there was a certain rightness when her head was higher than anyone else's, began to eat her apple pieces with enthusiasm. Jack looked at his wife.

'Thanks,' he said. 'There's nothing I love more than having both ears violently twisted whilst a pair of iron heels rhythmically shatter my breastbone.'

'That's all right, then,' she answered equably. 'I like everyone to be happy. I'll get the coats. And don't pinch the last of the chocolate biscuits, Jack. I know exactly how many there are.'

She left the kitchen and there was a silence

broken only by Flora eating apple. Toby finished his quarters and beamed at his father. Jack winked back at him companionably.

'Tell me, Tobes,' he asked thoughtfully, 'have you come across the word "witch" yet?'

CHAPTER ELEVEN

Nest woke suddenly, heartbeat unsteady, struggling into awareness as she tried to see the clock. Even before she could read its illuminated face she knew that the night was over. The thickness of the curtains could not completely block the light-fingered morning as it groped between the gaps in the heavy folds, touching the room alive with rosy colour, stroking mahogany and glass until they reflected a sheeny lambency. The house was wrapped in absolute silence. On such a morning the deep cleave would be filled with a creeping mist, only the highest treetops rising above drifting fog, whilst the sea, lying quiet beneath its clammy blanket, waited for that warming radiance that now traced its way into the darkness of Nest's room.

In the first months after the accident, her helplessness had brought nightmares to her waking and sleeping hours. What if the house should catch fire? Or if there should be an intruder? Her inability to move quickly or defend herself manifested itself in sweating terrors, which Jack and Mina had tried hard to allay by practical means: a very good smoke alarm system, bars at her windows. The large morning-room, barely used since Lydia's death, was the obvious choice for Nest's quarters. Next door to the kitchen, it had been quite easy to plumb in a small bathroom and equip it for her needs. The fact that it was on the ground floor made access simple for her, yet increased her night-time fears. Mina refused to allow her to lock herself in but the bars had helped.

'It's so *stupid*,' Nest would cried vexedly, almost weeping with frustration. 'I'm OK until I go to bed. It's the dark . . .' and Mina remembered a younger Nest, screaming in the night after *Hans Brinker* was read aloud during the children's hour: the chapter 'The Red Lion Becomes Dangerous' tells how the young Dutch boys disturb an intruder. The vision of the robber, creeping quietly, creeping slowly across the moonlit floor, knife in hand, remained with small Nest long after lights were out and, after the nightmare, she'd been allowed to sleep in Mina's bed for the rest of the night. Since the accident, she'd gradually adapted to this aspect of her disability but she was still prey to terrible dreams and waking horrors.

Now, even as she peered at the clock, she stiffened into immobility. Someone was in the room. Tense and alert, blood singing in her ears, she strained to see the darker, denser shape near the door. It waited, motionless, yet, in the breathless silence, Nest's heightened senses detected confusion on the part of the intruder. For a brief moment she wondered – hoped – that this might be a peculiarly vivid dream but, before she could dismiss the thought, there was a movement: a stealthy turning of a handle, a wedge of light lying across the floor before the door closed again with a tiny but audible click. Instantly Nest was washed in a drenching sweat of relief, her locked muscles unclenching painfully. She swallowed several times, her eyes closed, and began deliberately to inhale long deep breaths. Presently, she pushed back her covers and began the slow process of dressing, and, later still, wheeled herself into the kitchen for breakfast.

The room was filled with bright, comforting light and Nogood Boyo came to greet her. She leaned from her chair to stroke him and wished her sisters 'Good morning'.

Georgie was immersed in a catalogue but Mina folded and put aside the *Spectator*, smiled at Nest – she never commented on her sister's nocturnal miseries, preferring to dwell optimistically on the pleasures of the day ahead – and poured herself another cup of coffee.

'There was an e-mail from Jack last night,' she told Nest. 'They're all coming on Saturday for the whole day. And Lyddie's coming too. Isn't that good news?'

Nest lifted the kettle onto the hotplate, responding to Mina's evident delight with a raising of spirits.

'Great,' she answered cheerfully. 'Isn't it, Georgie? How long is it since you saw Toby and Flora? Flora's baptism, was it?'

'*What* a day that was,' remembered Mina. 'That lovely chapel. It was such a good idea having her christened at the school, wasn't it?'

'Do you remember, Georgie?' persisted Nest, as Georgie rather fumblingly turned a page, frowning to herself. 'Do you remember Flora?'

'Of course she does,' said Mina anxiously, her happiness evaporating a little in the face of Nest's odd insistence. 'And darling Toby.'

'When are they coming?' asked Georgie. 'When . . . ?'

She fell into an odd, listening, posture; eyes vacant, head slightly cocked, and Mina looked at Nest in dismay. Nest wheeled herself to Georgie's side and put a hand on her wrist; she saw that there were fresh egg-stains on the brown jersey and her sister's hair was tangled and unbrushed.

'Georgie,' she said gently, and shook the flaccid wrist, 'Jack and Hannah are coming on Saturday. Good, isn't it?'

Georgie's glance travelled slowly from her wrist up to Nest's face. 'I know a secret,' she said. She began to smile a little, secretly, cunningly. 'I know a secret.' Her voice was stronger now, the old singsong intonation, and Nest knew a tiny stab of fear. She looked at Mina, who was watching Georgie with an expression that mirrored her own sudden anxiety, and she released her sister's wrist abruptly.

Mina pushed back her chair. 'Yes,' she said with forced brightness. 'On Saturday. What fun it will be,' and, calling to the dogs, she went out into the garden. After a moment, Georgie returned to her catalogue as if nothing had happened and Nest wheeled back to the now-boiling kettle and, very thoughtfully, began to make herself some coffee.

'It was Georgie,' she said to Mina, some time later when they were alone together in the drawing-room. 'You never come into my room without knocking. It was morning. Who else could it have been?'

'She gets confused,' said Mina. 'You know she does. Oh dear . . .'

'But why stand there in the dark without speaking? I was terrified.' Nest's fear was manifesting itself in anger. 'If she's going to start creeping about I shall have to lock my door. She might do it in the middle of the night next time. Have you any idea how frightening it is to wake up and know there's someone in the room with you?'

'Yes, well, no, but I can imagine,' answered Mina distressfully. 'Oh, I am so sorry.'

'It's not your fault.' Mina's dismay made Nest feel guilty. 'Obviously it isn't. But I can't cope with this.' Silence. 'Mina. Do you think Georgie might know . . . something?'

The true fear was out in the open now. Mina's eyes met Nest's briefly and slid away.

'I . . . don't know.'

'But no-one else knew,' said Nest urgently. She

glanced at the closed door and instinctively lowered her voice. 'Only you and me and Mama.'

'I certainly never told Georgie,' said Mina firmly.

Nest stared at her. 'Do you think Mama can have told her?'

'I can't believe that she would have done but that's not to say that somehow Georgie didn't . . . hear something.'

'Oh, my God!'

'Look,' said Mina quickly, 'let's not panic. She's obviously suffering from delusions of some kind. Dementia . . . I don't know what it is but it's stupid to start jumping to conclusions. It's probably something she just thinks she knows. After all, there are other secrets.'

'Other secrets?'

'Well, not secrets,' said Mina quickly. 'Not . . . real secrets. This is just Georgie being . . . Georgie.'

Nest turned to stare out into the garden. 'I hope you're right.'

'And please don't lock your door,' pleaded Mina. 'I'd be so worried. If you hear anything just ring your bell. That's what it's there for, after all. I realize that this time you were completely taken by surprise, but next time—'

'I hope there won't be a next time,' said Nest grimly.

She wheeled herself out through the french door onto the terrace and Mina was left alone. She sat quite motionless except for one hand which, gently and quite unconsciously, continued to stroke their mother's rosewood sewing-box, standing where it had always been, beside her chair.

Timothy manages one more visit to Ottercombe before vanishing again into Europe. Ambrose and Georgie, by now, are firmly fixed in London; each manipulating the other to attain his or her own ends. Petrol rationing and restrictions on travel give them excellent excuses to avoid the long journey to Exmoor but, somehow, Timothy finds the means: travelling by train to Barnstaple, catching the last connection to Parracombe and walking the rest of the way, nearly four miles, across the moor. He arrives late on a wild March evening and only Lydia and Mina are still up to greet him. His skin is burned dark brown by a harsh foreign sun, his hair bleached liked straw, so that, to Mina, he seems as exciting and romantic as she has always remembered him.

Lydia is unable to contain her relief and joy, speeding across the hall and into his arms, holding him tightly. Timothy has been trained in a tougher school and is able to smile at Mina, shielding Lydia whilst he stretches a hand to her daughter.

'Were you anxious?' he asks her, his eyes creasing into a smile. 'Did you fear for me, crossing the moor at night, wondering if I might meet Carver Doone or Tom Faggus?'

Mina laughs, delighted at his ability to connect so quickly, touched that he remembers how her whole life is a world informed by fictional characters.

'I was worried,' she admits, 'when you telephoned from Barnstaple and then the pips went and you were cut off. We both were. We knew you'd have to walk from Parracombe but I told Mama that this was nothing compared to what you're used to.' She smiles indulgently upon her mother, who is calmer now although her eyes are strangely brilliant, her cheeks flushed. 'But we didn't tell the Tinies, did we, Mama, or they'd never have gone to bed at all?'

'I expect you'd like something to eat.' Lydia schools her voice into a steadiness she does not feel and he smiles down at her. Their glances lock and linger, her hand tightens on his sleeve, but Mina is already leading the way into the kitchen.

'We're very lucky,' she calls back to them, 'that we have a farm so close. They give us cream and eggs and cheese. And Jenna – do you remember Jenna? – sometimes brings us a chicken or some rabbits that Seth catches. I think it's better to be in the country in wartime although Georgie thinks we're very dull. Did you see Papa and Georgie in London?'

'No.' By now they have joined her in the kitchen. 'No, there was only just time to catch the train. They are well?'

'Oh, yes.' As the kettle boils on the range and she prepares some simple food, Mina chatters happily. 'They survived the Blitz, at least, although Mama tried to make Georgie come home. She thought it was a great adventure and insisted on staying with Papa. She'd like me to go to London but Mama needs me and I teach the children, although Henrietta and Josie are getting too big and they'll be going away to school in the autumn. Timmie goes over to Trentishoe for lessons with the vicar. Papa says he must go away to school soon too . . .'

Her chatter dies away as she becomes aware of the silence behind her. They both smile at her as she glances over her shoulder but she senses a tension.

'You must be terribly tired,' she says to Timothy. 'We've been collecting wood in the cleave all afternoon so there's a fire in the drawing-room. Why don't you take your supper through on a tray? It's all ready.'

'That's a lovely idea. Even with the range alight it feels so cold in here.' Lydia is indeed trembling as she embraces Mina. 'Goodnight, my dear child. It's very late and it will be a busy day tomorrow. Away you go to bed, now.'

'The house is full.' Mina kisses Timothy too. 'Our cousins are here with their babies. You've had to go into Papa's dressing-room next to Mama. It's quite small but we've made it comfortable, haven't we, Mama?'

'Very comfortable,' smiles Lydia. 'Have no fear. He'll sleep well tonight.'

She glances almost mischievously up at Timothy but his face has a brooding, almost impatient expression. Watching them, despite her sharing

131

in Timothy's homecoming, Mina feels suddenly excluded, no longer a participant. Lydia picks up the tray and Timothy follows her across the hall; neither of them glance up as Mina climbs the stairs and passes along the gallery, whispering a last 'Goodnight'.

The children are wild with delight when he appears at breakfast time. Even Henrietta and Josie, who are trying to outdo each other in the attempt to be sophisticated young women, forget their quarrels and readily resume their familiar relationship with him. He brings each of them a pretty, flowered silk scarf – blue for Henrietta, green for Josie, but otherwise identical. Delighted that he has not classed them with the Tinies, awed by the soft beauty of the silk, they rush away to find some garment that might be worthy of a marriage with such splendour.

'How clever of you,' says Mina with relief, 'to give them the same thing, otherwise they would fight.'

She does not see the tender glances Lydia and Timothy exchange, nor does she guess that there has been a certain amount of collusion with regard to the presents. Timmie has a model of a Spitfire, which renders him quite speechless with excitement, and Nest is given a charming rag doll, with a whole selection of clothes for it to wear.

'Imagine all those things being in that small holdall,' marvels Mina. It does not occur to her, now that she is grown-up, that she might have a present. Nor does she suspect that Mama has been given a gift privately, and she watches the Tinies with genuine pleasure as they examine their toys. Timothy waits until she is alone before he takes his opportunity.

'I have something for you,' he says, as she stands peeling potatoes in the scullery. Jean and Sarah have taken the younger children down to the beach and the house is quiet. He hands her the package and watches her face as she quickly wipes her hands on the towel before she takes the book out of the bag. The mere fact that it is a book, doubly precious in these times, causes her to gasp with delight but when she sees the title, then 'Oh, *not* an M. J. Farrell,' she cries. 'Oh, this is the nicest thing you could have given me. I loved *Taking Chances* and *Devoted Ladies* and I've read them so many times they're falling to bits. This must be her latest one. Oh, thank you,' and she flings her arms about him and hugs him tightly. 'You've written in it, haven't you?' She checks anxiously and then grins at him again. 'I can't wait to start it.'

'You'll have to wait a little longer,' he smiles, touched as always by her warmth and her likeness to Lydia. 'I want you to take some photographs for me.'

'Me?' she asks, surprised but flattered. 'I'm not terribly good at it,' she warns him. 'I cut off people's heads and feet, but I'll try.'

'Good girl,' he says. 'Most of the children are down at the beach but Nest and Mama are about. You can practise on them and when the others come back you'll be an experienced photographer.'

She looks again at the book, imagining the treasure it holds, and puts it carefully back into its bag.

'Come along,' he says, 'before we lose the sunshine,' and she follows him through the hall and out into the garden.

It is Ambrose who breaks the news, four months later; telephoning from London on a sultry July afternoon when the children are at the beach. Suspecting nothing, he feels that it is *he* who requires sympathy: he has, after all, lost a very good friend.

'One of the best,' he says, over and over, until Lydia feels that she might slam down the receiver. 'Poor old Timothy, I always thought he was indestructible. I shall really miss him. They don't make 'em like that any more. One of the best . . .'

When Mina arrives back, Lydia is sitting in the drawing-room, dry-eyed, her hands stroking and smoothing the last letter, which had arrived a week before. She stares at Mina, frowning a little, her eyes blank.

'Mama . . . ?'

'He is dead,' she says almost matter-of-factly. 'Dead.'

Mina knows at once that she is speaking of Timothy, not Papa, and she goes quickly from the room into the hall, where the children are disentangling shrimping nets from buckets and arguing together.

'Take them into the morning-room,' she says to

Henrietta, 'and then go and find Jean or Sarah and ask them to give you all some tea. Keep them quiet if you can, Henrietta. Mama is not well.'

In the drawing-room, Lydia is still sitting motionless in her chair beside her sewing-box. Mina picks up a stool and perches close to her, taking the letter so that she might hold Mama's hands and placing it carefully on the top of the sewing-box. They sit together in silence, Mina gently cradling the icy hands, whilst the sun sinks slowly behind the cliff and the garden is filled with shadows.

No word is spoken: the tears come later.

CHAPTER TWELVE

'Sorry,' said Nest later, when they were clearing up after lunch. 'I had a complete sense of humour failure. I'm sure you're right and it's just that she's so confused. Anyway, there's no reason to take it out on you.'

'I've been wondering whether I should tell Helena that we simply can't cope.' Mina emptied the washing-up water away and wiped round the sink. 'If it's a deteriorating process then it may go in stages. Today we can manage, tomorrow we can't. I shouldn't have agreed to it at all.'

'*We* agreed,' Nest pointed out. 'It was a joint decision. It was just her coming into my room—'

'I know,' said Mina quickly. 'I'm sure she meant no harm. And you were always over-imaginative.'

Nest began to chuckle. 'I think we both were. All those books we read. I can't begin to count how many characters I was in love with. Mr Rochester. Steerforth. Ralph Hingston – do you

136

remember Mama reading *Portrait of Clare* to us? How I adored Ralph.'

'Oh, goodness, yes.' Mina put away the last plate and paused, remembering. 'Albert Campion. Berry. Richard Hannay. And Peter Wimsey . . .'

'No.' Nest shook her head, nose wrinkling. 'No, not Wimsey. He was rather mere.'

Mina grinned at her. ' "Personally I am a bit parshial to mere people",' she quoted and they laughed together, a whole shared past flowing richly between them.

'What's the joke?' Georgie was watching them from the doorway.

'Oh, nothing much.' Nest fought down an unworthy impulse, remembering the tiny, bitter, childhood struggles for power, resisting the temptation to exclude her oldest sister. 'We were talking about all the people we'd been in love with. Just being silly.'

'It's funny you should say that.' Georgie came further into the kitchen, smiling at them: a sly, knowing smile. 'I was only thinking earlier about Tony Luttrell. Do you remember him, Mina?'

'Yes,' said Mina after a moment. 'Yes, of course I remember him.'

'I think I remember him too.' Nest frowned thoughtfully. 'Although I must have been quite young. How odd! I remember him with Mama, being terribly upset . . .' Too late she caught sight of Mina's face, grim with hurt, and, confused and surprised, hurried to repair the blunder. 'We were thinking of going out, Georgie,' she said. 'We're

137

going to the Valley of the Rocks. I wonder if Mother Meldrum's Tea Rooms is still open . . . ?' She could hear herself gabbling, aware of Georgie's watchful, almost amused gaze flicking between them.

'I'm sure it will be.' Mina seemed to have regained her serenity. 'With weather like this it'll be open until after half-term at least. We might be able to have a walk so bring a warm jacket, Georgie. I'll go and find the dogs, Nest, and then we'll get your chair into the camper.'

They drove slowly up the steep drive, turning left, eastwards towards Lynton, over the high road on the edge of the Down, which plunged precipitously into the Channel. This afternoon, the water dazzled in the autumn sunshine, the silky skin of the sea rippling lustrously until it met with the sheer grey cliffs where it broke in gentle creamy foam against the unyielding rock. The dying bracken streaked the moors with shades of russet and amber, camouflaging the shy, tawny deer, and shaggy, heavy-headed ponies kicked up their heels or cropped the close-grazed turf. Below them a raft of gulls, snow-white against the sapphire waves, drifted inshore whilst others screamed derisively from their precarious roosts on the high stony ledges.

As the camper, holding left at Holdstone Down Cross, plunged into the narrow lane that led to Trentishoe church, Nest was thinking of the expression on Mina's face. Staring out at the tall bushes of spiky gorse in bright brimstone flower, watching a flock of chaffinches fluttering above the beech-mast, she still felt as if she had unintentionally pried into something very secret.

Nest thought: Tony Luttrell. I *do* remember him.

She clung to the back of Georgie's seat, murmuring soothingly to the dogs, as they bumped sharply downhill beside the church, passing beneath the ragstone wall of a high-perched cottage and the old farmhouse with its recently converted outbuildings, into the deep, single-tracked cleave. Images were forming in her head: a young man standing on the terrace, laughing with Mina and Mama, a cigarette cocked lightly in the fingers of one hand whilst the other gesticulates, embellishing a scene that he describes to them; a thin face with a long, mobile mouth. Tony Luttrell: how odd that Georgie should think of him after all these years.

'I'd forgotten,' said Georgie slowly, as the road dipped into the wooded lanes of the Heddon Valley, 'I'd forgotten how beautiful it is.'

The other two smiled, her appreciation binding them briefly together so that they travelled for a while in a peaceful, harmonious silence, between the stone-faced banks topped with neatly clipped beech hedges, the turning leaves glowing coppery gold.

Unreeling like a silent film, the pictures continued to project onto Nest's inner eye: a young

Mina with Tony Luttrell in some kind of uniform, sitting together on the sofa in the drawing-room, and, once, very smart in a dinner jacket whilst Mina clings to his arm in a cloudy, rose-coloured chiffon. Nest frowned, cudgelling her memory, aware that a sense of affection informed these memories, recalling that she too had liked him. He had been kind, she thought, playing racing demon with her and Timmie and – oh, yes! – he'd owned a little open-topped sports car, so dashing and romantic. They'd taken turns to sit in the driving-seat, pretending to drive it. Timmie had worn Tony's pale yellow, washed-leather string gloves, far too big on his small hands.

Nest smiled to herself as the camper slowed to negotiate the bustle outside the Hunter's Inn where a coach-party stood; some looking hopefully towards the National Trust shop, some of them booted for serious walking.

'We could have tea here on the way back,' suggested Mina. 'Jan always takes good care of us and Georgie would like Charlie, the peacock, don't you think, Nest?'

'Mmm? Oh, yes, probably. Let's see what the time is when we get to Mother Meldrum's, shall we? Do you remember the wild peacocks, Georgie?'

'Of course I do.' Georgie sounded sulky, irritable as always when she was treated as a visitor rather than a local. 'Of course I remember them.'

The fragile harmony was in danger of being shattered and Nest was prey to a familiar guilty uneasiness.

'Sorry,' she muttered. 'Sorry. Silly of me . . .' and bent to pat Polly Garter, curled on the blanket at her feet.

'Not far now,' said Mina pacifically, as they chugged across field-topped cliffs above Woody Bay, and Nest eagerly craned back towards the west to see a tanker, out of Avonmouth, passing slowly down the Channel; on the further shore, the hills of Wales dreamed tranquilly; insubstantial and mysterious.

Georgie stared from the window, soothed again by the beauty and the peace, her mind temporarily, happily, rooted in the present. She tensed a little in her seat as Mina slowed the camper on the mossy bridge so that they might watch the waterfall tumbling down a rocky cliff-face, where alder and hazel leaned together and hart's-tongue fern and pennywort clung in crevices.

'There's the folly,' she said presently, pointing excitedly to the Duty Point Tower, standing above Cuddycleave Wood.

She fell silent again but remained alert as Mina stretched to pay their toll and the camper moved slowly on, past Lee Abbey and into the narrow valley road between the craggy, piled rocks. Voices from her childhood murmured in her ears; memories of other journeys in the car with restless siblings, and Mama, always ready to protect Papa from irritation with a game: I-spy or spotting. 'I wonder who will be first to see a pony?' or 'A choccy for whoever spots a buzzard,' and Georgie, sitting with her nose pressed against the window, watching, determined to be first.

'Castle Rock,' she cried triumphantly, now, pleased to be first again, determined to prove her local knowledge. 'Look, Mina. Do you see the goats? Up there on Rugged Jack?'

Mina, too grateful for this exhibition of sanity to deprive her of her triumph, spoke sharply to Captain Cat – who was inclined to resent the goats – and allowed Georgie also to notch up the White Lady, thus completely restoring her sister's good humour.

Watching the wild goats, bearded and horned, playing amongst the boulders on the gorse-covered slopes, Nest's memory still reeled slowly across nearly sixty years: Tony pleading with Mama, his face tight with despair, and, later, Mina weeping. Why? Had Mama refused to give her approval to the match? Why should she?

The past, however, refused to give up its secrets and, presently, seeing that Mother Meldrum's was open for business, they stopped to have some tea.

That evening, with Georgie in bed, exhausted by the day's outing, and Nest finally settled, Mina went gladly to her room, the dogs clattering about her feet. There had been no message from Elyot yesterday evening and she was beginning to fear that she might have been too forward in suggesting a visit to Ottercombe. Perhaps he was finding it difficult to frame a refusal that was both polite and convincing?

'Po-po-po,' the air escaped her lips on an

outward exhalation of breath as she undressed slowly. Manhandling the camper through the steep countryside was beginning to be an effort for her, and her neck and arms ached alarmingly, yet she dreaded the time when she might be unable to drive. How would they manage, so far from shops, so isolated, if she had to give up driving?

Mina thrust these fears away, comforted as always by her familiar belongings, murmuring love words to the dogs as they stirred and yawned upon their beds. Despair – the enemy within – was always tensed, ready to muscle into a moment of cheerfulness, to wrestle down a fragile content-ment. She undressed slowly, rather painfully, grateful for the warmth from the radiator. Central heating, like electricity, had come late to Ottercombe and Mina could still remember icy rooms, dressing beneath the bedclothes, huddling round the fire in the drawing-room. Only the kitchen with the range, later replaced by an oil-fired Esse, had been really warm.

Now, as she cast off her clothes and reached for the long fleecy wrapper, a tiny flickering excite-ment fluttered beneath her ribcage. She tidied up, deliberately prolonging the expectation, setting the magician marionette dancing and turning on his hook, and then went into the alcove. Anxious now, she switched on the com-puter, moving the mouse, eyes fixed on the screen: five unread messages – and one from Elyot. Foolishly weak with relief she opened it, scanning it quickly for signs of any change, and then read it slowly, her heart light again.

From: Elyot
To: Mina

Things are not too good here. Yesterday, the carer came in to look after Lavinia whilst I took a few hours off to get out into the country and stretch my legs. The weather is more like May than October, isn't it? I had a wonderful walk in the hills, so refreshing and uplifting, but unfortunately, on my way home I clipped a parked car and still feel ridiculously shaken by the episode. The owner, a young man, was uncomplimentary about 'old buffers' being allowed on the roads and I felt strangely humiliated. Worse, when I got home, I found that Lavinia had been very difficult and the carer was rather worried about her, suggesting that she was deteriorating and that I might not be able to cope for very much longer.

I can tell you, my dear friend, that once she had gone I was prey to the most terrible depression. Coming on top of my silly accident, this news managed to destroy all the recharging to my batteries that the exercise had achieved. What shall I do when I can no longer drive? How could I possibly put Lavinia into a home and walk away from her? I was too low to talk to you last night – I don't sound much better now, do I? – but I

144

needed to make contact. At these moments the only people who can really help are those who are in a similar position and your offer of a few days' holiday has been like a tiny sparkle of light at the end of a very long dark tunnel. Bless you for it. Even if it never happens, the thought of it is keeping me sane – just.

I hope all is reasonably well with you?

Mina sat for some moments, deep in thought. Presently she began to type, in her careful, two-fingered way.

From: Mina
To: Elyot

How strange, Elyot, that our experiences seem to bear a close comparison of late. Georgie and Lavinia are clearly suffering from the same kind of mental problems and she is beginning to make trouble – well, Georgie always did that! But it's these swings from past to present that unnerve me. She upset Nest by going into her room early this morning, not doing anything, or speaking, but simply standing in silence in the dark. Poor old Nest, who has always been highly strung, nearly died of fright and was very upset. The trouble is, it seems impossible to confront Georgie simply because I don't know how it might take her. Mentally, she's clearly unstable. Nowhere near as bad as it is for you, I know that, and, anyway, Georgie is not my responsibility. If I insisted, Helena would come and remove her, but she is my sister. The trouble is that she's worrying Nest, talking about a secret. Well, we all have those, don't we, but there is something rather serious here. I only wish I knew which secret Georgie is thinking she knows. Oh dear! How odd that makes us sound but it's such a relief to talk to you about it.

As to the driving, yes! My terror too. I was so tired after our trip this afternoon, and, like you, I had terrible fears about how long I could keep going. We can't let it get us down. I know you've read *The Screwtape Letters* but I wonder if you've read Bernard Haring's *Hope is the Remedy*? His Uncle Screwtape is the Super-Skunk, presiding over a Universal Congress of Skunks, and their agenda is to transform their enemy, the Church, into a perfect sacrament of pessimism. He knows that Christians – and that goes for most people too – cannot survive if pessimism is injected and hope destroyed. We can't afford despair, old friend. One day you'll come to Ottercombe, I feel quite sure of it, and, meanwhile, we have this luxury of communication.

Didn't you tell me that your son was due home from abroad later this year? That's something to hold on to, isn't it? And we have Jack and his family, and Lyddie visiting on Saturday. They will certainly cheer us up. Forgive me if I'm beginning to sound dangerously trite but I know how close to the edge we both are.

Stay in touch, Elyot. You are much in my thoughts.

His reply came swiftly.

From: Elyot
To: Mina

My dear Mina, you have restored me. I haven't read *Hope is the Remedy* but I shall make a point of doing so now. I think I need it!

Goodnight and God bless you.

Mina breathed deeply with relief and a vague, warming happiness. Smiling a little she began to open her other messages.

CHAPTER THIRTEEN

Earlier that same evening, Lyddie had been
hurrying through the narrow streets, hoping to
get to The Place before the rain started in earnest.
A soft, grey mist rolling in from the west had hung
like a gauze curtain before the sinking sun,
quenching its splashy, burning splendour so that
the colours blurred and ran together, gold and
scarlet and amethyst staining gently into a
delicate, pearly dusk. Lyddie had watched it from
the field gate in the lane above the town, whilst
the Bosun pottered nearby, waiting for the last
rosy flush to be extinguished before returning
home to change into something that would give
her confidence for supper at The Place. During
the last two days, since the row over the letter, a
kind of truce had begun to stretch between them
and Lyddie was finding the strain of behaving like
a polite stranger difficult to maintain. She'd been
rather shocked – and then frightened – to discover that Liam seemed almost indifferent to the

loss of their happy relationship. That evening, after the row, she'd found it impossible to stroll into The Place as if nothing had happened. How could she see him like that, in public, after what had happened between them?

He'd returned home in the early hours of the morning and had been surprised to find her waiting up for him.

'Why aren't you in bed?' he'd asked, almost irritably – and when she'd gone to him, hoping to soften him, to explain why she'd been unable to come to The Place, he'd said that it was too late for emotional scenes and they'd both best get some sleep. Silenced, humiliated, she'd trailed upstairs behind him, wondering if he'd relent once they were in bed together. He'd turned on his side away from her, at once, and had been asleep in minutes. She'd lain, stiff and unhappy, wide-eyed in the darkness, listening to his regular, unforced breathing. Presently, she'd crept out of bed and gone downstairs to make some tea, drinking it with one arm round the Bosun's neck. He'd been delighted to see her, charmed by this break from routine, and was rather sorry when she went back upstairs, ascending away from him into the darkness. Towards dawn she'd fallen into a heavy sleep and, when she'd wakened, Liam had gone.

His note was on her desk: 'It's going to be a busy day – we've got the VAT inspector in the office. See you this evening for supper as usual.'

She'd seen it as an olive branch and, anxious to build on even this small peace-offering, had gone, as usual, for supper. Liam, however, had remained in the office for most of the evening and even Joe had worn a preoccupied expression that did not encourage any kind of intimacy. As they'd walked home, she'd almost been afraid to ask Liam too much about the inspector's visit, lest he interpreted her interest as unwarranted curiosity, but had managed to intimate that she wished that they could find some way back to their usual ease of manner. It was clear that Liam had been drinking, something he rarely did when he was working, and, although he was more approachable than he had been the previous evening, nevertheless there was an odd indifference, almost a brutality, about him that unnerved her. This time he made love to her with a passion that held no tenderness whatever and yet she still clung to him, determined to break through this stranger's façade to the real Liam, whom she loved.

Once again, he fell asleep immediately but at least, this time, there remained some semblance of an embrace and, comforted by his warm, relaxed body, she was able to sleep. He brought her a mug of tea in the morning, but the constraint was still there, although she'd tried to smile at him, to indicate her love.

'So what time are you away to your cousin Jack?' he'd asked – and, when she'd told him she'd cancelled her visit, he'd looked quite put out.

'How could I go when we're like this?' she'd pleaded. 'Can't you see that it would have been impossible?'

'Mother of God!' he'd exclaimed. 'What a child you are' – but then he had relented and stretched out a hand to her.

'I was going to take the day off to go to Dorset,' she'd said, holding his hand tightly, 'so couldn't we spend some time together? Take the Bosun and go for a walk somewhere? It looks as if it's going to be a glorious day.'

'I couldn't possibly,' he told her, looking away from her disappointment, disengaging his hand. 'The VAT inspector's not done with us yet, I'm afraid. I'll be stuck in the office with him till lunch-time at least, maybe longer.'

'But you'll be home this afternoon?'

'I hope so. If not, then I'll certainly be able to have supper with you this evening. Is that a date?'

'Oh, yes,' she'd said, grateful for this much at least and responding to his lighter tone. 'I'll be there.'

So here she was, the Bosun padding at her side, hurrying to be indoors before the rain increased. She was a little earlier than usual but this was deliberate. She was hoping to be at her seat in the snug before the café filled up. She knew she was being foolish but she flinched at the thought of facing the glances of the now-familiar clients, of threading her way between occupied tables, believing that those who knew her might guess from her expression that all was not well between her and Liam. It came as a tiny unwelcome shock to realize that she still counted herself so much on the outside; no warmth or true friendliness

151

awaited her here; only polite greetings and the knowledge that any fall from grace would delight one or two regulars. Of course, there was Joe . . .

She paused inside the door, fumbling with the Bosun's lead, glad to see The Place was nearly empty. Two men sat on stools at the bar near the door talking quietly together, the background CD – an Aretha Franklin recording – giving them conversational privacy. Lyddie straightened up and looked around her as if for the first time, approving the black-and-white tiled floor, whitewashed rough-stone walls and the large gilt-framed mirrors. Comfortable, cushioned basket-weave chairs were set at the round, black-stained beech tables, which each had its posy of fresh flowers and a candle in a wrought-iron holder. The long bar, with its high stools, stretched the length of one wall and the snug was right at the back, just outside the kitchen door. In one corner a narrow staircase curved to an upper floor where the offices, storerooms and lavatories were situated. Discreet wall lights gave an intimate glow, the place was fresh and clean and inviting, and, through the glass panes of the kitchen door, Lyddie could see the kitchen staff working amicably together as if in a silent movie, cut off from the small world outside the sound-proofed door.

Passing between the tables, she was nearly at the entrance to the snug when she heard the conversation, low-pitched but tense. The words were not clear but the tone was; she recognized the voices of Joe and Rosie – and they were arguing. The background music made it impossible to hear, or to make her approach heard, and Lyddie paused anxiously, wondering what she should do. The Bosun, however, had no such finer feelings. He shouldered his way past her and wagged cheerfully into the snug, confident of his welcome. The voices ceased abruptly and, by the time Rosie emerged, Lyddie had moved back into the body of the room and was busy taking off her long raincoat.

'Oh, hi!' She smiled at Rosie as if surprised to see her. 'It's beginning to rain quite hard. We only just made it in time. I thought there was nobody here.'

Rosie watched her for a moment, not speaking, until Joe came out of the snug behind her and Lyddie was able to smile at him too, as naturally as she could.

'I'm a bit early,' she was beginning – and then, to her relief, a couple came in, exclaiming at the weather, and Rosie moved behind the bar.

'Come and sit down,' Joe said, smiling back at Lyddie. 'You *are* a bit earlier than usual, and Liam's still in the office, but you must have a drink and then I'll go and tell him you're here. I know he wants to eat with you this evening. I've had instructions.'

Her heart was warmed by his words, and by his welcome, and courage flowed once more in her veins. She sat down in the corner of the snug, the Bosun stretched just outside, and waited for her drink.

'So.' He put a glass of wine in front of her and slid onto the opposite bench. 'How are you? I didn't have a chance to talk to you last night, we were too preoccupied with the man from the VAT, but I think he's finished with us and we've passed all the tests with flying colours!'

He was friendly, easy in his corner, yet Lyddie still sensed uneasiness beneath the joky exterior.

'I'm worried about Liam.' She said the words without really thinking about them; they seemed to jump from her lips like the toads from the princess's mouth, and she watched his expression change.

'Worried?' Joe never drank when he was working, so, having nothing to occupy his hands, nothing to sip whilst he thought up some light response, he folded his arms across his chest and frowned a little. 'What's to worry about? He seems fine to me.' But he would not look at her, shifting, instead, sideways onto the table, one leg stretched along the bench, so as to stare out of the doorway of the snug.

'I don't know.' She rested her arms on the table. 'I hoped you'd be able to tell me. He keeps the whole business side so private but there's something on his mind.'

She noted that he looked relieved, watched him relax slightly. 'Oh, that's Liam all over,' he said. 'Even I don't know what's going on when it comes to the business. It's his baby, always has been. No good getting upset about it.'

'It's not quite that.' She wondered how much

she could confide in Joe. 'The thing is, I've been wondering if the business needs money. If— Oh, hell, I don't know how to put this. We've had a bit of a row about it, actually.'

She looked so miserable that Joe swung his leg off the bench and faced her directly across the table.

'OK,' he said. 'I know you saw a letter. Liam told me something about it and I think he was over the top about it, if you want my opinion. You're his wife, after all, and I think he's too obsessed – well, possessive, anyway – about The Place. It's his whole world and you're going to have to try to accept that. But there is no need to worry about the financial side of it. Honestly. It's not unusual to raise money against your own property when you're in a partnership. It means that the liability is equally shared. We've got to modernize the kitchen and that's the long and short of it. I'm doing the same, raising money against my flat, and Rosie's not too thrilled about it, I can tell you.'

'Is that what you were arguing about?' she asked, comforted by his matter-of-factness.

He flushed, clearly embarrassed, and she cursed herself that, in her relief, she'd been so tactless.

'Anyway,' she said quickly, covering the lapse, 'it's simply that I might have some money coming to me, you see, and I wondered if I could help him.' She shrugged. 'You know, stop him having to borrow.'

'Liam's a control freak,' Joe told her. 'He likes to do everything himself. It's crazy if you've got some money and you're prepared to let him use it – but that's Liam!'

'And who is it taking my name in vain?' Liam appeared in the doorway, smiling at their discomfiture, stroking the Bosun's head. 'What lies is he telling you about me?'

It was clear that, between Aretha Franklin and the people now filling the café, Liam had heard only the last few words and Lyddie swallowed in a dry throat and took a quick, nervous sip at her wine.

'I was just telling her what a mean, arrogant bastard you are.' Joe got up, grinning easily. 'But I'm sure she knows that by now, poor girl.'

'She does indeed.' Liam took Joe's place, lifting Lyddie's hand to his lips. 'I don't deserve her at all but you knew that anyway.'

Joe turned away, laughing. 'I'll get you a beer,' he said, 'and then you can tell me what you want to eat.'

'It's the truth of it,' Liam agreed, still holding her hand. 'I'm a mean, arrogant bastard. Can you forgive me at all?'

'Oh, Liam.' She was so overjoyed to see him easy and charming, so loving as he looked at her, that she knew she'd forgive him anything. 'I'm really sorry about the letter. It was quite wrong of me—'

'Shall we forget the old letter? The VAT man has gone, the saints be praised, and I feel like a reprieved man. Could you manage another drink?'

'Yes, please,' she said gratefully. 'Oh, I could.'

He leaned to kiss her, quickly to begin with, and then lingeringly, until Joe, coming back with a menu, was obliged to bang on the table to gain their attention, so that the three of them laughed together and harmony was re-established.

CHAPTER FOURTEEN

Driving to Ottercombe on Saturday morning, Lyddie still felt all the relief and happiness that making up with Liam had brought her. Within her relationships, Lyddie dealt in absolutes: she was incapable of living with strife, unable to ignore surly tempers or icy silences. She liked open discussion, however painful, and preferred communication to the bottling up of discontent. Misunderstandings could so easily blow up into full-scale resentment, irritation could develop into intolerance, and she believed that every relationship worth nurturing needed attention to detail. She'd discovered fairly early on that not everyone worked in the same way and she was quite content to leave those who did not agree with her to their own principles, though, as yet, she had not been prepared to compromise her own.

Now, despite the relief and happiness, she was

experiencing the first stirrings of anxiety. She was forced to admit that there was a whole part of Liam's life to which she had no access: a no-go area that was closed to her. Had this been clear from the beginning or had she wilfully misled herself because she'd wanted him so badly? Even now, although Liam was full of apologies for his outburst and the current of love was flowing once more between them, Lyddie was obliged to face the fact that he had not budged an inch from his original position. The Place was his and she had no part or say in it. The subject of the loan to be raised against the house, along with her own offer, had been simply despatched straight back into that no-go area; it was as if these matters had never been raised and, despite her policy of negotiation at all costs, Lyddie had found herself unable to resurrect them. She knew why: the resumption of their loving, warm, easygoing pattern of life had been too precious to risk. He'd shown her his weapons – withdrawal of love, silence, coldness – and she'd quailed before them.

She tried to convince herself that it was early days, that Liam could not be expected to change overnight with regards to his passion for his business. After all, she knew what it was like to love one's job, she'd worked with professionals who juggled their work and their families; she knew that there had to be a certain amount of compartmentalization and a great deal of self-discipline. Five years of Liam's life were bound up in the wine bar: it had been his whole world. She needed to make allowances, to give him space to adjust. Part of the cause of the row, she also told herself, had been to do with the VAT inspector's visit; the timing had been most unfortunate and it was now obvious that Liam had been pretty uptight until the accounts had been given the all-clear. How quick he'd been then to make amends, to acknowledge his faults and to sweep away all her apologies for opening his letter. Nevertheless, it was also clear that that particular subject was closed, off limits, and, in her silent acquiescence, too grateful for his love to risk it again, she had surrendered her own principles.

As the car fled along the A39, leaving Hartland Point and Bude to the west, circumnavigating Barnstaple and speeding away again towards the turning at Kentisbury Ford, Lyddie tried to convince herself that she was exaggerating, that they were both recovering from their first serious row, and that Liam would slowly relinquish his grip on the business and allow her to enter into it with him. She must be patient. The fear remained, however; a tiny shadow cast across her happiness.

Both Mina and Nest were aware of it as they watched her playing with Toby and Flora or laughing and talking with Jack and Hannah. There was a febrile quality to her brightness that worried both of them but they were too concerned about Georgie to attach too much weight to it. They guessed that it might have something to do with

Liam and, whilst they both felt the impotence of being obliged to stand back and watch a beloved child suffer, they also knew that marriage to such a one as Liam was bound to be hedged about with difficulties. They, like Lyddie's colleagues in London, could see past the charm and sexiness, beyond the fascination and the challenge, to the determined, driven, restlessness that possessed Liam's soul; but then, they were not in love with him.

After lunch, however, Georgie was beginning to behave oddly enough to keep them both alert. She'd begun the day well, appearing to have a reasonable grasp on the proceedings. Nest managed to avoid irritating her, reminding herself not to fall into the trap of asking her sister if she remembered Hannah and the children, talking instead with Mina about the little family whilst the three of them had breakfast. Georgie had not contributed but appeared to be listening and taking it in.

'After all,' said Mina philosophically, as she and Nest cleared up afterwards, 'Jack and Hannah know the score. I doubt they'll be offended if Georgie muddles them with someone else, and the children won't understand anyway.'

'As long as she doesn't . . .' Nest hesitated, 'you know – blurt something out.'

Anxiety curdled Mina's gut. 'The thing is, we don't know what it is she might blurt out.'

Even as they stared at each other fearfully, a commotion was heard outside: Jack and his family had arrived. The sisters hurried through the hall, the dogs racing ahead, and out into the garden. Jack had already released Toby from his seat and he came hurtling round the front of the car to greet the dogs, whilst Flora could be heard struggling with Hannah and wailing, 'No! No!' and, 'Get down! Get *down!*' as her mother undid the straps of her chair.

Jack kissed his aunts and looked tolerantly upon his family. Flora had now fought her way both out of the car and from Hannah's restraining grasp and stood swaying uncertainly on the gravel, her gaze fixed upon the dogs.

'Which is Nogood Boyo?' asked Toby, kneeling amongst the three of them. He thought the name was exceedingly funny. 'Why is he called Boyo? Why is he no good?'

'Because he's a very naughty person,' explained Mina, 'and he's Welsh.'

'What's Welsh?' asked Toby, puzzled, stroking Nogood Boyo's head and submitting to being licked upon the cheek. 'Why is he Welsh?'

'Don't,' murmured Jack. 'Please, Aunt, just don't. After "no" and one or two other unsavoury words of the moment, "why", "how" and "what" follow in quick succession. It won't stop with defining "Welsh", I promise you. Next it'll be Dylan Thomas, his life and work, and after ten minutes you'll be giving a dissertation on *Under Milk Wood* and then how will you explain Polly Garter, I wonder?'

Mina tucked her hand under his arm, chuckling.

'I was always taught that one should answer children's questions,' she said, 'but your father and Nest gave me some very bad moments when they were small, I admit.' To Toby she said: 'Boyo's a Sealyham. That's the kind of dog he is. And Sealyhams come from Wales.'

'Dogs are different makes, Tobes,' Hannah told him. 'You know that. The Bosun doesn't look like these, does he? That's because he comes from Switzerland. See?'

'And the secret, at this point,' said Jack, beaming at his aunts, 'is that when he answers "No", we all pretend we haven't heard him. Now who was it mentioned something about coffee?'

'Come on in,' said Nest, feeling more light-hearted than she had for several weeks. 'You are hopeless, Jack. It must be due to Hannah that the children are so good.'

'My yoke-mate is a miracle of patience,' he said, dodging a blow from his wife with a dexterity born of practice. 'But teaching small boys all day long instils a high degree of self-preservation. Ah, here's Aunt Georgie. Good morning, Aunt, and how are you?'

Georgie allowed herself to be kissed, stared fixedly at Hannah for a moment and stood watching the proceedings as Flora was whisked upstairs to have her napkins changed, Toby reflected upon the rival merits of orange juice and milk, trying to decide which he might like best, and Nest and Mina chattered and joked with Jack. As usual, they relaxed quickly into the happy, carefree aura

163

that he always so successfully created and, in the midst of their jollity, Lyddie and the Bosun arrived. Georgie was drawn smoothly into the conversation and even Flora, once she was allowed to have her juice sitting on the floor beside the Bosun, responded with a sunny amiability that charmed her older relatives.

Lunch passed without too many alarms but now, as they sat drinking coffee in the drawing-room with the french doors open to the terrace, Mina grew aware of the change taking place in Georgie. She'd managed one or two fairly sharp observations during lunch – which because of lack of space had been a buffet arrangement with the children at the kitchen table – but now that particular expression, which Mina was learning to dread, was transforming Georgie's face. Confused, even anguished, Georgie sat contemplating her family. In the drawing-room, the scene of so many family occasions, she seemed to drift in time, staring first at Toby, now at Flora, in puzzlement. She turned her eyes to Jack and saw Timmie sitting talking – but to whom? Was it Nest who sat beside him, leaning towards him, listening intently, as they had so often sat together in the past? Yet here was Nest, wheeling her chair into the circle, reaching for her coffee . . .

A child paused to look up at her, a small fair-haired boy with Timmie's eyes, puzzled by her unnatural immobility. Georgie stared back at him, remembering. Of course, these two tinies were Timmie and Nest and the other two, the grown-ups, must be Timothy and Mama. She chuckled to herself . . .

'I know a secret,' she said to the child – but, before Toby could take her up on this, Mina turned quickly, thankful that the ebb and flow of conversation had covered Georgie's words.

'Toby,' she said, 'take this cup to your mother, darling. Carefully, now. Don't spill.'

Distracted, Toby carried the coffee to Hannah and then flopped down beside the Bosun, stroking his smooth head and kissing him upon the nose.

'I wish we had a dog,' he murmured plaintively, and his parents rolled their eyes despairingly at one another.

A discussion about the fors and againsts of bringing up children with dogs around started up, and a tiny 'po-po-po' of relief escaped Mina's lips, but she felt tense and fearful, as if awaiting a blow of some kind. Nest, catching her eye, raised her brows questioningly but Mina felt unable to respond lest someone should see her. She smiled reassuringly at Nest and glanced again at Georgie. She had the look of one who had been unfairly thwarted; she hunched her shoulders, as if bridling, and her lips were compressed. Yet there remained an air almost of triumph; the air of one who wielded a secret power and relished it.

Lyddie was explaining, now, that she didn't work on her computer, that she used it for typing and filing but that she didn't edit on it.

'It's a different way of working,' she was telling

Jack, 'and I have actually turned down work because it's on disk. I'd have to learn it and, somehow, I just don't want to go there.'

'You should be more flexible,' he said teasingly. 'You should be ready to embrace new technology. Look at Aunt Mina and her e-mail.'

'Well, there you are.' Lyddie smiled affectionately at her aunt. 'But then, Aunt Mina has always been a trend-setter. She's a yes-person.'

'Absolutely right,' declared Jack. 'That describes her perfectly. A yes-person.'

'Oh, no.' Georgie had been wriggling in her corner, listening intently, watching for an opportunity. 'Not always, were you, Mina?'

Mina clasped her hands together. 'I don't think I know what any of you mean,' she countered lightly, praying for some kind of distraction.

'Not always,' insisted Georgie eagerly. 'You didn't say "yes" to Tony Luttrell, did you?' She began to smile, watching their faces, seeing surprise fading into anxiety and curiosity, enjoying the sudden, uncomfortable silence.

'Much too long ago to be interesting.' Nest used the voice that had once quelled classes of young students to good effect. 'Aren't you going to take these children down to the sea, Jack? The poor old Bosun is waiting for that walk you promised him.'

'The sea! The sea!' chanted Toby, scrambling to his feet, whilst Flora, who had been enjoying a little doze on Hannah's lap, woke suddenly and began to wail. The party broke up rapidly and Georgie was left alone, sitting on the sofa, still smiling.

'I know a secret,' she murmured – but there was nobody left to hear it.

CHAPTER FIFTEEN

Early in the evening, after the younger members of the family had gone, Mina, in her turn, walked down to the sea with the dogs.

'Will you be OK?' she asked Nest. 'It's just that I need to be alone for a bit. Georgie's asleep so I think you can safely relax.'

'I'll be fine.' Nest watched her anxiously. 'It's you I'm worried about.'

Mina managed a smile. 'No need. I shan't be long.'

She pulled on her blue Guernsey cardigan, picked up her stick from the brass holder by the front door and went away, along the terrace and through the small wicket gate that opened on to the path to the sea. It was rocky underfoot, stepped with roots from the trees that climbed the steep sides of the combe, and Mina walked carefully. The dogs were well ahead – scrabbling after a squirrel, who leaped and swung to safety in the branches of a tall beech – racing for the sheer joy of running with a thousand scents to lure them onwards. The stream tumbled along beside them, in full spate after the recent rain, cascading over the smooth, rounded boulders, lapping at the ferny banks. The dogs' high, excited barks were drowned in the sound of its rushing, although Polly Garter trotted back to encourage her mistress onward to the sea. Mina was scarcely aware of her; she was travelling back in time, remembering a springtime fifty-five years before.

It seems contrary to Mina that she should meet Tony Luttrell at a party given by the Goodenoughs; those Sneerwells whom she dislikes so much.

'Do come, Mina,' says Enid, having driven over one afternoon in the early spring of 1943 with the faithful Claude. 'It's not a terribly smart event. Just a little get-together with some officers of the SLI. I suppose you've heard of the Somerset Light Infantry?' she says lightly to Lydia, whom she considers almost mentally deficient, buried away at Ottercombe. 'They've been busy defending our Somerset coastline but I understand that they'll soon be off on a more dangerous mission.'

She likes to imply that she is in the know and Lydia, who has had a visit from one of the officers in regard to the beach at Ottercombe, is nevertheless quite happy to allow Enid her sense of superiority.

'We need some pretty girls,' says Claude with his sneering smile. 'There's a terrible shortage of them, don't you know? We need Mina to swell the ranks.'

'And what about Henrietta and Josie?' asks Enid. 'Surely Henrietta is old enough for parties? Will they be home from school for the holidays?'

'Oh dear.' Lydia grimaces a little. 'It will have to be both or neither, I'm afraid. There is only a year between them, you know, and I simply couldn't stand the fighting if Henrietta goes but not Josie.'

'And will Mina mind the competition?' Enid raises her thin brows teasingly.

Lydia looks at her daughter, knowing her dislike of the Goodenoughs, not wishing to see her upset or coerced.

'Of course I shouldn't,' says Mina, almost relieved, feeling that there will be safety in numbers. 'It sounds rather fun. But Josie is only fifteen, you know, and they can both be a bit silly, sometimes. I hope they'll behave themselves.'

'Quite like the Bennet sisters,' sniggers Claude. 'Now, are you an Elizabeth or a Jane, I wonder?'

'Mary Quilter's coming,' says Enid encouragingly, feeling that Claude has gone far enough and anxious that her party should be a success; three pretty girls, even if two of them are young and silly, are better than one. 'You know Mary, don't you? Her brother is an officer in the SLI. It will be fun, I promise you.'

Mina feels a flicker of excitement. 'But how shall we get over to you?' she wonders. 'I suppose we could cycle to Parracombe and catch the train to Lynton. Or maybe Seth might give us a lift . . . ?'

'Don't worry about transport,' says Enid kindly. 'We're all clubbing together with our petrol coupons so that one person can do a round trip. It'll be a bit of a squash, mind, but that's part of the fun, isn't it? We've decided that we deserve a little bit of excitement. Now that's settled, then.'

Once they've gone, Mina looks apprehensively at her mother.

'It will be fun,' says Mama comfortingly. 'And you don't get much fun, Mina. I'm only sorry that you'll still have Henrietta and Josie to keep an eye on. You have quite enough of that kind of thing here. Although it's so much quieter, now that Jean and Sarah and the babies have gone.'

'I don't mind them coming. Actually, I'm rather pleased. I should feel terribly shy all on my own. You have to remember that I shall hardly know anyone there.'

'You won't have time to feel shy with Henrietta loose,' predicts Mama. 'And now we must think about something to wear. I have some pretty things that should make up into something nice for you. There's that lovely green shantung, which suits our colouring so perfectly. It's much too long, of course, but we can do something about that. We'll telephone Georgie and ask her what the latest fashion is in London. Do they still have fashions, I wonder, in wartime?'

'But that's one of your best frocks,' says Mina, startled. 'It would be such a shame to cut it.'

'Nonsense.' Mama touches her lightly on the cheek. 'I shall never wear it again. Let's tell the Tinies that you've been invited to a party. They'll be so thrilled.'

'And what about Henrietta and Josie?'

'They must wear their school party frocks,' answers Mama firmly. 'Quite suitable for girls of their ages. And please don't mention it in your letters to them. No need for them to know until they come home.'

Mina feels that this is a shame – her sisters will lose all the thrill of anticipation – yet she knows that it is a wise decision. There will be no time for them to fall out over small pieces of finery or quarrel about whose garment is the prettiest.

The Tinies are, indeed, excited by the forthcoming party. *The Midnight Folk* is being read during the children's hour and they are enacting the story privately. Having endowed the young hero, Kay Harker, with a sister, Gerda – a subconscious nod to *The Snow Queen* – they spend their time searching for the Harker treasure. The owl in the woods is Blinky and the fox that they see in the gorse-covered slopes above the cleave is Mr Rollicum Bitem Lightfoot. They are rather at a loss, however, for substitutes for the evil Abner Brown and terrifying Sister Pouncer.

'We could use the Sneerwells if they came oftener,' says Nest sadly, 'but it seems rather unfair to use Mina and Mama.'

'We'll simply have to,' Timmie answers robustly. 'It can't be helped and, anyhow, they needn't know. We'll use Henrietta and Josie when they come home for Easter.'

'If only we had some cats,' grieves Nest, 'for Nibbins and Blackmalkin and Greymalkin. Jenna says Tiddles has had kittens but Mama says "No" because of her asthma.'

The party distracts them a little. Timmie wants to know all about the SLI and Nest is enchanted by the pretty frock that is being made up for Mina – 'Shoulders are square,' Georgie tells them firmly. 'I'll send some shoulder-pads down and a pattern' – and Mina takes time to sew a short, flaring skirt out of the spare pieces of shantung for her small sister. Nest takes off the inevitable gingham, passed down from her older sisters, and swirls happily before Mama's long looking-glass.

Two weeks later, squashed into Claude's roomy, dark green Rover 16, Mina feels almost sick with excitement. Her long, shining black hair is swept upwards, held in place with tortoiseshell pins, although feathery strands escape to slide around her throat, and the soft silky shantung feels deliciously sensuous against her cool white skin. Happiness and expectation lift her above the wrangling of her younger sisters, who are still arguing over which of them should have been allowed to wear the most respectable pair of party shoes. They are only silenced when the car stops at the eleventh-century church at Martinhoe to pick up another two members of the party, and they travel on in an amicable, rather shy silence until they arrive at the Goodenoughs' house, high above the little town of Lynton.

As they put their wraps in the guest bedroom,

and Henrietta and Josie barge each other in an attempt to stand before the glass, Mina catches a glimpse of herself between their elbows. The minimal amount of make-up Mama has allowed lends a glow to her cheeks and emphasizes her eyes, which stare back at her, huge in her small, oval face; the high-piled hair gives height and sophistication, and the softly falling folds of silk accentuate her slenderness. Her sisters turn away, sweeping her with them, and they hurry down into the wide, brightly lit hall – 'I wish *we* had electric light,' says Henrietta discontentedly – and into the drawing-room, where some of the other guests are already assembled.

'Ah, here they are at last,' cries Enid Goodenough, with a show of affection that surprises all three girls. 'Now, come along and meet these young men who have all been waiting for you.'

Dazed by so many strange faces and names, Mina smiles, shaking hands again and again, until the young officer who has been part of a small circle of people in the corner turns to meet her. His blue eyes light up, as if she is, indeed, the one for whom he has been waiting, and he takes her hand in his warm fingers.

'Hello,' he says. 'Isn't this fun? I'm Tony Luttrell and you must be one of the beautiful Miss Shaws.'

For all of that April, and for part of May, the cleave and the beach, and the down high above the channel, become their private sanctuary. Here they walk, arms entwined, amongst the uncurling bracken, looking down upon the waves rolling in, driven by a westerly gale, to beat against the tall, grey cliffs; or, on hot afternoons, they sit close together on one of the flat boulders that edge the beach, watching the sleek otters chasing and rolling in the surf, water droplets flying and flashing in the sunshine; or, on still, quiet evenings, they stand beneath the trees, the scent of bluebells all about them, locked in long, dizzying embraces that shake them both and make them long for more. The frenzied, urgent needs of wartime lovers, and the changing world beyond this small corner of Exmoor, have left Mina untouched, and Tony, only twenty-one and yet to be in any real danger, is no more experienced than she, so it seems the natural course for him to approach Lydia so as to ask formally for Mina's hand in marriage.

The interview takes place one May evening in the lamp-lit drawing-room. The french windows stand open to the soft, warm air and a thrush is singing in the wild garden.

Lydia listens gravely to Tony's stammered declaration of love, careful not to smile at his earnestness. During these last four weeks she has grown deeply fond of him, her maternal instinct, reaching out to his youth, warmed by the sweetness he shows to her beloved daughter. He brings the Tinies little gifts, enters into their games, and the affection with which he treats Lydia goes some way to healing her own unhappy, grieving heart.

'I shall have to speak to my husband,' she tells him, 'but as for me, my dear boy, I think you know how delighted I am.'

'The unit will be going away soon,' he tells her anxiously, 'and we should like to be engaged before I go. Is it possible that you might speak to Mr Shaw soon?'

'Very soon,' she promises him, 'but he will want to meet you, Tony, and it is difficult for him to get away from London. The formal engagement might have to wait a little longer.'

'But we have your blessing?'

Lydia gets up from her chair, casting aside her needlework, and goes to him, embracing him as if he were one of her own children. 'You have my blessing,' she tells him. 'As long as you continue to love her as you do now.'

She leaves them in peace, sitting together by the fire, weaving their dreams of future bliss, until Tony drags himself away, his few hours of leave over. Mina goes out with him, as usual, to see him off, listening to the little sports car roaring away up the drive and out onto the high road over the moor.

Now, fifty-five years later, down on the beach, Mina sat on a rock watching the dogs playing at the water's edge, thinking of that love and remembering how it transformed her quiet, placid life. Shaken and moved beyond even her imagination, his love had been everything that she'd ever dreamed of: the culmination of every romance that she'd read. She'd adored him, investing in his youthful, charming chivalry every last ounce of her love and trust. Only much later could she imagine the irresistible atmosphere that possessed the young men of the newly raised 9th Battalion; the excitement and the urgency as they trained for the invasion of Normandy. The young must boast their way to maturity and, now, she was able to understand how his fall from grace had been simply a part of the whole 'live now, for tomorrow we die' war mentality that she'd experienced for herself only when, finally, she went to London to stay with Georgie.

Mina sat on in the fading light, tears on her wrinkled cheeks, her heart heavy with regret and pain. How could he have lived up to such adoration, such worship? And why, oh, why, when the unit returned in November, on its way to coastal defence in Berwick-upon-Tweed, had he been foolish enough to tell her of his brief affair with an older newly widowed woman in Cornwall?

'It was nothing,' he'd cried, his voice breaking now that he saw her shocked, hurt face. 'Nothing at all. I missed you so much and she'd lost her husband . . . Oh God! Can't you see that I'm telling you because I can't bear for anything to be between us. It was nothing. It's over. Please, Mina . . .'

Unable to understand, with their love debased, ruined, lying in tatters between them, she'd sent him away with a cold, proud face that only just managed to hide her anguish.

As she walked home in the twilight, hardly aware of the moths dancing, ghost-like, beneath the branches, and bats darting above her head, Mina recalled that last meeting: their shyness after six months' separation, the expectation and the terror. Nervous as she was, his foolish young-man bragging might have been forgiven had she been more experienced, more generous, but the thought of the widow in Cornwall stood mockingly, triumphantly, between them, destroying confidence and trust.

Mina thought: How strange that it should still hurt.

Suddenly, through the deepening dusk, a deep-pitched booming reverberated fitfully, an unearthly insatiate moan, the stuff of myth and legend. It was the disquieting 'belling' of the red stag, whose stentorian roar was challenged by another bellowing call a short way off. As she opened the gate into the garden Mina listened for the clash of antlers, strangely disturbed by the eerie, throbbing roaring, but the only sound was the trembling hoot of the owl echoing in the shadowy cleave. She paused for a moment, her hand still on the latch, and then followed the dogs, who ran ahead, looking forward to the warmth and comfort of the kitchen and their supper.

CHAPTER SIXTEEN

Lyddie parked the car in the only space left in the narrow road, coaxed the weary Bosun out onto the pavement and went into the house to change. Saturday nights at The Place were rather special: tables had to be reserved and a certain formality of dress was observed, although there was no specific rule. It seemed that there was a kind of implicit understanding amongst the clientele that Saturday nights were different and they took a certain pleasure in making an effort. Lyddie enjoyed the opportunity of dressing up and, this evening, chose a soft, velvet, figure-hugging dress in such a dark navy blue that it was almost black. The hemline flared around her slender calves and the scalloped edge of the boat-shaped neckline was bound with navy satin ribbon. She showered quickly, brushed her black hair until it flew about her face and then chose some pretty silver bangles, which the three-quarter-length sleeves showed to advantage. Grey stockings and navy suede pumps completed the outfit, and she paused to look at herself in the glass, gaining confidence from the reflection that smiled back at her. She picked up her long, well-worn, wool and cashmere coat – her London coat – and ran quickly down the stairs.

The Bosun, who had fallen asleep again in the hall, lifted his head and stared at her in disbelief as she urged him up. He'd spent the day fending off three small dogs and two children, been hauled from pillar to post, encouraged to swim in blood-chilling water and now, after another long journey in the car, he was being dragged out yet again. Good grief, he hadn't even had his supper! Struggling into a sitting position he sat for a moment, swamped with self-pity, until he heard the familiar sounds of biscuits being poured into a bowl and the grind of a tin-opener. Brightening a little he stood up and pottered into the kitchen. Ah, yes! His supper was being prepared. His tail waved very slightly and his tongue came out and polished up his chops a little. He felt that after all the demands that had been placed upon him in the last few hours he deserved some kind of nourishment. He ate heartily whilst his water bowl was being filled, and then drank some of the cold fresh water, looking forward to resuming a good, long sleep. However, before he could take up his favourite position, stretched out in the hall, the lead was being clipped about his neck and he was being hurried through the windy streets.

'You know you'll like it when you get there,'

Lyddie told him encouragingly as he padded wearily at her side. 'You love it when people tell you how wonderful you are. You're getting to be a sort of mascot.'

This was perfectly true. The regulars greeted him cheerily as the Bosun and Lyddie went in together, delighted to show the few new punters that they were 'locals', an impression they hoped to build on later when Liam made his round of the tables to chat. In the summer, The Place had been written up with enthusiasm in the *Independent*, and now a rumour was circulating that Jonathan Meades might be paying a visit: the locals were thrilled and everyone wanted to be in on that particular act.

Lyddie made her way between the tables to the snug, surprised at how nervous she felt at the thought of seeing Liam again. Despite the reconciliation she felt a fluttering anticipation that was not wholly joyful: there was some almost imperceptible change. Joe was behind the bar and he smiled at her as he pulled a pint, although his greeting was lost in the babble of voices and background music. She took the Bosun with her to the snug, pausing briefly at one or two tables so that he could be patted and admired but not allowing him to be a nuisance, and made him sit out of the way of the path from the kitchen and the bar. He was very glad to slump down, nose on paws, raising his head politely to acknowledge his most ardent admirers, but ready for a nap. Lyddie shrugged herself out of her coat. She knew that

Joe would bring her a glass of wine when he had a moment; meanwhile she sat on the outer edge of the bench where she could see the bar and a few of the tables.

Linda was on duty tonight, helping Joe behind the bar, and Mickey came swinging through the kitchen door, two plates held shoulder high, and winked at her as he passed. Lyddie wondered where Liam was but she didn't have the courage to go upstairs to the office, or into the kitchen to see if he were discussing the menu with Angelo, the chef, and she wondered if she would ever see herself as anything more than a privileged guest. During a brief lull, leaving Linda in charge of the bar, Joe brought her a drink and leaned beside her, looking out over the rapidly filling tables.

'Thanks.' She raised the glass to him. 'Is everything OK? You look a bit fraught.'

'Oh, I'm OK.' He didn't return her smile. 'Liam'll be down in a minute. He's just finishing off in the office.'

She sipped her wine, feeling oddly uneasy. 'It's busy tonight, isn't it? Is Rosie in? I don't see her anywhere.'

'No, she's not in.' A pause. 'She's not working here any more. Didn't Liam tell you?'

'No.' She stared up at him, shocked. 'But why? Has she got a better place somewhere?'

'I don't really know. We've split up. I don't know her plans. She's staying with a friend for a while.'

'But that's awful. I'm so sorry, Joe.' Lyddie

remembered the low, furious voices, Rosie's look as she came out of the snug with Joe behind her, and reached out to touch his crossed arms, not knowing what else to say.

'It's been coming for a while but I have to say that it's still a bit of a whammy.' He remained standing above her, remote, unapproachable. 'Here's Liam.'

Before she could speak to him again Joe moved back behind the bar as Liam crossed between the tables, raising a hand to this one, nodding to another, but not pausing until he reached the snug.

'So here you are. Safely back again. And how are the Aunts? And Jack?' He bent to kiss her, then leaned back again to study her. 'Your eyes are blue tonight, do you know that? I've never known a woman whose eyes change with the colour of her clothes.'

She was foolishly pleased with such an un-characteristically public display of affection, aware of the glances of several of the women diners, and tried to think of something sensible to say.

'I'm sorry to hear about Rosie,' was all she could think of. 'It's such a shock. Poor old Joe.'

'Well, that's just life, isn't it? Some you win, some you lose.'

He sounded philosophical, indifferent even, in the face of Joe's misfortune, and she looked surprised. He read disapproval in her face and leaned to kiss her again.

'If you ask me,' he murmured against her ear,

'he's well out of it. Joe can do better than that, I've always thought so.'

'Well, probably.' Lyddie, who believed this herself, could hardly argue with him. 'But it doesn't mean that he's not cut up about it.'

'Sure.' Liam nodded, straightening up and looking about as if he'd had enough of the topic, assessing the atmosphere of the bar, his eyes missing nothing. He glanced back at her. 'Could you manage some supper, do you think?'

'Yes. Yes, I could.' Lyddie was faintly annoyed by his indifference to Joe's plight. 'Unless, of course, it's time for the royal walkabout.'

His eyes narrowed a little, amused, acknowledging her thrust. 'Let 'em wait,' he said, and sat down opposite. 'Tell me about your day while we decide what to eat.'

Later that evening, Nest sat in bed, propped about by pillows, her book lying face downwards on her knees. She'd been unable to concentrate on the book, seeing Mina's face on its pages, hearing her voice.

'We were so cut off here, you see,' she'd said, sitting at the kitchen table, holding her mug of hot tea. 'Isolated as we were, the war was simply a dreary, boring time of endless shortages. We were often cold and hungry but we were never truly scared. Mama was so reclusive, she hardly ever listened to the wireless and was always careful not to let the little ones be made frightened. Ottercombe was another world. It wasn't until I went up to London, in nineteen forty-four, that I first experienced the greediness for life: the frenzy for extracting the most out of every single minute. Georgie and I talked about Tony. Actually, she was very sweet to me. She was in her element: the town mouse dispensing wisdom and guidance to the newly arrived country mouse.'

'Did she think that you should have forgiven him?'

'Part of her did.' Mina was trying to remember. 'She could sympathize with how it might have been for him. The other chaps egging him on, the pressure and that genetic imperative which we interpret as "I don't want to die before I've had sex" feeling which is so prevalent in times of real danger. But part of her didn't want me to be the first to be married – Georgie always needed to be the first – but, to be fair, she also wanted me to have a good time. She thought that I'd been buried alive down at Ottercombe and she genuinely wanted me to enjoy myself. She felt that I deserved it.'

'Wartime London, just before the invasion, must have come as a fearful shock.'

'Oh, it did. But it was a relief too not to have any time to think. And I used it to take my mind off Tony. He'd started to turn up at Ottercombe whenever he could get any kind of pass or leave, and the strain was frightful. I had to get away.'

'That's the bit I could remember,' agreed Nest. 'His pleading with Mama.'

'I didn't understand, you see. I was still living in the thirties. The war made a huge chasm in the world we knew but I discovered it too late. And, anyway, I was barely nineteen. The only men I knew were in books, cardboard and paste; a real flesh-and-blood one was beyond my ken. I knew nothing, then, about the complexities of human nature. How priggish I must have been!'

'You were never priggish,' protested Nest. 'Of *course* it was a shock. It was just a pity that you reacted to it so drastically.'

'Ah, yes. You mean Richard?' Mina shook her head, swirling the remains of the tea around in her mug. 'Yes, I was a fool. You were much wiser when it was your turn.'

'We were both fools. But Richard Bryce, Mina. Did you really think you were in love with him?'

'Oh, po-po-po . . .' She leaned back in her chair, thinking about it. 'I suppose I felt that it didn't really matter in the circumstances. And Richard was kind and very good for my morale – and he had no parents to put a brake on it. He fell for me like a ton of bricks and his fellow officers were so excited about it. It was rather as though I were marrying all of them, not just Richard. The wedding and everything was entirely unreal, like some great stage production. Wild and romantic and crazy, typical wartime stuff. It was only then that I began to realize a little of what Tony had experienced when he was down in Cornwall. That sense of unreality allows one to behave quite out of character; a game that has nothing to do with real life.'

'And then,' Nest took the story up when Mina fell silent, 'Richard was killed when the King

David Hotel in Jerusalem was blown up. It always sounded so odd, it being a hotel. Of course I was only twelve but I overheard Mama talking on the telephone and I could see it quite clearly inside my head. A big white building with pillars and palm trees and camels. Although I never quite understood why Richard was staying in a hotel in Jerusalem.'

'It was the British HQ,' said Mina. 'Jordan had been granted independence. The war was over. How cruel life is.'

'And you came back to Ottercombe,' said Nest, after an even longer silence, 'and in the autumn I went away to school. But you seemed so calm about it all. Not like you were after Tony.'

'I am ashamed to say that there was almost relief at Richard's death.' Mina set the mug back on the table. 'Once he'd gone back to the Middle East I realized what a fool I'd been. He was a stranger, a nice, kind stranger, but a stranger, and the thought of spending the rest of my life with him was terrifying. By his death I was released and because of it I've felt guilty ever since. Stupid, isn't it?'

'Did you ever think of getting in contact with Tony again?'

An almost humorous look smoothed away Mina's expression of self-disgust. 'The Sneerwells went out of their way to tell me that he was happily married,' she said. 'It was too late.'

'Lord,' said Nest at last, 'what fools we mortals be.'

'It's late.' Mina glanced at her watch and pushed back her chair. 'Much too late on top of an exhausting day. Away you go to bed. I'll clear up here while the dogs have their last run.' She bent to kiss Nest, her eyes still shadowed with memories. 'God bless.'

So Nest had wheeled herself across the hall into her room and begun the long preparations for bed. At last, longing for sleep but still unable to concentrate on her book, she'd settled herself more comfortably, switching off the light, putting the book on the bedside table, closing her eyes against the pictures that still danced before them.

Tony's little sports car is parked on the drive and Mama sits in the drawing-room watching him with anguish as he paces to and fro before her, the fist of one hand twisting and twisting into the palm of the other, his face wretched. There is no sign of Mina. Outside in the hall, Nest can hear his voice.

'*Please* let me see her, Mrs Shaw. I must try to explain to her. It was nothing, you see. Nothing that counted.'

'My dear boy, I have tried to talk to Mina. I *do* understand, I promise you.'

'Do you?' In his eagerness he stops pacing and sits beside her, half-turned so that he can see her face. 'Do you, really? Then can't you explain it to Mina? We were all behaving rather foolishly, you see. The training was very intense and we began to get an inkling of what the real thing might be like. This woman had lost her husband at Dunkirk and she was lonely.' He peers at her anxiously lest he should offend her, longing for her to understand him. 'There were several of us all having a drink together and it got a bit out of hand. She started to get a bit weepy and then . . . well, the others were egging me on. You know how it is?'

Mama covers his restless hands with her own. Her face is sad as she watches him, rather as she might look at one of her own children.

'You see, Tony, the whole point is that Mina can't understand it. She is a romantic and this is her first love. To her it was the most precious thing in the world—'

'And to me!' he cries passionately. 'This was . . . outside all that. I must try to make her see it my way.'

'I don't think she's capable of separating it.' Mama holds his hands tightly. 'Oh, not because she is cruel but because it is beyond her experience. Nothing she's read or known could possibly have prepared her for it. I've talked to her. I've tried to explain how, in times of war, other energies and needs can take over and we break the usual rules that govern ordinary life, but she can't get to grips with it. This love was something fragile and beautiful and it's been smashed.'

He bends over their joined hands, sobbing so bitterly that, outside the door, Nest is frightened. Tears come to her own eyes for Tony – and for poor Mina too. Something terrible must have happened for Mina to allow Tony to be so unhappy.

'Why did you tell her?' Mama's voice is full of compassion. 'My dear boy! Whatever made you do it?'

Tony swallows, wiping his eyes on the backs of his hands, still clasping hers tightly so that she can feel the tears.

'I was shy about seeing her again. I know it sounds silly but I was. I felt shy and nervous and uncertain of myself. There was something else too. I'd changed a bit, down in Cornwall on exercise. I'd begun to feel I was really part of the war and I was proud of it. I hadn't done the other thing before, either, so that when I drove down here and saw Mina again there was an unreality about it that was almost frightening. There seemed to be two separate worlds – hers and mine – and for a moment I couldn't mesh them together. It was important that she knew I'd changed, grown, and that I wasn't just a kid any longer. I wanted her to know that I was a man now, and so, before we could adjust ourselves properly, these crass things were coming out of my mouth. It was only when I saw her expression that I suddenly realized what I was doing. Everything swung back into focus but it was too late.'

'My poor boy. Can't you see that Mina will not be able to believe that you could possibly love her if you can be like that with another woman? It would need a much more worldly woman than Mina is to be able to accept it. That woman in Cornwall has taken something vitally important, which Mina thought was hers, and you, apparently, gave it to this woman very willingly. Mina's trust and pride is smashed to pieces.'

'Oh God . . .' he begins to sob again, whilst Mama comforts him, and Nest turns away to look for Mina.

She is huddling in the corner of the morning-room sofa, weeping silently. Nest watches her through the crack in the half-opened door, wishing that time could roll back to those happier earlier years.

This autumn, Timmie has been sent away to school and Nest misses him quite dreadfully; she creeps into his room to look at his Meccano constructions; staring up at his model aeroplanes suspended in continuous flight from the ceiling, touching with tender fingers his old knitted soldier propped against the pillow. During those weeks before Tony's return, Mina has done everything she can to keep Nest occupied: letters are written to Timmie, plans made for the games to be played in the holidays; suggestions for his Christmas present to be discussed. Suddenly, however, Mina is no longer interested in these diversions. Her eyes are swollen with tears and she seems unable to concentrate.

'Try not to worry her,' says Mama. 'She's had some bad news. No, of *course* not about Timmie, you foolish child. It's nobody you need to worry about.'

Now, peeping through the crack in the door, Nest decides that at least she can try to comfort her big sister. Slipping into the room, she climbs up beside Mina and curls beside her, resting her head against her shoulder, saying nothing. Presently, Mina wriggles her arm free and draws her nearer so that they sit close together, silent but sharing.

CHAPTER SEVENTEEN

'Is it your turn,' asked Jack hopefully, his voice muffled by pillow, 'to make the Sunday morning coffee?'

A long, low groan issued from the further side of the bed and Jack rolled over on his back the better to listen to it.

'I think,' he said aloud, but as if to himself, 'that that was a "yes". Oh, good.'

He settled himself more comfortably but, before Hannah struggled out of her cocoon of quilt to disabuse him of this assumption, a steady, rhythmic roaring could be heard, and, presently, a pattering of feet. Jack instinctively braced himself as the bedroom door was flung wide.

'Flora's awake,' announced Toby, 'and she pongs. It's really yucky.'

'Tobes is beginning to develop a real flair for the Obvious Remark,' Jack murmured to his wife. 'Have you noticed? Don't let me keep you, though. Hurry away. Oh, and do switch the kettle on before you de-pong our child.'

'It's your turn.' Hannah held on to the quilt. 'You know it is, Jack. Go and do something, for Heaven's sake, before she explodes.'

'It *is* your turn, Daddy,' Toby reassured him. 'Mummy did last Sunday because I was sick in the night from Hamish's birthday and nobody went to church because you didn't want to take Flora on your own.'

Jack struggled into a sitting position and stared at Toby indignantly.

'So much for male solidarity,' he said. 'Thanks, mate. Oh, and don't expect any support from me next time you embark on your "Oh, I wish *we* had a dog" stuff.'

'Jack, just shut up and go and deal with her,' moaned Hannah urgently, burrowing further into the feather quilt. 'You can argue with Tobes in her bedroom. Go away.'

Jack shrugged himself into a long towelling robe and followed his son across the landing. Flora, her face puce but tearless, stood clinging to her cot-rail, wailing loudly. At the sight of Jack she paused, drew a ragged breath and began to hiccup.

'Uh-oh!' said Toby with dreadful satisfaction. 'She'll have those for ages now. Sometimes they can make her sick.'

Before Jack could think of a suitably quelling reply, he was overcome by the pungent odour emanating, along with the hiccups, from the cot. He closed his eyes, shuddering.

'Dear God!' he muttered. 'How am I supposed

to eat breakfast after this? Come on, Tobes, you know the routine. You can help me. Where's the mattress thing? Oh, good man! That's it, lay it right there. Now, up you come, princess.'

Later, he made coffee whilst Flora sat contentedly in her high chair with a chocolate biscuit ('Mummy *never* lets us have those before breakfast. She'll be *very* cross.' 'Then don't go telling her and upsetting her, OK?'), her hiccups quite abated, and Toby, having finished his biscuit, examined a new plastic dinosaur from the cornflakes box.

'I've got three of these all the same,' he said sadly, studying the back of the carton. 'I'm collecting them but I only ever get these ones. Why don't we get some of the others?'

'It's called Sod's law, chum,' said Jack, his good humour restored by hot, black coffee. 'It's the same law which says it's my turn to get up this morning and it's why you've got your knickers on back to front. No future in that, Tobes. Now be a good chap and watch over your sister while I take some coffee up to Mummy. OK? Shan't be long.'

He went out of the kitchen and there was a short silence.

'You've got chocolate all over your face,' Toby told Flora.

She observed him placidly as she carefully licked the chocolate from the biscuit and dropped the soggy crumbs over the side of the chair onto the floor. Caligula sniffed at them fastidiously, then disappeared through the cat-flap into the garden. Toby watched for a moment, imagining his mother's face when she saw the mess later.

'*Not* very helpful, darling,' he said aloud to himself, in Hannah's voice, and set the dinosaurs to fighting on the table, making growling noises, and Flora chuckled as she watched, stretching sticky fingers towards them.

Upstairs, Jack stood the coffee on the bedside table and looked down on the small piece of Hannah that he could see.

'I'm not asleep,' she said, muffled. 'Are they OK?'

'Quite OK. Coffee's there if you want it.'

'Thanks.' She fought her way out of the quilt and reached for the mug.

'Everything's under control,' he said. 'Sleep a bit if you want to.'

'I might,' she said, drawing up her knees and pushing her hair back behind her ears. 'Jack, I've been thinking about us getting a puppy. I didn't want to say anything in the car coming back from Ottercombe yesterday because of Tobes but it was such fun seeing the kids with the dogs, wasn't it?'

'It was.' Jack was smiling. 'I have no problem about having a dog, Han, but it's you who'll bear the brunt. Are you sure you haven't got enough on your plate already? I shan't be able to do much about puppy-training during term-time.'

'I thought we might wait until the Christmas holidays,' she told him. 'Then we've got three weeks off to break it in ready for next term. I think it would be good for the boys too; help them settle in and take their minds off being homesick.'

Jack bent to kiss the top of her head. 'I think it's a brilliant idea. Tobes will be out of his mind.'

'We'll have to decide what breed is best for a houseful of children,' she mused, sipping her coffee thoughtfully.

Jack beamed at her. 'I've heard that Dobermanns are *very* partial to children,' he said. 'Or is it Rottweilers? You know the joke? What dog has four legs and an arm? But maybe they've just had a bad press.'

'Go away,' she said. 'Go and watch over our young. I'll be down in a minute. And don't say anything about the puppy yet. I want to see Tobes's face when we tell him.'

Later that same morning, wheeling slowly, Nest progressed from the sunny courtyard along the mossy path that wound through the wild garden; crossing the small stone bridge, below which the stream flowed, and passing beneath the last of the tall, silky plumes of the pampas grass, spared as yet from Mina's secateurs. In summer, here in the shelter of the cliff, the feathery cream and the pink foliage of aruncus and astilbe tangled with tall green ferns and purple loosestrife, whilst hypericum crept over their roots, carpeting the damp ground with its small round woolly leaves and yellow flowers. Early in the year, snowdrops and primroses grew amongst the roots of the tall beeches and, in late spring, lily of the valley and snake's-head fritillary bloomed amongst the coarse grass that bordered the stream.

Here, where the culvert carried the flow of water down into the valley, the umbrella plant spread its red and brown serrated leaves underfoot, thriving with the rheum and rodgersia amongst the ghostly, delicate boles of the silver birch, and, in a cranny of the cliff hidden by salix and wych-hazel, the pied wagtail built her nest. Pausing, turning her chair a little in the autumn sunshine, Nest watched a charm of goldfinches, dipping and fluttering with their dancing flight above a clump of thistles, and suddenly, further down the valley, a mallard broke into its hoarse, comical 'rarb-rarb' cry. As she wheeled herself onward, she recalled the games that she and Timmie had played in this enchanted garden with its secret places and wild, dramatic setting. Could there possibly have been a more wonderful place on earth for two imaginative children? Few books were beyond their scope for re-enactment, although, reasonably, there had been an occasional disappointment due to a lack of vision on the part of the adults.

It is in the Christmas holidays of 1943 that Timmie is given his first Arthur Ransome, *Swallows and Amazons*, and, after the first reading, the beach is easily transformed into Wild Cat Island, although Mama refuses to let them have a sailing boat. In vain they plead: the currents on this north Somerset coast are much too dangerous to allow two small children to act out their fantasy stories to the limit and they must be content with the rock-pools, in which to swim, and the cliffs to climb. After Christmas, once Mina has gone away to London and Timmie and her sisters have returned to school, Nest is left with Mama. Now, alone for hours at a time, she enters almost completely into the world of make-believe, her vivid imagination fuelled by the stories that Mama reads to her during the children's hour. Preoccupied with her own loneliness and anxiety, Mama has begun to read other things than the beloved story-books. Curled beside her on the sofa, before the fire, Nest listens to Alison Uttley's *The Country Child*, her heart beating fast as she passes, in spirit, with little Susan Garland coming home from school through the Dark Wood. She peeps fearfully at the Rackham illustrations as Mama reads *Goblin Market* – although she loves the picture of the children called to hear their mother's tale – and always, in Nest's mind, it is Mina she sees as the brave Lizzie who saves her sister from the wicked goblin men. She experiences a strange, yearning restlessness, a tingling of blood in her veins, when she hears for the first time the poetry of Thomas Edward Brown and O'Shaughnessy's *Music and Moonlight*, and the lyrical prose of Richard Jefferies.

All through that late winter and early spring she wanders like a small wraith, verses and phrases singing in her ears, images crowding in her mind, dazed by the glory of the English language, groping towards ideas she cannot, at nine, hope to understand. She misses Mina just as much as she misses Timmie; inexplicably touched by Mama's gentle melancholy, yet her soul on fire with a mysterious fusion of nameless, poignant longings and wild excitement. When the snowdrops show their delicate, drooping heads beneath the naked beeches in the wild garden and the lemon flowers of the winter aconite are scattered amongst the grass, Mama moves on to *Jane Eyre* and Nest falls in love with Edward Rochester, whose tragic, romantic image becomes the receptacle for all of her unformed passion. As the March gales pile mountainous seas against the tall grey cliffs, and snowstorms sweep from the Bristol Channel across the moor, Nest stands at her bedroom window, listening to the restless surging of the waves as eagerly as though, at any moment, she might leap out to become part of all that elemental, untameable magic.

The Easter holidays bring her companionship again in the form of Timmie and, once again, they play out their small dramas, though, this time, they are enacted against the background of a perpetual battle waged between Henrietta and Josie. The two girls are locked in a rivalry that drives their mother to despair and fascinates their two young siblings. Henrietta, barely twelve months her sister's senior but as old as Eve, can generally run circles round the less complicated, more direct Josie. The two of them are invited to one or two parties and Henrietta is allowed to go to a tea-dance – with a school friend and her brother – which sends Josie into a sulk for several days. The brother, a sweet-tempered, naïve seventeen-year-old destined for the army in the autumn, is quite besotted by Henrietta's wiles yet is far too well brought up to ignore Josie.

The quick-tongued, clever Henrietta torments Josie with her conquest but Josie, experiencing the agony and the ecstasy of first love, for once refuses to be browbeaten into second place.

A tennis party sets the scene for a full-scale battle: Henrietta has avoided telling Josie that she is invited until the very last moment, guessing that it will be too late for her to go.

'It's not fair, Mama,' cries Josie, near to tears. 'My tennis things need washing and I haven't anything to wear. She's done this on purpose because she wants to be with Lionel on her own.'

'Oh, honestly!' Henrietta looks at Mama, round-eyed with amazement at her sister's apparent madness, inviting her mother's approval. 'How can I be alone with *anyone* at a tennis party? And, anyway, it's embarrassing, Mama, to see her making sheep's eyes at him all the time. She's just a little girl, after all. He thinks it's a terrific joke.'

'He does not! He likes me. It's you who plays up to him, draping yourself round him—'

'That will do.' Mama, for once, is cross and the girls fall silent, biting their lips, waiting for her decision. 'It was very wrong of Henrietta not to tell the truth about the invitation and I am almost inclined to refuse to let either of you go . . .' Josie puts out her tongue triumphantly and Henrietta turns white with fury '. . . except that Lionel will already be on his way to collect you. If this happens again, Henrietta, I shall forbid any more parties, and perhaps, Josie, it will teach you to keep your clothes in good order. This time, I'm afraid, you will have to stay at home.'

Henrietta flounces away, secretly overjoyed with her success, whilst Josie, frustrated and bitterly disappointed, flings her sister's newly whitened tennis shoes into the slimy depths of the waterbutt. In the row that follows, even Timmie is frightened and Nest is in tears. Finally, Lydia threatens that if Henrietta and Josie do not behave she will tell Lionel the whole truth about their shocking behaviour so that the girls, flung together into an unwilling confederacy, stammer their way out of trouble as best they might. Lionel, puzzled by their confused explanations, insists that, of course, they must both go with him to the party. Shoes and a tennis-skirt, he tells them with youthful confidence, can be supplied by his sister. Besides, he adds as if this clinches it, his mother is expecting them. Neither Henrietta nor Josie wishes to lose face before this innocent boy, who is just as charming to Lydia and Nest as he is to the two quarrelsome contenders for his affection, and, after this, the battle in his presence is waged with silent jabs and pinches or with furious glares, which slide into the sweetest of smiles when he glances their way.

The feud continues, gaining impetus, and the two Tinies stare aghast when, at the height of their passions, Henrietta empties a teapot half full of the dregs of cold tea over Josie's freshly set hair and, in retaliation, Josie slashes the skirts of Henrietta's best party frock. Tears and shrieks rend the peaceful cleave whilst Mama pleads and remonstrates in turn. Much though she misses Timmie, Nest is almost relieved when the summer term begins and she is alone again with Mama.

'We miss Mina,' says Mama. 'There's something *steady* about her.'

Fifty-five years on, Nest smiled to herself as she wheeled over the lawn and onto the gravel. Yes, beneath Mina's warmth and apparent agelessness there was a serenity that remained unchanged even when it was challenged by grief or despair. All the family, at one time or another, had leaned against it and drawn strength from it. As Nest had this thought, Mina appeared from the open doorway, Georgie behind her.

'Lovely news!' she cried, making a fearsome face for Nest's benefit which denied the loveliness of the news and made Nest grin privately. 'Helena and Rupert are coming to see us. Won't that be fun?'

CHAPTER EIGHTEEN

Lyddie telephoned the local office of the courier service she used, asked for her parcel to be collected, and began to pack the completed typescript, along with her notes, style sheet and the letter to the editor, into the publisher's Jiffy bag, before putting that inside the courier's special plastic bag. She filled in the form on the top page of a book of blanks they'd given her and carried the parcel downstairs. Ever since a typescript had gone astray she hadn't trusted the Post Office and now she was obliged to wait for the delivery van. As she put the kettle on for a cup of tea, the Bosun watched her hopefully but she shook her head at him.

'You'll have to wait until he's collected this,' she told him, showing him the package – and he heaved a sigh and settled down outside the door in the hall.

Lyddie huddled a little in her long green knitted coat as she waited for the kettle to boil. As winter drew on, her small room was increasingly cold – especially on sunless days. Perhaps, after all, some kind of heating should be installed; the electric fire was out of the question, with the Bosun keeping her company, but a radiator of some kind might be the answer. In fact, the whole house could do with central heating. There was a very efficient woodburning stove in the long downstairs room, which was kept alight for most of the winter and helped to warm the small house, but their bedroom, next door to Lyddie's study, was very chilly.

As she made her tea, Lyddie had a new idea. Perhaps the money from the house in Iffley could be used to install central heating. It would add to the value of the house and make their lives more comfortable; surely Liam couldn't object to that? The kitchen was in a small extension at the back of the house, making an L-shape at the end of the long room, and the back door led into a tiny yard, which Lyddie had filled with pots and tubs of flowers. Now, she carried her tea into the other room where she could sit at the table and look out into this little area. The back wall and the wood-shed were washed the same creamy-pink as the extension walls and, with the chrysanthemums and hebes making a late, colourful display, it was a delightful little scene. In the summer, roses and honeysuckle climbed the wall and the wood-shed roof, but now, with November approaching, there was little left of their earlier glory.

Watching the robin pecking up toast crumbs,

Lyddie wondered why she felt this very real need to contribute – apart from her own earnings. Why not just put the money somewhere safe, when it should come along, and save it for an emergency? Wrapping herself more closely in her long green coat, her hands clasped around the hot mug, Lyddie allowed herself to look at the situation dispassionately. The truth was that, even after two years in Truro, she had this odd sensation of unreality. Just occasionally she caught herself thinking: What am I doing here? or had an unsettling feeling that she was waiting for something. Most of the time she was too involved in her work to be thinking of anything but the current typescript. Even with the lists she made, a great deal had to be held in her head as she worked, each and every line of typescript to be thoroughly checked for punctuation and spelling, every fact noted, so there was little time to brood on the state of her marriage. In one year she might work on thirty-five typescripts – the turn-around was very quick – so she couldn't accuse herself of having too many hours on her hands in which to magnify or distort her emotions. Yet there was this strange sense of expectancy: that this was temporary and something else was going to happen very soon.

Lyddie set down her mug and, pulling the long, soft wool about her, went to kneel before the stove. She opened its glass doors and began to lay the fire with some kindling and one of the fire-lighters from the box beside the log-basket. Soon she had a little blaze going and closed the doors so that the flames would pull up into a blaze. Sitting back on her heels she watched golden tongues licking round the scraps of wood, mesmerized for a moment by the curling, greedy fire, before standing up so as to wash her hands at the kitchen sink. She dried them on the roller-towel behind the door and went back to the table, picking up her mug again, frowning as she tried to analyse these sensations of impermanence.

Perhaps this feeling of unreality was because of the odd life she and Liam led. It was impossible, with The Place, to live as other young couples did: making supper together; going out for a meal or down to the pub; booking seats for the theatre or having an evening at the cinema. She was beginning to realize that the glorious day when Liam and Joe could afford a full-time bar manager, so as to relieve them from their heavy work-load, would be long in coming. It was being borne in upon her consciousness that Liam, at least, had no desire to be free of his work: he loved it; it was his life. Because of her early readiness to adapt, to be content with spending evenings in the snug, she had allowed the future pattern of their marriage to be set. Yet what else could he have done? There *was* no bar manager to give them evenings off and – after all – would nagging have had any effect except to cause unhappiness and discontent?

Lyddie sighed. The point was that she'd enjoyed it. Going to The Place after a long day of isolated concentration, sitting joking with Joe in the snug, eating delicious food she hadn't had to buy, prepare or cook, was a wonderful change from that unhappy year in London after James had left for New York. How well she could remember coming back to the small flat, after a long day and a gruesome journey home, only to find that she was out of food and much too weary to go out again to shop, so that she'd eat some toast and mindlessly watch some television before falling into bed. It was her work as an editor and the relationships she'd had with her friends at the publishing house that had made life worthwhile. Now, she still had her work but it was difficult to make new friends when one either had to entertain them alone or take them to The Place, where Liam might – or might not – be available to sit and chat with them.

At this point, however, she shook her head. To be honest, it was not really a lack of friends that she was missing – she still kept closely in touch with those few special friends and occasionally went to London to see them – it was this inability to come close to Liam that was beginning to affect her. It was as if his inner self were kept inviolate, unknowable, and, even for her, he was not prepared to make exceptions. His delightful charm, his wicked tongue and knowing eye disguised a secret personality, a depth that even Lyddie could not penetrate.

'Are you sure,' her closest friend, Caroline, had asked, 'that you really want to do this? Oh, I can see that he's drop-dead sexy, and he's terribly funny, and clearly an achiever . . . but he doesn't let you get too close, does he?' And Lyddie, foolishly flattered to think that only *she* had access to the private Liam, had assured her that she knew what she was doing.

Now, trying to be scrupulously fair, she reminded herself that the row over the letter had unnerved her, that these feelings of unreality – as if I'm on some kind of *holiday*, she thought – might simply be a result of the fact that this was an entirely different way of life. Thousands of people – hoteliers, restaurateurs, and those involved with tourism – lived in this oddly fragmented way and managed perfectly happily; yet this truth brought no comfort. The fact remained that Liam was content to go on exactly as he was, with no intention of allowing her more closely into his life. Her need to contribute was simply a desire to be included, to be involved; to break through his protective shell and force him to acknowledge her as an equal in this whole partnership. The row had pointed up her anxieties and it was difficult to return to that previous innocence; that belief that, soon, things would change: that a bar manager would be employed, she would be involved financially, and they would become truly partners, talking openly and freely, sharing their emotions and fears.

The affair of the letter was closed and Liam certainly bore no grudge, there was no lingering resentment or coolness – but no progress had been made either. They were back at square one.

Yet things had subtly changed: the honeymoon period was over but there seemed no clear way forward; all paths at present were marked 'No Thoroughfare'. The difficulty was that Lyddie was beginning to be less able – less willing – to remain passive. Her instinctive reaction to consider Liam's point of view, to weigh up his reactions carefully, was beginning to crumble in the face of her own needs. This insecurity – a result of James's defection – was not a genetic part of her character and, beneath the fear that she might lose Liam too, her sense of fair play and her determination were re-emerging. More, a longing for his child was beginning to possess her, distracting her from her work, and, after all, might this not be the natural answer to their impasse? Perhaps Liam's indifference to children, his reluctance to discuss the possibility of a family, was simply due to his obsession with The Place? A new mind-set was needed but how to approach it . . . ?

A ringing at the doorbell startled her and woke the Bosun, who staggered up and barked confusedly at Lyddie's long mackintosh, hanging from a peg in the hall, before realizing his mistake. After a moment he came in and stared at Lyddie reproachfully, unused to having his sleep so rudely disturbed, and she picked up the parcel and hurried out to open the door.

'When is Helena coming?' asked Georgie, for the fourth or fifth time since the telephone call, and

Mina answered patiently, 'At the weekend, not long now.'

'And don't forget Rupert,' murmured Nest wickedly. 'Dear Rupert's coming too.'

In a corner of the sofa Georgie had already relapsed, as she so often did, toes restlessly tapping, shoulders shrugging, even her face twitching – now frowning, now pouting – as if she could hear a tune in her head, or, rather, as if she were having a long conversation with an unseen adversary.

'Why adversary?' asked Mina when Nest had propounded this idea.

'Because she seems so fractious,' answered Nest, after a moment. 'You don't feel that she's enjoying herself but that it's some kind of contest.'

Mina had considered this. 'That sounds about right,' she'd said at last.

Meanwhile, Georgie sat wrapped in her private world whilst Nest knitted the toys and small garments that she sent to the local Women's Institute for their charity stall, and Mina did the crossword. The logs had burned into silky, ashy embers and the wind, howling up in the cleave, rattled at the windows and echoed eerily in the chimney.

'Yes, Rupert's coming too,' agreed Mina absently. 'Who wrote *Of Mice and Men*? Nine letters with a B in it.'

'Steinbeck,' said Nest. 'The thing is that it's rather easy to forget dear old Rupert, though, isn't it?'

'Terribly easy,' said Mina, still absently, busy writing in the word – and then, realizing what she'd said, glancing up, first guiltily at Georgie and then reproachfully at Nest, who grinned back at her.

'Just testing,' said Nest. 'Away with the fairies.'

'But not always,' warned Mina.

'No, not always.' Nest put her knitting aside and yawned. 'Bedtime. Would you like a hot drink, Mina?'

'Yes, please.' Mina took off her spectacles and folded up *The Times*. 'Goodness, is that the time? I'll let the dogs out.' She raised her voice a little. 'Hot chocolate for you, Georgie?'

Recalled from her inner world, Georgie looked up at her intelligently enough but Nest could see that, even now, it was still second nature for her to frame her answer carefully. There was seldom, with Georgie, a warm, uncalculated response.

'As long as it's not as milky as last night,' she said. Her face took on the slightly fretful, faintly frowning expression that indicated that one had been weighed in the balance and found wanting.

'Oh dear.' Mina sounded cheerfully apologetic. 'Wasn't it quite right? Would you like to do it yourself?'

This was something of a challenge for all three of them. The last time Georgie had made herself a hot drink, Nest had wheeled herself into the kitchen to find milk boiling over the Esse, no sign of Georgie, and Mina's favourite milk pan ruined.

'Well, if you can't manage to make a cup of hot

chocolate . . .' Georgie was struggling to get out of her deep, comfortable corner, mumbling complainingly to herself, whilst Nest had already gone ahead to begin the night-time preparations. Mina put the guard across the fire, collected her spectacles and her book, checked that Georgie had taken her belongings with her and shut the door behind them all. The dogs followed her across the hall, looking forward to their last potter in the garden, and, by the time she reached the kitchen, Nest was already managing the hot drinks, observed closely by Georgie.

Mina went past them, out into the windy night, watching the dogs disappear into the wild garden. Between the flying wracks of cloud, torn apart by sharp gusts, she could see the bright stars, whilst the music of the tumbling waterfall, cascading into the stream, joined with the roaring of the gale in the trees up on the steep-sided cleave, and, beneath it all, the insistent, groaning groundswell of the sea.

Invigorated, refreshed, she called to the dogs, who appeared one by one, and they went back into the sudden hush of the kitchen. Georgie had already gone, carrying her mug of chocolate, and Nest was putting the pan to soak, Mina's mug waiting on the Esse to keep it warm.

'That was naughty of you,' she said, bending to kiss her goodnight. 'Saying that about Rupert. Very risky.'

'I know,' said Nest unrepentantly, 'but, you know, Mina, there are times when I *want* to do something outrageous. To break out of this damned prison; to dance and run . . .'

She looked away, the passion dying from her flushed face, biting her lips, whilst Mina watched her helplessly, knowing from past experience that nothing she could say would ease the pain.

'On the other hand,' said Nest, wheeling towards the door, 'I think I'd rather be physically crippled than mentally crippled. I'm not really making fun of Georgie, you know, it's just a kind of letting off steam. Oh God, the frustration! And now, the fear on top of it. Sometimes, I think I might explode with it all. Anyway, none of it's your fault. Sorry, Mina. Goodnight.'

Distressed, Mina climbed the stairs, the dogs at her heels, clutching her mug in one hand, spectacles and book in the other, but, once the bedroom door was closed behind her, the tension slipped away and she entered into her little sanctuary with hopeful cheerfulness. The hot drink, a talk with Elyot, a chapter of her book; these were all pleasures to be savoured, along with the warm welcome that the dear and familiar objects offered and, later, the comfort of the bed, made luxuriously cosy with the electric blanket; a present from Hannah and Jack.

'Po-po-po' – each breath dispelled some tiny anxiety as the drink was placed carefully beside her computer and the dogs settled and curled themselves on their beds. She undressed, remembering other nights with candlelight and icy sheets, and hurried herself into the fleecy robe, murmuring a grateful prayer for the comfort she presently enjoyed. Tonight, she decided, returning to the alcove, switching on the computer, sipping the hot, sweet chocolate, tonight Elyot would not be reserved as a treat. No, tonight he would be first: she needed him. Her thin shoulders sagged with relief when she saw that there was a message from him, and she opened it eagerly.

From: Elyot
To: Mina

My dear friend
How are you? Not blown away, I hope? We've had a better day, today . . .

CHAPTER NINETEEN

Nest, however, could not sleep. The demons, against which she struggled with reasonable success during the day, returned at night to torment her. Frustration, resentment, guilt and despair: these were her night-time companions. As she sat in bed, propped about with pillows, she wondered if Georgie's presence was good for any of them, even for Georgie herself. It seemed to Nest that, back here at Ottercombe, in the home of her youth, Georgie's confusion was increased. Last weekend, she'd watched Jack's children, and Jack himself, with a kind of painful intensity that had been quite upsetting to witness. It was clear – or so Nest thought – that she was travelling between the past and the present, trying to make sense of it, and failing. Sometimes she confused Mina with Mama, although for much of the time she was quite bright and alert. Nevertheless, she was dangerous. She'd already disinterred Mina's love for Tony Luttrell; what else might she decide to uncover? It was clear that Mina was nervous, although she still denied that Georgie knew as much as she pretended.

'She always enjoyed that sense of power,' she'd said comfortingly. 'Hinting at things and putting us all on edge. But when it came down to it, it was only things she'd imagined or half heard.'

'The trouble is,' Nest had answered, 'if you have a guilty secret then that kind of thing makes you distinctly nervous. People have been murdered for behaving like Georgie.'

The blurting out of Mina's secret had seriously upset Nest. Not only was she furious for Mina's sake – it might have been very embarrassing and distressing for her – it had made her frightened on her own behalf. In Nest's opinion Georgie could not be trusted, and there was an end to it.

'But what can we do?' Mina had said despairingly. 'I shall ask Helena to take her away if you're really frightened.'

'The trouble is, she might say something to Helena or Rupert. Or to anyone!' Nest had looked quite wretched. 'I don't think I shall ever feel safe again.'

'If you feel like that, then I shall talk to Helena at the weekend,' Mina had answered firmly. 'After all, at my age there are limits to how much I can do. She and Rupert must understand that. My first responsibility is to you and I can see that this is beginning to stress you.'

Nest had shaken her head, torn between her own fear and pity for Georgie.

'Let's wait and see,' she'd said.

As she sat in bed she fretted at her inconsistency yet, each · time she saw Georgie's vacant, lost expression, her heart contracted with compassion and she knew that she must cope with her own anxiety for a little longer. Knowing that a bad night lay ahead, Nest gave up any attempt at stoicism and took a sleeping-pill. Settling herself as comfortably as she could, she allowed her thoughts to drift, giving way at last to the memories she'd buried for so long.

There are so many changes after the war. Georgie is married, now, to a young man at the Treasury, whilst Henrietta and Josie, still quarrelling, go to London and find jobs: Josie as a secretary in a department of London University and Henrietta in a small antique shop owned by a very wealthy, titled woman. To begin with, the first floor of the London house is turned into a flat for them but, when Ambrose dies of lung cancer just after his fifty-fourth birthday, the house is divided formally and the rest of it is let. Georgie promises to keep an eye on her two younger sisters and, when Mina returns to Ottercombe after Richard's death, it is clear that Lydia is very happy to sink into a semi-invalidism. Her world has changed: Ambrose dead, Timothy dead, one daughter is married and another a widow. It seems that she no longer has the will or the energy to control the lives of her two strong-minded, single daughters and she lets them go to make their own way in this new, strange world.

Mina comforts her. 'Georgie will keep an eye,' she tells her, 'and there are friends of mine who will help them out if they have problems.'

Lydia is content to believe her; Josie and Henrietta have worn her down during the last years of the war and she is delighted to have Mina home again. They settle down peacefully together to long periods of quiet, only enlivened when Nest and Timmie come home for the school holidays. For these two it seems that the old, happy days have returned. Soon they grow out of their make-believe games and begin to explore further afield than their beloved cleave: walking inland over the moor; cycling along the coastal road to Countisbury, shouting with excitement as they free-wheel down the steep slopes, groaning as they trudge up the hills, bent double over their handlebars. They go to the tiny village of Oare and explore the church, where Lorna Doone came to be married to John Ridd, and stand together at the altar where Lorna was shot down by the villainous Carver Doone. They descend from the wild, wind-blown coast road to the sudden, sheltering peace of wooded valleys and eat their picnic on the banks of the East Lyn or on a sunny, heather-covered slope, watching stonechats and whinchats flitting above the rounded grey stones. The only place forbidden to them is the wild, peaty bog-land called the Chains where, because of the pan of iron just below the surface, it is wet even in high summer and unwary walkers can sink up to their knees between the coarse tussocks of grass.

Timmie, it seems, is destined for the army; he has all the eager zest for exploration and adventure that so defined his godfather, and Nest, watching him grow strong and tall, is filled, in turn, by pride and fear.

'Does he have to be a soldier?' she asks Mama one morning just before a new term. Mina has driven Timmie to the barber in Combe Martin – 'Off to Sweedlepipe,' she says. 'Must get that hair cut!' – and she and Mama are alone. 'Supposing there's another war?'

Mama's eyes look beyond her – as they so often do these days – to a far-off summer afternoon when she once stood in the hall, smiling at Timothy, holding his hand as he said, 'I apologize for arriving unannounced . . .'.

'Mama?' says Nest questioningly – and Mama, returning to the present, takes a quick breath and touches her lightly on the cheek.

'There is nothing we can do, my darling,' she says gently. 'He would be unhappy doing anything else.'

Mina understands how she is suffering, and tries to comfort her, but Nest returns to school knowing that there are very few holidays left that she and Timmie will share.

In the autumn of 1951 Timmie goes to Sandhurst and Nest embarks on her last year at school. Now, with Nest at seventeen and Mina at twenty-eight, the two sisters are closer than they've ever been. Lydia seems to have withdrawn to those bygone years of the thirties; she drifts, happily vague, content with gardening or reading, quite ready for a little outing, with Mina at the wheel of the small Austin. Occasionally, Georgie visits with baby Helena, or Josie and Henrietta descend. Josie is now engaged to a young nuclear scientist and, since she no longer is a threat, Henrietta and she have become rather closer. Henrietta continues to play the field. Glamorous, amusing, confident, she has plenty of admirers but no special one. Despite her air of elegant sophistication she can be wickedly, cruelly funny and she makes Nest and Mina laugh until they cry, with her naughty imitations of Georgie's Tom and Josie's Alec.

'Too yawn-making for words,' she says, wrinkling her nose after one such performance. 'Tom is only interested in the National Debt and Alec is bored by anything that isn't in a test tube. He makes a point of despising normal people. He's only happy in a laboratory. Poor old Josie. They might be off to America, did she tell you?'

Nest is fascinated by her beautiful, modern, older sister and is beginning to think that it will be fun, when she leaves school, to go to London and try her wings. Yet Henrietta has none of the deep-down stability of Mina, nor the shared love of books and language, and it is still with Mina that Nest feels happiest. Henrietta has a febrile quality, a quick-witted lack of tolerance that means that those who are caught in her spell must be continually on their toes so as to stay in favour. During the Christmas holidays, with time to spend with her younger sister, Henrietta senses future competition and she is quick to lay the foundation for any developing relationship.

'Do you really think that all that hair hanging down your back suits you? Makes you look peaky, *I* think. Perhaps a perm would liven it up,' and, 'Goodness, I forget how behind the times you are down here. I hope you won't wear those frumpy clothes when you come to London. I know rationing's been grim and Utility's ghastly, but even so . . .'

By the time Henrietta has gone, Nest feels faintly breathless and quite inadequate. She anxiously inspects her meagre wardrobe and bunches her hair about her head, peering at herself in the glass.

'Do you think I should have my hair cut off?' she asks Mina, who comes in with some aired laundry.

Mina meets her anxious eyes in the looking-glass, sees the old-but-good tweed skirt laid out on the bed, and knows that Henrietta's one-upmanship has been at work.

'No, I don't,' she says positively. 'It looks wonderful, all long and silky. Much nicer than a dried-out frizz. I notice Henrietta keeps hers long, although she always wears it up these days. You know, that is really *such* a nice tweed. Beautifully cut. Makes you look so slim.'

Nest is comforted but decides that perhaps London can wait until the Easter holidays. She and Mina embark on a feast of Nancy Mitford's books, new words and phrases enter their vocabulary, and Lydia smiles to see them so happy together.

When the Easter holidays come, however, the possibility of going to London is postponed yet again. Lydia has a recurrence of her asthmatic troubles and Mina is much preoccupied with looking after her, leaving Nest to deal with mundane jobs about the house and much of the cooking. Nest is quite happy and, one soft, warm afternoon in early April, she wanders down to the beach. In the cleave familiar sights greet her eyes – a spray of budding white blossom on the wild pear tree, the drooping purple heads of the dog violet, pale green catkins hanging from the silver birch – whilst she listens to the distant laughter of the yaffingale and, closer to, the chiff-chaff utters its two random notes followed by a soft chirring call.

As she passes out onto the beach she stops, startled by the sight of the figure of a man, lying stretched on a rock, his face turned up to the sunshine. Out in the bay a small boat bobs, sails furled casually on the deck, and a wooden dinghy is pulled up on the shingle. Once or twice small boats have taken shelter in the cove from sudden squalls but never before, to her knowledge, has the sailor come ashore. Nest moves forward cautiously, to take a closer look, but she disturbs a gull, fishing in a rock-pool, who flies up with a raucous cry. The man raises his head, shielding his eyes against the sun, sees her and slews round on the rock, staring.

She stands still, watching him: his cord trousers are rolled above his ankles, he wears a thick, oiled fisherman's sweater and old sand-shoes on his feet.

'Hello,' he says, not moving from the rock. 'It's hot as June in this cove and I couldn't resist it. Have you come to tell me I'm trespassing or are you simply a passing dryad?'

She is transfixed by his light Irish voice and the utter beauty of him, so wild and casual there upon the rock.

'No,' she says at last, foolishly.

'No to which?' he asks teasingly. 'To the dryad or the trespassing? Or is it both?'

She smiles, then, possessed by a sudden glorious upswing of spirits. 'You *are* trespassing,' she says, crossing the beach towards him. 'But I won't tell on you.'

He laughs, not standing but waiting until she reaches the rock. His knees are drawn up now, his arms linked loosely around them as he watches her approach. His red-brown hair glints in the sunlight and his eyes are a dark, bright blue.

'And me hoping you were a dryad,' he says ruefully. 'Wouldn't it just be my old luck? So you own this magic place, do you?'

'Well, not me,' she answers, looking down at him, confused, breathing fast, already wanting to touch the crisp hair and rub the salty fold of his jersey between her fingers. 'My family own it.'

'Do they so?' His voice is warmly intimate, his glance keen. 'And will you share it with me for this afternoon, lady?'

'Oh, yes,' she answers simply, so sweetly, that he jumps up and makes her an old-fashioned bow.

'My name is Connor Lachlin,' he says.

'And mine is Nest,' she answers – and holds out her hand.

When he takes it – and carries it briefly to his lips – she feels that she might faint with wild, longing joy and, when they sit together on the rock and he retains her hand in his warm one, she knows how, at last, between a moment and a moment, the world can change for ever.

CHAPTER TWENTY

Nest stirred, her dreams disturbed. Drugged with medication, unwilling to waken, yet she was aware of someone standing close to her. Her eyelids, weighted with sleep, fluttered open but it was too dark to see anything clearly and past images still crowded upon her vision. A denser shape detached itself from the shadows and leaned over her; she felt the breath upon her face and did not know whether she still dreamed. Her body, heavy and relaxed, was incapable of movement yet she knew fear and tried to speak.

The form still hovered above her and she was aware of hands lightly moving upon her. Her skin shrivelled and shrank from the touch, her muscles contracting in horror, but she could not lift her arms or make any sound apart from the groaning that issued from her dry throat.

'Mama.' The word was little more than a whisper. 'Why is it dark in here, Mama? Why are you lying down in the morning-room?'

Trying to rouse herself, Nest felt herself to be swimming in treacle, and 'No,' she tried to say. 'No, I am not Mama . . .' but the words would not be formed.

'I know a secret, Mama. *Your* secret.' The whispering voice was horrid in its knowing confidentiality. 'Why don't you speak to me? Shall I tell your secret, Mama?'

In an enormous effort of will, Nest raised her arms – oh! how heavy they were – and feebly gripped Georgie's wrists.

'It's me!' she muttered. 'It's me. Nest. Not Mama. It's Nest . . .'

Exhausted from the effort, she fell back against her pillows, dimly aware of a new quality of silence: surprise, perhaps, and confusion.

'Nest?' Georgie seemed to be considering this. She began to chuckle a little. 'Nest. I know about you too, Nest. I know a secret. Shall I tell?'

'No!' cried Nest – but the shout that rang in her head was merely a whisper and she closed her eyes as a great weariness overtook her, sweeping her back to where she longed to be, no longer aware of Georgie or of the door opening quietly and then closing, very softly.

She dreamed again, her arms still outflung upon the quilt, her eyelids fluttering as she watched the past replay itself before her.

During that week, whilst Mina is occupied with Lydia, Connor sails to the cove nearly every day. He is staying in Porlock, at a small cottage owned by a friend, and the boat is part of the deal.

'It's a chancy old coast,' he tells Nest, 'but when you've sailed off the west coast of Ireland you should be able to manage the Bristol Channel.'

He is a professor of history at one of the Oxford colleges and is at least ten years older than she is: a fact that worries him a little as the days pass.

'As if it matters,' she cries. 'Think of Maxim de Winter and the girl in *Rebecca*. Age isn't important.'

She attributes to him all the manly graces which, nearly ten years before, Mina has bestowed upon Tony but Connor is not an impressionable young man with no experience: in fact, his holiday in Porlock is specifically to put distance between himself and a girl who is pursuing him. To be fair, he has not wilfully led her on – nevertheless he has not discouraged her too much either. Connor likes to be loved. With Nest, however, he sees all the responsibility of encouraging a much younger, innocent girl; a girl, moreover, with a respectable family at her back.

'I think I should meet them,' he says, 'Mina and Mama. I'm behaving like a thief, lady, and I feel uncomfortable with myself.'

His principles only serve to make her love him more, yet she postpones the meeting, fearing that somehow the magic will be spoiled. One morning she tells Mina that she is going for a long ride and sneaks away on her bicycle, meeting Connor on the road over Trentishoe Down. He cannot resist the spice of adventure or the romantic secrecy, and the bike is hidden in the furze whilst they flee away in his old convertible, travelling roads she once passed over with Timmie, laughing and singing together as the warm west wind streams through their hair and stings their skin alive to every light touch between them.

At Brendon they stop for a pint and a sandwich at The Staghunters, and she tells him of the pony fair held here each October, and afterwards he must take her to Oare church again so that she might show him the narrow Gothic window, just west of the screen, through which the wicked Carver shot at Lorna in her dress of 'pure white, clouded with faint lavender'. He teases her for living in her books, she calls him her 'Penfriend from Porlock', and, when he kisses her, those innocently imagined love scenes with Ralph Hingston or Edward Rochester are washed clean from her mind for ever.

Once he returns to Oxford, Nest wishes that she had allowed him to meet Mina and Mama. She sees now that it was childish and, more importantly, it means that there can be no letters or telephone calls. Even Mina would be shocked – or more probably hurt – to think that Nest has been deceiving them for nearly two weeks. If only he'd met them she could now be having the comfort of his letters and the bliss of hearing his voice. As it is, they have had to part in a deeply unsatisfactory manner.

Yet, as she sits on the beach on 'his' rock, watching the sun setting into the glowing west, tall cliffs carved black against the streaming banners of flame, the sea burnished with a liquid gold, she cannot quite regret it. How could such magic be part of the humdrum world? It is precisely because it is the stuff of fairy-tales that it has no place in the ordinariness of daily life. Nest relives each moment of their meeting. She reinvests each glance and word of his with her own ardour, reclothing him with all the characteristics with which those paper lovers were endowed whilst clinging to her memories of this flesh-and-blood male. Later, standing at her bedroom window, watching the cleave fill with moonlight, listening to the nightjar, her heart is brimming with joyful hope. Something must occur to make this a true story; with all her youthful confidence she wills this to come to pass. Miracles, happy endings, *do* happen and it is on such people as her and Connor, who believe that they can, that the grace falls.

So she is not surprised, on her return to school, when she is invited by a friend to stay for half-term. It is not the first time that she and Laura have visited each other's homes but, this time, Nest is suddenly aware of other opportunities. Mina responds positively to her request: Mama is better but low in spirits and needs to convalesce. It will be nice for Nest to be with young people for a few days and, after all, adds Mina, anxious lest Nest should feel unwanted, the summer holidays are not far away. She will be home soon.

The school is strict: visitors have to be vetted, letters are checked. Even if Nest said that Connor was her cousin there would have to be a telephone call to Mama to verify this, just as her permission would be sought if Connor asked to take Nest out for the afternoon. The headmistress is quite *au fait* with the wiles of young women and she takes no chances; she is, after all, *in loco parentis*. Going home with Laura for half-term with Mina's permission, however, is quite acceptable and Nest sees that, if she wants to make the most of this opportunity, she must take Laura into her confidence.

Laura is thrilled: it is simply *so* romantic. A letter is smuggled out to Connor and a reply awaits her when she arrives at Laura's home on the outskirts of Gloucester. A meeting is arranged. It is easy for the girls to travel into the city together where Laura will shop, have some lunch, go to the cinema matinée, and then meet up with Nest again for the journey back.

'Good job it's *Brief Encounter*,' says Nest, on the train. 'I've already seen it. Just in case your mother asks questions about it, I mean. It's a wonderful film and Celia Johnson is just heavenly. It's terribly sad, though: you'll cry buckets. I hope you've got masses of handkerchiefs.'

Laura feels Nest's arm, pressed against her own, trembling with excitement and looks at her with sympathy and envy.

'I can't wait to meet him,' she says.

Nest stares from the train window, biting her lip. This has been the condition of Laura's being party to the deception ('Mummy would kill me if she found out') and Nest hopes that Connor won't mind. He has been less than fulsome about the plan and she is alternately beset with nerves and possessed by a fierce, wild excitement. Now that it is actually happening and she will see him in a few minutes, the terror exceeds the joy and she shivers as she contemplates her actions and imagines her mother's face if she were to find out. Presently, however, courage and high spirits flow back; after all, what can it harm if Laura meets him? Soon Nest will be free of school, in six weeks she will be eighteen, an adult, and this foolish need for secrecy will be over. So she tells herself as the train rattles into the town, forgetting that she has ever thought that she and Connor could never be part of the humdrum world: that they were separate and apart from dull reality. It is all about her, here in the carriage: the tired woman with the heavy shopping basket; a man, frowning as he reads a newspaper; a young mother crooning to her child as it wriggles on her lap. Beyond the train window she sees cars, offices, factories and, beside her, Laura's warm body presses against her own as they sway and jolt along. All this is real enough.

They pass through the barrier into the sunshine outside the station – and he is there; leaning against the car, legs crossed at the ankles, waiting.

'Golly gosh!' murmurs Laura, awed by the impact of a mature male – he certainly makes her brother's friends look raw by comparison – and Nest feels an uprush of pride.

When he stretches a hand to her, however, her pale skin is suddenly stained blood-bright, but he kisses her lightly on the cheek and shakes Laura's hand with a blend of natural courtesy and wicked deference that makes her his slave for ever. She watches them drive away, her envious smile still lingering about her lips, and then turns away, contemplating the long, lonely day ahead.

Once they are alone, Nest's shyness continues to rob her of speech. She steals sidelong glances at him, trying to relearn him as he weaves his way competently through the traffic. The casual holiday clothes are replaced with a tweed sports coat and flannels, the sand-shoes by polished brogues. He looks older, more serious: very real indeed. Nest swallows in a dry throat and he glances across at her, his eyes crinkling into a smile. Instantly, the flame of confidence is reignited and she settles more comfortably, content to wait until they arrive at wherever it is he has ordained that they should spend the day.

When he stops the car, in a quiet spot at the edge of a hill overlooking rolling farmland, and turns to her, however, shyness returns and she stares ahead through the windscreen, unable to meet his eyes.

'Do you not think that this is a bit rash?' he asks gently. 'Not that I'm not delighted to see you, of course.'

She glances at him quickly, made fearful by his question, so clearly anxious for reassurance that he takes her face between his hands and kisses her until the blood hammers in her ears and she clings to him. Gently he takes her hands in his own, folding them quietly together.

'I've brought a picnic,' he tells her, his voice deliberately light, 'made of all the right stuff, believe me, or as near as I could get to what you'd consider suitable for such an occasion. Though nectar was in short demand and they were fresh out of lotus . . .'

She is laughing, adoring him, but he hasn't finished with her.

'We'll have a perfect day,' he tells her, more seriously, 'but this is the last one, lady, until I meet your family. You don't do this to me again.'

She promises, too happy and relieved to protest, but even though the picnic is delicious and the sunshine blesses them with its warmth, there is some difference that she cannot quite define. The ease they shared is gone, the holiday magic slightly tarnished, as reality presses in on their idyll. The invisible cloak that seemed to contain and protect them on Exmoor seems to be slipping and, when she suggests that they find somewhere to have some tea, he is not too keen. In the little tea-shop he withdraws even further: the intimacy vanishes; his tone is light, social, amused. She feels that she is still a schoolgirl being given a treat by an older member of her family, a cousin perhaps, and, going to the cloak-room, she peers into the tiny mirror, stares down at the shirtwaister dress, wondering if she looks too young beside his elegant, confident maturity.

When she returns she sees too the look the waitress gives him, knowing and complicit, and she wonders, with a new terror gripping her heart, whether in her absence Connor has been flirting with her. Their invisible cloak has been torn away indeed; oh, how distant, now, the beach and the moor; how natural and easy their love was, then.

'So,' says Connor, back in the car, unaware of her churning gut and destroyed confidence, 'will you give me an address or a telephone number so that I can meet this family of yours?'

She nods miserably and he puts a finger under her chin and turns her face towards his own.

'If you still want to,' she mutters – and he laughs and kisses her.

'For my sins,' he says, 'I do. So now which of them do I drop in on? You have sisters in London, isn't that the way of it?'

'No, it ought to be Mama and Mina.' She feels better now, sitting straighter, thrusting away her unworthy fears, ashamed of herself: he wants it to be above board and she has been so ready to misjudge him. 'But they're such a long way away.'

'I'm going down to Porlock again for a weekend. I'll drop in.'

'What will you say?' She stares at him, fascinated by his insouciance.

'Oh, that's not a problem. I shall say that I met you through your friend Laura at a party, and you told me to call on them when I was down next. How does that sound?'

'It sounds wonderful.' She is renewed again, full of delight. 'They'll love you, of course.'

He smiles drily. 'Of course. And you could be writing them a letter, just to say you've met this chap who might be passing through. Mention Porlock but keep it light; a coincidence, that kind of thing. But no contact between us until I've done it. Now, do you promise me that?'

'Oh, yes, I promise. Only how—'

'No questions. Just leave it to me. Don't you trust me, woman?'

'Of course I do.' She melts towards him, yearning for his embrace, weak with longing.

'I'm taking you back,' he says at last, 'and you'll never know what it's costing me. It's a medal I should be getting for it. Comb your hair and make yourself ready to meet that pop-eyed friend of yours. That's good. Give me a last kiss now. We'll say our goodbyes here, not in public at the station . . .'

'I love you,' murmurs Nest, trying the words for the first time, but he is busy reversing the car out of the parking space and doesn't hear her.

CHAPTER TWENTY-ONE

It was Friday evening before Lyddie summoned up the courage to speak to Liam about her idea for installing central heating. Just as on Saturday evenings The Place had a special atmosphere, so on Friday evenings it tended to let down its hair and a merry, end-of-week jollity pervaded it. When she arrived, there was already a crush at the bar but Joe waved to her cheerfully and several regulars stopped the Bosun to make much of him, exclaiming at his size and asking her questions about his diet and how much exercise he required. To her surprise, Liam was already installed in the snug and he stretched out an arm to pull her down beside him.

'What a racket!' he said. 'We're getting quite a rowdy element in here on Friday evenings. I'll have to put the prices up.'

'I like it,' Lyddie said, kissing him. 'It's fun, although it seems busier than usual. Were you waiting for me?'

'I was,' he answered. 'Someone's having a birthday and I think we'll get our order in before they want to eat. That way I can give Joe a bit of a break later on.'

'That's fine by me.' She let him help her out of her coat. 'We've had a very long walk and I'm starving.'

'I feel guilty about giving you that animal,' he said, leaning to stroke the Bosun, who had settled in his usual place at the end of the table. 'All this walking you have to do!'

'I need it.' Lyddie folded the coat and put it with her bag on the opposite bench. 'I sit down all day, remember. A long walk in the morning and then again in the evening is good for me – as well as him. Anyway, if I didn't he'd be impossible. He's still a very young dog. If I didn't wear him out before I started work he'd be an absolute pain. Luckily, he's very placid and he's big. He's glad to have a good long rest during the day.'

She saw that he was distracted, looking towards the bar, and glanced in the same direction. A pretty blonde girl was working beside Joe and, as they watched, he smiled reassuringly down at her and she pulled a face at him, clowning terror.

'Who's that?' Lyddie turned to Liam, surprised.

'That's our new girl, Zoë. She's done the work before and she's keen but this is her first night so we're keeping an eye on her.'

'Rosie's replacement?'

He nodded, watching Zoë serve a customer.

'She seems to be on the ball all right, but it's early days.'

Lyddie bit back the impulse to say, 'I didn't know you'd replaced Rosie already,' and saw Joe give Zoë an approving nod. She asked a question and he bent to show her something below the bar, their heads close together.

'Well,' she said thoughtfully, 'perhaps she'll be taking Rosie's place in more ways than one.'

Liam smiled. 'Always the romantic. And why not? So what are you going to eat?'

They sat together, companionably, sometimes talking, sometimes watching the ever-changing scene beyond the snug. After they'd eaten, Liam went to relieve Joe at the bar so that he could have some supper.

'How's Zoë doing?' she asked him, once he was settled on the bench opposite. 'She looks very competent.'

'She's good. She knows the job, it's just a question of finding out where things are, getting the hang of the layout, that kind of thing.'

She looked at him as he forked fettuccini into his mouth, longing to ask how he really was; wondering if he'd heard from Rosie. He glanced up, caught her expression and smiled at her.

'Are you OK?' She smiled back at him. 'You look tired.'

He raised his eyebrows. 'What's new? I *am* tired. Tired of working fourteen hours a day.'

'But no hope of a bar manager yet?'

He shook his head at her warningly. 'I'm not

239

going down that road. I don't like being caught in the crossfire between a husband and wife. It'll happen one day.'

'I suppose so.' She glanced towards the bar, watching Liam sharing a joke with one of the regulars. They roared with laughter, happy and at ease, and Lyddie sighed. 'The thing is that Liam actually never seems to be tired. On the contrary, he seems to thrive on his work; the more he does the more it seems to energize him. Odd, isn't it?'

'There are lots of people like Liam,' he answered. 'It's a kind of genetic instruction. A driving force. If they stop, they die.'

'Don't say that,' she said. 'I don't want us to be like this for the rest of our lives. I want us to spend some time together occasionally, have a holiday, start a family, that kind of thing. Like ordinary people do.'

He looked at her compassionately. 'But Liam's not an ordinary person,' he said gently. 'Something drives him. You must know that by now.'

'Yes,' she said. 'Yes, I know that.'

When Liam came to sit with her again, and Joe disappeared, carrying his plate into the kitchen, his vitality licked over him like a flame; even his hair seemed to tingle with it. He kissed her, glossy with goodwill, slipping an arm about her shoulders, and Joe grinned at them as he came back through the kitchen swing-door.

'You two ought to have a curtain across, some-times,' he said. 'It's indecent the way you carry on in public,' and they laughed back at him as Liam bent to kiss her again.

'The atmosphere here goes to your head,' she told him.

'And not just the atmosphere,' he answered. 'Did I tell you that you look beautiful tonight?'

Mickey brought them some coffee and they sat quietly together, drinking companionably.

'I had an idea earlier,' she said at last, 'about putting in some central heating. You're right about my room getting cold. I know I could use the electric radiator but it's terribly expensive. What about biting the bullet and putting in proper heating? It would increase the value of the house, wouldn't it?'

'It would.' He was staring down at his coffee, stirring it thoughtfully. 'But have you any idea of the cost?'

'No,' she said slowly, 'but we could get an estimate.' A pause. 'I could use the money from the house for it. What do you think?'

Another pause. She glanced at him; he was still stirring his coffee, the spoon moving round and round, and she had the impression that he wasn't listening to her at all, that his whole attention was somewhere else. Part of her was relieved that he hadn't immediately vetoed the idea or lost his temper; part of her was puzzled. He spoke, however, before she could repeat the question.

'It's a thought,' he said. He took a draught of the coffee and leaned back, stretching, a smile touching his lips. 'Definitely a thought.'

She drew a long breath, feeling herself relax. 'Good,' she said.

'And I must go and talk to the punters,' he said and chuckled suddenly. 'What did you call it? My royal walkabout?' He swallowed some more coffee and stood up. Squeezing past, he smiled down at her, sending her a little wink. 'I'll be back.'

She settled comfortably, quite weak now that the moment was over, still astonished at his amiability. After pouring some more coffee, she sat quietly, watching him as he moved amongst his customers; a nod here, a pat on the shoulder there, a compliment to a pretty woman, a longer conversation with some favoured regulars. After a moment she was aware of someone watching her and, glancing across to the bar, she saw Joe looking at her with an odd expression of mingled affection and compassion.

Mina carefully set out the pieces on the backgammon board, put the dice ready in their cups and waited for Nest to position her chair comfortably. In the corner of the room, Inspector Morse, with the faithful Lewis, was solving Oxford's crime whilst Georgie watched alertly, muttering excitedly from time to time.

Mina threw a five, Nest a two, and Mina began to move her counters.

'Georgie came into my room again last night.' Nest spoke quietly but normally, knowing that the noise of the television would mask her actual words, not wishing to attract attention by sounding conspiratorial.

'Oh, no!' Mina fumbled with her dice as she put them back into the cup, looking at her anxiously. 'What happened?'

'I was out for the count.' Nest threw her dice. Double four. 'To begin with, I wondered if it was a dream. You know what it's like when you take a sleeping pill? You feel drugged.' She began to move her counters. 'She thought I was Mama, lying down in the morning-room. She couldn't understand why.'

She finished her move and Mina threw her dice, six and four, and frowned at the board.

'Did she say anything . . . well, anything silly?' Mina's hand hovered over a counter.

'She said that she knew Mama's secret and asked if she should tell it.'

Mina's hand trembled a little; she moved her counter quickly and then put both hands in her lap.

'And did she?' she asked, quite casually. 'Did she tell this secret?'

Nest made her move, taking one of Mina's undefended counters as she did so.

'No,' she answered. 'I managed to catch hold of her. She was leaning over me, you see, whispering.'

Nest watched Mina give a tiny shudder as she threw her dice. 'How horrid for you.'

'It was, rather. I managed to grapple with her. And then I said that it was me, Nest.'

'Oh, trust me to throw a double six when I can't use it. Your turn. So what did she say then?'

'There was a bit of a silence. Then she said, "I know a secret about you too," or something like that. "Shall I tell it?" she asked me.'

Nest deftly moved her counters out of an imminent danger and glanced across the table at her sister. Mina looked old and tired; her frailty filled Nest with love and remorse.

'And did she?' Mina could barely frame the words. 'Did she tell you what she knows?'

'No.' Nest shook her head. 'I shouted at her. Well, I think I did, it was all so hazy, but perhaps it was stupid of me. I'm beginning to think that it would be more sensible if we confronted her and found out exactly what it is she *does* know. If anything.'

'No,' said Mina quickly. 'No, I don't think so.'

They stared at each other across the forgotten game and, quite suddenly, loud music and the sound of commercials crashed ear-splittingly into the room. Nest winced and, just as suddenly, there was silence.

'Sorry,' said Georgie cheerfully. 'I turned the thingy the wrong way.' She got up and came towards them. 'I've seen this one before. It's the don who did it. Funny, isn't it? You'd never expect the things that happen in Oxford, would you? I always thought that Oxford dons were such *respectable* people.' She peered at them, eyes bright. 'Shall I get the tray in while the commercials are on? The coffee's all ready, isn't it? Just pour boiling water in the jug?'

She went away. Nest bit her lip and Mina reached to touch her hand.

'I was dreaming about Connor, you see.' Nest spoke rapidly. 'Remembering those years after the war and Timmie going off to Sandhurst. Mina, do you remember the day Connor called on you here that very first time?'

Mina took a slow, deep breath, her gaze drifting away from Nest's face, looking back to a long-past June day.

'Yes,' she said gently. 'Yes, of course I do. We were in the garden after lunch. I was putting out some bedding plants and Henrietta was talking to me. She'd brought out a garden chair and was sitting smoking, chatting while I worked. Mama was resting. Henrietta was being naughty about Mama disapproving of her slacks. You know how old-fashioned Mama was about things like that? They were quite beautiful, I have to say, in a delicious navy-blue linen. Superbly cut, of course, and she was wearing a bright yellow shirt . . .'

'Go on,' said Nest grimly. 'I can imagine the scene.'

'Well, Connor came walking down the drive – of course we had no idea who he was – and introduced himself and explained that it had seemed rather pushy to sweep in with the car and so on. He apologized for calling unannounced but said he'd been passing and that he'd met you at a party and you'd told him to drop in.' She paused, thinking back, cudgelling her memory.

'Go *on*,' whispered Nest urgently, listening for Georgie.

'Henrietta was enchanted by him. She got up and said something like, "I didn't know my baby sister had such good sense," and introduced herself. He took her hand and bowed over it but you could see,' Mina's voice was dragging, hesitating – 'Go *on*!' said Nest fiercely – 'that he was bowled over by her. I have to say that she looked sensational. She was so . . . breathtakingly English. A dark-haired Grace Kelly. It was as if he'd been suddenly blinded. It was the true *coup de foudre* – I recognized it because I'd been there once, myself – and he shook my hand in a complete daze. I offered him some tea and he said that he'd love some – oh! but he was charming with that faint touch of the Irish – and Henrietta carried him off to help her make it. I think she was afraid that I might make eyes at him.' Mina paused. 'You must remember,' she pointed out, 'that he was much more our generation than yours.'

'You don't have to remind me,' answered Nest bitterly. 'Once he'd clapped eyes on Henrietta I must have looked like a raw, tongue-tied schoolgirl. That's what he said when he wrote to me, you know? Not in those words but it's what he meant. Oh, he didn't mention that he was dating Henrietta, of course – I found out about that much later – but he talked about the difference in our ages. Cradle-snatching, I think he called it. He took me out to tea first, if you remember?

246

He wanted to do the honourable thing and tell me face to face but, afterwards, he wrote to me, to confirm it, you might say. I think he suspected that I'd simply refused to take it in, that I'd go on hoping, and he was absolutely right. In the letter, he repeated what he'd said in that wretched tea-room, that he'd given it a great deal of thought and he'd realized that it would be wrong of him to let our friendship develop any further. He said that the romantic way we'd met had put a whole false impression on it and that I'd soon find that my feelings for him were simply infatuation, a schoolgirl crush. He was very, very kind.' She stared across the neglected backgammon board at Mina. 'I learned that letter by heart,' she said bleakly.

'Here we are!' Georgie was back with them, carrying the tray. 'Oh, it's started again.' Mina and Nest stared guiltily at the silently mouthing, gesticulating Morse. 'You should have shouted.' She looked at them reproachfully.

'Well, if you've seen it before I expect you'll soon pick it up,' said Mina pacifically. 'We got carried away by our game.'

Georgie stood the tray on the low table by the fire and came to look at the board.

'Looks a bit messy,' she said critically. 'Remember the day when I gammoned you, Mina?'

'Yes,' said Mina, smiling. 'I remember it very well. It was jolly clever stuff. You'd better get back to Morse and I'll pour the coffee and make Nest's tea.'

Captain Cat and Nogood Boyo came from their beds, ears pricked hopefully, and she fed them a morsel of shortbread, murmuring her love words to them and taking a piece to Polly Garter, who was still curled on her beanbag. By the time she got back to the board, with her coffee and Nest's mug of herbal tea, the moment of confidence was past and they played in silence, each locked into her thoughts of the past, until the game was over.

CHAPTER TWENTY-TWO

Helena and Rupert arrived late on Saturday morning, by which time all three sisters were in a state of nervous tension. Georgie was, by turns, either capriciously critical of the arrangements made for their comfort or petulantly indifferent, as if she'd suddenly remembered exactly why she was at Ottercombe in the first place. Nest had slept badly, reliving those days of Connor's rejection but unwilling to take another sleeping-pill, and looked exhausted. Mina, ploughing steadily onwards, disregarding Georgie's sudden switches of mood but anxious for Nest, was still trying to come to some decision as to whether or not she should insist that Georgie should be removed.

The previous night she had sent an e-mail to Elyot.

From: Mina
To: Elyot

My dear friend I am in a state of guggle. There is no doubt that Georgie has opened Pandora's box and all our skeletons are tumbling out. Or am I mixing my metaphors? First me and Tony Luttrell, now Nest and Connor. I simply do not know what to do for the best . . .

From: Elyot
To: Mina

Wait, wait until the moment shows its hand. These things so often resolve themselves and we need the patience to let ourselves be carried. Oh dear! How simplistic that sounds – and so much easier written than done! Don't I know it. Just don't give in, dear old friend, but let me know how the day went – if you have any strength left by the end of it . . .

So Mina had gone to bed, determined to take his advice, holding Lydia's carved, wooden rosary, allowing the beads to slip between her fingers, until a measure of calm possessed her weary brain and she'd slept. She'd risen refreshed, surprisingly peaceful, but Georgie's mood-swings and Nest's look of patient suffering gave rise to anxiety that she was unable to control. It was almost a relief when Rupert and Helena arrived and they all went out to meet them.

'Mother!' Helena swung herself enthusiastically out of the car and hurried to the waiting Georgie as if they'd been kept forcibly apart for months. 'How *are* you?' She held her at arm's length. 'Looking *very* well.'

She beamed tenderly into Georgie's sulky, watchful face and Nest felt an overwhelming urge to burst into hysterical laughter. She caught Mina's eye but Mina stared back at her expressionlessly, daring her to grin, although Nest knew that she too longed to chuckle. Rupert was approaching, having carefully locked and alarmed the car – 'Does he think that there are car thieves hidden in the garden?' asked Mina indignantly, later – and smiled graciously upon them. He kissed each of them lightly on the cheek and took Georgie's unresponsive hands.

'Well, Ma-in-law,' he said jovially, with all the brutal condescension of a senior master to a young and foolish pupil, 'have you been behaving yourself?'

Georgie stared up at him: humiliation stiffened her jaw and squared her thin shoulders whilst the colour flowed into her pale cheeks. She freed her hands, firmly but politely, and turned away from him.

Mina and Nest looked at one another – 'It was at that point,' Nest said, afterwards, 'that I knew we couldn't ask for her to be taken away. My God! He is such a pompous prat of a man!' – and both broke into speech, urging the whole party into the house.

251

It was clear that Helena was ashamed of Rupert's patronizing behaviour, though she refused to side against him. Too many of Georgie's cruel cuts and slights over the long years had sliced away at her love for her mother until only the bare bone of filial affection was left for this elderly woman, who had consistently withheld any shred of diplomacy or generosity with respect to her daughter or her husband. Helena knew that Rupert was at his worst with her mother and her family and, embarrassed though she might be, yet she could understand that it was his own past humiliations at her mother's hands that reinforced his own least likeable mannerisms in her presence.

Georgie had heard the words 'As you sow so shall you reap' but it had never occurred to her that they would ever ultimately apply directly to *her* and, now, she turned into the house, mortified, resentful and powerless. Mina, who had some idea of the reasoning behind the behaviour of all three of them – and a certain degree of sympathy for both Helena and Rupert – was nevertheless a prey to sibling solidarity and was relieved to see that Nest, for the same reason, was firmly supporting Georgie.

It seemed, after all, that Elyot was right: the moment had showed its hand and the situation was resolved almost before they'd begun. Nothing occurred to change their minds. The meeting, having got off to an unfortunate start, continued to deteriorate. Helena, refusing to disapprove of

252

Rupert's continuing pomposity yet attempting to restore Georgie's pride, fell between all the stools. Her desperation to shield her husband whilst ameliorating the situation with her mother became too painful to watch and, after lunch, Mina announced that she was taking the dogs for a walk down to the beach. For one brief moment, Nest was truly tempted to break her self-imposed rule and ask to go with her but Mina, not guessing this, added that this was Nest's rest time.

'I expect that the three of you would like to have some time together,' she said brightly and, without waiting for anyone to agree with this optimistic statement, she seized Nest's chair and pushed her firmly out of the drawing-room and into her bedroom, closing the door behind them.

For a moment they stared at one another fearfully, almost as if they expected one of the others to come rushing after them, before Nest let out a gasp of relief whilst Mina collapsed on Nest's bed.

'Do you realize,' asked Nest, presently, 'that we have nearly *twenty-four* more hours of this hell to get through?'

'Don't,' said Mina. 'Just don't. At least you can plead exhaustion or pain, or something, and escape.'

'Poor Georgie,' said Nest. 'Oh, wasn't it horrid? She looked so utterly humiliated.'

'Yes.' Mina hesitated for a second, wondering whether she should attempt to put forward Helena and Rupert's point of view but decided against it. It was as if she had been given an answer to her prayer and, that being so, it would be wrong now to cloud the issue. 'Poor old Georgie. I think, after all, that she'll be better off in that home.'

'So do I,' agreed Nest at once. 'Anyway, did you hear Rupert say that they're off for a week's holiday? In which case it looks as if we haven't much choice. Honestly, Mina, Rupert is the *end*!'

They talked together for a little longer but by the time Mina set out on her walk, the decision had been taken.

From: Mina
To: Elyot

. . . and, to be honest, nothing happened to make us change our minds. It's very sad that they don't get on better as a family but it's too late to turn the clock back and, after all, Georgie will only be with us for three more weeks. It was odd, and very endearing, to see Nest's volte face in the light of Georgie's humiliation. I pray that nothing happens now to make her regret it. I can't really imagine anything that could precipitate such a disaster . . .

At half-past ten on Monday morning, after a long walk beside Malpas creek, round the ornamental lake and home again, Lyddie settled a weary Bosun in the yard, checked his bowl of cold water and gave him a biscuit. He looked at her pathetically, ears flattened, but she patted him briskly and gave him a quick kiss on the nose.

'I shan't be long,' she told him, 'but I simply *have* to do some clothes shopping and I can't drag you round with me. You can have a good, long sleep and we'll go out again later. *Good* boy!'

He watched her go back into the kitchen and heard the key turn in the lock; when he heard the front door slam and her footsteps going away, he sighed heavily and began to crunch his biscuit. Ten minutes later he was deeply asleep.

Lyddie heard the cathedral bell chime the third quarter as she passed down Pydar Street. It was a bright, crisp October morning and she was glad of her wool jacket although the cold air was invigorating. Even after her long walk with the Bosun, she felt full of energy and was enjoying a sense of freedom. An author had been late submitting his manuscript, a long novel, and Lyddie was in the unusual position of having a two-week slot booked and no work. For some reason she couldn't quite define, she hadn't told Liam about this unexpected bonus: she'd decided to chill out a little, to do some shopping and perhaps pop in to The Place at lunch-time: something she very rarely did.

She spent some time in the Body Shop and then headed for the Mounts Bay Trading Company, where she bought a charming silk and wool cropped jersey and hesitated longingly over a narrow, elegant skirt in dark green, soft merino wool.

'I'll think about it,' she told the assistant laughingly. 'No, no, don't tempt me any more! Put it back on the hanger. I'll have some coffee and brood on it.'

She hurried out into the bright sunshine, back to Boscawan Street, wondering whether to check out the Jaeger shop in Lemon Street before deciding on the merino skirt. There was a small queue at the bank and she glanced at her watch as she waited to draw some money: it was nearly half-past eleven. Should she have coffee at the *patisserie* in Lemon Street or go to The Terrace? Lyddie pushed her card into the slot, tapped in her code and waited. Of course, she could have coffee at The Place – but almost instantly she rejected the thought. It was much more likely that Liam would spare half an hour to have lunch with her than to stop for coffee. After all, he'd have to eat at some point – and it would be fun to have a little extra time together.

For the last few days he'd been on brilliant form: amusing, tender, passionate. She'd begun to believe that the 'No Thoroughfare' sign was beginning to come down and a new way forward was opening up to them after all. She'd decided that the time was very nearly right to talk to him about her longing for a child: to suggest that it was time they started a family. Putting the cash into her purse, peeping at her new jersey, remembering last night, with its long, languorous hours of glorious, heart-stopping love, Lyddie thought: I am *happy*. She paused for a moment, aware of nothing but untinged, pure joy; a few seconds in which nothing else existed but this upward-winging sensation. The man behind her in the queue shifted and cleared his throat and Lyddie smiled blindingly at him before turning away.

She was passing the narrow entrance into Cathedral Lane when she saw them: Liam and Rosie, silhouetted at the other end of the passage. Liam had his hands up, rejectingly, whilst Rosie seemed to be remonstrating. Lyddie was past, actually looking in the window of Monsoon, when her mind did a kind of double take and she realized what she'd seen. Or had she? She stepped back to look into the lane just as Liam turned away, heading towards The Place, Rosie staring after him. Her stance was defeated, frustrated, and she thrust her hands into her pockets before she glanced round and saw Lyddie. She stiffened, hesitated, and then, ineluctably drawn, each walked to meet the other. They met outside Abacus.

'Rosie,' said Lyddie warmly, 'how good to see you. I was so sorry to hear that you'd ... left. How's it going?'

Rosie stared at her with that familiar intense, calculating look and then smiled wryly. '*Is* it going?' she asked. 'That's the question.'

'Oh dear.' Lyddie felt both sympathetic and responsible, guessing that Rosie had been asking for her job back and that Liam had refused. She wondered how much the split-up with Joe had to do with her leaving The Place and whether she was regretting the whole thing. 'Look, I was just going to have a cup of coffee. Do you feel like joining me?'

'Why not?' Rosie seemed to be debating with herself as much as with Lyddie. 'Yes, OK. We'll go to The Terrace.'

With white cane furniture and mirrors, and the ivy in its hanging baskets, The Terrace was charming – yet totally unlike The Place.

'I always feel faintly guilty when I come in here,' said Lyddie when they had their coffee in front of them on the small round table. She chuckled. 'It's rather like being unfaithful, if you see what I mean?'

'Well, you needn't let that worry you, need you?' asked Rosie flippantly.

Lyddie was puzzled, sensing some subtle challenge beneath the casually uttered question. 'How do you mean?' she asked.

'I mean why should *you* worry about being unfaithful.' Rosie watched her, still unsmilingly, and then shrugged impatiently. 'I *mean*' – she emphasized the word as if implying that Lyddie were being unnecessarily stupid – 'that you're married to the expert.'

'I don't understand you.' Lyddie tried to speak lightly. 'Sorry. Look, you seem a bit upset—'

'No, *you* look.' Rosie leaned forward, blocking Lyddie's view of the other customers. 'Open your eyes for once. It's about time, after all. I've always thought that you should know . . .' She sat back again, eyes narrowed, assessing her. 'Perhaps you *do* know that Liam's cheating on you.'

Lyddie smiled disbelievingly. 'Cheating . . . ?'

'Oh, for God's sake!' Rosie looked away for a moment, her hands clasping in an odd wringing movement, and then stared at Lyddie. 'Joe always said you never guessed but I didn't really believe him. Christ, Lyddie! You've seen him with the customers, with the women.'

'Yes,' agreed Lyddie carefully, 'and I *did* wonder if he'd been with one or two of them before we were married—'

'One or two?' Rosie gave a short explosive laugh. 'Jesus! And the rest.'

'I don't believe you.' Lyddie sounded quite calm, although an icy hand seemed to be twisting and gripping in her gut. 'Oh, not about Liam going with some of the women in the past. He was a free man, after all, why shouldn't he? But I think that all this is because he won't give you your job back—'

'We're *lovers*, Lyddie. Me and Liam. We were lovers long before you blew into The Place on that *bloody* summer's day and turned his head with your class act . . .'

'All the more reason for you to be—'

'Please,' Rosie interrupted wearily, 'oh, *please*, don't let's pretend that I'm doing the woman scorned bit. I left The Place of my own free will. Liam and I have been having it off for the last year – yes, there was a break for a while after he married you – but now there's someone new. Oh, I haven't been given the push, Liam's not like

259

that. The more the merrier where he's concerned. He likes a harem. It lends spice, a bit of competition. Christ! Lyddie, don't look like that. Where the hell did you think he was when he said he was going to the bank every day, or the cash and carry?'

'And Joe?'

'Joe?' Rosie looked baffled at the question and then shook her head. 'You really want some convincing, don't you? Joe and I were never serious except for a short time after you and Liam got married. When Liam and I started to go to bed together again, Joe kept up the pretence because he didn't want you to be hurt. He was furious but he can't do anything about it. They're partners and that's that. The Place is more important to them than anyone, haven't you found that out yet? I told Joe I was going to tell you before one of those other cows that Liam hangs out with spills the beans but he was very angry with me. That's what we were arguing about that night when you came in out of the rain.' She looked aside from Lyddie's white face. 'It's *not* spite,' she said urgently. 'It's just . . . You need to know before anything else happens; someone else deciding to drop him in it. He has one hell of a magnetic pull, does Liam, but one of the others might just tug free and decide to get her own back. You're not very popular, you know, waltzing in and pinching him from under our noses.'

Lyddie remained silent; she even drank a little coffee, although her hand trembled and the cup rattled as she replaced it in its saucer. Rosie watched her admiringly, consideringly.

'I'm not sure you believe me, even now,' she said. She leaned forward again. 'Tell me,' she asked casually, 'would you agree if I said that, just these last few days, since Thursday, let's say, Liam's been really sparkling, right up there, know what I mean?' She smiled. 'Yes, I see that you would. Know why? The reason's very close to home and she's called Zoë. You can tell when Liam's pulling someone new. It goes to his head like champagne and he wants everyone to share the bubbles. He was at The Place yesterday afternoon, wasn't he? Right? And he couldn't possibly get home. Right? I bet you haven't seen the set-up in one of the storerooms upstairs, have you? Just in case someone's ill or has to stay over? No, well, it's bloody useful. And that's where he was yesterday afternoon and I bet you had one hell of a night with him!'

Once again she looked away from Lyddie's shocked, vulnerable expression, biting her lips with frustration.

'Look,' she said at last, 'don't take my word for it. Go there now and see for yourself. He won't be expecting you. I'm sorry, Lyddie. I am, really, because you're a sweet person and he should have left you alone. But I love him too, and he was mine before he was ever yours.' She stood up quickly, swinging her bag over her shoulder, staring down at Lyddie. 'And now,' she said bleakly, 'you'll never know, will you? You'll look at them all with new eyes. The ones who smile at him and, even worse, the ones he doesn't take too much notice of, and you'll never know.' She gave a tiny bitter laugh. 'Well, join the club.'

She whirled away, out into Boscawan Street, and Lyddie sat on, her hands still trembling, sick to the stomach. Mechanically, she finished her coffee and, presently, she found that she could stand up, pay the bill, and walk out into the sunshine. Her mind a careful blank, she crossed the road and stepped briskly through Cathedral Lane, towards The Place. She paused just inside the door. It was fairly quiet, just a few late morning shoppers having coffee, and there was nobody behind the bar. Zoë stood at the entrance to the snug, smiling down at someone hidden from sight inside. As she watched, Lyddie saw the hand that came out to draw a sensual, lingering finger round the bare space between Zoë's jeans and short, cropped T-shirt. She leaned towards the owner of the finger, laughing now, and Lyddie drew back quickly as Liam swung himself into view and, after a swift but even more intimate touch, pushed Zoë affectionately but firmly aside and disappeared into the kitchen.

Some people, coming in for lunch, screened Lyddie's escape and she hurried away, her cheeks burning, her heart knocking in her side. Walking fast she broke every now and again into a stumbling run, until she was safely home with the door closed behind her.

CHAPTER TWENTY-THREE

Overnight, the wild westerly gales, driving onshore behind the high tides, piling the sea against the rock-bound coast, had refashioned the beach and scoured the pools. Seaweed had been flung far beyond the usual high-water mark and the dogs ran excitedly amongst the brown, shiny kelp, examining the spoils. Behind them, Mina moved more slowly, collecting smooth, twisted pieces of bleached, salty wood, which later would sizzle with magical red and green and blue flames when she lit the sitting-room fire. Further down the beach, Georgie stooped over a pebble, turning it carefully in her fingers before putting it in her pocket. She was beginning to develop a fondness for inanimate things: a stone, a short length of string, an old stub of pencil. These would be placed together in odd, meaningless, still-life patterns that she would touch tenderly from time to time, or re-examine more closely with a kind of possessive affection.

Now, as Mina watched her, Georgie's attention was caught by something half buried in the wet sand. She crouched to dig deeper, disinterring the object from which she brushed the gritty shale.

'Look!' She straightened up, the wind whipping her voice away as she turned to look for her sister. 'Look what I've found.'

Mina hastened down the beach curiously. 'What is it?'

'It's a toy car.' Georgie was delighted. 'Do you see? The rubber wheels are gone, and all the paint, but you can see quite clearly that that's what it is.'

Mina peered at it, not touching it, sensing that Georgie was not ready yet to let it out of her grasp.

'So it is.' She laughed incredulously. 'One of Timmie's, d'you think? Fancy finding it after all this time. I wonder how long it's been buried? Oh, of course, it might be one of Toby's.'

'No.' Georgie shook her head at once. 'It's too old. No, it's Timmie's. I recognize it. Timothy sent it for his birthday when he was about seven, at the beginning of the war. He was quite mad with joy about it. So was Mama. Surely you remember? There was such excitement when the parcel arrived. *She* had a letter, of course.'

Mina felt, quite suddenly, an odd sense of still-ness. The hoarse shrieking of the gulls overhead, the pounding, rhythmical crash of the insatiable tide upon the shore, the wild barking of the foraging dogs; all these sounds seemed to recede as she looked at Georgie. Her sister's expression was compounded of simple pleasure and a knowing, amused scornfulness as she examined the toy car. Silence stretched between them.

'Did you read her letters?' Mina asked at last. 'Mama's letters from Timothy, I mean. Did you, Georgie?'

Instantly the expression changed: replaced by the shrugging, bridling motion of the shoulders, the sly, twitching face movements, as if she heard another conversation in which she was already justifying herself to an unseen accuser.

'Did you, Georgie?' insisted Mina.

'Letters?' Georgie looked up from the toy, whose silvery, sand-blasted surface gleamed dully in a shaft of wintry sunlight. Her eyes were watchful but quite sane.

'She kept them in her sewing-basket, in a little, shallow, secret drawer.' Mina turned to look out across the channel. 'Odd how the Victorians loved secret drawers, isn't it? I saw her by mistake, putting a letter away. I thought it was the Tinies playing in the drawing-room. Do you remember how they'd hide just before lunch-time and one of us would have to find them?' She chuckled a little. 'I can see them now, standing quite breathless behind the long curtains with their sandals showing at the bottom. They never *could* guess how I found them so quickly. Did you see Mama putting the letters away too?'

'I heard something.' Georgie was willingly drawn into the remembering game. 'A little, sharp bang. I was lying down on the sofa and she didn't know I was there. I was home from London for a weekend or a holiday during the war. Quite early on, I think it was. After the blitz, though.'

'And you heard the drawer shut?' Mina edged her back to the point.

'Yes. I looked over the back of the chair but she was going out of the room.' Georgie paused, thinking about it. 'I was curious,' she admitted, after a moment. 'There was something, you know . . . *furtive* about it. It was unlike Mama. She was always so tranquil, wasn't she? But she looked so odd, secretive but excited too, that I felt a little flutter of . . . well, a "What's she up to?" kind of sensation.'

'So you went and had a look?' Mina's voice invited intimacy.

'Well, I did. It wasn't difficult to find the spring-catch. Goodness, I couldn't believe it when I saw them all stacked together. There were dozens of them, weren't there?'

'There were quite a lot,' Mina agreed. 'Most of them were from abroad, of course . . . Did you read them too?'

'Some of them.' Georgie's glance crossed Mina's and slid away. 'Enough of them to see what had been going on between them.'

'But you didn't tell anyone?'

'No.' Georgie sounded defensive, almost as if Mina was accusing her of dereliction of a duty. 'Of course, I was less shocked than I might have been before I went to London but, somehow, this rather old-fashioned love affair was quite in keeping with the times. Timothy off in the far-flung outposts of the Empire, doing his bit, while Mama waited for him at home.'

A pause.

'You didn't feel that Papa should have been told?'

'No, I didn't!' answered Georgie at once, almost indignantly. 'It didn't take me long to discover what had been going on for all those years with that frightful widow whilst Mama and the rest of us were shuttled off to Ottercombe. He preferred her to *us*, his own family. To be quite honest, I felt a sense of *satisfaction* that Mama had been playing him at his own game, if you want to know.' She looked slyly at Mina. 'Did *you* tell him?'

'I didn't read them until after she'd died,' replied Mina gently. 'And he was long dead himself, by then. He would have made a terrific row, widow or not, so I suspected that, if you'd known about them, you'd kept it to yourself. Anyway,' she chuckled a little, 'you like to have secrets, don't you?'

Georgie looked down at the toy again, hiding her own secret smile. 'Sometimes,' she said pertly, almost childishly. 'Timmie loved this car, you know. He took it everywhere with him. I hid it once, just to pay him out.' Her smile faded a little. 'He was Mama's favourite. And Papa's. *I* was the eldest. *I* was their first-born but, because he was a boy, they loved him most. Sometimes he needed a lesson.'

'I don't think he was really their favourite.'

Mina was dismayed by this relapse. 'I think they loved us all differently.'

She spoke soothingly, trying to hide the tiny spasm of distaste at Georgie's disclosure – a young woman of seventeen or eighteen hiding a child's toy for spite – and her sister looked at her again, her eyes bright.

'What a joke, wasn't it? Timmie, so blond and tall. Not a bit like any of us and Papa so proud of his handsome, only son.' She began to laugh. 'Everyone remarking on how *different* he was. But all the time . . .' her laughter was edging out of control, 'but all the time . . .'

'I know,' said Mina quickly. 'I read the letters too, remember.'

Georgie stared at her, tiny bursts of laughter still escaping from her lips, her eyes confused now.

'It's a secret,' she muttered vaguely.

'Yes,' said Mina quickly, urgently. '*Our* secret. Nobody else must know.'

Georgie turned away, smoothing the little car with her fingers, mumbling to herself.

'I want to go home,' she said.

She set off, stumping away across the beach, and, sighing with frustration and anxiety, Mina collected her bag of firewood, called to the dogs and followed her on to the path.

It was almost dark before Lyddie realized how cold the house was becoming. She had taken the Bosun out rather earlier than usual, striding purposefully through the streets as though by sheer physical effort she could conquer the numbing horror that pervaded her mind. Even if she had not witnessed the telling little scene at The Place, yet she might have accepted the truth that Rosie showed her. It was so obvious, once she'd been told. Walking the lanes, her hands jammed into her pockets, the Bosun running beside her, she'd felt scorched by humiliation. She remembered, with shrinking mortification, the looks of those other women and was able to put quite a different interpretation upon them. How blind she'd been; how foolish!

Now, as she lit the stove, crouching before it as she fed it with sticks and then larger logs, she tried to determine how much of her hurt was pride and how much damaged love. Those women – oh! how many? – like Rosie had colluded with Liam to deceive her and she had gone in and out, happy, sure in her love, despite her twinges of jealousy, whilst they laughed behind their hands. The tiny scene with Liam and Zoë was burned like pokerwork into her mind's eye: wherever she looked she saw it, superimposed. It was the manifestation of all the pictures that Rosie had drawn for her. She knew that she would be quite unable to enter The Place again and wondered, in a moment of panic-stricken despair, where she should go and what she should do.

She made herself some tea, just for the reassurance of doing something ordinary and normal, and drank it sitting at the table. The Bosun roused himself from his sleep and looked at her hopefully, so she fed him, talking to him as she usually did, and, afterwards, he lay down again, stretched on the floor beside her. When the telephone rang she didn't answer it but watched it in an almost detached fashion. The answer machine and fax were in her study but she made no attempt to listen for a message, remaining where she was at the table. When it rang again an hour later she continued to ignore it but, by now, a terrible restlessness was beginning to possess her: the need to decide what she should do, accompanied by a paralysing inability to think properly.

As she crouched beside the Bosun, drawing comfort from his bulky warmth, she heard the key in the lock and, in one short moment, Liam was in the room. She stared up at him, shocked suddenly out of her numbed condition by his physical presence. Vividly, she became painfully aware of all that she had lost, seeing clearly that nothing could ever be the same again. She stumbled to her feet, still staring at him, and saw too that he was furiously angry. Even in her misery she sensed that the anger was not directed at her; it flowed past her, pouring from him in waves of energy so that his eyes were unnaturally bright and his hands flexed and clenched as he looked at her.

'Why did you not answer the telephone?' he asked abruptly – and she frowned a little in surprise, rather like a pupil set a totally unexpected question during an examination.

Speech seemed impossible – there were no

words for this situation – so she continued to stare at him, as if she were learning a whole, new person.

He sighed, his eyes flickering about the room, weighing up what he might say.

'When you didn't come in for supper, and then you didn't answer the telephone, I began to get worried.' He'd decided to get straight to the point. 'It was Joe who told me. You had coffee with Rosie, I hear?'

'I had rather more than coffee.' She was thankful that her voice sounded quite normal. 'She decided that it was time that I should know that I was living a delusion.'

'I love you. That's no delusion. We're married. That's a fact.'

'Yes.' She couldn't deny it. 'My delusion was in imagining that you were being faithful to me.'

'Oh, Mother of God!' It was a sigh of weary impatience, his anger dissipating into irritation. 'You have to understand that none of them matter. It's you I love. Do you not see that? I could have married any of them but I married you . . . What's amusing you?'

'It's just that I thought you might be more original. But I'm not really amused. There's nothing at all funny about being told that your husband is a philandering bastard by his chief mistress.'

'But you had no difficulty in believing her?'

The brief descent into hurt innocence didn't sit well on him and Lyddie smiled faintly.

'Oh, but I did,' she assured him. 'Tremendous difficulty. I could believe that you and she had had an affair before we were married – after all, why not? But I thought she was getting her own back, you see, for being given the sack. I didn't realize she'd gone of her own free will.'

'Rosie's a chancer, always has been.'

'Oh, I can believe that. But it doesn't mean that she's a liar.' There was a silence. 'So does that mean that you're denying it?'

In the longer silence that followed her question, Lyddie felt all that had once been confident and secure in her begin to crumble.

'No,' he answered at last. 'There'd be little point in that. I'm saying that it's unimportant. It needn't affect what we have together.'

'But it does!' she cried. 'Do you really think that I can walk into The Place ever again? That I can sit there calmly eating my supper whilst you slink around the tables mentally screwing whichever female customer takes your fancy and drooling privately over the barmaid you were knocking off earlier up in the storeroom?'

He made a fastidious grimace and she saw that, fantastically, some puritanical streak deep in him hated her outspokenness. A surge of pure anger, untinged with self-pity, rinsed her clean of any insincere emotion.

'I saw you earlier,' she told him. 'I came to The Place at lunch-time and saw your behaviour with Zoë. And her response to you. Do you suggest that I should come along and sit in the snug whilst she laughs behind her hand as Rosie has done for the last year? Do you really think that I'm that strong, Liam? Or that I'm capable of such heroic acts of humiliation on your behalf? Do you actually think you're worth it?'

He was silent. She could see that the knowledge of her lunch-time visit to The Place had shaken him and that, behind his bleak expression, he was thinking of what he should do next.

'Do you have any suggestions to make?' he asked at last.

'I gather you're not contemplating changing your ways?' she asked lightly.

'Oh, I might contemplate it,' he said truthfully, 'but it wouldn't last. I did try for a while, after we were married, but . . . well, it didn't work out.' He raised his hands, palms outward. 'No point making promises I mightn't be able to keep.'

'Well, ten out of ten for honesty.'

He looked as if he might try further persuasion – but changed his mind.

'I've got to go back,' he said – 'You amaze me!' she said sarcastically – 'would you prefer it if I stay the night at The Place? Give you space to decide how you want to play it?'

'Why not?' She shrugged, part relieved, part oddly disappointed. 'I understand you've got very comfortable accommodation.'

'I'll be back in the morning,' he said un-emotionally. 'Around ten.' And before she could reply he went out quickly, closing the door gently behind him.

CHAPTER TWENTY-FOUR

'Did you remember the car, Nest?' asked Mina, after Georgie had gone to bed. 'So odd, finding it after all these years.'

'Oh, yes.' Nest, wheeling across the kitchen, paused to look at it where it stood on the dresser. 'Anything from Timothy was a treat, wasn't it? Those postcards he sent and the unusual presents. I still have a beautiful Peruvian doll he gave me for a birthday. I think we all envied Timmie having him as a godfather. I probably remember him least because I was youngest but I still have this feeling about him. A sensation of someone special and charismatic that we all loved. Or am I endowing him with childish fantasy?'

'No,' said Mina. 'Oh, no. Timothy was very special indeed. I'm glad you can remember him. After all, you can't have been more than seven when he was killed.'

'It's more this feeling inside than a clear picture of him.' Nest screwed her eyes tight shut, as if she were trying to summon Timothy up from the past. 'He seemed so tall, taller than Papa, and fair. But I suppose everyone seems tall when you're seven years old. Oh, and I remember Mama writing to him, telling him about Timmie and how he was getting on.'

'Yes,' said Mina, after a moment. 'She wrote to him often, especially during the war. The letters went to a special BFPO address. Anyway, I just wondered . . . about the car.'

'I don't remember Timmie losing it.' Nest's brow furrowed. 'He must have had it for some time when it finally went missing otherwise there would have been a frightful row. He mislaid it not long after he first received it and he was quite distraught. Luckily it turned up.'

Mina, remembering Georgie's confession, said nothing. Nest, a tray balanced across her knees containing her needs for the night ahead, turned her face up for her goodnight kiss and went wheeling away across the hall. Mina switched off the lights and climbed the stairs; as she reached her bedroom door the telephone began to ring. She hurried into her room and snatched up the extension from its rest.

'Aunt Mina? It's Lyddie. I've only just realized that it's rather late for you. I'm so sorry. Did I wake you?'

'Gracious, no, child,' answered Mina cheerfully. 'I'm about to do my e-mails. Shan't be in bed for hours yet. How are you?'

'It's . . . um. I'm OK but there's a bit of a

problem this end.' A pause. 'Would it be terribly inconvenient if I came over for a few days?'

'Of course it wouldn't, my darling,' said Mina warmly. 'Do you want to talk now or wait until you get here?'

'It's just I've had a bit of a shock.'

Mina could hear that she was near to tears and her heart beat fast with anxiety.

'Oh, darling, are you all right? You don't have to say a word. We shan't pry, but if we can help you only have to say the word. You know that.'

'Yes, I know.' Another pause. 'It seems that Liam's been sleeping around. You met Rosie when you came down, didn't you? Well, she told me. They've been lovers for the last year and there are others. It was she who told me . . .'

'But have you confronted Liam?' asked Mina sharply. 'It might be that she—'

'Oh, yes,' said Lyddie miserably. 'We've had it out and he doesn't deny it and, anyway, I . . . saw him with someone.'

'My poor darling.' Mina was horrified. 'Oh, I *am* so sorry. How perfectly wretched for you. When will you be here?'

'I'm going to try to get some sleep and I shall leave early in the morning. I hope to be with you by about ten o'clock, if that's not too early?'

'Of course not. Come any time you like. We'll be waiting.'

'Aunt Mina?' carefully.

'Yes, my darling?' gently.

'You can tell Aunt Nest, if you like, but not . . .' waveringly.

'I quite understand. Don't worry,' firmly.

'Bless you. See you in the morning.'

'Drive carefully, Lyddie.'

Mina replaced the receiver and stood for some while staring at nothing in particular, her face anxious. Nogood Boyo scuffed his plastic toy around her feet, growling at it with pleasurable fierceness, whilst Captain Cat watched with a certain disdain. 'Give me a real, live rat, any day,' his contemptuous look implied. 'We didn't have silly toys in *my* day . . .' Polly Garter was already turning round and round on her beanbag, stretching luxuriously before curling into a ball.

'On your beds,' said Mina. 'Go on, boys. Beds.'

They obeyed reluctantly; Captain Cat implying that he was going, anyway, of his own accord; Nogood Boyo dragging the toy with him, still shaking it excitely. Captain Cat turned his back pointedly on his offspring but Nogood Boyo was enjoying himself far too much to notice.

In her alcove, Mina read her e-mails: one from Helena, thanking her for a lovely weekend, which made her grimace, and one from Jack, which made her chuckle. At last she opened Elyot's offering, settling more comfortably, ready for a session.

From: Elyot
To: Mina

Your account of the weekend was very amusing. And also touching. I have no experience of sibling friendship or rivalry but I was moved by the way you and Nest are planning to stand firmly by Georgie in spite of the threat she holds over you. At least it's not for too much longer.

After a period of peace here, we've had another setback. Lavinia has unaccountably taken against our GP, a thoroughly decent fellow, and I am at my wits' end. She seems to suffer from quite horrid delusions about him which, though I sympathize with how distressed she must feel, I try to dispel by explaining that she's imagining things. This upsets her even more and she accuses me of siding against her, etc., etc. On top of this, I've had my eye test. Ever since that accident, I've felt quite nervous when driving and now the dreaded word 'cataract' has been used. The foolish thing is that, in losing my confidence, I'm more likely than ever to have another accident. Lavinia, however, hates to be left alone for very long, even with friends, so long journeys by public transport aren't really an option. I really fear that the day is approaching when we shall have to give up this place and move into the town, or even into sheltered accommodation. It's the uncertainty that is so exhausting. And as Lavinia's confusion and mistrust grows, so the circle of help I can call on shrinks. Today I might leave her quite happily with a friend whom, within five minutes of my departure, Lavinia is unable to recognize. I return to a scene of real drama: Lavinia sobbing, angry with me, frightened: the friend, affronted, indignant, even cross.

It's interesting to see how soon friendship cracks in the face of rejection – even when the one who rejects is so clearly not in her right mind. Sympathy, compassion, attempts to understand, vanish very quickly indeed. It is all taken very personally and there is not enough love to make allowances. What an indictment that is! And I am just as bad as the others. I want to shout at her – even, in the worst moments, to strike her – simply in order to make her listen to me. Lavinia was always strong-minded, draconian in her views, hot-tempered, and it's rather as if all her other gentler qualities are being squeezed out by these more dominant traits, which grow and multiply now there is no longer the thin veneer of civilized behaviour to restrain them.

My dear old friend, I shouldn't be saying these things, even to you. I spend too much time alone trying to understand this terrible thing that is happening to us, to analyse it, in an attempt to deal with it more adequately. I can't tell you how much the thought of you soldiering on at Ottercombe sustains me. I feel, from your descriptions of the house and the cleave, not to mention Nest and Georgie, that I know you all, that you are friends to whom I could come in the ultimate despair. But the Super-Skunk hasn't got me yet, never fear! William will be home in a week or so – oh! how much comfort that thought brings! – although he has worries of his own.

Anyway, enough of us! Let me know how you are. Fully recovered, I hope, from the weekend?

Mina read this several times with a growing and quite irrational resentment for the unknown Lavinia. She brooded on her reaction for a while. Clearly her sympathy must be with Elyot whom she 'knew' – as it were – rather than with his tiresome wife. It was much *easier* to side with Elyot, who always came over as sane, rational, cheerful in the face of adversity, rather than with Lavinia, who, let's face it – even in her heyday – hadn't sounded particularly attractive, unless, of course, you had a thing about pigheaded, narrow-minded, intolerant bigots . . .

Mina pulled herself up sharply. It was extraordinarily stupid, she reminded herself, to start getting possessive about a man she'd never met and was unlikely to meet. Of *course* he would show his best side to her, of *course* he would gain sympathy where he could. Yet – a tiny voice murmured – he spoke of shouting at Lavinia and even wanting to strike her. That was surely a natural reaction about which he'd written openly and without guile.

'A good slap would probably do her the world

of good,' muttered Mina crossly – and then burst into a fit of giggles. For goodness' sake! Here she was at the age of seventy-four behaving like a jealous teenager.

'And remember,' she told herself, 'you've never even seen him. Oh, I know you have your mental picture of him: military bearing, thick grey hair, distinguished. Rather sexy, twinkly eyes. Well, dream on, as Jack would say. He's probably four foot two and as bald as a coot. "Sans teeth, sans eyes, sans taste, sans everything",' and, having pulled herself together, Mina began to compose her reply.

From: Mina
To: Elyot

Hello, Elyot

Oh dear, things sound a bit grim at your end. Not so much the cataracts – beastly, but can be dealt with relatively painlessly, I understand – but more about poor Lavinia. It is utterly wretched for both of you but I wonder if it's wise to try to make her see the truth about her GP and so on. It might well go against the grain to go along with these fantasies but, in opposing her, you might well a) make her even more determined to insist upon them and b) undermine her confidence in you. It's important that she feels that you are on her side and, after all, does it matter if you pretend a little? Your GP sounds as if he would quite understand – I expect he sees and hears the most outrageous things – and I wonder if you should have a talk with him about it. You don't have to go into every small detail but I doubt you'll shock him. A situation – which might well get worse – where you are on opposing sides can do no good for either of you. I fear that you might already be in a no-win situation and the important thing is to keep hold of the love and confidence which is between you.

Oh dear, Elyot! I've just reread this and feel that I sound like a rather second-rate cross between Mother Teresa and Mary Whitehouse. Have you noticed how terribly easy it is to moralize about other people's dilemmas? Well, the shoe might well be on the other foot soon. I've just had a telephone call from Lyddie who is coming home for a few days. Her husband, it seems, has been playing the field and she's clearly in need of a little TLC. The timing couldn't be worse and poor Nest will be in a terrible state. It's the unpredictability of it all. All I can say is, watch this space.

CHAPTER TWENTY-FIVE

'The timing couldn't be worse,' said Nest, her face drawn and strained. 'And Helena and Rupert about to go on a week's holiday.'

'Try not to anticipate trouble,' said Mina gently. 'Lyddie is only here for three days. Just a breathing space.'

'That *bloody* man,' cried Nest. 'I never liked him. He's so smooth and charming. Always smiling. One shouldn't trust people who smile all the time.'

'Oh, Nest.' Mina couldn't help chuckling. 'It's too late to do the "I always said his eyes were too close together" thing now, I'm afraid.'

Nest stared at her for a moment and then burst out laughing. 'Mama used to say that,' she said, 'do you remember?' – and they laughed again until Georgie came upon them, looking for her breakfast.

'What's the joke?' she asked amiably.

Once again, Nest found herself making the

283

effort not to answer 'Nothing', thereby excluding her sister. Instead she said, 'We were remembering how Mama used to say that you couldn't trust people whose eyes were too close together. So silly, really.'

'But probably true,' said Georgie. 'There's always a grain of truth in the old saws. Is it porridge this morning, Mina?'

Nest and Mina exchanged a glance of relief at this apparently sane approach and prayed that it might last.

'If you like,' said Mina cheerfully. 'Oh, and Lyddie's coming later on this morning. She's staying for a day or two. Just a little break between books.'

'Oh.' Georgie looked slightly put out. 'But I wanted to go to Lynton this morning to get my new library book.' She frowned. 'Did I say that it was in?'

'Yes,' said Nest quickly. 'Quite right. The librarian phoned yesterday afternoon. There's no reason why you shouldn't go to Lynton to get it.'

'Of course not,' agreed Mina. 'I'll drive you over later.'

Her eyes met Nest's privately – 'and keep her out for as long as I can' implicit in the glance – and Nest felt a lessening of tension. As they ate breakfast she wondered if it would be possible to keep Georgie and Lyddie apart for most of the time, although it would be a strain, but, even as she considered ways and means of achieving it, the dogs began to bark and they heard Lyddie's voice in the hall.

Mina reached her first, hugging her tightly, holding her close.

'How lovely for us,' she said. 'My dear child . . .' She looked into Lyddie's eyes and held her again, murmuring little love words as she did to her dogs.

Coming behind her, wheeling slowly, Nest could hardly bear to look at the pain on Lyddie's face. She took the outstretched hand and clasped it tightly until Lyddie bent to kiss her.

'I'm not doing very well,' she muttered, tears threatening again, and Nest swallowed her own pain and anger on Lyddie's behalf and gave the hand a little shake.

'We'll have a chat very soon,' she said, 'if you want to. Can you manage in front of Georgie?'

Lyddie nodded, straightening up, trying to smile, and the two older women looked at her with affection and encouragement, enfolding her in their love, communicating their strength.

'It's the Bosun.' She tried for a lighter note. 'Shall I let him out? You know how Captain Cat terrifies him and he's already anxious because he knows that things aren't . . . quite right.'

'Of course he must be let out,' cried Mina, 'and if Captain Cat can't behave himself I shall shut him in the woodshed. Go and get him and then come and have some coffee. I'm just about to take Georgie off to Lynton, and you and Nest will be able to have a good old talk or whatever. I'll let the dogs out for a while and you can bring the Bosun in so as to get him settled. They'll be fine. Give me a shout when you've got him into the hall and I'll let mine out of the kitchen door. That'll faze 'em.'

The Bosun was delighted to be set free, rushing away over the lawn, into the secret garden and then back again, tail waving, tongue lolling. He seemed relieved to be at Ottercombe, despite the potential anxiety of a run-in with Captain Cat, sensing the possibility of a security that had been absent for the last twenty-four hours in Truro. Presently they went inside, giving the all-clear to Mina, who opened the kitchen door with relief so that the three barking dogs, mad by now with inquisitive frustration, shot like furry white arrows into the courtyard, round to the front of the house and began to search for the intruder.

'I'll take them with me when we go,' said Mina, bending to stroke the Bosun's head. 'Don't worry, they'll settle down. Poor old fellow, you must be worn out.'

The Bosun flattened his ears, responding to the sympathetic tone, managing to look both pathetic and brave. He *was* exhausted: woken early from sleep, dragged off for a walk whilst it was barely light and then hurried into the car for a two-hour drive. His tail beat hopefully against Georgie's chair and she looked at him consideringly whilst Mina slipped him a biscuit or two as a reward for his suffering. He crunched happily and Georgie patted his head.

'You *are* a big chap,' she said admiringly. 'He'll like a walk down to the beach, won't he?'

'I'm sure he will,' agreed Mina, 'but Lyddie needs some coffee and you and I have to go to Lynton. Do you need anything else besides your library book?'

'I don't know.' Georgie looked distracted. 'I can't remember . . .'

'It doesn't matter.' Mina was very calm. 'We've got all morning to wander round. Go and get yourself ready while I make a shopping list.'

Once she'd gone a constraint fell upon the three of them, covered by the necessity for coffee to be made for Lyddie whilst Nest agreed that she'd like some more, so that a small bustle ensued and each of them was careful not to look at the other. The atmosphere was lightened by the appearance of the three dogs at the kitchen door, where they stood in a row, staring indignantly through the glass at the Bosun as he lay stretched full length on the floor, deeply asleep.

'Ever been had?' Mina remarked to nobody in particular – and even Lyddie laughed. Georgie appeared in her coat and hat, carrying a capacious bag, and Mina collected her belongings and hurried her away. There was the usual commotion as the dogs were encouraged into the camper, the engine started up and, finally, there was silence.

Lyddie drank some coffee, blew her nose and stared at the table. Nest watched her sympathetically.

'If you don't want to talk that's fine by me,' she told her. 'You don't have to, you know. You might just want to think things through on neutral territory and give yourself some space. Do whatever you want to.' She turned her wheelchair away from the table so that she could see Lydia's rockgarden, and sipped some more coffee.

'That's what's good about you and Aunt Mina,' Lyddie said. 'You're like contemporaries. It's odd, really. I couldn't think where else to go. Roger and I have never been really close and I hardly know Teresa. I thought about Jack and Han but it didn't seem fair with their house-load of children. In Truro there's no spare space for moments like these, you see. No spare room to retreat to or a second living-room. And I just didn't know how to handle it. Did Mina tell you?'

'She said that Liam had been unfaithful with Rosie and probably one or two others.' Nest continued to look out into the courtyard. 'We gained the impression that he didn't deny it.'

'No, he didn't deny it,' said Lyddie bitterly, 'nor did he feel that change was an option.'

'It does rather make for an impasse,' murmured Nest.

'I was thinking about it for most of the night and for the drive here.' Lyddie pushed her mug aside and put her head in her hands. 'The thing is, you see, we lead such a strange life. I can't just go back to how it was. Rosie's right when she says that I shall never know now which of those women he's been with. And I feel so humiliated. How could I walk into The Place again, knowing what I know?'

'How clever of Rosie, wasn't it? Those words were a death-knell to your relationship.'

'He didn't bother even to make a stab at protesting. He seems to feel that, because he married me, I shouldn't mind. "The rest mean nothing." I quote.'

'And, as far as he's concerned, that's possibly true. The rest probably come under the same heading as a pint of beer or a good long walk. Necessary at that moment, briefly satisfying, but easily replaceable.'

Lyddie's chair scraped on the slates. 'But you don't think that I should go along with that, do you?' She sounded anxious. 'How would *you* feel if the man you adored was having it off with someone else?'

There was a silence. The Bosun groaned in his sleep, stretching, whilst beyond the glass door a robin pecked at some toast crumbs.

'I should feel gutted,' Nest said at last. 'I should feel betrayed, sick with jealousy, and utterly gutted. I wouldn't want anyone to see me, I would feel incapable and helpless, but the worst and most humiliating thing of all would be the fact that I still loved him and wanted him more than anything else in the world.'

'That's much too close to be a guess,' said Lyddie, after a while. 'So what did you do when it happened to you?'

'I didn't have too many choices,' answered

Nest, 'and we weren't married. It was a different situation but if you're asking if I fought my corner the answer is no. I was too humiliated and I couldn't bear for anyone to know.'

'Well, that's a luxury I don't get,' said Lyddie grimly. 'I feel quite sick when I think of all the nights I've gone bouncing into that bloody wine bar and everyone's been thinking, poor fool, if only she knew, while those women . . .' She swallowed. 'How could he do that to me?'

Nest shook her head. 'It makes you wonder if he thinks the same way as other people, doesn't it?' she asked. 'It's like cruelty to helpless children. It makes you wonder how people's minds actually work. It's as if there must be a bit missing somewhere or as if they genuinely feel that they have a divine right to operate outside the usual rules by which most people live. You can see that Liam is driven by some restless urge to achieve and this might be all of a piece with the sexual urge. It explains his passion for The Place and his will to make it succeed. At its best it's amoral rather than immoral. It's utterly tunnel-visioned, and everything – and everyone – is sacrificed to the greater plan.' Nest glanced at Lyddie and was shocked by her white face and shadowed eyes. 'You look exhausted,' she said. 'My poor darling, could you sleep, do you think?'

'I couldn't sleep last night,' Lyddie admitted, 'and I'm absolutely bushed. My head feels as if it might split open at any moment.'

'Take some paracetamol and go to bed,'

suggested Nest. 'If it doesn't work, get up again and we'll think of something else.'

'I might just do that. Now that I'm here, and I've got it off my chest, I do feel as if I could sleep. No, don't worry. I've got painkillers. Am I in my usual room? Great. I'll see you later, then. And, thanks, Nest.' She bent and kissed her cheek. 'You've been brilliant.'

It was only after she'd gone that Nest realized that, for the first time, Lyddie had dropped the prefix 'Aunt'. She smiled a little; perhaps it was a compliment. She sat, still gazing out, listening to the Bosun's regular breathing and thinking about Connor.

CHAPTER TWENTY-SIX

It is Mina who, unaware of the real situation, arranges for Connor to take Nest out to tea just before the end of term. His letter to Mina, thanking her for his afternoon at Ottercombe, suggests it – very casually – since he will be near the school during the following weekend, 'if your mother is happy about it,' he adds, 'and Nest's headmistress allows it.'

Nest is relieved to hear that Connor has managed to visit Ottercombe but Mina's letter unconsciously strikes a warning note that makes her uneasy: 'He's great fun and made us laugh. Mama was very taken with him but not as much as he was with Henrietta, who was down for the weekend. Anyway, he's sent a bread-and-butter and asks if you'd like to go out to tea . . .'

'You seem to have been a great success with my family,' she says lightly, once they are settled in the tea-shop in the little local town. There are other families with their daughters at nearby tables and she is obliged to behave with a decorum that she doesn't feel at all. 'Mina says Mama was very impressed with you.'

'She's a lovely woman.' He seems calm, quite at ease, but she senses his tension. Fear seizes her and her fingers tear and crumple the paper napkin in her lap. 'I can see where you get your looks, you and your sisters.'

'We're all very alike.' She wants to take his hand, touch him, make him look at her properly, but from the corner of her eye she sees little Lettice Crowe's mother, smart in navy foulard, watching them, trying to be noticed. 'So what did you think of Mina?'

'Ah, Mina.' He smiles in the old familiar way that twists her heart. 'She's a darling, so she is. I would have recognized her anywhere from everything you've told me about her. She's a rare soul.'

'And Henrietta? Do you think she's a rare soul? I hear you met her too?'

The arrival of the tea gives Connor a moment in which to rally but Nest, watching his face, knows that her premonition is a true one. He smiles briefly at the waitress and sits forward in his chair, pretending to rearrange the cups, checking the hot water. At last he looks at her and the truth is there in his eyes for her to see.

'Yes,' he says. 'I met Henrietta.'

As he picks up the tea-strainer and the pot and fills the two cups, Nest knows that she could never have done it with so steady a hand. At this moment the full ten-year age-gap stretches its whole length between them: he is controlled, steady: she knows that at any moment she might cry. She thinks of Henrietta, of her beauty, ready wit and sophisticated confidence, and is miserably aware of her own immaturity. He places the milk and sugar near at hand and pushes her tea towards her.

'Drink it.'

The quiet, bitten-off command causes her to glance up at him. With a slight jerk of the head, he directs her attention to the other interested families and she responds instinctively, sipping her tea obediently, lifting her cup with a trembling hand and setting it back in the saucer with only a tiny clatter. He fills the teapot from the hot-water jug and offers the tiered stand of cakes, turning it slowly, almost teasingly, as though to tempt her appetite. She stares at them: rock buns adorned with glacé cherries, a long chocolate eclair, oozing synthetic cream, in a paper frill, an assortment of iced squares topped with crystallized orange pieces. Revulsion heaves in her stomach and she swallows with difficulty at the thought of the sticky sweetness. Connor continues to turn the plate, watching her. She takes a rock bun, the least offensive, and puts it on her plate.

'I wanted to see you,' he says gently, 'because I needed to tell you myself, not by a letter. And it's not just to do with Henrietta. I'm too old for you, Nest, and you know that this is something that's worried me from the beginning. When I met your family it underlined it. I'm Mina's contemporary, older than Henrietta even. It never occurred to them, even for a second, that there could possibly be anything but a chance acquaintance between us, triggered by the fact that I had friends at Porlock. They still regard you as a child – oh, yes, I know you're nearly eighteen – but suddenly I saw it with their eyes and I realized what I'd done.'

He leans forward, smiling very slightly, as if telling her a story; deliberately disguising the tension of the moment from her school friends and their parents. It is a grotesque parody of the intimacy for which she yearns and she sees now why he was careful to seat her so that she is partly protected from their interest. Mrs Crowe is still trying to catch Connor's eye.

'Cradle-snatching, they call it.' His warm, flexible voice makes it sound almost amusing. 'I can't do it, Nest. It was one of those magic interludes which happen out of the real world but shrivel once they're exposed to harsh reality. I knew that when I met your family.'

She takes another sip of tea and crumbles the corner of the rock bun. Her sheltered life at Ottercombe and at school has not equipped her for this kind of experience. If they were alone, she could plead with him, hold on to him, try to change his mind, but what can she do here in this flowery, genteel environment surrounded by her watchful peers?

'Try not to be too hard on me. It's not easy, Nest, I promise you, letting you go.'

Oddly, it's the plea for sympathy that stiffens

her spine. She pushes her plate aside, dropping the remains of the napkin upon it.

'I have the most terrible headache,' she says, quite clearly, so that others might hear if they're listening. 'I'm terribly sorry, Connor, but I can't manage any cake. Do you think we might go back now?'

She smiles at her friends as she passes between them on her way out, ignoring Mrs Crowe's ostentatious gesture of concern, and they drive the half a mile to the school in silence. He is too intelligent to risk any further conversation which might lead to tears or appeals or recrimination: he conceals his own sadness, knowing that she needs all her pride and courage to get back inside with her dignity intact.

A few days later, she receives a short letter from him, a repetition of the things he has already said – kind but firm – but still she cannot quite take it all in: she loves him too much. In fact she is back at Ottercombe, more than a month later, before Nest truly believes that it is over, that he will not telephone or suddenly appear, telling her that it was all a dreadful mistake. She makes up scenarios in which he returns to her; she rushes to answer the telephone and to pick up the post, longing to tell Mina the whole truth but unable to admit it even to herself. Then, on the morning of 15 August, Mina receives a letter from Henrietta.

As Mina reads Henrietta's letter aloud – but carefully edited – to Lydia, as they are at breakfast in the morning-room, Nest understands at last that it is finished.

'"Connor and I are seeing rather a lot of one another" – You remember Connor, Mama? He came to visit us here.– "and he comes to London quite often. We've discovered one or two mutual friends and he's invited me to a party in Oxford next weekend, which sounds rather fun . . ."'

Nest is gripped with such agonizing jealousy that the rest of the letter passes unheeded. She pictures them together knowing that now she has no chance at all of regaining his love. Once he has spent a period of time with the most glamorous of all her sisters how could she possibly hope to compete?

Mina finishes the letter, folding the sheets and putting it beside her plate, whilst Nest stares into a bleak emptiness; a future that no longer contains Connor. The rain, beating against the windows, lowers her spirits further.

'I can't remember a wetter summer,' says Lydia. 'The lawn is like a sponge.'

'Lots of the rivers are flooding,' says Mina, 'but surely it can't go on like this much longer. Even our own little stream is over its banks.'

There is some kind of melancholy satisfaction to be had from the walk to the beach, although Nest watches anxiously as a duck with her ducklings is swept at high speed on the current; tumbling against boulders and overhanging branches, they scramble almost comically in their mother's wake, seeking a quiet shelter in a peaceful backwater. Following them, Nest is so preoccupied that it is some time before she truly appreciates the weight of water flowing down from the high moors. All manner of tiny springs gush from the rock-face as though – as the locals say – the rocks are being squeezed, swelling the stream as it cascades to the beach. To begin with, the drama of the scene, the ceaseless roaring of the water, the crying of the gulls, is in keeping with her mood. Nevertheless, she has an odd sense of foreboding; as if, today, nature's force is too great for her. Usually its implacable size and power brings solace, putting her puny fears into perspective, but today there is a rising ferocity in the sheer noise of it: the water tumbling from the cliffs, the waves crashing onto the beach, the increasing heaviness of the rain drumming on the rocks.

When she arrives home, she is relieved to see that Mina has already lit the drawing-room fire.

'Mama is restless,' she tells Nest. 'It's this wretched weather. It's madness to have a fire in August but I think we need it. I'm just getting tea ready so take off that soaking mackintosh and go and talk to her. Try to remain cheerful or she becomes anxious. Nothing specific, it's just how she is. If only this wretched rain would stop!'

The rain, however, does not stop; it increases as evening wears on and, at about half-past eight, there is a cloudburst and five inches of rain fall in one hour. Up on the Chains, no longer able to penetrate the unyielding ground, the torrents of water pour off the moor, gathering all before them as they hurtle towards the sea; huge boulders and savagely uprooted trees smash into bridges and carry them onwards so that, finally, the debris represents one huge battering ram. Houses and buildings are demolished as though they are cardboard; the West Lyn – changing course, destroying roadways, a chapel, shops, houses – rushes to join the East Lyn River. They swirl violently together, twenty feet deep, bearing along one hundred thousand tons of boulders, building a dam twenty-five feet high, until the pressure becomes too much and the great tide gives way in a mighty roar, sweeping houses, cars and animals far out to sea.

At Ottercombe, using old sandbags to keep the water out of the kitchen, watching the swollen stream pouring across the lawn and rising to the bottom of the terrace, Mina and Nest are too anxious for their own safety to give too much thought as to what might be happening further up the coast. It isn't until the morning that the devastation becomes apparent – on Lynmouth Street hotels and houses have disappeared without trace, the road buried deep in silt and strewn with boulders, whilst half a mile out to sea, hundreds of great trees stand upright supported by their enormous roots, torn from the ground – and the acts of heroism begin to be told, along with the tales of tragedy.

The women at Ottercombe listen, shocked, to their wireless, read the newspapers in horror and give grateful thanks for their own safety. For Nest, her personal grief becomes a part of a larger mourning and, for ever afterwards, the twin disasters of the Lynmouth Flood and losing Connor are inextricably entwined.

CHAPTER TWENTY-SEVEN

From: Mina
To: Elyot

Dear Elyot

What a household we are! Lyddie arrived just after breakfast looking haggard. Oh dear! Things are clearly every bit as bad as we feared. I took Georgie off to Lynton – which is another story! – leaving Nest to be quiet with Lyddie. We hoped that Lyddie might be able to talk her problems through with her and, apparently, this was the case although Nest is finding the whole thing very painful, as you might imagine. You won't know that there has been a long pause between the last sentence and this one. My dear Elyot, it shocks me to think how much I have trusted you. I have made a present to you of so many of our secrets, by so doing lifting part of the burden from my shoulders but putting us all into a vulnerable position. The odd thing is how easy it has been to become intimate with someone I have never seen. I know it took a little while for us to become true confidants but, nevertheless, the ease with which I've grown to trust you is frightening and I can see why parents are anxious about their children talking on the Internet. Would it be as easy by telephone? I don't think so. Or at least, not quite so quickly. We've all had those odd moments with strangers, a sudden outpouring of a worry, knowing that each will go her separate path very shortly, but I have come to depend on your advice and encouragement in a quite different way. Writing seems to lend a natural familiarity.

Anyway, Nest is finding it difficult. 'How would you feel if the man you adored went off with another woman?' asked Lyddie, or something like that. Well, Nest told her exactly how she'd felt and is now in a fit of anxiety lest Lyddie should question her more closely. Oh, how deceit and self-image does make prisoners of us all! Yet it hasn't been Nest's fault that she's practised deception all these years. It was forced upon her. Still, we managed to get to bedtime without any more terrors although we're like cats on a hot tin roof. The thing is, Elyot, I can feel it coming: a kind of nemesis for us all. Nest felt it first, of course. All those weeks ago when Helena telephoned to ask if we could look after Georgie until the nursing home was ready for her, Nest felt the first stirrings of it.

As for Georgie . . . Well, you might not believe this, Elyot, but this morning I lost Georgie! Oh, the horror still grips me, although I find I can't help laughing too. She was in merry pin, all dressed up for Lynton, and only the sharpest eyes would have noticed that she was wearing matching shoes but in different colours. One black, one brown. We went off very cheerfully, dogs in the back, nice, bright morning. She was sharp too, remembering places very clearly as we went along. Have I said to you that I wonder whether coming to Ottercombe is the worst thing we could have done for Georgie? Well, I think it is. She's been hauled back into the past and you can see her struggling to remain rooted in the present. It seems to me that it is easier for her to drift back, that she remembers things from forty years ago more readily than she can remember what we did yesterday. Maybe that's part of the dementia. Of course, nobody has dementia any more, do they? And especially not **senile** dementia! Oh dear, what a politically incorrect word 'senile' is – **much** better to mask it with the smarter, more acceptable, name of Alzheimer's. The point is, are the two diseases the same?

Whatever the truth is about that, Georgie certainly seems ready to slip into the far past and remembers many odd things. This morning we talked of Papa dying just after the war and how she tried to keep an eye on Josie and Henrietta whilst they were still single. Quite lucid, even amusing, and this is the tragedy of it all. So we arrive in Lynton, park the camper and set off to the library. We are at the age, dear Elyot, which brings out the best in our nice local people and we are assisted, waited for, smiled upon. And very nice it is too. The shopping is put into the camper but it is not until we get to the café and we are having some coffee that I remember that I need some bread. I tell Georgie that I must dash out to buy some and tell her not to go anywhere until I come back.

I rush away, buy the bread and when I get back – no Georgie. The waitress, rather surprised by my anxiety, said that she'd suddenly remembered something and went off. Now though I might have been startlingly indiscreet to you, my dear friend, I have not yet made the local people aware of our personal problems so I could do little more than check that she'd paid the bill – she had! – and hurry out onto the pavement. Which way had she gone? I run this way and that, panting along, checking her favourite places. No Georgie. People glance oddly at me and I see myself in a plate-glass window, a bundly old lady, red-cheeked, hat awry, scarf flying. Lynton is not a big town and before too long I have covered all the main streets. I even check the health centre. Suddenly – oh, let it be true! – I wonder if she has returned to the camper. She might, even now, be sitting peacefully inside, waiting for me. I begin to run – why didn't I think of it before? I never lock the camper lest some accident should happen and the dogs couldn't be got out. After all, if anyone needs a battered ten-year-old vehicle, complete with dog-chewed seat cushions, then, poor souls, their need must be greater than mine! But she is not inside. Captain Cat barks encouragingly, Nogood Boyo stares anxiously through the window at me, but no Georgie.

It is only as I make one last desperate search before going to the police station that I see her, standing on the pavement in a small side-road, staring up at a terraced house. Something, the way that she is standing, prevents me from calling out impatiently to her. I walk towards her. 'I wondered where you were,' I say calmly, as I approach. 'Are you OK?' She turns, her brow puzzled, sad. 'I've been looking for Jenna,' she says wistfully, 'but I can't find her. They say they don't know her here.' Jenna, the girl who looked after us when we were children, has been dead for more than ten years. She and her husband moved into Lynton in the sixties – into this very house, in fact, where the curtain twitches aside as a suspicious face peers at us. I take Georgie's arm. 'Jenna's moved,' I tell her – it's not altogether a lie although I hope she won't ask where, it's a fair step to the cemetery – 'and we must be getting home.' She comes along, willingly enough, and I ask if she might like a little trip along the coast or to Simonsbath, to distract her. By the time I'd got her settled and found that Nogood Boyo had gnawed the end off the loaf I could have burst into tears. As we set off, I saw a mind's-eye image of the pair of us: two potty, white-haired old biddies, wrestling an aged camper round the steep bends – and quite suddenly, I have to say, I began to laugh and laugh. Georgie, bless her, joined in and the dogs barked wildly until I pulled up at Brendon Two Gates to get my breath. 'That was fun,' observed Georgie cheerfully. 'Now where shall we go next?'

So, Elyot, a thumbnail sketch of our day. How has yours been, I wonder?

From: Elyot
To: Mina

Dear Mina
I have to say, dear old friend, that I laughed too, although I felt **such** a twinge at the picture of Georgie outside Jenna's house. This kind of situation is one with which I can identify only too easily. This flipping between normality and – well, what shall I call it? – 'losing the plot', as William would say. For us, sadly, those periods of lucidity are decreasing. We have hours of repetition: the same question or a single word, which is utterly maddening yet so pitiable.

However! I have taken your advice and stopped trying to persuade Lavinia that her wild imaginings about our GP are simply not true. I go along with it now, and merely murmur something agreeable or nod or look suitably shocked. I have to say that it goes against the grain – which is foolish, I know – because it seems that I am colluding in lies against an admirable, hard-worked and very tolerant man. At the same time, I suspect that he wouldn't be the least bit surprised at how poor Lavinia is feeling about him. He's seen it all before, no doubt. My real anxiety is that she refuses to see him. At present we drift along in this twilight world but, like you with your nemesis, I fear that something will happen shortly over which I shall have no control. The point I want to make, though, is: yes, you were right about accepting the situation and 'going with the flow'. Lavinia is calmer and, because she no longer has to persuade me to believe these horrors that cloud her mind, she dwells on them less and is more readily distracted from them.

My dear Mina, I too am amazed at the ease with which we've slipped into such comradeship. We've come a long way from that chat-room, haven't we? To be honest, I believe that we've both managed better in our different situations because of this ability to let off steam. Perhaps it is because we cannot see each other that we are able to confide in each other so openly. Like you, I have wondered about the aspects of disloyalty and have decided that what we are doing is no different to being 'counselled' or other like things. We discovered that we are of the same generation, of like mind, and our friendship developed quite naturally from there. Maybe it was foolish to be so trusting but I think that time has proved that we were justified and you have nothing to fear from me. You have given me far too much comfort for me to begin to contemplate the possibility of harming you. Not that I can imagine how it could be done. But I know how you feel. We haven't just told each other about ourselves; we have told about those who are close to us and sometimes we feel we are betraying a trust. Well, so be it. We have done it out of love and concern for them, in an effort to understand and to gain strength to continue with the task.

So, I offer you a toast: to family life.

CHAPTER TWENTY-EIGHT

'The thing is,' Lyddie said, 'the really unbelievable thing is that I still love him.'

Her three-day sabbatical was nearly over and she planned to return to Truro after lunch. Meanwhile she was kneeling on the kitchen floor, business-like in jeans and thick roll-necked jersey, brushing the recumbent Bosun. He groaned occasionally, and stretched luxuriously once or twice, but for most of the time he lay passively, tired by a long early-morning run over Trentishoe Down. After breakfast, Mina and Georgie and the dogs had walked down to the beach whilst Nest remained with Lyddie in the sunny kitchen, watching the grooming process.

'Well, of course you do,' agreed Nest. 'It would be odd if you didn't. Love isn't nearly so convenient as that. I've often wondered how it must be for those poor wives of serial murderers, suddenly discovering this whole other side to someone they love. How do they deal with it?'

309

'I suppose it doesn't have to be a partner.' Lyddie was distracted from her own pain for a moment. 'It might be a parent.'

'Yes,' said Nest, after a moment. 'It might be. Or a child.'

'The helplessness of little children is appalling,' said Lyddie. 'Jack said that he lives in terror of something happening to Toby and Flora. The worst thing is, he said, that you're constantly having to encourage them to do things that might hurt them so that they extend themselves otherwise you would make them prisoners. Having to decide whether they're ready for the next big step. How terrifying the thought of parenthood is!'

'There's something worse than that,' said Nest grimly – and fell silent.

Lyddie looked at her curiously. 'What?' she asked.

'Watching other people making those decisions for one's own child,' answered Nest at last.

Lyddie, looking thoughtful, resumed the long sweeping strokes so that the Bosun's black and tan coat gleamed.

'That's twice,' she said. 'First you talked about your lover being unfaithful and now you say that, about children, as if you really know.'

Nest stared at her, as she crouched beside the sleeping dog. Her small face, pale beneath its shining mop, was full of innocent affection – she looked like a child herself – yet Nest knew instinctively that the moment had come at last. Her hands clenched upon her lap in terror but she spoke out bravely.

'I *do* really know,' she said. Her heart seemed to flutter in her throat. 'I had a child, you see, years ago.' She looked away from the expression of surprise on Lyddie's face, concentrating on her story lest she should lose courage. 'It wasn't so simple, in those days, to be a single parent. Apart from the stigma there was none of the financial support that can be claimed now and you had to be very well off to provide child-care while you earned a living. I taught English – well, you can remember that – and at the time I worked in the private sector . . .'

'Did they throw you out?' Lyddie sounded so indignant that Nest managed a faint smile.

'No,' she said. 'The headmistress was a very fair woman. And very sensible. She gave me a sabbatical. I became pregnant in the autumn and took the spring and summer terms off. If anyone at the school suspected they never said anything and I was very glad to have work to go back to the following September.'

'But what did Grandmama say?' Lyddie was sitting back on her heels, the grooming forgotten, shocked but full of sympathy for this beloved aunt. 'And Aunt Mina? Did she know?'

'Oh, yes. Mina knew. Your grandmother was horrified, to begin with, but it was Mina who calmed her down. As much as anything it was the terrible stigma of having an unmarried pregnant daughter. That's probably so difficult for you to imagine in these enlightened days, but even in the middle sixties it was a disgrace . . .'

'But the father,' interrupted Lyddie. 'Couldn't you . . . ? Was he . . . ?'

'He was married.' She spoke so low that Lyddie got up and came closer, sitting down on the chair beside the table, the brush still in her hand.

'Oh, Nest . . .'

Nest looked at her. 'It wasn't an affair,' she said with difficulty. 'Nothing like that. It was just once. But I loved him, you see.'

Her face crumpled a little – and then she smiled again, shaking her head at Lyddie's quick impulsive gesture.

'You mustn't be sorry for me,' she said. 'Wait. I'm trying to think.'

'So Grandmama made you have the baby adopted?' Lyddie prompted her gently, full of compassion.

Nest took a deep breath, her eyes looked unseeingly out into the courtyard and she nodded.

'Mmm.' She steadied her voice. 'It was agreed that . . . the baby must be adopted. Even Mina pressed for it. Everyone decided that it was the best thing for— The best thing.'

Lyddie got up, dropping the brush, and came to kneel beside Nest's chair: in the face of this pain her own suffering receded.

'How awful.'

'It was awful.' She stared down at Lyddie's hand, warm upon her own, and then into the green-grey eyes that watched her so lovingly.

312

'But who was "everyone"? Did all the family know?'

'No, not all. Josie and Alec had gone to America by then and Georgie was with Tom doing some kind of exchange posting in Geneva. Timmie was with the army in Germany but he knew. Timmie was a great comfort.'

'And Mummy? Did she know?'

Nest stared round the kitchen, out into the courtyard and, at last, back at Lyddie.

'I've thought this through a million times,' she said, 'and there is no way except plain truth. Yes, Henrietta knew. She knew because it was she who adopted my baby girl.' She watched confusion give way to realization and the sudden wash of colour flood into Lyddie's cheeks. 'Forgive me, if you can, for breaking the silence now. It's just—'

'*Your* child?'

'Henrietta had great difficulty in carrying a baby. She had several miscarriages and she couldn't have any more children after Roger.' Nest spoke quickly, as if by words she could alleviate the effect of such a bombshell. 'And she so longed for another baby . . . Oh God! This is awful.' Nest tried out various phrases and rejected them; they were, ultimately, simply pleas for pity. She felt weak and ill but strove to hide it from the girl who still kneeled beside her, her eyes wide with shock.

'I could say all the obvious things: we felt it was the best thing for you; you had a better chance with Henrietta and Connor; you were staying within the family.' She gave a little gasp of self-disgust. 'None of it is relevant to how *you* feel, I imagine. The trouble is, I don't *know* how you feel. Utterly shocked, well, of course. Betrayed?' Nest swallowed in a dry throat.

'And my father?' asked Lyddie after a moment. 'Was it the man you talked about who left you?'

Nest looked down, surprised to see that Lyddie was still clasping her hands. She rallied herself for this next hurdle.

'Yes,' she said. 'I loved him.' Somehow this was important, terribly important. 'And he . . .' She could see all the pitfalls, knew that Lyddie, in her present raw state, would judge according to her own lights . . .

'And he was married.' Lyddie finished the sentence for her – but almost calmly, as if she were making her own assessments, coming to her own conclusions.

'It was Connor.' Nest couldn't bear to hear her guessing. 'Your father is . . . was your father. He and I—' She stopped: how to tell this without condemning Connor as an adulterer? 'He and I . . .'

'Were in love before Henrietta came on the scene.'

They both started as Mina spoke from the doorway behind them, their joined hands clutching convulsively together.

'Georgie's pottering in the garden with the dogs.' This was clearly to reassure them and she smiled at Nest. 'I have a feeling that you've been telling the story the wrong way round. You know

314

the rule? Begin at the beginning? It sounds as if you've started at the end. Come, child.' She held a hand out to Lyddie, who climbed stiffly to her feet. She looked dazed. 'Nest needs to rest and I have things to tell you. When you've heard the whole of the story you and Nest shall talk again.'

She slipped an arm about her shoulders and led her out of the kitchen and up the stairs. After a moment Nest wheeled herself across the hall into her own room and closed the door behind her.

As soon as she was alone she began to tremble. That it should happen like this after more than thirty years of silence; after these last few weeks of heightened anxiety and strain. The moment had offered itself and she'd taken it; the relief was enormous. She gulped down great, ragged draughts of air, steadying herself, trying to control the shaking of her limbs. What had Lyddie actually said? How had she reacted? Mina had come to her rescue as she always had; right from the beginning when, in the early days after the flood and the arrival of Henrietta's letter, Nest had taken her fully into her confidence. Mina might be able to make more sense of it to Lyddie just as she had, somehow, made sense of it to Mama all those years ago.

She stands between Nest and the appalled expression on Mama's face.

'It's not the end of the world,' she says firmly. 'Is it, Mama? This happens to all kinds of people. Doesn't it, Mama?'

There is an intensity in the question that slowly penetrates Mama's shock until she blinks and turns away.

'Yes,' she says, 'yes, of course; nevertheless . . .'

'We'll deal with it,' Mina says, smiling comfortingly at Nest. 'Let's not panic, shall we?'

Afterwards she says, 'Why did you just come out with it like that, you idiot? Why didn't you warn me first?'

Nest shakes her head, tears threatening, unable to speak. It is Mina who guesses. 'It's Connor's, isn't it?' she asks.

'It was only once, honestly.' Nest shivers uncontrollably like a sick dog. 'It was at Jack's christening. Connor came straight from a conference, remember? Roger was ill and Henrietta couldn't get away.' She cries out in frustration and anguish. 'It was the only time.'

Now, as she edged herself out of her wheelchair and on to her bed, reaching for her medicine, Nest recalled all the meetings and family gatherings; the humiliations and despair. Only Mina had known the whole truth; watching helplessly but steadily as Nest attempted to stifle her stubborn love for Connor, Mina had suffered with her, made her laugh, given her courage.

'One more time,' she'd say firmly, regarding a family ordeal involving Connor. 'If you could do the wedding you can do this.'

The wedding had become the bench-mark; the reference point.

316

CHAPTER TWENTY-NINE

'But of *course* you must be a bridesmaid,' cries
Henrietta. 'Of *course* you're not too big. I know
little ones look sweet but I must have you. Mina's
going to be too busy arranging it all with Mama.
And Georgie and Josie have the babies to worry
about. Anyway, I must have my little sister. If it
hadn't been for you, Connor and I might never
have met!'

She turns to him with a sparkling look, slipping
an arm through his.

'That's true,' he says lightly.

Nest can hardly look at him, unable to bear
those possessive gestures and caresses that bind
him to her sister. She listens, though; listens to
hear by what terms he addresses Henrietta. She
calls him 'darling' but he never uses endearments
in return. Nest finds some bitter consolation in
this, treasuring those moments when he called
her 'lady' and bewitched her with his voice. He is
careful to raise no expectation in her breast –

there are to be no backward glances – but neither does he raise suspicion by ignoring Nest. He treats her with all the casual affection of an elder brother and she must learn to see him, greet him, sit beside him, with apparently friendly indifference.

The wedding is a different kind of torture. As chief bridesmaid she must be seen to sparkle: to show her delight in her sister's happiness and to listen to Connor's speech, in which he tells the guests how beautiful she looks and jokes about marrying into a family with more than its fair share of beautiful women. She sits looking back at those happy, kindly friends, smiling brightly at this one and that, laughing at his jokes, and only Mina's face shows that *she* understands. Across the room her expression is grave but steady, secretly acknowledging the pain but somehow sending courage to Nest. The groom's present to her is a silver and coral bracelet, delicate and beautiful – 'Like you, lady,' he says quietly, lifting her wrist with the bracelet encircling it and briefly kissing her hand. Henrietta breaks suddenly upon this breathless moment so that Nest's heart hammers violently in her side, although Connor remains cool.

'He insisted upon choosing it himself,' she says proudly, admiring the bracelet. 'Aren't I lucky to have a husband with taste?' – and Nest can only nod and smile again until she feels that her cheekbones must shatter with the ache of it.

'It's the helplessness,' she says to Mina later. 'How do you learn to stop loving?'

'You don't,' answers Mina grimly – and, not knowing about Tony Luttrell, Nest thinks she's talking of Richard and gives her a consoling hug.

Timmie does everything he can to help, inviting her to parties, balls, introducing her to delightful young men who fall gratifyingly in love with her; but none of them is Connor and, after his brand of lovemaking, all of them seem crude and immature.

She trains to be a teacher, has several brief relationships, but it is during those years of her twenties that she becomes closer to Mina than ever before. To begin with, she teaches at a school in Barnstaple, Mina driving her to Parracombe to catch the train each morning, collecting her each afternoon. They take long rambling walks, work in the garden, look after Lydia. Mina is pursued at one point by a much older man, a widower, who refuses to take no for an answer. He lives with his older sister and his two children in Lynton and presses invitations upon Mina to visit them. Nest nicknames him Mr Salteena – 'Because,' she says, 'he is an elderly man of forty-two who is fond of asking people to stay with him. And his whiskers are black and twisty.' They subside into fits of laughter, giggling together like children, puzzling Lydia by odd literary references, capping lines of poetry, singing the lyrics from *The Mikado* and *Ruddigore*.

It is Henrietta who tries to encourage Nest to spread her wings, to move away from Ottercombe.

'It's different for you,' she says privately to

Mina. 'You spent those few years in London and married Richard. You had your own life – not much of one, I admit, but you had it – before you buried yourself down here. Oh, don't think we're not grateful, me and Josie and Georgie, that you're prepared to look after Mama, but to be honest, Mina, I think you're actually quite content. Nest's ten years younger than you are and, apart from her training college, she's never been away. She's twenty-five and soon it will be too late. A friend of ours teaches at a school in Surrey, a really super boarding school for girls, and she told me that they need an English mistress for the juniors. It's a really good post. Persuade her to try for it. She'll live in but at least she'll have the opportunity to meet new people. Do try, Mina. It's not right for her to simply fade away down here. You'll miss her, of course . . .'

It is that last sentence, implying a certain selfishness on Mina's part, that spurs her to talk to Nest. Perhaps she is ready for a change, perhaps she too sees that she might never have a life outside Ottercombe; for whatever reason it is, Nest applies for the job and gets it.

'If you hate it,' says Mina, as the parting draws near, 'you can always come home. And we'll have the holidays . . .'

Once she is in Surrey, Nest inevitably sees more of Henrietta and Connor. They invite her during half-term, introduce her to their friends, and Nest has to struggle against a reopening of the painful scars that have healed over the wound of her love. There is still a kind of restraint between them,

320

especially if they are ever alone together, and occasionally, very occasionally, as the years pass, she catches his look: a tender, almost puzzled glance, as if he has begun to question his actions. She is afraid, however, of reading too much into it, of destroying her fragile but slowly increasing peace of mind, and she avoids him as much as possible. She manages to deal with family birthday parties, weddings, Christmases, hiding her tenacious love successfully, until the weekend of Jack's christening.

Ten years of wise self-preservation done away with in a single evening!

Timmie's wife, Anthea, has rejected the garrison church for her son's christening and has decided that he shall be baptized in her family's church in the small Herefordshire village where she grew up. Those members of the family who can attend the afternoon service, and the jollities afterwards, book in at the local hotel, apart from Lydia and Mina who are to stay with Anthea's family. When Nest, rather late in the day, tries to reserve a room at the local hotel, they advise her that all their rooms are fully booked but suggest a charming pub a mile or two away, just over the Shropshire border.

It is while she is preparing to go down for her lunch at the pub that she sees Connor's car swing into the car park. Hidden by the curtain, she watches him get out and slam the door. He glances briefly up at the half-timbered building and she sees that his face is preoccupied, rather grim. Turning away, she paces the room, her arms folded across her breast, her head lowered in thought, and all the while a tense excitement rises inside her. Presently, she picks up her jacket and goes down to the bar where she discusses the lunch menu with the landlord, orders an omelette and asks for a whisky. When Connor appears she is still sipping it, sitting at a small table by the window.

'So there you are.' Clearly he expected to see her. 'What are you drinking? Scotch? Yes, I think I'll have one of those. Do you need a refill?'

She shakes her head and watches him go to the bar. He looks good in his smart suit and the beating, throbbing excitement increases so that she takes another sip to steady her.

'What a farce it all is!' He is back, putting his glass down, sitting opposite. He still looks faintly irritated, partly amused. 'Your family!' he exclaims.

'I thought you and Henrietta were staying at the hotel,' she says calmly.

'We were,' he answers, 'except that Roger has developed some childish ailment and she can't come. When I got to the hotel Georgie and Tom were having conniptions because they hadn't booked, didn't think they'd need to at the end of October, and there was no room for them and dear little Helena at the inn. I offered them our room at which point the receptionist – grateful, no doubt, to be rescued from Georgie in full spate – sent me along here. She said that one of the party was already booked in and obligingly told me which of them it was.'

'And so here you are.'

It is the whisky, perhaps, that has lifted her into this oddly confident, carefree mood. He looks at her, his smiling eyes narrowed consideringly, so that she feels rather breathless.

'So here I am,' he agrees.

What was it about that afternoon and evening, she is to wonder afterwards, that worked the magic and flung them back headlong, so that ten years of constraint vanished so completely? Well, obviously the absence of Henrietta was a contributory factor – and, just as crucially, the absence of Mina. When Nest and Connor meet up with the party at the hotel, to walk the short distance to the church, they hear that Lydia has had a bad attack of asthma and she and Mina cannot come.

'What a shame,' cries Georgie fretfully. 'And Tom and I are flying to Geneva in a fortnight. I'd counted on seeing them here before we go. Now I shall have to go down to Exmoor, as if I hadn't enough to do . . .'

Nest catches Connor's eye and they laugh secretly, delightfully, together in spirit as they were once before.

'Filial devotion's such a wonderful thing,' he murmurs, cupping his hand around her elbow as they walk up the church path.

'You're such a cynic,' she answers, trying not to shiver at his touch.

323

'Me, lady?' He looks shocked. 'The saints forbid!'

As the afternoon lengthens into evening the game between them changes subtly. Anthea's family are generous hosts and there is much laughter and revelry. It seems perfectly natural for Connor and Nest to spend these hours together as any couple might and, without their usual duennas, they adopt a joky yet privately aware closeness that none of the rest of the family questions. Constraint relaxed by wine and champagne, years of enforced familiarity eased into intimacy, once they are back at the inn the long period of frustration and loneliness resolves itself into one long night of passionate release.

CHAPTER THIRTY

Nest was wakened by Mina bringing her a cup of tea. She struggled up on her pillows, blinking away her dreams, struggling to remember.

'Lyddie,' she said anxiously, 'how is she? What did she say?'

Mina stood the tea on the bedside table. 'Lyddie has gone back to Truro. No!' as Nest exclaimed distressfully, 'not in a fit of rejection. Nothing like that. She was going anyway. Remember?'

'Yes, of course I remember. What a fool I've been, Mina. To burst out with all this now when she's got so much on her plate . . . How did she react?'

Mina arranged the pillows more comfortably behind Nest's shoulders and perched on the side of the bed.

'She was surprisingly balanced about it,' she answered gently. 'Clearly it's a huge shock but she listened to the whole story, asked sensible questions and said, very reasonably, that it was going to take a while to sink in.'

'Oh, Mina. Two shocks in less than a week! She must be reeling. Should she be driving, d'you think?'

'It will give her something to do. To be honest, it would have been difficult for the pair of you to meet over lunch, wouldn't it? This break will be good for both of you. She sent her love to you . . .'

'Did she?' asked Nest eagerly. 'Did she say that?'

'Yes she did.' Mina looked with compassion at Nest's strained, pain-lined face. 'I wouldn't make up something so important, you know that.'

'No,' said Nest, after a moment. 'No, you wouldn't.'

'You and Lyddie have more than thirty years of loving between you. That can't be discounted. She's not a child. She'll be quite able to see the situation fairly and squarely but she'll need time to adjust.'

'On top of finding out about Liam I should think it will be a very long time.'

'I'm not so certain,' said Mina slowly. 'She thought it was very brave of you to tell her. She said, "Everyone has a right to their own history." I think, oddly, her own problems will give her an added insight. It's always those who have never suffered nor failed who are the most intolerant. Lyddie will be fair – she won't mis-judge you, I'm certain of it – but that doesn't mean that it isn't a shock.'

'Of *course* it is!' exclaimed Nest. 'Good grief!

Discovering that your mother isn't who you thought she was!' She shook her head. 'How do you come to terms with it? How often I've asked myself that question when I've wondered if I should ever tell her the truth.'

'Mmm.' Mina looked thoughtful. 'And is she right, do you think? That everyone has a right to their own history?'

'Well, I'm very glad *she* thinks so, in which case I hope she won't be upset that I've kept it from her for so long. But in general terms? Well, if I believed it I suppose I would have told her once Connor and Henrietta died. Before then, they'd both made me swear not to tell her. It's a very complex subject with so many implications. It happened now simply because of the strain. And to think that after all that it wasn't Georgie in the end who let the cat out of the bag.' Nest groaned. 'All that terror . . .'

'Georgie was the catalyst,' said Mina. 'She played her part. And now you are going to sleep. You look exhausted and I'm not surprised at it. Drink your tea and then try to rest. All is well. The worst is over.'

'Do you think so?'

'Yes, I do.' Mina leaned forward, kissed Nest's cheek and stood up. 'Take your tea and stop fretting. She knows. She sends her love to you. The worst is over.' She hesitated, watching Nest sip her tea. 'Just out of interest, how *did* it actually start? What made you suddenly decide to tell after all these years?'

Nest frowned, thinking back. 'We started talking about love, about how it was impossible just to switch it off, no matter what the person had done. And we went on to speak of parents and children and how awful the responsibility is when it comes to letting your children grow and be free. And, for some reason, I said that it was worse watching other people exercise those decisions over one's own child. Lyddie jumped on it and it just went from there. The moment was right. That's all I can say.'

'I am very glad. I can see now that it's the best way, to be open, and the time was exactly right for it. Now try to sleep.'

Mina crossed the hall and went into the kitchen. There was no sign of Georgie but the teapot was empty and the kettle was boiling itself dry on top of the Esse. Mina snatched it up, cursing beneath her breath, and took it into the scullery to refill it. It sizzled as she took the lid off and poured in some cold water but she was too preoccupied to be cross with Georgie for long. She was thinking about Lyddie.

'*Everyone has a right to their own history.*'

Thoughtfully she set the kettle back on the Esse and went to find the dogs.

Lyddie, travelling west, was crossing the Torridge Bridge at Bideford. She was driving automatically, only some small part of her mind concentrating on the traffic, until it suddenly occurred to her that she couldn't remember the previous part of the journey at all. It had passed as if in a dream. She slowed down a little, glancing in her mirror, seeing the Bosun's comfortable bulk as he leaned against the grille, staring out at the countryside as it fled away behind him.

'This has been the worst week of my life,' she told him – and he turned his head to look at her, listening with pricked ears to her voice.

But was that true? she asked herself. Hadn't it been worse – or at least as bad – when she'd heard the news that her parents had been killed in a car accident? The shock had been cataclysmic, unbearable, yet it was an unpalatable truth that time had eased the pain, removing the tragedy to a further point where it might be dwelt on at a distance, as it were, with sorrow but without that same agony that she'd experienced at the time. It made her feel guilty when she acknowledged this but 'It must be so,' Jack had said once, talking about the death of his own father. 'How else could we function if we continued to bear that kind of loss every hour of our life?' This had comforted her, made her feel less selfish and uncaring. There were poignant moments – her wedding had been one of them – when she needed them terribly, missed them unbearably, yet it was true that gradually she'd learned to live with the sadness and the loneliness.

'And now?' she murmured aloud. 'And now – well, what? I can't seem to think straight.'

It seemed impossible not to think of Henrietta in any other light than as her mother: the nurturing and caring; the loving actions that make up a childhood: all this belonged to Henrietta. Yet Nest was her biological mother. The extraordinary thought 'Does it matter?' slipped into her weary mind and she felt a stab of guilt. Perhaps, because Henrietta had been dead for more than ten years, it was possible to let these two images juxtapose: Nest on the one hand; Henrietta on the other: both women who had loved and cherished her in their different ways.

'Nest lost everything,' Aunt Mina had said. 'First she lost Connor – and you are able, now, Lyddie, to really understand what that means – and then she lost you. She had no choices. Mama was absolutely determined that you should be adopted and Connor pressed her hard. Naturally, neither Mama nor Henrietta had any idea that you were Connor's child but you can imagine what it must have been like for Nest, beleaguered on every side. Connor wanted you desperately and yet what could he do? Should he leave his wife and child so as to support you and Nest? Either way it was an appalling decision to have to take. Someone had to lose and Nest drew the short straw. She paid very heavily for her one moment of need. She never stopped loving him, you know, and I believe that he loved both of them; that to Connor they were opposite sides of the same coin. And, to do Henrietta justice, she was delighted to help Nest by taking you as her own child and she was never less than generous in including Nest in your upbringing – as far as it was reasonable without harming you. There was only one occasion—'

She'd stopped then, and Lyddie, still trying to assimilate all these things, had not pursued it, intent on another line of thought.

'So Daddy wasn't an unfaithful kind of man, not really?'

'No,' she'd answered readily. 'Oh, there were plenty of opportunities but neither of them took them. Connor was not in any way a libertine. If he hadn't been so scrupulous over the fact that Nest was ten years younger than he was, and still at school, it's very likely that they would have married. Henrietta was the mature fulfilment of all that Nest promised and he was knocked sideways by her. He made his decision and stood by it. Nest never quite got over him, that was the tragedy. Oh, she made a pretty good fist of it but nobody else ever quite measured up to Connor.'

Remembering, glancing away to the sea at Widemouth Bay, Lyddie felt another wave of sympathy for Nest. She could imagine all too clearly how hard it might be to recover from loving the one man you adored. How was it to be done? She found herself thinking about Rosie. In an odd way, she'd played Henrietta to Rosie's Nest.

'He was mine before he was ever yours,' Rosie had cried – but Rosie was not prepared to back down: Rosie intended to make a fight of it. Had Liam ever really loved Rosie? Did he love her still? How cold, how sick she'd felt when she'd imagined her father being unfaithful; for a moment she'd thought of Liam and a sense of revulsion had swamped her as she'd imagined her father cheating and lying, betraying her mother.

'I can't imagine Nest as my mother,' she'd said desperately. 'It's not . . . not possible. Mummy was my mother. It's not that I don't love Nest. I do, she's been terrific to me, but I can't *do* that.'

'You don't have to,' Aunt Mina had answered firmly. 'Nest won't expect you to change how you feel about either her or Henrietta. Of *course* she won't. It would be impossible. And unnecessary. She is Nest, a person in her own right, and she has her own relationship with you. It would be foolish to say that nothing will change now but the past is the past, unchangeable. All she will hope is that you can continue to go forward without hating her for the deception and for giving you such a shock.'

'I could never hate Nest,' she'd said after a moment – and had been surprisingly relieved to know that this was the truth. 'She's meant too much to me for that. But I don't want to try to think about her in this new light. It's . . . not right.'

'I agree with you,' Aunt Mina had said at once. 'Henrietta was your mother in all ways except biologically. If that sounds odd then I think you know exactly what I mean. There is more to motherhood than simply producing the baby. Nest asks for nothing except that you shouldn't condemn her or, more importantly in her eyes, your father. Why do you think she hasn't told you before? After Henrietta died, for instance?'

'So why now?'

Aunt Mina had drawn a deep, deep breath, letting it out again with the characteristic 'po-po-po'. 'You might well ask. After all the years of silence it seems almost cruel that she should drop such a bombshell when you have already had an appalling shock. The simple truth is she was afraid someone else might tell you first.'

'Who else knows?' Lyddie had felt an unexpected surge of real fear and anger. 'Who . . .? Does Jack know?'

'Nobody knows,' her aunt had answered calmly. 'I am certain of it. The trouble is that your Aunt Georgie has some inkling of one or two things that happened in the past and is making rather a thing out of it. Nest has become almost paranoid about it and has convinced herself that Georgie is going to blurt out some secret or other to you.'

'And might Aunt Georgie know?' Lyddie had suddenly realized how much she would hate others knowing whilst she did not.

'I think it's highly unlikely. You have to understand that your grandmother would have died rather than anyone beyond the immediate protagonists should know anything about it. Georgie and Josie and Timmie and their families were all abroad during that time. Timmie knew that Nest was pregnant – but not about Connor – and I had to know because Nest came here to be with us, but nobody else knew. Georgie was always a bit of a troublemaker; she liked to ruffle feathers and now, especially, she's very confused. Nest has been carrying this secret for a long time and I think it's simply that the strain had become too much for her.'

'It must have been awful. Such a secret.'

'Such a secret,' her aunt had repeated with a sigh. 'A terrible weight to carry, continually questioning which is the right course to take. If you are not harmed I must admit that I am delighted that the silence has been broken at last.'

'I shall be OK,' Lyddie had answered. 'And I'm glad I know. Everyone has a right to their own history.'

'There's one last thing,' Aunt Mina had said with an effort. 'I think it's important. Do you remember that Henrietta wanted you to join her in that boutique of hers when you left university?'

'Oh, I certainly do. There was a frightful fuss about it. It was a crazy fad.'

'Connor, most unwillingly, took out a big loan against the house to buy the lease and get the shop stocked and, when the business started to lose money, Henrietta was insistent that you should work with her so as to save on wages. Connor and Nest were absolutely against it. It was the first time Nest had ever interfered . . .' She'd paused. 'There's this last thing that you should know. During that final car journey the three of them were arguing very strongly about it. Nest has always felt that if she hadn't been so vociferous, so anxious that you should not be coerced into giving up your chosen career, Henrietta might have concentrated harder on her driving and the accident might never have happened.'

Lyddie had stared at her. 'But . . . that's crazy.'

'Possibly. She felt unbearably guilty that she survived and, in the pain and depression that followed, she got it out of all proportion. I mention it to you because you should know that her punishment ever since that day is that she has never once been down to the beach. More than ten years. She always loved the sea so much and she took this form of punishing herself.'

'Poor Nest.' Lyddie had been stricken with compassion. 'Oh, poor, poor Nest. But it could have been *anything* that caused the accident. More likely Mummy was trying to light a cigarette. She was always a menace doing that and the car used to go all over the place.'

'I felt you should know,' Aunt Mina had repeated. 'You need not mention it to her but if you can show that you forgive her for all the subterfuge, she might at last be able to forgive herself.'

There was a long silence.

'We need to talk, Nest and I,' said Lyddie at last, 'but not just yet. I'd like a little time to digest all this very carefully and adjust to it. But I think I shall go back to Truro now, Aunt Mina. I think it would be a mistake to meet casually over lunch and I told Liam I'd be home by late afternoon. Give Nest my love, won't you, and tell her I'll be back soon?'

'And Liam?' Aunt Mina had asked gently. 'Have you been able to come to a decision?'

Lyddie had shaken her head rather desperately. 'But I need to see him,' she'd said. 'Don't forget to give Nest my message.'

Her aunt had kissed her and hugged her tightly. 'I shan't forget,' she'd promised.

And now, here she was, driving back to Truro, wondering what Liam would say to her – and what she would say to him. Her heart contracted with fearful apprehension and, for a while, the thought of the approaching meeting thrust all other more recent revelations from her mind.

CHAPTER THIRTY-ONE

He was waiting for her when she finally arrived; sitting at the table by the window, reading the newspaper. He must have heard the key in the lock, the dropping of her case in the hall, yet when she went in with the Bosun he made a show of continuing to read for a second before glancing up with a kind of pleased surprise.

'Well, hello,' he said to her – and, 'Hello, you,' in a different voice to the Bosun as he wagged across to greet him, demanding attention.

'Hello.' She stood rather awkwardly just inside the door. Liam could cover his awkwardness by ruffling the Bosun's ears and playing with him but Lyddie had nothing to do. She looked about the room, and at him, and experienced her third shock. He was a stranger: handsome, sexy – but a stranger. Even the room looked changed. It seemed smaller and utterly unfamiliar. She frowned, trying to make sense of it, wondering if her mind was playing tricks. After all, it had been an extraordinary week and she was very tired.

'Would you like some tea? Or something stronger?' He was standing up now, watching her, but he made no move towards her. 'You look bushed.'

'I *am* tired,' she admitted – and realized with another tiny jolt that it would be completely impossible to tell him about Nest's revelation. It would be like exposing one's deep, most private self to a kindly but indifferent acquaintance. She felt a sense of isolation accompanied by a feeble desire to burst into tears. 'Thanks, some tea would be great.'

It was important to be alone for a few moments so that she might get a grip on herself; she felt incapable even of ordinary conversation. He made no attempt to come in and out of the kitchen as he would have once – wandering to and fro, asking how the Aunts were, demanding her news, no detail too small – and she sat at the table in silence trying to cudgel her recalcitrant brain into intelligent thought. Deep down, though, a secret fear was growing.

She listened as he talked to the Bosun, filling his bowl with cold fresh water whilst making the tea. There was the sound of noisy lapping and, presently, the Bosun shouldered out of the kitchen, went through to the hall and flung himself at full stretch upon the floor, groaning pleasurably. Liam put the mug before Lyddie on the table and went to sit down again. It occurred to her that they had not embraced; he had not even touched her shoulder or made any gesture towards physical affection. The fear grew a little stronger. She raised her head and looked at him across the table. He looked back at her, the pleasant, unmeaning smile playing round his mouth, his eyes bright and blank. As her look intensified he raised his eyebrows a little, a quizzical quirk as if questioning her interest. She was simply too tired, too emotionally unstrung to be subtle.

'So you haven't missed me, then,' she said flatly – and picked up her mug.

It was a statement rather than an enquiry and his eyes flew wide open in genuine surprise before the mask was dropped again. 'And who told you that?'

'Oh, I'm just guessing. How's . . . . everything?'

'*Everything,*' he emphasized the word almost mockingly, 'is just fine.'

'And everyone?'

'Now, who would you be meaning by "everyone"? That's a bit ambiguous.'

'Oh, well,' she cradled the mug in her hands, pretending to ponder. 'Joe? Rosie? Zoë?'

His smile slipped visibly and his eyes were unfriendly. 'Could that be a leading question?'

'I imagine you've seen them?'

'I work with them, remember? It would be odd if I hadn't.'

'Has Rosie been given her job back, then?'

His expression was hostile now. 'She has not.'

'Ah. You haven't seen Rosie, then?' The pause

was a shade too long. 'I take it that means "yes".
Well, I guessed she wouldn't miss an opportunity.'

'It's you who left,' he reminded her. 'You didn't
have to go.'

She looked at him with a kind of smiling disbelief. 'You're saying that it's all my fault?'

He shook his head. 'I'm not saying anything.'

'But you saw Rosie.'

He was losing his carefully controlled patience.
'Yes, I saw Rosie. I've known her for a long time,
remember. Long before you came on the scene.'

'So she took pains to tell me. And I have this
feeling, Liam, that you wish you'd stuck with her.'

The silence was even longer and, this time,
Lyddie did not break it. She sat watching him, the
fear blossoming inside her.

'She accepts me for what I am,' he said at last,
almost sullenly. 'She takes the package.'

Lyddie swallowed some tea and put the mug
carefully on the small round mat. These coasters
had been a wedding present: six different
cartoons of a shaggy dog. She stared at it, remembering her wedding day, how she'd felt, and was
suddenly overwhelmed by a devastating sense of
loss.

'I was thinking,' she said, turning the mug
round and round on its mat, not looking at him,
'on my way down. Thinking about how it could be
done. I'm not like Rosie, you see. I can't just share
you around. I can't *do* that. But supposing we were
to make a fresh start? Go somewhere new to both
of us and you were to create another wine bar?'

She looked at him at last and caught his stare of complete incredulity.

'Mother of God,' he said at last. 'Are you crazy? And what about The Place, do I just walk away from it?'

'Joe could take it over. You could do it again in another town. Why not? It happens all the time. Shops, bars, start with one and then two and then chains of things in the end.' Suddenly she remembered their first conversation and how he'd answered when she asked why he'd called his wine bar The Place. 'You could call it The Next Place or The Best Place.'

For a second, just for a fleeting moment, she watched him catch the vision, saw the glow of it touch his face alight before it died and his eyes were bleak again.

'We couldn't afford it,' he said, 'even if I wanted to. Joe couldn't run it alone and it wouldn't stand a bar manager's salary yet. Anyway, we'd never get another loan to start a new place.'

'What if we used the money from the house in Iffley for the new place?'

He laughed and shook his head. 'I wondered how long it would be before that was dragged in. A drop in the ocean . . .'

'You could sell this house.'

'Have you forgotten I've got a huge mortgage on it? Forget it.'

Another pause.

'You said "even if I wanted to" just now.' Lyddie spoke slowly. 'That's the whole point, isn't it? You don't want to change, or leave The Place and, if you're really honest, I think you don't want us even to try, do you?'

'I can't see what all the fuss is about. You were perfectly happy before. Nothing's changed.'

'Oh, but it has,' she said quickly. 'Everything's changed as far as I'm concerned.'

'I'm the same person I always was.'

'Oh, yes, but, you see, I didn't really know the person you've always been. I only knew a part of you and I fell in love with that part. But now I know that you lie and cheat, that I'll never know in future whether you really are going to the bank, or the cash and carry, or a meeting with the accountant, or whether you're upstairs in the storeroom with the new waitress. That's quite a change.' She watched him for a moment. 'You really can't see it, can you?'

He shrugged. 'So what do you want to do?'

'I've already told you what I'd like us to do.'

'It's out of the question.'

She was silent, the fear mushrooming so that it filled her with misery.

'I knew it was over when I came in and saw you,' she said at last. 'It was as if you were a complete stranger. As if, in those three days, you'd changed completely.'

He looked away from her. 'You shouldn't have gone away,' he said.

'What does that mean?' she cried. 'If I'd stayed would you now be considering my suggestion for a new start?'

'No,' he answered. 'No, I wouldn't. But it gave me the time to see that . . .'

He hesitated so long that she guessed his meaning. 'It gave you time to see that you don't need me enough to change for me. For us.'

He nodded, still not looking at her. 'Something like that.'

'And how much input did Rosie contribute to your decision?'

'Rosie's always been there when I needed her.'

It was as if he'd struck her across the face. 'And how many times was that during these last two years?' she asked furiously. 'My God! And I thought we were so happy.'

He frowned almost distastefully, as if she were in some way offending his sensibilities, and looked at her at last.

'You're right,' he said. 'It has changed, I see that, but,' he opened his hands and then let them drop, 'I see no point in talking about it.'

'Fine,' she said. 'Great. So that's it, is it? Two years of marriage down the pan, just like that.'

'I've got to go,' he said, and stood up. 'Sorry. I'm really sorry, Lyddie. I made the mistake of falling in love. Oh, I did. You were different, you see. Clever with words. Aloof. Just that bit unattainable and it was a challenge. But I don't need it. I know that now, not if it means rows and arguments and questions. I can't hack all that stuff. Rosie knows me. We're on the same wavelength. She knows how I feel about The Place and puts up with it. She accepts that I need variety now and then. She doesn't like it but she doesn't complain. She knows that I don't want kids and neither does she. She'll go along with what I do and what I want.'

'And what do I do?'

'Well.' He didn't quite shrug it off. 'You've got your work and, after all,' he gave a little laugh, 'there's always the money from the house in Iffley.' Even he seemed to feel the brutality of his quip and he bit his lip. 'Sorry,' he said. 'That was cheap. I'm no good at this stuff, I'm afraid. You've always got the Aunts as a stopgap.'

'Thanks,' she said. 'So I have.'

'I'll be at The Place,' he said, 'if you need me. You'd better speak to your lawyer.' He paused, his jacket hanging over one shoulder, head lowered. 'And thanks, Lyddie.' He looked at her, grimaced. 'It was great while it lasted.'

She heard his footsteps pass the window and die away. The Bosun came in and looked at her hopefully. She stared back at him, wondering if it were remotely possible that she should be capable of standing up, let alone walking, but, after a moment, she got up and fetched her coat and they went out into the evening together.

344

CHAPTER THIRTY-TWO

'Of course she must come,' said Hannah. 'Of *course* she must. The kids could go to Mum for a couple of days.'

'It's just for two nights and then she's going to Ottercombe until she can sort herself out,' said Jack, who was sitting on the sofa with Caligula lying on his chest, purring loudly. 'Apparently she's got to get back to work again by next weekend – she's booked up until Christmas and she doesn't want to let anyone down. Lucky that this late delivery happened. The editor she works for has agreed to give it to another copy-editor if it turns up this week.'

'She daren't lose her contacts, I can see that,' agreed Hannah. 'She'll need her work. But can she live on it?'

Jack shook his head. 'I've no idea. Roger pays her interest in her share of the house. That should help.'

'Poor Lyddie. It's so devastating to find out that

345

someone you trust has been cheating. It destroys your self-confidence, apart from anything else. Did you suspect anything?'

'Well, she seemed fine when we saw her at Ottercombe, didn't she? In fact I thought she was on rather good form.'

'Almost too good?' suggested Hannah. 'Rather over the top? And remember when she couldn't come to stay – I wonder what that was about? It's always easy to be wise after the event but Liam always struck me as being a bit of a handful.'

'The trouble is that there is absolutely nothing that one can do to help. Nothing can take away the pain or the reality of it. Why is loving people so damned agonizing?'

She smiled at him. 'I had no idea when I married you that you were such a complete mother hen. I should have guessed when I saw all those little boys trailing after you, "Sir, I've lost this . . ." or, "Sir, I've done that . . .", and you behaving like a dear old nannie.'

'I am nothing like a dear old nannie,' he answered indignantly. 'I'm an absolute brute to the little monsters. Good grief! They're terrified of me.'

'Oh, yes,' she agreed mockingly. 'Scared to death. Like Hobbes the other evening, for instance? Reading him a story at ten o'clock at night?'

'He misses his mum,' said Jack defensively, 'and I didn't want him to wake the others . . .' – Hannah snorted disbelievingly – 'and he'd had a rotten day.'

'You're a big softie and they all know it,' she

said, grinning at him. 'Marshmallow right down to the centre. Flora had you sussed when she was three days old.'

He grinned too. 'Our daughter has an unerring instinct for a weak spot,' he agreed. 'Attila the Hun could take her correspondence course.' A pause. 'Will your mother cope OK?'

'Oh, now *don't* start fussing about that,' cried Hannah, exasperated. 'She manages them brilliantly and they love being with her. You know they do.'

'Yes, I do,' he admitted.

'Well then. I'll give her a buzz and, if it's OK, I'll take them over when I pick Tobes up from playschool. I think it would give Lyddie a freer rein to talk things over if we're on our own. There's nothing worse than being interrupted every five minutes when you're feeling like that. The best thing we can do for Lyddie is to concentrate on her. That's quite impossible with Flora in the house.'

'You're absolutely right,' he said. 'I'm going to watch the news and I'll make you a cuppa when you've finished talking to your mum.'

'That sounds great,' she said. She paused at the door, looking at him affectionately. 'Did I ever tell you that I have a thing about mother hens?'

'It's too late for soft soap,' he answered with great dignity. 'My feathers are already ruffled.' He flexed his shoulders, as if puffing himself up, and clucked several times like a meditative hen. 'Haven't you noticed?'

347

'Looks great,' she said admiringly. 'I'll be back later to check out your quills.'

She disappeared and Jack sighed heavily, as if shocked, reaching for the remote control. 'And people ask where Flora gets it from,' he murmured to Caligula. 'Well, we all know who rules the roost in *this* house,' and he switched on the television, swung his feet up on the sofa and closed his eyes.

At Ottercombe, Mina was preparing for bed. Lyddie had telephoned to tell them that Liam didn't want a reconciliation, except under the terms of complete surrender on her part, and so, she'd said, she had no course but to leave Truro and to ask if she could stay with them until she could decide what she should do next. Saddened though they were by the news, Mina and Nest had been deeply relieved that Lyddie wanted to come back to them. It showed, as nothing else could, that she'd accepted her past even if she had not yet had time to assimilate it thoroughly. She was going to see Jack and Hannah first, just for a few days, she'd said; a plan that her aunts had encouraged. They had absolute faith in her cousin and his wife, knowing that they would allow her to talk and sustain her.

'Roger simply must get his act together with his mortgage,' Nest had said. 'Thank goodness that the big loan Henrietta took out for her boutique was paid off by the insurance. It was so foolish of Connor to go along with that business.'

'Henrietta wouldn't give in,' Mina remembered. 'She was absolutely set on it. Even to the point of sacrificing Lyddie on its altar.'

Nest had looked at her, suddenly alert. 'Did you tell her about the accident?'

'I told her,' answered Mina carefully, 'that you'd all been heatedly discussing the question of whether she should work at the boutique and that you'd always feared that it was because of the high feelings that Henrietta wasn't concentrating.'

'But that's not all of the truth,' Nest had said sharply.

'Maybe not,' Mina had felt it necessary to be firm, 'but that's all you can tell her. The cause of the accident is between Connor and Henrietta and you. Not Lyddie. It would be quite wrong to involve her in it. She cannot forgive you on their behalf, she can only be dragged down by it. To tell the whole truth, in my opinion, would be self-indulgent.'

Nest had stared at her, almost shocked. 'Self-indulgent?'

'Yes,' she'd cried. 'Can't you see that? It can do no good except to relieve *your* feelings. She'll feel obliged to absolve you and she will simply be left with the burden of the knowledge and all the horror to live through again. It would be cruel. You must continue to live with this part of the story, Nest. If Lyddie is ready to accept all the rest of it, and to move forward, then you must forgive yourself at last and go with her. It's over.'

She'd seen Nest swallow, her hands tighten on

the arms of her chair, and, feeling a brute, she'd left her.

Now, as she brushed her soft white hair, a little 'po-po-po' escaping her lips, she wondered if she'd been right. At her feet, Nogood Boyo quartered the carpet, looking for his toy, whilst Captain Cat watched him alertly from his basket. Earlier, overcome with irritation, he'd sneaked the toy away, hiding it behind the curtain, and now he peered, ears cocked, as his single-minded offspring searched determinedly. Beneath her stool Mina felt his excited breath on her ankles and bent to look at him.

'What are you doing?' she asked. 'Silly Boyo. What are you looking for?'

Fearing possible collusion, Captain Cat tensed on his bed but his mistress was too preoccupied to guess what Nogood Boyo was after and left them to it whilst she went into the alcove. She clicked and scrolled, intent upon the screen, and finally opened Elyot's e-mail.

From: Elyot
To: Mina

A good day. William is home! Oh, the relief and joy of having him safely with us. Lavinia has reacted so positively. She recognized him at once and, although she was confused as to where he'd been, she was fairly lucid. She seems to have completely forgotten about Marianne, his ex-wife – which under the circumstances is just as well –

but his unexpected appearance is doing Lavinia so much good. I'd been afraid to forewarn her in case something should go wrong but now I believe it was probably the right thing to do. The happy shock seemed to trigger something in her brain so that she is – I nearly said 'quite her old self', which is far from true, but she is so bright that it does my heart good. I'd almost forgotten her smile. She has a quiet brooding look these days, and smiles rarely.

Sadly, it was all too soon before the question of our GP was brought up. I'd warned William about it and he is sympathetically non-committal, which is the best line to take. How right you were about that! Nevertheless it cast a tiny shadow over our happy reunion. William looks well and has leave until after Christmas when he takes up a posting with the Ministry of Defence. It will be good to have him back in the country for a while and, although I don't intend for us to be a burden to him, I know I shall be able to rely on him for support and – oh! so important – to make me laugh. Like you, my dear old friend, he has that blessed, happy ability to raise the spirits.

Enough of us. How are things at Ottercombe? Such good news that the skeleton is out of the cupboard. You have been very discreet, and rightly so, but I have guessed that it was a fairly large cadaver from the depth of your anxiety and, now, by the measure of your relief. Don't imagine

for a moment that having William with us makes me any less anxious to hear from you as usual.
Elyot

Mina sat for some moments, considering. It was good to think of him enjoying the company of his son and heartened by Lavinia's new-found brightness; it would be selfish to tell him about Lyddie's predicament quite so quickly. Yet she found herself longing to tell him, rather shocked by her need, realizing how much she'd come to rely upon him. She typed quickly lest she should weaken.

From: Mina
To: Elyot

All is well here and you are right to suggest that my relief is enormous. Nest looks better than I have seen her for a very long time. A degree of peacefulness possesses her at last – and not before time. Georgie has had one of her quiet days, rather as if she is puzzled by something that she can hear but we can't. No dramas at least!

I am so pleased to hear how happy William's arrival is making you. You deserve a break, dear Elyot, and it is lovely to think of you all together. What a treat to have him home for Christmas, not only because he is your son and he has been away for a long time, but because it will ease some of the load from your shoulders.

Enjoy this time together. We'll talk again tomorrow. Goodnight.

Mina closed down the computer, took off her long fleecy robe and climbed into bed. She switched off the bedside lamp and lay staring into the darkness.

'Everyone has a right to their own history.'

After a while she reached for Lydia's rosary and began to pass the smooth, cool beads through her fingers but still she found it impossible to sleep.

CHAPTER THIRTY-THREE

Nest too was lying awake, thinking very carefully about the things Mina had said earlier. She had been right to explain the accident in those terms to Lyddie; right in saying that she, Nest, must live with the truth without the luxury of Lyddie's forgiveness. Lyddie could not absolve her of her guilt and it would be cruel to put such a burden of knowledge upon her. It was bad enough for her to know that she had been the topic of conversation, that it was anxiety about her future that might have been a factor in Henrietta's momentary loss of concentration.

Nest shut her eyes against the picture of Connor's profile, his head turned towards her. They'd been returning late from the house of a mutual friend where some celebration or other had been taking place, Henrietta driving. Nest had only agreed to go, staying overnight with Connor and Henrietta, simply because Connor had asked her to plead Lyddie's case with Henrietta. For the first time in more than twenty years he had invoked her support, visiting her at the school in Surrey, asking her to persuade Henrietta out of her scheme.

'Lyddie would be wasted,' he cries. 'She's done well at university and now she's been offered a job with a major publishing house. She's over the moon about it. The real problem is that Henrietta's worried about the repayment of the loan and feels that Lyddie should be prevailed upon to help us out. There's all this talk about loyalty and family ties and so on. Henrietta has this mad idea that Lyddie won't need much in the way of wages as she'll be able to live at home and so she'll save on having to pay her full-time assistant. What future is that for Lyddie, I ask you? And she thinks having her in the shop will bring in young people and give it a shot in the arm. She can't understand why Lyddie isn't thrilled to bits at the thought of it. *Why* was I so crazy as to have gone along with the idea of a boutique in the first place? I won't have her sacrificing Lyddie's future . . .'

She watches him sympathetically, agreeing wholeheartedly that Lyddie should not miss her chance in London, but wondering how it is that the birth of their daughter so effectively killed all her passion for him; as if a sword had fallen, slicing the ties that once bound her to him.

How hard, how very hard it is, to give up her child, and yet, when she finally agrees to 'the terms and conditions' as she bitterly refers to

them, that period at Ottercombe is among the
happiest of her life. She feels so fit, so well,
'although,' she tells Mina, after her return from
the doctor's surgery, 'I'd have you know that I am
an *elderly primate.*'

Mina makes a face. 'Good heavens,' she says. 'It
makes you sound like some kind of gorilla' – and
they laugh together.

Even Mama, once everything is settled – 'once I
knuckled under,' says Nest – becomes affectionate
and sweet-tempered again.

Perhaps the acceptance, the giving in, is the
mainspring of this release of a new kind of
contentment. The horror and the fear, the terror
for her child's future – and her own – gives way to
a calm confidence. At Ottercombe, it is as if she's
stepped out of the world, hidden from its
censorious gaze, and is able to offer herself wholly
to this wonderful new experience without thinking of the future. The three women pick up the
threads of the life Nest had left five years before
and she sinks contentedly into the warmth of
Mina's caring. She walks for miles over the moor
and spends hours watching the sea, revelling in
the softly stealing, all-pervading sense of peace
that its unceasing movement always brings to her.

Timmie visits as often as he can, bringing
Anthea and small Jack, lending his support. He,
like Mama, has no idea of the identity of Nest's
lover and it is never discussed. He simply offers
encouragement and unconditional love, as is
Timmie's way. They all adore Jack, especially

Lydia, who loves to hold him on her lap where he sprawls, relaxed and sleepy. When Nest cuddles him, feeling his warm heavy weight, touching his flushed cheek and feathery hair, it seems impossible that she should not hold her own child like this. Yet some sense of self-preservation refuses to allow such thoughts to develop, pushing them gently but firmly away so that quietude fills her soul again and soothes her heart. It is agreed that she should be allowed to choose her child's name and Nest has no doubts in her mind: if the baby were a boy he is to be named Timothy; if a girl, Lydia.

During that winter and into the early spring, Lydia succumbs as usual to attacks of asthma and bronchial problems. Nest listens to her racking coughing and watches her increasing frailty with anxiety, thinking of those war years, when Mina was living in London, and Mama read aloud *The Country Child* and O'Shaughnessy's poetry. The positions are now reversed and it is she who reads to Lydia as they sit by the fire in the drawing-room whilst Mina sews or knits small garments for the baby.

'Do you ever get lonely?' she asks Mina one evening, after Lydia is in bed. She remembers how she'd gone away to start a new life five years before, leaving Mina with Lydia isolated at Ottercombe, and she feels a pang of guilt.

'Lonely?' Mina considers the thought. 'I don't think so. I have Mama who, as you see, requires quite a lot of care and, to be honest, I think I'm a naturally solitary person and I have the house and garden to look after. I've always had this passion for books, for stories. I live in them, you see, and the people are quite real to me. They are my friends and I've always found their worlds much more satisfying than the reality outside.'

Yet when the outside world imposes itself upon her, Mina responds with courage and cheerfulness. Nest knows that during her own bad times, first losing Connor, then those empty, agonizing weeks – mercifully few before she'd had to start the new term – after Henrietta takes the baby away, and, later again, the months immediately after the accident, it is Mina who holds her firm, instilling the will to go on, forcing her back to life.

Nest stirred restlessly, glanced at her bedside clock – nearly half-past one – and decided that she needed a hot drink. She edged herself out of bed, pulled on her dressing-gown and got herself into her chair. Opening the door quietly, listening for a moment, she wheeled across the hall and into the kitchen. She was sitting beside the table drinking camomile tea when Mina came in.

'Oh dear,' she said. 'You too? Not brooding, I hope?'

'I was a bit.' Nest set her mug down. 'Thinking back to the accident, you know. Trying to decide whether Henrietta actually took in what I said. I keep going over it. It was a soaking night, terrible rain, if you remember. The wipers were going and the traffic was quite bad; the tyres swishing on the wet road. I was almost shouting, well, we all were.

Connor and I had drunk too much and Henrietta was in a state because she was beginning to see that she might not get her own way. She wasn't used to that and she was starting to panic. She was very defensive, cross that I was involved, and she knew that Connor had roped me in so as to support him. She was snappy. "I may not be Lyddie's mother," she said, very sarcastic, and, quite without thinking, I said, "No, but Connor *is* her father . . ." I remember stopping short, clapping my hand over my mouth, and she turned her head very sharply and they looked at each other. And then the car just clipped the lorry coming in the other direction and we were spinning and spinning out of control. I'll never forget the terrible sounds . . .'

Mina had her arm about her, cradling against her breast, rocking her.

'She might never have heard you,' she said. 'Guilt can distort the truth. She might simply have turned her head to hear better.'

'Possibly.' Nest took her hands away from her face. 'Anyway, I agree with you about Lyddie not knowing. You are absolutely right about that. I just wish I knew how she's feeling about . . . the other thing.'

Mina straightened up, pushing her hands into her dressing-gown pocket, her fingers encountering the rosary where she'd put it quite unconsciously earlier, when she'd decided to come downstairs. She stood for a moment and then took a deep breath, 'po-po-po', and dropped the rosary on the table beside Nest's mug. Nest looked at it.

'That was Mama's, wasn't it?' she asked, momentarily distracted. 'Didn't Timothy give it to her?'

Mina put the kettle on the Esse and chose a mug. 'Not as such,' she said, 'although it *was* Timothy's. It came to Mama with the rest of his things after he died.'

'That was odd, wasn't it?' Nest picked up the rosary and let the beads slip through her fingers. 'Why Mama? Didn't he have a family?'

'Not as far as I know. All her letters to him came back with it and a few other things. Timothy didn't own a great deal, as far as I know. The flat he rented in London had been bombed and he hadn't much with him when he died. Just his rosary and the letters and a few photographs.'

'I remember letters arriving from him.' Nest was smiling a little now, remembering happier times. 'And occasionally presents for us.'

'Timothy had the gift of empathy,' said Mina. 'He grew to know us all and his presents were very distinctive and absolutely right. He was an explorer and a soldier and I think that he was doing secret service things in the war. He was Papa's friend and he came home with him one day and stayed for nearly a month. It was the summer before Timmie was born and one of the happiest summers I can remember.' She poured boiling water on her sachet of tea and waited for a moment. 'We all simply adored

360

him. It was Timothy who gave us our names.'

'How do you mean?' Nest looked startled, completely distracted now, as Mina had intended, from the horrors of that ten-year-old accident. 'Gave us our names? How could he?'

'Before Timmie was born we were called by shortened versions of our names. At least, by Papa we were. Mama tried to prevent it and she called us by our full names but Papa was trying to make a point. I didn't realize at the time but I see it now.' She hesitated a little, dropping the sachet into the rubbish bin, stirring the tea thoughtfully. 'There was a little streak of brutality in Papa. Oh, not a physical cruelty but a hardness, an insensitivity. He never considered how anyone else might feel and didn't particularly care if he hurt. He called us George, Bill, Henry and Jo. I can remember that day, you know, when Timothy arrived. We came up from the beach and Papa introduced us. He used to call us the bandar-log, jokingly. "Here are the bandar-log," he said, and then he told Timothy our names. "But why?" Timothy asked. He looked puzzled, almost distressed. "Such pretty children," he said. And Papa said, "It's the next best thing to having boys," or something like that, and I saw Mama's face. So did Timothy. It was as if she had been struck. He began to give us different names, kinder and more feminine.'

'And what did Papa say?' asked Nest, rapt as always by Mina's story-spinning.

'The thing was that he loved Timothy too.'

Mina came to sit at the table. 'Everyone did. He was irresistible: we all fought to sit next to him or hold his hand. We saved up our treasures to show him and did drawings for him. And he looked so handsome. Do you remember? Very tall and fair with a brown face. He looked as if he spent all his time in the open air and he was very tough and yet there was this kindness.' A little pause. 'You know about Papa's widow in London, of course,' – Nest nodded – 'but I was never sure how much Mama knew about her. Nothing in those early days, I'm sure, but I can see that he used her asthma attacks as an excuse to get us out of London whenever possible. Not that this was any punishment to her – she adored Ottercombe – but I wonder if she might have missed Papa, or adult company. She'd had several miscarriages and she was never very strong but Timothy warmed her into life. Does that sound silly? She flowered and grew in his company and he was a buffer between all of us and Papa's insensitivity. We were all in love with him, I think, not just Mama.'

Nest glanced up quickly from the rosary, which she was threading through her fingers.

'Not *just* Mama?' she repeated questioningly.

'They fell in love,' said Mina dreamily. 'I didn't understand then, I was too young, but I know it now – and, anyway, I read the letters.'

Nest was wide-eyed. 'Were they love letters?'

'Oh, yes. Once I'd read them everything fell into place. That amazing summer, before Timmie was born . . .'

'Wait a moment,' said Nest slowly. ' "Before Timmie was born." You used that phrase just now. That's it, isn't it? This is the secret that Georgie knows. You said once, "There are other secrets," and then you clammed up. I see it now. A boy after all those girls and Timmie was tall and fair – even his name! Oh, I know that Timothy was his godfather, but even so. I'm right, aren't I? Timothy was Timmie's father. Good grief, fancy Mama—'

'It's not *quite* right,' interrupted Mina gently. 'Although it's what other people believed too. The wretched Sneerwells were always hinting at it. But it wasn't quite like that although there is a tiny truth in it. Timothy relaxed Mama, he made her happy and confident, and I think it was because of that she was able to conceive. But Timmie was Papa's son. It wasn't until the following year that Timothy and Mama became lovers. It's you who are their child, Nest. You were the love-child, the baby he adored but couldn't acknowledge.'

She stopped speaking and the silence flowed into the kitchen, filling the spaces.

'*Timothy's* child?'

'She loved him so much.' Mina felt it was important that Nest should know this. 'It's odd how history repeats itself, isn't it? Mama and Timothy. Me and Tony. You and Connor.'

Nest looked at her and Mina saw that there was no horror or distress on her face, only a kind of awed amazement.

'Tell me everything,' she said. 'Start again and tell me everything you know.'

CHAPTER THIRTY-FOUR

Lyddie dropped her case on the bed and looked around the small room. There was only just enough space for the chest of drawers and a chair beside the bed.

'Thank goodness there's a hanging cupboard built into the wall,' Hannah said. 'It would have been impossible to cram a wardrobe in here – it's hardly more than a cupboard – but at least visitors haven't got to share with Tobes or Flora.'

'It's great.' Lyddie looked appreciatively at the vase on the chest, with its arrangement of autumn berries and beech leaves; the folded fluffy towels on top of which lay a new tablet of deliciously scented soap. 'Thanks, Han, it's brilliant.'

'Come down when you've got yourself sorted.'

She disappeared and Lyddie unpacked the little case, squeezed it between the foot of the bed and the wall, and set her spongebag beside the tilting-glass on the chest. Before she'd left Truro she'd packed the contents of her office – laptop, reference books, charts – into the car, given her four favourite and most useful editors her mobile telephone number and sorted out her winter clothes. She would have to go back, of course, but she needed to make this a significant break; a gesture that indicated that she was making a new beginning.

The Bosun had looked anxious as he'd watched his space in the back of the estate car being eroded but there had been enough room for him to jump onto his own bed, which was flanked by a box containing a week's rations and his dinner bowl. When she'd left London some of Lyddie's belongings had gone to Ottercombe and a few things to Oxford and, as she drove to Dorset, she felt a deep sense of relief that she had a second home to which she might flee. Roger and Teresa would have been willing to put her up for a while but the house in Iffley no longer seemed like home. Teresa had put her mark very strongly upon it and, anyway, neither of them were as dear to her as Mina and Nest, or Jack and Hannah.

As she drove to Dorset she wondered, as she often had in the past, why it should be that she'd been so much closer to Jack than she'd ever been to Roger.

'Roger doesn't know?' she'd asked Mina anxiously.

'No, no,' she'd answered soothingly. 'He was only three or four years old. No, Roger has no idea of it.'

She realized, on that journey from Truro, that it

would be easier to disclose Nest's revelation to Jack than to Roger, although she'd begun to see that it would be impossible to tell anyone at all. After all, it was not her secret to tell; there were too many people involved. However, there was more to it than that. Although she could imagine the comfort it would be to share it all with Jack, she knew that it was too early, that she needed time to digest it, to discover her own true feelings about her new identity, before she could open it up to other reactions. Nevertheless, it was an odd sensation to think of Roger as her half-brother as well as, bizarrely, her cousin.

Lyddie had shaken her head, confused but not particularly dismayed. It had always been difficult to get close to Roger; he was very self-contained and he had a waspish, sometimes cruel, tongue, which wounded although he'd smile and say, 'It was only a joke,' and appear contemptuous of her sensitivity. From her earliest memories Jack had been a warm, friendly child; caring and thoughtful for others' needs and always very funny. At least Jack was still her cousin, nothing changed that.

He was waiting for her when she'd finished unpacking and came down to the kitchen, sitting on the floor with his back against a cupboard, his legs stretched out in front of him, talking to the Bosun, who sat beside him gazing with a blend of amazement and affection into Jack's face. Lyddie burst out laughing and, immediately, the tiny knot of fear and pain in her gut began to unwind and dissolve.

'Caligula upset him,' Jack was explaining. 'Dogs are very sensitive people and Caligula was very rude. Wasn't he?' he asked the Bosun, who licked Jack's nose gratefully and beat his tail upon the floor.

'Quite mad,' observed Hannah resignedly. 'But don't let it worry you. I suppose you realize that the Bosun is going to cause havoc when the boys get back after supper. Bedtime is going to be a very interesting experience.'

'I've only ever been here in the holidays,' agreed Lyddie, 'or at half-term. Oh dear, we'll have to hide him in the garage.'

'You'll do no such thing,' replied Jack indignantly. 'His nerves are quite lacerated enough already. The boys will be delighted. I can't wait to see their faces. Has Hannah told you that we're going to get a dog?'

'No.' Lyddie smiled, delighted at the thought. 'Goodness, Tobes must be out of his mind at the prospect.'

'He doesn't know yet.' Hannah poured Lyddie's tea. 'We decided to wait until the holidays begin to give us a flying start with the house-training and I couldn't cope with the thought of his asking every five minutes how long it was to the end of term.'

Jack gave the Bosun a hug and climbed to his feet. 'You look very tired and rather fraught,' he studied Lyddie closely, 'and later on you shall have a very large drink. I'm not really allowed to start until the little darlings are all in bed. Not allowed to be drunk in charge of a dormitory.'

'But that doesn't mean that *we* can't,' said Hannah firmly, nodding encouragingly at Lyddie. 'Anyway, he's only here to say hello before he goes off to supervise prep and then supper. We can't wait for him.'

'Such unselfishness,' observed Jack to nobody in particular.

Lyddie chuckled. 'Sounds good to me. Never mind, Jack. You'll soon catch up.'

'I thought you might walk over to the school with me,' he said. 'Stretch your legs after the drive and give the Bosun a gallop.'

'I'd love to,' she said. 'That's a really good idea.'

'Let her finish her tea,' said Hannah. 'I'll sort our supper out. Oh, how wonderful not to have to preside over the children's tea!'

'Speak for yourself,' said Jack gloomily. 'Have you ever seen a hundred and fifty small boys between the ages of eight and twelve masticating in unison? No? Well, don't bother. It could put you off food for life.'

Later, as they paced across the smooth turf beneath the chestnut trees, where each autumn the boys gathered conkers, Lyddie tucked her hand in his arm and he smiled down at her.

'Poor old love,' he said. 'Want to talk?'

'I'll tell you something strange,' she said. 'I feel sick to my stomach when I think how Liam's behaved, and I still want him and feel that it's a tragic waste, but behind all that is a sense of . . . well, almost relief. Oh!' she cried in frustration.

'It's so *difficult* to explain this because it sounds as if I don't care and I do. My heart flips when I think of him, and I feel bereft, but the whole way through, Jack, there was this weird feeling of unreality. Can you understand that? Like I was on a holiday where none of the normal rules of daily life applied. Oh, I was working, and that was real enough, but it was odd, working at home all day and then going to The Place every evening and joshing with Joe. I told myself that thousands of people live like that, running hotels and pubs, but it still seemed unreal.'

'Was the difference,' suggested Jack, after a moment, 'that most other hoteliers and restaurateurs are in it together? It's a common interest. They start it together, have their own roles within it, and their whole lives are bound up in it and controlled by it. You told me that Liam never invited you to play any part in his work, that he actively discouraged it, in fact. You got on with the work you'd been trained for, alone at home, and then used The Place purely as a wine bar every evening. I often wondered how you would carry on like that, to be honest. Where did children fit into the scheme of things, for instance? You could have only become more and more isolated. The hours are so antisocial – or, at least, antifamily – that I wondered whether, at fifty, you'd still be working alone all day and then sitting in a wine bar every evening whilst Liam lived his own life on the side.'

She looked up at him. 'Did you suspect that Liam was cheating?'

He frowned, formulating his thoughts. 'I had this feeling that he was playing a part. You know, all that gliding around chatting to the punters and putting himself about in that particular way he has – a kind of cross between a high-class major-domo and Peter Stringfellow. Sorry.' He glanced down at her, pressing her hand with his arm. 'I'm not trying to be offensive, it's just that he *is* a bit of a poseur and a very attractive one, by the way. I can imagine that women really fell for him.'

'Well, *I* did.' Lyddie sighed. 'I think you're absolutely right. There was no chance of real family life, no weekends, no holidays. Perhaps that's why, in this very odd way, it's almost a relief. Not that it hurts less.'

'No, but it gives you something to work towards,' said Jack. 'That it was, really, a mistake, I mean. You can hang on to that. I have to say that I did wonder if it was a bit quick after James.'

'I'm beginning to lose my confidence,' said Lyddie. ' "To lose one man might be regarded as a mistake", et cetera.'

'Absolute rubbish,' he said. 'What about third time lucky? I shall insist on vetting the next candidate.'

'So you don't think it's wrong of me to give up on marriage to Liam?' She was surprised at how important his answer was.

'It sounds as if you hadn't much option,' he replied. 'You've offered him a way forward and he's rejected it. I can't think what else you *could* do.'

'You don't think I should just go along with it?'

'No, I bloody don't,' he said forcibly. 'Good God, Lyddie! Don't be daft. However much you love him, nobody could expect you to passively accept such a role. He's put his cards on the table and you have to take it or leave it. Well, you're leaving it.'

She smiled, hugging his arm. 'Thanks, Jack.'

'I'm not sure why I have your gratitude but you're welcome. Will you be OK with the Aunts for a bit?'

'I think so. At least I shall be able to work. I'm glad now that I didn't make Roger sell the house all those years ago so that I could have my share. He couldn't have afforded, back then, to buy me out. Now he can and it will be very useful. It's been like a nest-egg, all this time.'

'You could go back to London, to your old job, or one like it.'

'I have thought about it.' She hesitated. 'I need time to think it through. I can do that at Ottercombe.'

'Nowhere better to recuperate than with those two old darlings,' he said affectionately. 'Look, if you take the way through the shrubbery it'll take you round the outbuildings, back onto the path home, and it'll give the Bosun a good run. Will you be OK?'

'Of course I will. Bless you, Jack, you're such a comfort.'

He smiled down at her. 'You're doing the right thing,' he told her. 'Hang on to that. See you later. We'll have more speaks this evening.'

She watched his tall figure walk with long strides towards the sprawling Georgian building, saw the small boys toiling in from the rugby pitch waving to him, calling to him, and felt a huge love for him.

'Come on,' she said to the Bosun. 'You can't go with him but he'll be back later' – and she turned away, her hands in her pockets, her heart eased from some of its pain.

CHAPTER THIRTY-FIVE

Nest was sitting by the fire in the drawing-room. It was a bleak and dismal November afternoon, a raw wind blowing the drizzle against the windows, and it was good to turn one's back on it and stare instead at the comforting flicker of the flames. The dogs and Mina had gone down to the beach, despite the weather, and Georgie, tired after a morning's shopping in Barnstaple, had gone upstairs to rest. It was good to be alone in this peaceful room, freed finally from the weight of the secret that had lain on her heart for more than thirty years; alone to think about all the things Mina had told her. Was it simply Mina's skill at story-spinning that had enabled her to listen so calmly and, if not immediately accept this new startling evidence, at least be able to begin to come to terms with it without anger or fear? Was this how Lyddie might feel? Had Mina woven her spell there too? Never had Nest been so grateful for Mina's gift. She'd spun the events of the past

into a rich tapestry, threading each strand carefully together so that the characters emerged,
vivid and exciting against the bright, familiar
background of the cleave and sea or moving
within the old house as if it might be yesterday.

Nest looked down at the things she held in her
lap: some photographs; an Easter card; the rosary.
These were the only objects left behind by her
father, except, of course, for his letters, which had
been returned with these other effects. There
had not been many letters between the two of
them, twenty perhaps in all. She'd read them
chronologically, remembering as she did so Mama
opening his letters at the breakfast table: the
flimsy sheets rustling as she turned them, folding
them away in the envelope, and the way her hand
had strayed to touch it as if reassuring herself that
it really existed. Given their circumstances, the
letters were almost shockingly indiscreet:

'Oh, my darling,' she'd write. 'How can I bear
this endless separation . . . ?' and his replies,
which always began 'My dearest love,' and covered
sheet after sheet with the outpourings of his love.

'I am expecting your child and I feel nothing
but the deepest joy. Oh, why am I not afraid? I am
so happy . . .'

There had been no question that she should
leave Ambrose who, as luck would have it, arrived
at Ottercombe a few weeks after Timothy's visit so
that there was never any doubt in his mind but
that this was his own child. It was clear that Lydia,
even for Timothy, would never have contemplated

374

leaving her children and equally clear that he had never demanded it of her:

> . . . for what kind of life could I offer you, my heart's love, which could give you the stability and security required for you and your beloved children. How can we take our joy at their expense? They are very dear to me and, if we harmed them in any way, our love would be dust and ashes . . .

She answered him.

> . . . to know that this is your child gives me the greatest happiness, and I have your namesake too, your godson. When I look at Timmie I remember how we first met and you stood in the hall saying, 'I apologize for arriving un-announced,' and I knew that I would fall in love with you . . .

Nest had been shocked by the naïvety and the simplicity of these letters: they were like two children standing in awe before this amazing gift of their love. At first, Nest had read avidly, gulping the words down hungrily as she relearned her own history; later, though, she'd been ashamed.

'I feel as if I've spied on them,' she'd said to Mina. 'It doesn't seem fair, somehow. They were so . . . so *innocent*, if you see what I mean.'

'Oh, I know exactly what you mean,' she'd agreed ruefully. 'I felt it too, but when Mama died I didn't know what should be done with them and by then, you see, I'd begun to guess the truth. Towards the end she began to talk about him, to believe that he was here with her, and it wasn't difficult to work out certain things. It felt wrong to destroy the letters without quite knowing if I had the right. In the end I read them and decided that I should keep them, just in case.'

'I'm so glad you did,' said Nest fervently. 'The odd thing is that, although I feel this kind of disloyalty, I also feel strangely proud to have been the product of such love. Gosh! That sounds a bit naff, doesn't it . . . ?'

'No, it doesn't,' Mina said quickly. 'It doesn't at all. There isn't one of us who wouldn't have been thrilled to have Timothy as our father. You *should* be proud.'

'I wish,' Nest had said, after a moment, 'that Lyddie could feel the smallest bit of that in her position. And not for any reason except that it would help her, as it's helping me, to come to terms with it, to accept it.'

'I think you'll find that those thirty-odd years of love and friendship which you have given Lyddie will earn much more than her acceptance. It makes it easier too that Henrietta has been dead for over ten years. Perhaps that sounds brutal but it will be less complicated to adjust with her memories of Henrietta at a distance and it's the love which counts in the end. Lyddie hasn't got to choose or worry about disloyalty; she simply has to continue to allow herself to receive your love.'

Listening to the wind casting handfuls of cold rain against the window, Nest looked again at the treasures she held. First, a photograph of Lydia and Timothy with seven-year-old Nest standing between them: one sandalled foot resting upon the other, with a rag-doll clasped in her arms, she watched the person behind the camera, her face eagerly intent; Timothy's hand was placed lightly about Lydia's shoulder so that she leaned slightly towards him, her hand on Nest's head. He was laughing, encouraging the photographer, whilst Lydia looked at Timothy, her face alight with love. On the back of the photograph in faded ink was scrawled, '1941. Lydia and Timothy with Nest at Ottercombe.'

'I probably took it,' Mina had said. 'Timothy certainly had a camera and he liked to take photographs. It was clever of them to manage it, though, without any of the rest of us being in it. My guess is that the others had probably been sent on ahead to the beach so that he and Mama could snatch the opportunity. You've seen all the others we've got with variations of us all with them. This is the only one I've ever seen with just the three of you.'

Nest stared down at it, willing herself to remember the occasion. Words from one of the letters slipped into her mind:

She's such a darling baby only, oh dear, Ambrose insists that she is to be called Ernestina!!! At one time he wanted Timmie to be named Ernest, after his father, and then, to my delight, decided that he should be named for you. But now he stands firm. Such a ponderous name for such a pretty, tiny scrap of humanity . . .

Nest tried to bring her father to mind but it was very difficult; he'd been such a distant figure, rarely at Ottercombe even after the war, and his death had occurred before she was fifteen. Yet she could still recall the presence of Timothy; that aura of excitement that clung to him, the security he represented.

'But I can't have been more than seven or eight when he died,' she'd said to Mina. 'It's odd, isn't it?'

'You can remember the atmosphere, I expect.' Mina had smiled reminiscently. 'When Timothy was here it was like Christmas, Easter and birthdays rolled into one. He was special.'

'Like Timmie. Or Jack?' suggested Nest.

'I've often wondered how much Mama's meeting Timothy, her thinking about him through that pregnancy when she was here alone with us, might have affected the child she was carrying. I know it sounds peculiar but I suppose it's possible that Timmie was *shaped* by their love in some way, which in turn passed on to Jack. To be fair, it would have been easy to believe that Timmie was their child but you only have to read the letters to see that they weren't lovers until the following year.'

Now, alone in the quiet drawing-room, Nest

passed her fingers gently over the battered photograph and looked at the second one: a portrait of Lydia, taken by the same camera and clearly by Timothy himself. Her tender look of adoration could only have been called up by him: beautiful, wistful, her lips curving into a smile. On the back was written: 'Lydia – 1934.' She would have been thirty-five years old. The last photograph was one with which Nest was familiar: Lydia sitting on a chair just outside the french window, her children gathered about her. She held the baby Nest on her lap, whilst Henrietta and Josie sat cross-legged on the ground at her feet. Timmie stood by her knee, Mina just behind him with her hands on his shoulders, and Georgie stood at Lydia's right, rather as if she presided over the little group. Nest stared intently at each face. Lydia smiled out peacefully, one hand gently cradling the baby's head, shielding it a little from the sun. Endearingly gap-toothed, startlingly alike, Henrietta and Josie grinned cheerfully, the small event engendering an unusual camaraderie. Timmie's look was slightly anxious, a knitted soldier held up – rather tentatively – as though he hoped that it too would be recorded for posterity. Mina's smile was warm, happy, clearly at ease; a contrast to Georgie's almost censorious expression. On the back was written, 'Ottercombe, 1936.'

Strangely moved, sighing a little, Nest placed the photographs together and looked at the Easter card. Beneath a simple colourwash of the empty Cross, bathed in sunshine, were the words: 'He is risen.' Inside Lydia had written: 'With love from us all at Ottercombe', and each of them had signed it. Georgie's writing was clear and careful, Mina's looping and generous, whilst the two younger girls' names were written in best school copperplate. Timmie had printed his name in shaky capital letters, twice as large as any of the others, and it was clear that Lydia had held Nest's fist on the pencil to so as to make her distinctive contribution. Opposite the names and the greeting was a printed verse:

> The tumult and the shouting dies;
> The Captains and the Kings depart:
> Still stands Thine ancient sacrifice,
> An humble and a contrite heart.
> Lord God of Hosts, be with us yet,
> Lest we forget – lest we forget!

She wondered what significance these words from Kipling's 'Recessional' had had for her father, and why he'd carried them, or was it simply that the card carried the love of all of his 'family' within it? As she pondered this, a voice spoke in her ear.

'What have you got?'

It was several seconds before Nest could control the violent shock and the crashing of her heart, so as to look up calmly at Georgie, trying to shield her treasures from that interested stare as she slipped them into the tapestry bag that held her spectacles and book.

'Nothing much.' She tried to keep her voice neutral. 'I didn't hear you come in.'

Georgie edged past Nest's chair and sat down at the end of the sofa.

'I couldn't sleep,' she said. Her gaze slid away from Nest towards the fire. 'The wind is getting up.'

'Mina should be home soon.' Nest took some deep, calming breaths and then, quite suddenly, she relaxed. She'd forgotten that Georgie had no power to harm her now.

'I think you can be quite certain,' Mina had said, when she'd given Nest the letters, 'that Georgie knows nothing about you and Connor and so has no idea about Lyddie. *This* is the secret Georgie knows. She's read them too.' She'd given a great gasp of relief. 'Po-po-po. How wonderful to have everything in the open at last.'

'Not quite everything. You're not suggesting that I should tell Lyddie,' Nest had looked anxiously at her sister, 'not on top of everything else . . . ?'

'No, no.' Mina had shaken her head. 'At least, not yet. Maybe the day will come for that, you must wait and see, but at least we can both relax a little now. It's you that Georgie associates with her secret, not Lyddie.'

Now, Nest looked at Georgie with compassion; her teeth were drawn, her reign of power was over.

'Do you remember Timothy?' she asked quite naturally.

Georgie looked at her slyly and started to

perform that strange bridling, shrugging movement, a little smile on her lips, her eyes sharp.

Nest thought: She's like a child who knows she has done something wrong, yet justifies it with this kind of 'see if I care' defiance.

'I know a secret,' Georgie said – and, from nowhere, Nest was caught up in a memory of a hot summer's afternoon: she and Timmie conducting a toys' tea-party under the trees on the lawn. Georgie was towering over the table and Timmie was frightened: she could feel his fear, running out through his hot hand into her own. Even when Mina appeared she could not restore the harmony; the happy atmosphere and sunny afternoon were scarred with the ugly stains of anger and cross voices and she, Nest, wept frightened tears wrung out of impotent helplessness and a sense of destruction: the foreshadowing of the transience of childhood and the loss of innocence.

Now, more than sixty years later, she leaned forward and touched Georgie's arm gently.

'So do I,' she said.

CHAPTER THIRTY-SIX

Walking back from the sea, Mina was experiencing an unusual blend of light-headedness and light-heartedness. The last few weeks, ever since Georgie's arrival, had taken their toll – dizzy spells and a terrible exhaustion – in a way that nursing Lydia and caring for Nest had never done. It was odd that such mental stress should be so much more deeply wearing than sustained physical effort. Towards the end, Lydia had become very demanding in terms of sheet washing and running up and down the stairs dozens of times a day; she'd required carefully planned meals and a great deal of company yet she'd rarely been fretful, never critical. She'd loved to have Mina with her – 'Oh good, you've brought your coffee up too, we can have it together' – and she'd always loved Mina to read aloud to her. 'Now, what is it this evening? Oh, yes, of course, *Twilight on the Floods*. Now, where had we got to?' The television had tended to make her anxious, finding it difficult sometimes to follow accents, or any fast-moving action, although she'd adored any kind of costume drama and refused to miss a second of Wimbledon.

Mina had been grateful for any respite that gave her the opportunity to rest, although Lydia needed to know that she was somewhere near at hand. She'd always been delighted to see her grandchildren, especially happy when they were all at Ottercombe together, and she'd written regularly and at length to Josie's boys in America, showing their photographs proudly to anyone who might spare the time to look at them. Each winter her asthma attacks and bronchial infections had grown a little worse, yet she'd clung to life with surprising tenacity. Mina had held her frail frame whilst she inhaled friar's balsam, a towel over her head and the bowl, and they'd laughed together, even then, about the indignities of old age. She'd been nearly eighty when a series of strokes put an end to her patient suffering.

Mina pulled up the hood of her jacket against the rain, hunching against the wind. Great beeches, some still retaining their tiny hoard of copper, groaned restlessly above her head whilst at their feet, amongst thick bare roots, mallards rested from the hurly-burly of the rushing water. The dogs scampered amongst the reeds and up the steep sides of the cleave, following the tracks of badger and deer, and when she called to them the wind caught her voice and tossed it lightly away.

She walked on, thinking of Lyddie and Nest,

praying that all would be well between them, remembering how Nest had worked to hide the pain of watching her daughter being loved and cherished by her sister whilst she was unable to play any part other than that of a fond aunt.

'Sometimes,' Nest had told her privately, desperately, 'I wonder if it would be better if I never saw her at all. I can't explain the longing to seize her and hold her and then, oh God! when Henrietta gives her to me I'm so afraid of breaking down, of simply getting up and running away with her, that I hardly dare think about it and I sit like a dummy, so busy keeping my feelings under control that it's a complete waste.'

'I have to say, Henrietta is being very good,' Mina had admitted. 'She had all those miscarriages so she knows a little of what you feel, but I agree that having the contact must be agonizing.'

'I've thought of going right away, perhaps abroad for a while, but Miss Ayres was so good about keeping my post available and being so broad-minded that I feel it would be terribly ungrateful. I used to ache for Connor,' she'd said, 'and now I ache for Lyddie.'

Mina had put an arm about her, hugging her. '*Used* to ache for Connor?'

'Yes.' Nest had looked at her, distracted for a moment. 'It's odd, isn't it? Once Lyddie was born it was as if a curtain came down on all that. I felt quite cold, detached. Perhaps it was some kind of instinctive, merciful self-preservation. I think I'd go mad if I still felt the same way about him. Even when I see him with Lyddie I feel nothing but a sense of relief that he loves her so much. It makes me sure that I did the right thing – given that I couldn't keep her.'

Pausing to pick up some twigs and small branches, brought down by the gales and useful for kindling, Mina sighed with relief as she revelled in this new sense of freedom from the weight of secrets. Standing up suddenly, she felt quite light-headed again, and had to put her hand against a mossy tree-trunk to steady herself.

'Isn't it odd,' Nest had cried almost indignantly, once she'd read the letters, 'that Mama should have become pregnant by Timothy and yet was so horrified when it happened to me? So determined that I couldn't keep my baby, behaving as if it were all so shaming.'

'I think you have to take several things into consideration,' Mina had answered carefully. 'First, and this is quite important, was the passage of time between your pregnancy and hers. It's amazing how people forget, how, looking back, it seems that it was quite different for them. Distance lends enchantment to the view. There was a deeply romantic element which she couldn't see in your case. If you'd been in a long-term relationship, had been madly in love, Mama might have reacted more understandingly. As it was, it was necessary to play that side of it down and you were obliged to make it all sound rather chancy. Poor Nest, you were bound by a loyalty which we couldn't explain to her. Second, and even more importantly, she was a married woman with the protection and status of a husband.'

'Even so,' Nest had said, rather sadly, 'I think she might have been a bit less Victorian about it, given the circumstances.'

'I think she was utterly true to her Victorian upbringing, double standards and hypocrisy.' Mina had tried to make her laugh. 'And you must admit that, once it was settled that Henrietta should take the baby, she couldn't have been sweeter.'

'It's OK,' Nest had grinned at her, 'I'm not going to go all hurt at this late stage, it's just all so incredible. I can't see myself breaking this one to Lyddie for a very long time, if at all. I think she's got enough on her plate.'

'Well, I agree with that but it gives you an even stronger bond, doesn't it? And one day, who knows, you might be able to share it with her.'

'Possibly. Our next meeting is going to be quite nerve-racking. I keep imagining that her generosity is too good to be true, as if she hasn't really taken it in, and when she does . . .'

'Of course she's taken it in. That's nonsense. I think she'll have much more difficulty coming to terms with Liam's defection.'

'I wonder what she'll do.' Nest had looked sombre. 'Do you think she'll go back to London?'

'Back to her old job?' Mina had shaken her head. 'I simply don't know. I can't imagine what would happen to the Bosun if she does. Jack might have him. They're hoping to have a puppy. Or we could have him here.'

'Captain Cat might not like that.'

'Captain Cat might have to lump it!'

They'd chuckled together and now, as Mina opened the kitchen door and she and the dogs went inside, she paused to give him a pat as if to make up for her callousness. She sent them to their beds to dry off a little, put the kettle on the hotplate and went through to the drawing-room. Nest was nowhere to be seen but Georgie was sitting at the end of the sofa, slumped a little, her head dropping forward on to her chest. There was a stillness about her, an immobility, and when Mina spoke her name she did not move. Heart in mouth, Mina went forward and bent over her.

'Georgie,' she said huskily – and swallowed in a suddenly dry throat. 'Georgie?'

Her sister opened an eye and looked at her.

'Where on earth have you been?' she asked grumpily. 'It must be long past tea-time.'

Mina straightened up and took a deep breath, controlling an urge to smack her hard.

'The kettle's on,' she said. 'It won't be long.'

Back in the kitchen she found that her hands were trembling as she lifted up the teapot.

'Only one more week,' she told herself grimly – and began to make the tea.

From: Mina
To: Elyot

. . . although I have to say that afterwards I simply had to laugh. Probably nervous hysteria.

Goodness, what a time it's been. Nest came into the kitchen and wondered what on earth was going on, the kettle boiling its head off and me sitting weeping with laughter. I have to say that for one terrible moment I thought Georgie was dead and, to be honest, I think my reaction was pure relief. Nest made the tea in the end and when we got back to the sitting-room Georgie was sitting up, almost aggressively perky, although I believe that she is beginning another stage of deterioration.

I shall be glad to be free of the responsibility – which sounds terrible because she is my sister – but I am getting too old for all these alarums and excursions. Lyddie will be back soon and poor Nest is very fidgety but it will be a great treat to have her with us until she's decided what she is going to do. Her money from the house near Oxford could set her up in some small flat – but where? I think that, legally, she's entitled to something from the house in Truro and even from the business but I guess that both are in thrall to the bank and Lyddie is not the kind to demand an eye for an eye. She can stay here for as long as she likes, of course . . .

From: Elyot
To: Mina

Take care of yourself, old friend. You deserve a good long rest. I am very glad to have William here to do the driving for me, my confidence is low at present and it's a great relief. Make certain that Lyddie has a good lawyer – not that it's any of my business . . .

CHAPTER THIRTY-SEVEN

'I'm not sure that it's been good for me being with you two,' Lyddie said, as she and Hannah drove into Dorchester to do some shopping. 'You are so right together. It points up everything I've lost.'

'Are you sure?' asked Hannah. 'I mean, did you actually have it in the first place with Liam? That absolute rightness?'

Lyddie stared out through the windscreen at the rain drifting across the gently rounded hills.

'I suppose not,' she said at last. 'Not ever quite like you and Jack – but there were moments . . .'

'Of course there were,' said Hannah remorsefully. 'Sorry. I'm really not trying to belittle what you had. It would be utterly wrong to pretend that Liam is some kind of monster and you were never happy with him. So many people do that, have you noticed? They convince themselves that things were never right and they deny all the happy times.'

'I think that's more the case with the partner that has decided to go rather than with the one who's been left,' said Lyddie thoughtfully. 'It seems necessary for the one who's leaving to justify their actions to themselves – and to others – and so it becomes almost essential to persuade everyone that there were all kinds of problems. It's silly, really, although perfectly understandable.'

'It *is* silly,' agreed Hannah, turning the car from the narrow lane into a wider road, 'because all your friends generally know exactly how it's been and it's impossible to make them believe it. Maybe it's easier to kid yourself. On the other hand, there are the cases where the reverse applies. You watch friends being made thoroughly miserable and you wish the scales would drop from their eyes and they'd have the courage to get up and go.'

'Is that what you thought about me?' asked Lyddie rather sadly.

'No, love, of course not.' Hannah put out her hand briefly and clasped Lyddie's folded ones. 'You *were* happy. The thing is, it's impossible to judge who might be right for someone you love. I have friends who are deliriously happy with people who would bore me rigid or drive me mad in ten minutes.'

'So what did you really think about Liam?'

There was a short silence.

'Truth?' asked Hannah cautiously.

'Truth,' agreed Lyddie firmly.

'When I first met him I thought, well, lucky old Lyddie! He is, let's face it, a very attractive man, but, after a bit, I began to sense that there was something driving him along a one-way track and that nothing and nobody was going to get in the way of his objective. I was worried that he'd find marriage too demanding and that you'd be abandoned at some wayside station. For instance, I simply couldn't imagine Liam as a father, which would have been fine except that I knew that children were definitely on your agenda, and, anyway, it seemed such an odd way for you to live. You know what I mean? Spending all day working and then going to the wine bar. There was no privacy, no weekends or evenings for you to be yourselves. I worried about that.'

'But Liam himself?'

'Well, I feel this tormented restlessness about him. He's vital, very alive, but there's something desperate about it. Like he's watching himself perform, acting a part and, underneath it all, a terrible obsession. As long as you're prepared to sacrifice yourself to it you'll be fine. Step out of line and you'll be dumped. I think that in another age he might have conquered worlds, or gone with Scott to the Antarctic, but there again . . .' She paused and Lyddie looked at her, sitting straight, her hands lightly on the wheel, her brow furrowed in thought.

'But there again?' Lyddie prompted.

Hannah bit her lip. 'I was going to be brutal,' she said anxiously.

'Well, go on. I expect I can take it.'

'I was going to say – but there again perhaps not, because there's something *little* about Liam. I suspect that those types whose natural position is leading, conquering, discovering, often have a sexual appetite to match.' She shrugged. 'Not always, of course, but I can see that it might be all of a piece. A kind of ruthlessness which Liam has certainly displayed. He has charisma but at the same time I just have this feeling that he will only ever be a big frog in a small pond.' She gave a quick sideways glance. 'Have I upset you?'

'No,' replied Lyddie, remembering Liam's face when she'd spoken about a chain of wine bars: how he'd seen the vision and then instinctively drawn back from it. 'Well, only my pride a bit. You feel a twit, don't you, when you've been taken in?'

'Oh, hell!' exclaimed Hannah. 'Look, anyone might have been taken in: he's a gorgeous-looking chap. Who wouldn't have been knocked sideways? *I* was. It was only over a period of time that I began to . . . *suspect* him.'

'It's a relief, really,' said Lyddie. 'It makes me feel more sure that I'm doing the right thing. It's not easy, walking away from a marriage.'

'But I thought he was doing the walking? He's the one making the rules. And the rules are not fair ones, Lyddie. You can't accept a situation like this where one partner says, "I must have the freedom to do exactly as I please no matter how it hurts or humiliates you", honestly you can't. Marriage or not. Well,' she shrugged again, 'only if you can't live without him.' Another anxious glance. 'Do you feel that might be the case?'

Lyddie took a deep breath. 'Just occasionally,'

she admitted, 'I need him so much I almost feel tempted but I only have to think of Rosie or walking into The Place and I know I couldn't do it. I'm going to have to manage somehow.'

'Might you go back to London?'

'I simply don't know. I can't see it somehow; it's like starting again. Except that I'm not twenty-two any more and my friends mostly have partners or are married.' She shook her head and tried for a lighter note. 'Anyway, what would I do with the Bosun?'

'You know that needn't be a problem if you really wanted to do it.'

Lyddie smiled. 'Bless you. I wish I knew what was right.'

'Could you afford to live, doing what you do now?'

'Just about – as long as I get my money from the house and buy my own place, however small. Without rent or a mortgage I might just get by.'

'Will Liam sell the house in Truro? You should get something from that, surely?'

'It's heavily mortgaged already and I don't want to be demanding about this. He's got enough financial problems as it is.'

Hannah raised her eyebrows but said nothing for a moment.

'Don't make any important decisions until after Christmas,' she suggested presently. 'We'll come down to Ottercombe to see you all and have some fun and you could come to us for the New Year. What do you think?'

Lyddie gratefully accepted this offering as a breathing space and the talk turned to lighter subjects.

CHAPTER THIRTY-EIGHT

It was several days later before Mina wrote again to Elyot.

From: Mina
To: Elyot

And so the day is nearly upon us. It seems like several light years since I told you that Georgie would be arriving – and now it's all over. We've all survived it and, although her presence has triggered off so many memories and prised open some of Pandora's boxes, I can honestly say that I think, on the whole, it has been for the good. Nest looks much better – more content, younger – and she and Lyddie seem to be settling down to a new acceptance of their relationship, which is strongly underpinned by the affection they've always shared. For myself, I have been forced to come to terms with a foolish decision I took as a young girl and which has been buried ever since.

We've confronted these things together, Nest and I, and we've drawn even closer because of it. I wish I could tell you much more, dear Elyot, but these are not just **my** secrets and already you know so much of what goes on here at Ottercombe. I still feel certain that one day you will come here to see us all.

As for Georgie, well, now that her departure is at hand I feel unusually fond of her! More seriously, much though I feel saddened by the thought of her in a home I know that we couldn't keep her here. Even in these few weeks I've seen a deterioration and I simply couldn't be responsible for some disaster. Nest must be my first responsibility but there are moments – long, hard moments – when I feel very badly at the thought of letting Georgie go. I know that Helena will do everything that is proper – that sounds so cold, doesn't it? – but I also have the feeling that very soon she will not really know quite where she is or whether it matters. If that sounds as if I am trying to comfort myself, well, there might be an element of truth in it but I really do believe that she is losing her grasp on what is happening. Her 'foggy' moments are occurring more often and lasting for longer periods and she is a continual worry to me as to where she is and what she is up to.

Lyddie seems to be coping remarkably well although I suspect she misses Liam very much. She works very hard, which occupies her mind and saves her from too much brooding, but if you come upon her unawares you catch a glimpse of the misery she feels deep down. The dogs are learning to live together too. My darling old Polly Garter spends most of her time asleep but Nogood Boyo is thoroughly enjoying this new friend and clearly likes having some young blood about the place. He and the Bosun have some splendid games together and Boyo is learning to ignore his father's grumpiness and make his own decisions. He's developing a rather cocky swagger – it's definitely a case of 'me and my friend Bosun' – whilst the Bosun is also gaining in confidence and will actually come into a room where Captain Cat is in possession, although he still looks distinctly nervous and stays as far away from him as possible!

So how are things with you? Lavinia? William? All well, I hope?

From: Elyot
To: Mina

I can't tell you how deeply glad I am to receive your sitrep. I can well imagine how your feelings must war together regarding Georgie. Knowing you, my dear old friend, I feel you would be happier if you could gather her in beneath your capacious and comforting wing but you are right to resist it. I know to my cost that this wretched dementia creeps stealthily on, sometimes shuffling, sometimes sprinting, and you never know what might happen from one day to the next. Situated where you are – and how you are – you simply can't afford to take the responsibility. If something were to go badly wrong you'd never forgive yourself.

And if you detect a note of serious anxiety – even panic? – in my 'voice' then you are quite right. Quite suddenly, yesterday, Lavinia took a downward turn, which took the form of not knowing who I was, screaming in true terror when I approached her, fighting me. She tried to run away from me, wrenching at the front door in an attempt to open it, fell badly and has had to be taken to the cottage hospital. She has broken her wrist and sprained an ankle and is in an altogether wretched condition. As you know, this lack of recognition has happened before but it has been possible to calm her down eventually. This truly violent reaction was terrifying for both of us – unfortunately William was out shopping – and I cannot forget her expression of fear as she stared at me nor her pitiable state once she'd fallen.

I can't tell you how glad I am to have William with me now. Stay in touch.

From: Mina
To: Elyot

My dear Elyot
I was shocked to read your account of poor

Lavinia's lapse and her accident. What a devilish thing this is, isn't it, eating away at the mind, stealing away memory and rationality? I am so pleased that you have William at hand, and how good of you, at such a time, to share your experience so as to strengthen my own hesitant decision. You are right in suggesting that my instinct is to keep Georgie with me but I see now that it would be wrong to consider it – even if Helena and Rupert were to allow it, which is very unlikely.

But never mind me! My thoughts are so much with you. Is there anything I can do?

From: Elyot
To: Mina

Only be there to listen and to make me feel that I have a very good friend close at hand. I'm well aware that this accident has brought us to a new point from which there is no going back and made me face the fact that we couldn't have continued to jog along as we were. Even that state, now that Lavinia is settled in the hospital, seems desirable compared to this loneliness. I realize now that I was simply going from day to day refusing to look beyond the next meal or to face the future.

Thank God for William.

From: Mina
To: Elyot

Of **course** I am here – you know that. Oh, my very dear friend, how I feel for you. Of course you must be missing Lavinia terribly and I quite understand that you'd rather have gone on as you were with her at home with you. It is even harder when you've been depended on so much. Suddenly everything seems so pointless, a terrible emptiness turns the world grey, and life stretches futilely ahead. And I'm supposed to be comforting you!!! What can I say?

From: Elyot
To: Mina

Your very real understanding is a thousand times more valuable than meaningless banalities. As usual you have given me comfort and made me feel that I am not isolated. How terribly important this is and, though William is such a comfort, at these times we need those who have suffered in a like manner. Dear Mina, I cannot write any more tonight except to say how very grateful I am to you.

God bless you and goodnight.

From: Mina
To: Elyot

I know you won't read this tonight, and quite right, too. You need rest. I couldn't go to bed, however, without reminding you that we are here if you need us; if you think that a trip to Ottercombe might do you and William some good. I know once you told me that you live near Taunton so it's not too far.

Anyway! It might be much too early to think of such a thing and I'm sure you're spending a great deal of time with Lavinia at the hospital but the invitation is there.

Goodnight, dear Elyot.

CHAPTER THIRTY-NINE

Helena arrived late in the morning to fetch her mother; for the other three, waiting for her, the hours since breakfast had stretched interminably.

'It's not that I want to see the back of her,' Mina had assured Nest despairingly, 'it's simply that she looks so wretched. I feel like a traitor.'

'I know. I feel exactly the same but what can we do? You know that you couldn't possibly shoulder the responsibility of looking after her indefinitely.'

Lyddie watched them anxiously. She'd come down from her study to make herself some coffee and was distracted by their evident distress.

'Doesn't she want to go?' she asked.

They turned towards her, ready to share their fears with her.

'It's simply that she won't know anyone at the home and it will be so strange for her,' said Mina, her hands winding unconsciously together. 'To be honest, I don't quite know how much she knows.

I simply feel this sense of reproach emanating from her, as if she feels that this is her home and we're throwing her out. Being here has taken her – well, all of us – so far back into the past that I'm not sure she can remember what happened before she was here.'

'I'm sure she can,' said Lyddie gently. 'After all, she doesn't question who Helena is, does she? Or that she has some kind of right to fetch her?'

'No,' agreed Mina, after a moment. 'No, that's absolutely true, she doesn't. But I still feel that there's been some change.'

Nest bit her lip. She had a horrid feeling that the change had followed the conversation in the sitting-room when Georgie had said, 'I know a secret,' and Nest had responded, 'So do I.' After that brief exchange Nest had watched an expression of surprise, confusion and finally a kind of despair pass over her sister's face. The jigging of the shoulders and the sly smile, the tapping foot and inward glee had died away and she'd drooped, slumping into the corner of the sofa. She'd refused to answer or talk to Nest, turning her head from her so that, after a while, Nest had gone away. Yet she'd felt guilty that in confronting Georgie at last, she'd removed her power, defused the vital will to control.

For the remaining days she'd continued in that dull, listless mood; shuffling about, sitting in corners, unresponsive. When Mina told her that Helena would be coming to take her home – her lips stumbling at the word – Georgie had stared at her rather vacantly but had been quite ready to go with her upstairs to start the packing.

'The point is,' Lyddie was saying, 'that this is progressive. Anything might happen and you're simply not equipped for it here. She could wander off anywhere; up on the moor or down to the beach. You can't be her gaoler, Aunt Mina. She'll be very well looked after and probably love being with all the other people. We'll go and visit her. Now I'm on the insurance of the camper I'll drive you and Nest up and we'll stay in a hotel somewhere. It'll be fun.'

Mina stared at her, almost weak with gratitude. Whilst she would have vehemently denied any suggestion that she was not perfectly strong enough to care for Nest or to run Ottercombe, nevertheless this infusion of youth and energy was the most tremendous relief. The last few weeks had drained her more than she had realized and Lyddie's strong, practical support was like a tonic. She knew a sudden foolish desire to burst into tears.

'It sounds . . . wonderful.' She sat down dizzily, suddenly, on a kitchen chair and Nest wheeled over to sit beside her whilst Lyddie made the coffee.

'Rather good for you to be chauffeur-driven after all these years.' Nest was smiling at her. 'Just think. You'll be able to see things again which you can't when you're doing the driving. You know, all those little sudden glimpses of the moor or the sea when I shout, "Oh, look" – and you can't because we're going round a bend or something.'

'I was wondering . . .' But before Lyddie could tell them her idea the door was pushed open and Georgie came in. She looked round at each of them almost suspiciously and, automatically, Mina began to struggle to her feet but Lyddie spoke first and Mina sank back gratefully.

'Perfect timing, Aunt Georgie,' she said cheerfully. 'I'm making some coffee and I was just about to come and find you.'

Georgie frowned, looking round the kitchen, not answering, and Mina's spirits sank. Nest wheeled forward touching Mina lightly, comfortingly, on the arm as she passed.

'Are you looking for something?' she asked gently.

Georgie stared at her distrustfully, still with that tiny frown creasing her brows, and turned away to peer along the dresser shelves. Her hands fumbled over the surface, her steps were short, uncertain, and the other three watched in a kind of breathless, unmoving silence.

'Aaahhh . . .' She let out a sound that was little more than a long breath of relief.

'Have you found it?' Nest tried to keep her voice light, interested.

Georgie looked at her guardedly for several moments before opening her hand to show what it held. It was Timmie's little car, washed and scoured by a thousand tides, and Nest – for one terrible moment – wanted to seize it from her.

'I took it from him before,' Georgie said confidingly. 'He is Papa's favourite but I am his first-born. I shall hide it.' Her eyes travelled over Nest – puzzled now, as if surprised to see her in a wheelchair – and beyond her to Lyddie, who watched her compassionately. 'Mama?' she murmured. Her face, confused, even frightened, crumpled suddenly and Mina came quickly to her, taking her arm.

'Let's go and pack it so that it doesn't get lost again,' she said, 'and then we'll have that coffee.'

They went out together and Lyddie looked at Nest.

'Wow!' she said feelingly. 'That was scary. What was all that about the car?'

'It was Timmie's car,' said Nest. 'Timothy . . . his godfather sent it to him and Timmie adored it. Georgie found it on the beach a week or so ago. It had lain there for all those years but she remembered it. I was rather hoping to keep it, for various reasons, but there we are . . .'

'Oh, what a shame,' cried Lyddie. 'Was it a kind of keepsake because of you and Timmie being little together?'

'Yes,' said Nest slowly. 'Partly that and partly other things. Timmie and I were very close and I was very fond of him . . .' – 'and,' she wanted to say, 'because it was a present from my father and I have so little by which to remember him' – 'which is probably why I'm so fond of Jack.'

'Oh, they are such heaven,' said Lyddie warmly, 'Jack and Hannah, but it's good to be here, Nest.'

They looked at each other rather shyly, each remembering acts of love that spanned thirty years, but not confident enough yet to make any great gesture.

'I'm glad you feel comfortable with us,' said Nest. 'You're happy in your little study? That was Timmie's room, you know.'

'I love it,' said Lyddie. 'It's just the right size, not too big, and I've fitted all my things in. Aunt Mina's found a big table for me to work on and a bookshelf for all my reference books and things, and I've got my proper chair now. It was good of Liam to let me keep the car. I managed to bring back most of my stuff on this last trip.'

'But you didn't see him?'

Lyddie shook her head. 'I told him when I would be arriving and he steered well clear.' She gave a mirthless snort. 'I didn't know whether to be relieved or disappointed.'

'Both, I should think,' said Nest. 'It wouldn't be natural otherwise.'

'I had a moment's temptation to go into The Place. Just to go in like any ordinary customer and order some coffee, but my nerve failed me.'

Nest chuckled. 'I'm not surprised,' she said. 'Early days for that kind of courage.'

Lyddie looked at her, wondering how she'd managed to meet Connor as her brother-in-law, how she'd hidden her pain and her longing. She felt a surge of respect and fellow-feeling for Nest, a sense of grateful recognition, and knew that it was this that truly related people: this deep-down knowing and sharing. They smiled again, reaching tremulously towards this new level of trust and love but, before either could speak again, there was a sudden ringing of the doorbell, which sent the dogs ricocheting from their beds, barking madly, whilst the Bosun sat up and stared at them in amazement.

There was a sound of a door opening, a voice halloo-ing in the hall, and Helena was at the kitchen door.

'What excellent timing,' said Nest, pulling herself together. 'The coffee's just made. Did you have a good trip?'

It was clear that Helena expected some kind of mild reproach, an unspoken but hinted disapproval, and she was ready to adopt a brisk, defensive attitude but her fear faded in the feeling of warmth and goodwill that pervaded the kitchen and she was able to sit at the table with her coffee, admiring the Bosun whilst describing her journey. It was accepted that to drag the moment out would be foolish and, when Georgie appeared with Mina some minutes later, it was tacitly agreed that the two of them would hurry away.

'We shall stop for lunch quite soon,' Helena said, 'so that she doesn't get tired. And you must come and visit.'

'Oh, we shall,' said Lyddie cheerfully, 'we've got it all planned. You'll have to find a good hotel locally which can deal with wheelchairs, Helena, and send us the details. Goodbye, Aunt Georgie. See you soon.'

Lyddie's positive approach carried them through the painful farewells. Still looking puzzled, Georgie was kissed and hugged, put into the car, and Helena drove away.

The three of them stood together on the drive, staring after the car, suddenly at a loss. Mina, fighting tears, was swallowing hard, recalling the day that Georgie had arrived.

'Do you remember,' she'd asked her, 'how we used to go to the top of the drive to wait for Papa or Timothy and ride down on the running-board?' and the sunlit garden had been suddenly full of memories and Georgie's face had crumpled – as hers was crumpling now.

Nest was beside her, reaching to put an arm about her, and they looked at each other.

'I just know that I shan't see her again,' muttered Mina, swallowing painfully.

'I feel the same,' Nest assured her, 'but we shall. Not here, perhaps, but Lyddie is going to drive us up to visit her.'

She looked helplessly at Lyddie, who smiled and put her arms about them both.

'I certainly am,' she said cheerfully, 'but I'm going to need some practice with that old monster you've got, Aunt Mina, so I suggest a trip to Dulverton for lunch at The Copper Kettle. Trish will cheer us all up and the run over the moor should be wonderful on a day like this.'

'What a lovely idea,' said Mina, still near to tears. 'Oh, *what* a treat it would be. But can you spare the time, my darling?'

'I started work very early,' said Lyddie – who, finding sleep impossible, was tending to work half the night so as to distract herself from her thoughts of Liam – 'and I can work this evening. The important thing is to make the most of this glorious day before the light goes.'

They hurried inside to find their coats and, as Nest was shrugging herself into a warm fleecy jacket, Mina appeared.

'I think this is yours,' she said. She opened her hand and there, lying on her outstretched palm, was the little silver car.

Nest stared at it and then looked at Mina. 'How on earth . . .?'

'Never mind,' said Mina briskly. 'Soon it would have no meaning for her, even if Helena didn't find it first and chuck it in the bin, and it's important to you.'

'Yes,' said Nest, close to tears, 'it *is* important to me.'

'Put it away, then, and come along,' said Mina. 'We're going on an outing.'

The camper was beside the door when Nest wheeled herself out, closing the front door behind her.

'But what about the dogs?' Mina was asking anxiously. 'Oh dear . . .'

'The dogs will be just fine,' said Lyddie firmly. 'Now then, in you go, Nest. That's it. You're in the front with me, Aunt Mina, and you'll have to have Captain Cat with you. Dear old Polly's on her bed already, bless her. There now, in you go with Nest, Boyo, *good* boy . . .'

Presently they were ready. Captain Cat sat on Mina's lap, peering aggressively over her shoulder at the Bosun, who was already lying comfortably in the big space beside Nest's chair, whilst Nogood Boyo sat between his big paws with a smug 'me and my big mate' expression on his doggy face. Captain Cat gave a small woof of contempt and turned his back whilst Lyddie climbed in, adjusted the seat, and started up the engine. She grimaced at Mina, who beamed encouragingly back at her, and they jolted away up the drive.

CHAPTER FORTY

For a whole week the crisp golden weather held good and excursions became the order of the day: over to Simonsbath for coffee in the little café; lunch at the Hunter's Inn where the wild peacocks frightened the Bosun; a drive along the coast and through the Valley of the Rocks. Lyddie, tired as she was with lack of sleep and the pain in her heart, was nevertheless glad to be of use, to feel needed and – more than that – she was enjoying herself. Mina and Nest had always been important to her but now, living with them, she discovered the depth of their humour, the breadth of their courage, and her love for them was informed by this knowledge and grew deeper and wider with the discovery.

'They're terrific fun,' she said to Jack, one weekend not long before Christmas, when he drove his family down to see them.

'An exeat weekend,' he'd said on the telephone, 'the little blighters are going home, the

Lord be praised, so we could come down on Sunday if you can cope with us?'

Their arrival increased the sense of continuity and Lyddie was beginning to be aware of a slow healing.

'Well, of course they're fun!' he'd answered her, almost indignantly. 'We all knew that.'

'Of course we did,' she said, 'but I think I shall stay here for a bit, Jack. It's not just because I feel I can help them by driving them about and doing all the things that Mina probably shouldn't be doing at her age, but quite selfishly because they're helping me.'

'Quite right too,' said Jack. 'That's the tragedy of this present way of life. We no longer consider that older people have all these things to offer. Their courage and wisdom and experience is just brushed to one side. They're probably doing you much more good than you could do to them.'

'I agree,' she answered with humility. 'I *do* need them. And you too, of course.'

'Well, naturally,' he said, his voice losing its serious note. 'You couldn't manage without me, I'm quite aware of it. It's a gift I have, a burden nobly borne . . .'

'Oh, shut up,' she said, laughing. 'But I just wondered if it's right to stay. For all sorts of reasons.'

'I suspect,' he said shrewdly, 'that you're worrying lest they should come to rely on you and then you'll never have the courage to leave them. Is that it?'

'Something like that,' she admitted. 'Although, at this moment, I can't quite imagine wanting to go anywhere. I'm just afraid that I'm using Ottercombe as a refuge because I feel so wounded and, when I feel strong, I might want to do something else.' She watched him anxiously. 'It's this horrid feeling that I might be using them.'

'I think that you should rely on their common sense,' he answered firmly. 'Accept now for what it is and let go of fretting. Make the most of it so that all three of you are happy for this time and don't spoil it by trying to deal with imaginary scenarios which might never arise. OK?'

She grinned at him. 'Thanks, Uncle Jack,' she said demurely.

'So are you going to let me get you on the Internet like I did Aunt Mina so you can e-mail your friends? Come on, Lydd, why not join us in the twentieth century before it's too late? One more year to go! Take a chance, why not?'

'I might,' she said, laughing. 'I just might at that. Dear old Aunt Mina loves it. She chats to all her friends at night. I see her light on, really late, shining under her door.'

'Well, there you are, then. Go on! Then we could have speaks every day. Hannah loves it.'

'I'll think about it,' she promised. 'I really will.'

'Lunch is ready,' said Toby, appearing suddenly, 'and Mummy says it will get cold if you don't come *this minute.*'

'A directive I never disobey, do I, Tobes? Mummy's word is the Law and the Prophets rolled into one, especially when food is involved.'

'What's the law and the prophets?' asked Toby predictably.

'Ask your Aunt Lyddie,' answered Jack promptly – and vanished kitchenwards.

Toby beamed up at her. 'We're going down to the beach after lunch,' he told her. 'All of us with the dogs. I love the Bosun best of them all. I wish we had a dog. Can he swim? We're not allowed to today because it's too cold but Mummy says we can all go down to the beach. Well, all except Aunt Nest. She never goes to the sea, does she?'

Lyddie stared down at him, thinking of Mina's words. 'No,' she said slowly. 'No, she never does. I expect she has a little sleep after lunch.'

Hannah's clear voice echoed impatiently from the kitchen and Toby grabbed Lyddie's hand. 'Come on,' he said. 'Lunch.'

Later, as the beach party assembled, Lyddie said that she would stay with Nest and do the washing-up.

'Take the Bosun, though,' she said. 'Aunt Mina will keep him under control.'

There was a blessed silence, once the door had shut behind them all, and Lyddie smiled at Nest.

'Would you like to rest?' she asked. 'I'm very happy doing this lot on my own, really I am.'

Nest made a little face. 'To tell the truth, I would,' she admitted. 'Love them though I do, I find a few hours of them all quite exhausting. If you're sure . . . ?'

'Quite sure,' said Lyddie firmly. 'Off you go. I'll bring you a cup of tea later, if you like. Although you'll probably hear them all coming back.'

'I expect I shall,' agreed Nest.

She wheeled away and Lyddie was left in possession of the kitchen. She began to clear up methodically and, after a moment, found herself humming. These small, unexpected manifestations of happiness were still surprising to her and she moved quietly about, grateful that she was granted such a refuge.

By the time the lunch things were washed up and put away, the kitchen tidy and the kettle ready on the Esse, she heard the sounds of the returning party.

'It was the devil of a job getting them away,' said Jack, accepting his cup of tea, 'but we really should be on our way very soon. It's a long drive and the boys will be back this evening.'

Nest was roused and came to join them for the last ten minutes, before the children were packed into the car after tearful farewells to the dogs, and the grown-ups embraced each other with thanks and promises of future jollies.

'We'll get together somehow for Christmas,' Jack said, hugging Lyddie. 'We'll sort something out.' He bent to kiss Nest, holding her hand tightly for a moment, and then turned to Mina. 'Lyddie looks well,' he murmured, under the cover of the others' farewells.

'She does, doesn't she?' she answered eagerly. 'And it's such lovely joy having her here. My dear boy, you are *such* a blessing to us all.'

He looked down into her sweet, old face and bent to kiss her lips gently. 'Love you lots, darling,' he said tenderly. 'We'll have speaks later.'

'God bless you,' she said. 'Drive carefully.'

They went away up the drive, Toby's hand waving furiously at the window, and the three standing motionless on the gravel heard the car pull out and accelerate away across the moorland road.

'And now,' said Lyddie, 'you and the dogs have a little rest, Aunt Mina. I've lit the fire in the drawing-room. Pour yourself another cup of tea and go and enjoy it in peace.'

'It sounds wonderful,' admitted Mina, 'but what about you?'

'Ah.' Lyddie laid her hands upon the back of Nest's chair. 'Well, *I* think it's time that Nest and I went down to the sea.' She smiled at her. 'What do you think, Nest?'

The silence seemed to engulf them all and Mina realized that she was holding her breath. After a long moment Nest turned to look up into her child's face.

'I think that's a very good idea,' she said.

It was exactly as she'd remembered it, dreamed about it. The steep-sided cleave clothed with larch and oak and tall, noble beech, their bare, twiggy branches reaching to the tender blue sky; great thickets of rhododendron beneath the rocky shoulder of the moor; bright green ferns at the water's edge. The stream ran beside her through the narrow valley, flowing over smooth boulders and under willow, whilst ducks dabbled amongst the reeds and the sharp scent of gorse was carried on the breeze. Nest's hands clutched at the arms of her chair as she turned this way and that, each sight furnishing a hundred memories, until at last the cleave widened into the crescent-shaped beach, protected on each side by the high grey cliffs, and the stream travelled onward to its inexorable meeting with the sea.

The sea. Nest hardly realized that her chair had stopped moving; that she was sitting on a flat rock staring across to the waves that rolled in, crashing against the towering walls of stone and sweeping over the shaly sand. Voices were carried on the wind:

'We'll live here together when we grow up.'

'Have you come to tell me I'm trespassing or are you simply a passing dryad?'

'We have a new baby brother. Do you think Papa will love us any more?'

'It was nothing. Nothing at all. I missed you so much and she'd lost her husband . . . It's over.'

'Will you share this magic place with me for this afternoon, lady?'

She was quite unaware of the searing tears that streamed down her cold cheeks as she listened to the rhythmic beating of the tide and allowed the salty air to wash away her bitterness and pain. Presently she was aware of Lyddie kneeling beside her. Lyddie took her handkerchief and dried

Nest's cheeks and kissed her before she straightened up.

'We must go home before it gets dark,' she said gently. 'But we'll come again . . . won't we?'

'Oh, yes,' said Nest, struggling to keep her voice steady. 'We'll come again. And thank you, Lyddie.'

Lyddie tucked the handkerchief away, paused for one last look out to sea, and turned the chair for the journey home.

Mina watched them go, her warm heart full of gratitude: the miracle had happened, the acceptance made. She'd been watching the love between Nest and Lyddie growing steadily and now any reservations she might have had were finally lifted from her. Calling to the dogs, deciding that she could manage without another cup of tea, she went into the drawing-room, still feeling light-headed with the joy of it all. Unconsciously pressing her fingers to her old, withered lips, holding the kiss Jack had given her, she sat down in the corner of the sofa whilst the dogs flopped gratefully and wearily upon their beds. She stared at the brightly burning fire, thinking back over these past few weeks: jaunts in the camper, quiet contented evenings, walks with the dogs; and further back again, seeing scenes amongst the burning logs and hearing voices in the whispering flames.

'I'll tell you a story,' said the Story Spinner, 'but you mustn't rustle too much or cough or blow your nose more than is necessary . . .'

'I apologize for arriving unannounced.'

'He should be called Kim, not Tim. Kim, the Little Friend of all the World.'

'He is dead. Dead.'

'Is it possible that you might speak to Mr Shaw soon?'

Arousing herself suddenly, as if from a dazed sleep, Mina thought first of Timmie, going away to school and then into the army, and then of Jack and his small family. She murmured a prayer for their safety and wellbeing and, as a stronger wave of dizziness engulfed her, she had time to see quite clearly, and with deep joy, Lyddie smiling down at Nest; to hear her saying, 'I think it's time Nest and I went down to the sea,' and see Nest's answering look of love and trust. It was her last conscious thought.

CHAPTER FORTY-ONE

Walking in the early mornings with the dogs on the moor above the house, looking out to sea, Lyddie tried to come to terms with this new blow. Without Aunt Mina, she felt as if she'd suddenly lost her footing, trodden confidently out onto a step that was not there. In the ambulance, leaving Nest white-faced but determined – 'You *must* go! I can't be with her but she mustn't be alone. Please go with her. I'll be all right!' – she'd held Mina's cold, unresponsive hand and stared beseechingly into the calm, serene face. Waiting alone in the hospital, she'd known the truth, already learning to face a future that did not hold Aunt Mina.

The minute Jack had heard the news, telephoning Ottercombe to say that they were safely home, he'd driven straight back. Leaving Hannah with the children and the boys, and another master to take over his teaching duties, he'd come straight to the hospital at Nest's request and taken the whole terrible business into his hands.

This morning, the fourth after Mina's death, watching a tanker ploughing down the Channel, catching the rays of the newly risen sun, Lyddie could feel the tears running down the back of her throat.

'It's just that she's always been there,' she'd said to Jack. 'She and Nest, after Mummy and Daddy died. I can't quite imagine life without Aunt Mina.'

'She's left everything to you, Ottercombe, everything,' he'd told her. 'Did you know that I'm an executor? Aunt Nest has the right to live at Ottercombe until she dies but it's academic, of course. She could never manage there alone.'

'She isn't alone,' Lyddie had said. 'I shall be with her.'

Jack had watched her thoughtfully. 'Shall you stay at Ottercombe?'

'Yes, I shall. Even if I wanted to I couldn't possibly uproot her now. It's been the most terrible shock for Nest. On top of all the other knocks she's taken it would be the last straw. Anyway, I don't want to leave. I love it here and I can't imagine where else we could go. I had no idea that Aunt Mina had left the house to me, though.'

'She knew that you could be trusted to look after Aunt Nest and it's possible . . .' He'd hesitated.

'It's possible that she suspected that I might need a refuge,' she'd supplied rather bitterly.

He'd shrugged, still watching her compassionately. 'Maybe. When you talk of Aunt Nest's "knocks" do you mean the accident?'

'Well, yes . . .' She remembered with a sudden shock that Jack knew nothing of the true relationship between herself and Nest. It was odd to have secrets from Jack. 'Yes, of course. Do you think it's crazy? Us staying at Ottercombe?'

'Of course not,' he'd answered. 'If Aunt Mina could cope with it all, I'm sure you can, although you have to remember that you work full-time. There's a bit of money invested – Richard Bryce was a wealthy man, so that should help a bit. No, it's simply that Aunt Mina devoted her life to Grandmama and then to Aunt Nest and I don't want to see you sacrifice your life in the same way.'

'Was it a sacrifice?' she'd wondered. 'I can't think of anyone more content than Aunt Mina. And how wise she was, considering that she only spent a few years outside the cleave. We all turned to her at one time or another, didn't we?'

'Oh, I agree.' Jack had smiled at her. 'Aunt Mina was a communicator and one way or another she retained her intellectual integrity. She never shut herself off. I'm delighted that you'll be together, you and Aunt Nest, but I don't want you to forget that there's life outside Ottercombe, that's all.'

'I shan't do that,' she'd promised. 'Perhaps the time might come when we'll want to sell up and move into a town, that kind of thing. It's just that I don't want to do anything in a hurry and I don't want to upset Nest any more than she is now.'

'Fine.' He'd paused. 'Have you noticed,' he'd asked, 'that you don't call her "Aunt" these days?'

'No, I don't, do I?' she'd agreed after a moment. 'Odd, isn't it?'

High above the turbulent waters, a tiny silver aeroplane tracked across the sky, unspooling a silvery thread, which frayed and unravelled as she watched. Her shadow, long and thin, stretched ahead across the sheep-nibbled turf and she idly held her arms out a little, stiff and straight, and opened her fingers, two and two, so that they looked like long pointed scissor-hands. She made several cutting movements until suddenly, disgusted by her childishness, she thrust her hands deep in her pockets and turned back, calling to the dogs.

At Ottercombe, Nest was getting herself up by degrees. She sat on the edge of the bed, pulling on a long, warm flannel skirt in soft blues and red. It was Mina who had discovered the blissful ease of elastic-waisted skirts and trousers, sending away for catalogues, poring over them with Nest, insisting that she should remain stylishly dressed, boosting her confidence.

Sitting on the bed, Nest fought with the tears that threatened night and day. Mina was everywhere: working in the garden, cooking in the kitchen, reading beside the fire. Nest could still see her, in those dreadful days after the accident, dancing on the terrace, a puppy in her arms, holding up one of its paws elegantly as they swept to and fro; pouring a very necessary drink before dinner; pushing the wheelchair round the supermarket so that Nest could choose something special for her birthday, Nest clutching the wire basket on her knees.

'Christ . . . did not cling to equality with God . . . but emptied himself . . .' The verse came unbidden to her mind. Perhaps that was what the attaining to Christ's hard-won peace was about: an emptying of self, cheerfully, willingly . . .

She heard Jack moving about in the kitchen and steadied herself, continuing with the slow dressing process. What would she have done without Lyddie and Jack?

'I'm staying,' Lyddie had said firmly, generously. 'We belong together, you and I. We'll get through this somehow. You'll have to show me the ropes, mind.'

Nest was too grateful, too thankful, to make anything but a token protest about being a burden.

'And where would I go?' Lyddie had demanded. 'I hope you're not intending to throw me out? Anyway, someone's got to look after the dogs.'

Her cheerfulness did not deceive Nest and her heart went out to Lyddie.

'Does Liam know?' she'd asked Jack privately – and he'd nodded.

'Lyddie telephoned to tell him,' he'd said, 'but it's clear that he doesn't give a damn.'

He'd looked unusually angry, for Jack, and Nest had been filled with love for him. He was dealing with every aspect of the funeral and she was relieved to be spared.

'Just let me know anyone you think should be

invited,' he'd said. 'And I hope it's OK but I've checked her e-mail correspondence and sent a message out to some of the people in her e-mail address book. It seems wrong, I know, to read her letters but I wondered if there might be someone out there who's wondering what's going on. She had several regulars and one man, especially, called Elyot. Did she ever speak of him?'

Nest had shaken her head, frowning. 'I don't think so. She only ever talked in a general way about them. It was good for her to have people to speak to and I know that some of them were looking after disabled people like me.'

'Well, this chap seemed a bit worried not to have heard from her. His wife is ill in hospital, apparently, so I suspect she met him through some carers' chat-room. Looking at their e-mails it's clear that they've been very good friends. I'm going to print them off for you to read.' He hesitated. 'It probably sounds odd but I think you should read them too. Anyway, all her close contacts know now.'

'It's so good of you,' she'd said, tears threatening again. 'Sorry, what a fool I am!'

'Have a good weep,' he'd advised sympathetically. 'I do, regularly.'

Now, fully dressed and having got herself into her chair, she heard the sound of Lyddie's voice talking to Jack, and Nogood Boyo's high bark. It was Captain Cat who was feeling the loss of his mistress most; old Polly Garter was too old to be more than a little puzzled by her absence and

428

Nogood Boyo was too young, too infatuated by the Bosun, to worry a great deal, but poor Captain Cat mourned Mina quite heart-rendingly. He'd adopted Nest as his protector, sitting beside her chair and following her about, until Lyddie ruthlessly dragged him out for walks with the others. The four of them were learning to sleep amicably in the kitchen together at night but, oddly, Nest was glad of Captain Cat's companionship, his shared sadness, and she often lifted him onto her lap, murmuring to him, smoothing his warm white head, as Mina had in the past. He would be waiting for her now, with Lyddie and Jack.

Straightening her shoulders, schooling her lips into a smile, she wheeled herself across the hall and into the kitchen.

CHAPTER FORTY-TWO

By the day of the funeral the house had been cleaned from top to bottom; in the drawing-room the firelight was reflected in the gleam of rose-wood and mahogany; the scent of freesias filled the empty spaces; even the dogs' beds had been washed. As the family waited for friends to return from the church, the house seemed ready to welcome them, with its familiar, homely smells of log fires, flowers, beeswax and dog.

The rooms had responded to Lyddie's violent whirl of cleaning and polishing, dusting and scrubbing.

'It's good to have something to do,' she'd said – and had been instantly seized with compunction for Nest whose activity was so limited.

'I'll arrange the flowers,' she'd said, almost with pleasure at the prospect. 'At least I can do that.'

Hannah had arrived two days before, having left the children with her mother. 'I could possibly have managed Tobes,' she'd said to Lyddie, 'but not Flora. You need to be able to concentrate at times like these and I'm afraid that Tobes is in a very bad way. He adored Aunt Mina and I think it would simply be too much for him. In the end I decided to leave him too, and at least I can get on with the catering part without any distraction. How many are we going to be?'

'I'm not too certain.' Lyddie was trying hard not to burst into tears. It was odd how this grief suddenly came upon one, out of nowhere, twisting the heart. She swallowed the weight of tears in her throat. 'We've got eight of us in the house, I think. Me and Nest; you and Jack; Helena and Rupert, and Aunt Josie is flying over from Philadelphia with her youngest son, Paul. Roger and Teresa are driving down early in the morning. But I don't know how many people might turn up at the church tomorrow and then come back here afterwards.'

Hannah looked at her, noting the shadows beneath the eyes, the taut lines about the mouth.

'Have you done the beds?' she asked.

Lyddie nodded. 'We're all ready. Only the food to do, and Jack's collecting Josie and Paul from Taunton this afternoon. Helena and Rupert will be down this evening.'

'Then come and sit with me in the kitchen and help me make a shopping list. We'll go into Barnstaple and get everything and then have a quiet cup of coffee somewhere. Jack can keep an eye on Nest and the dogs.'

'I'd like that,' said Lyddie. Suddenly she longed

to be away from Ottercombe, to see that the world was still carrying on as usual, to forget – for a brief moment – that she would never see Aunt Mina's face again. 'Thanks, Hannah. That would be really good.'

Surprisingly, the arrival of Josie and Paul did much to lift the spirits. Josie had been away long enough for her grief to be a gentler affair; a warm recollection of happy times; of, 'Oh! and do you remember . . .?', which seemed to comfort Nest and animate her. She was fascinated by this tiny, thin, vital woman, very smart, very American, who looked so much like Henrietta, and to talk to her youngest son, Paul, who was quiet and good-looking with delightful manners. Jack and Rupert took him off into a corner with a bottle of whisky, whilst Helena told Lyddie and Hannah how Georgie had settled into the home.

'It was strange at first,' she said, 'well, we expected that, but she was very quiet, a bit bemused. She doesn't bother to answer us much or seem to know what's going on. I go in every day on my way home from work, and we both visit at weekends, but she doesn't take much notice of us. I really couldn't see any point in bringing her down with us.'

'Oh, no,' said Lyddie quickly. 'It would have been horrid. So confusing and frightening for her. At least her memories will be happy ones.'

'Poor Helena,' Hannah said sympathetically. 'I think these terrible times are worse for the carers and the watchers than the ones who have gone beyond anxiety.'

Helena looked at her gratefully. 'I sometimes think that too. But then we don't know what's going on in their heads, do we? They might be suffering in a way we know nothing about.'

Her eyes filled with tears and Lyddie took her hand. 'Don't,' she said, trying to smile. 'Don't you dare, Helena, or we'll all be at it' – and the three of them had laughed, albeit shakily, together.

'So many memories,' Josie was saying to Nest. 'Goodness, when I think back! Me and Henrietta fighting like cat and dog and Mina trying to keep the peace. Poor Mama! Of course, you and Timmie were just babies to us. Remember how we called you the Tinies?' Her face clouded. 'Oh, Nest. Timmie and Henrietta gone, and now Mina. All those years looking after Mama and then . . .'

'And then all those years looking after me?'

Nest was smiling but Josie grimaced. 'Still Miss Big-Mouth,' she said cheerfully. 'That's me! But Mina was a saint. *I* couldn't wait to get away after the war years. Stuck down here with nothing to do. It wasn't so bad in the early days of the war when we were small. Goodness, do you remember those wretched babies that came to stay with cousin Jean . . . ?'

'That's right.' Nest pretended to frown too, to cudgel her memory. 'And do you remember Timothy?'

Josie's brow cleared. 'Timothy,' she said gently.

'Of *course* I remember Timothy. He was like a visitor from another world. A fairy godfather. Oh, how we envied Timmie, Henrietta and me, his having Timothy as his godfather. Although he was so sweet to all of us, wasn't he? *Much* nicer than Papa. Surely you can remember him, Nest?'

'Yes. Yes, I can. But not so well as you, I expect. Being that much younger . . .'

'Sure. Well, he was something else, I can tell you. So good-looking and romantic. And all those places he went to . . .'

'Mina used to talk about him sometimes,' said Nest mendaciously, 'but she couldn't remember too much.'

'Well,' Josie settled herself more comfortably, her brain busy. 'Let me see now . . .'

'So,' said Rupert, swallowing some whisky. 'Everything under control?'

Jack glanced round at his womenfolk. 'I think so,' he said. 'I'll be glad, though, when it's this time tomorrow.'

Rupert gave his shoulder an affectionate pat. 'It'll be OK,' he said reassuringly.

Jack topped up Paul's glass. 'Drink up. I hope you can stay for a while. How would you like to see life at first hand in an English prep school?'

And now here they were, standing awkwardly about, waiting for the first arrivals. Food had been laid out in the kitchen, and on the gate-legged table in the drawing-room, and bottles of wine were opened, breathing on the dresser, or chilling in the fridge. Chairs had been collected from all over the house, and china and glass dug out from cupboards. The sound of an engine, a car bumping down the drive; Lyddie looked at Nest and they exchanged a reassuring smile, a nod of mutual encouragement, as Jack came through from the kitchen and went to open the front door.

Sitting just outside the drawing-room door, Nest watched them come. She'd been surprised at the numbers in the church: trades-people from Lynton, some locals from the outlying farms, a few family friends and one or two strangers.

Listening to the familiar words of the service, Lyddie's hand tightly clasping hers, Nest had tried to empty her mind, to keep her eyes away from the coffin. Visions filled her eyes: Mina pushing her in the garden to show her the first primroses: Mina singing as she drove across the coast road so that Nest could see the sea without feeling guilty; Mina talking to the dogs, her love murmurings followed by the little 'po-po-po' of sighing breath. Nest's throat had ached with the pain of it, her heart was heavy and cold as lead in her breast; only Lyddie's warm clasp had held her firm.

Now she smiled at these dear souls – who had in their way loved Mina – as she accepted their gentle commiserations, thanking them for coming. Above the heads of an aged farmer and his wife, who were telling her that they could remember Lydia, she saw two men enter the house.

They'd been at the church, right at the back, and, as she'd wheeled out, she'd glanced at them, thinking for a moment that she recognized the younger man. As the farmer and wife turned away, Nest watched the two men look about rather diffidently, saw Lyddie turn to greet them, holding out her hand with a smile.

The younger man took it, smiling down at her, holding her hand in his.

'I apologize for arriving unannounced,' he said – and Nest felt a tiny shock wave as though the two, standing there together, were locked in some eternal memory.

'*I apologize for arriving unannounced.*'

'My father can't drive at present and he asked me to bring him,' he was saying, still holding Lyddie's hand. 'You won't know who we are.'

As the older man moved forward to stand beside him, Nest wheeled swiftly forward.

'But I do,' she said – and joy lifted her heart, as though Mina had touched her lightly upon her shoulder. She looked from the young face to the older one, and smiled with warm recognition. 'You're Tony Luttrell,' she said, and put out her hand. 'Welcome back to Ottercombe.'

CHAPTER FORTY-THREE

In the days that followed, once Jack and Hannah had returned to Dorset, Josie and Paul to America, Helena and Rupert to Bristol, it was the promise of this new beginning that gave Lyddie and Nest courage to go forward.

'Although it's hardly a new friendship,' Lyddie said. 'After all, it's more than forty years old. Oh, how fantastic it is! I feel that Mina sent them along specially. And you recognizing him like that after all those years!'

'Well, I didn't recognize Tony,' Nest reminded Lyddie. 'It was William I recognized.' She chuckled. 'How silly that sounds. The thing is, he looks so much like Tony looked when I first knew him. Quite a bit older, of course – William must be in his late thirties – but it's there. When I saw them in the church I felt a sort of flicker but I was too overwrought to follow it through. It was when I saw him standing there with you . . .'

She fell silent, unwilling to go further, to speak

the words that William uttered, which her own father had said to Lydia so many years before. Lyddie was too absorbed to notice her withdrawal, so taken was she by this strange happening. She made Nest tell her Mina's story over and over.

'I'm not doing it as well as she would,' Nest would cry in frustration. 'It was Mina who was the story spinner,' and then Lyddie must hear the other stories, of Nest and Timmie when they were the Tinies, of Henrietta's on-going feud with Josie, despite their very real affection for one another; of picnics and the games they'd played, and of the stories that Mama had read them during the children's hour.

Lyddie would sigh with pleasure at the end of each telling, the thought of the life in the house stretching back, helping to heal her hurt from Liam and the loss of dear Aunt Mina.

'William might be over tomorrow,' she'd say casually – and she'd take the dogs down to the sea, trying to control the strange lifting of her heart at the thought of seeing him again.

'It's too soon,' she'd tell herself savagely. 'Don't be a fool! You did this with Liam after James . . .' but she knew that William was no Liam. His clear gaze and quiet smile betokened a quite different character and she felt at peace with him, relaxed and content. Both of them were recovering from broken relationships and neither was in any haste to rush into a new commitment. They were simply happy to spend time together, discovering one another. As they walked together in the woods, listening to the restless hush-hush of the waves on the shore, passing beneath the ghostly birches whose blood-red wands glowed in the late afternoon sunlight, a quietness stole upon her heart.

Nest too was comforted; not only by the sight of Lyddie and William together but by Tony's company. How extraordinary it was that he should reappear now, as a result of Mina's death, to be such a staunch comfort to her. He came with William when he could; Lavinia was failing and he tried to be with her for as long as was practicable each day.

'If only Mina had known who you were,' Nest had mourned when Tony explained how he'd received Jack's e-mail, described how he and Mina had 'talked'.

'I was afraid to tell her,' he'd said, his still-handsome face sad. 'It was so amazing when I first saw her name. She made no attempt to hide it. Why should she? I was more cautious when I started experimenting on the Internet and decided to use a part anagram of Tony Luttrell and call myself Elyot. It wasn't long before she mentioned Ottercombe and you, and then I knew. Oh, Nest, I can't tell you what I felt! How often I longed to tell her the truth. But I didn't know whether she still hated me and I was afraid to take the chance. I needed her too much.'

'She never hated you,' said Nest gently – and found herself telling Mina's story yet again, the whole truth of it, so that Tony was unable to contain his emotion and they sat together in the dusk, comforting each other.

'She needed you too,' she told him. 'You helped her through these last few years. You *must* know that.' She hesitated. 'I have to say that Jack printed off your "conversations" and showed them to me. Forgive me for that but it meant so much to see that she had all that love and support from you. Perhaps it was better this way, for all sorts of reasons.'

'Perhaps.' He blew his nose. 'I shall never forget that e-mail from Jack. It was exactly as if I'd lost her all over again. I simply had to come, just once, to see this house and you.'

'And now you'll come often, I hope,' she said. 'You and William.'

He looked at her, his eyes bright with unshed tears. 'It would mean so much. Thank you, Nest.'

So now, with Christmas less than a week away, they were waiting for more visitors: for Jack and Hannah and the children, and the puppy.

'I think it's utterly noble of you to have us all,' said Hannah, on the telephone to Lyddie. 'Poor Captain Cat!'

'He's learning to adapt,' said Lyddie robustly, 'like the rest of us. It's really good of you to come, Han. Don't think I can't imagine what it must be like to transport two children and all your Christmas this far.'

'We can't wait,' promised Hannah. 'Once Tobes knew that you had a chimney worthy of Father

Christmas he was ecstatic. A Christmas with *five* dogs? I ask you. What more could life hold?'

'I've been trying to make the house Flora-worthy.' Lyddie sounded anxious. 'When you look at it in terms of a crawling child, a house is a - minefield.'

'Tell me about it,' said Hannah drily. 'Don't worry, we'll be just fine. And you've got the tree?'

'In a bucket in the shed,' said Lyddie promptly, 'and lots of decorations. Oh, Han, I can't wait to see you all.'

'Ditto,' replied Hannah cheerfully. 'Jack's bringing the booze, by the way. Says he doesn't trust either of you with his delicate palate.' A pause. 'Quite,' agreed Hannah. 'I was silenced too. Then I hit him!'

Lyddie burst out laughing. 'Give them a hug from us. Speaks soon. 'Bye.'

Now a peaceful silence hangs over the house. William has arrived and taken Lyddie and the dogs off to the beach; everything is in readiness. Slowly Nest wheels her chair out of the shadows, the rubber tyres rolling softly across the cracked mosaic floor, and pauses outside the drawing-room. Brightly wrapped Christmas presents are piled upon the ancient settle and a jar of spindle-berries stands on the oak table beside the lamp, whose light glints on the big copper plate. Silence fills the high spaces of the hall and flows about her as she bends her head to listen, her eyes closed. She can no longer see Georgie and Mina, with Timmie propped between them on the sofa, nor Josie, working at her jigsaw on the floor, whilst Henrietta leans to look at the pictures in the book. Mama's voice is stilled, the children are gone.

Their story is finished; a new chapter is beginning.

THE END

Marcia Willett's new novel

THE BIRDCAGE

Will be published by Bantam Press
in August 2004

Here's a taster . . .

Prologue

The child, waking suddenly and finding herself alone, sat up anxiously amongst the makeshift bed of cushions and rugs. She could hear her mother's voice, echoing oddly – now loud, now quiet – a murmuring duet with a deeper voice, flaring and dying so queerly that she scrambled to her feet and went out into the passage. Small, tousled, without her shoes, she hurried along until she emerged into a Looking Glass world where painted gardens ascended into cavernous shadowy places, a flight of stairs revolved gently away, and walls drifted silently apart. A cluster of lights, perched aloft, lit up an interior as neat and bright as a dolls' house room, with cardboard books on painted shelves and shiny plaster food set upon the small table; she almost expected Hunca Munca to appear.

Standing quite still, just beyond the circle of light, a draught shivering round her legs, she watched her mother, who talked and smiled and stretched her hands to someone whose arm and shoulder, clad in severe dark cloth, could just be glimpsed; but, before she was able to run to her, a sudden surging roar pinned her in the dark corner. As it beat up, swelling then receding dizzily about her head, she squared her mouth to cry out in fear, and then there were people all about her, lifting her, soothing her, carrying the small struggling figure away from the woman who remained on stage as the curtain rose and fell, again and again. She yelled aloud in panic as she was borne off – 'Angel!' she shouted – but her voice was lost in the backstage bustle and she cried out again.

No sound came and she wakened – properly now – to the present, her head at an uncomfortable angle against the arm of the chair, her mouth dry. The fear was still with her, a sense of terrible loss clinging with the fragments of the dream, so that she passed her hands over her face as if to wipe away both the dream and the panic together.

'Sleeping in the afternoon,' she told herself disparagingly. 'What do you expect?' and glanced hopefully at her watch. Twenty-eight minutes past five. Once, not so long ago, this would have been a time of preparation, of nervous tension; swallowing black coffee, forcing down some bread and butter, before going to the theatre. There, the world beyond the stage door brought its own particular brand of comfort. Snuffing up the familiar theatre smell – dust, greasepaint, sweat – hearing the chatter in the dressing-rooms; a kind of comradeship and relief that sprang from the security of being where you belonged, concentrated the mind on the work ahead. Still nervous, oh yes! But excited now and part of the family: listening to the gossip as you sat at the mirror and applied the colour to your face.

Lizzie Blake straightened in her chair, shrugging her shoulders to ease the crick in her neck, stretching her long, still-glamorous legs. She rose from the armchair, humming. She'd discovered that humming held thought – and fear – at bay and she knew plenty of tunes. Today it was *South Pacific*: 'This Nearly Was Mine'. She waltzed into the kitchen, exaggerating the beat, hamming it up, humming and singing alternately, slipping back nearly twenty-five years. Lizzie filled the kettle and switched it on; not that she wanted a cup of tea but that dread, empty, early evening desert between five and seven had to be filled somehow – especially now that Sam was gone.

She hurried herself away from this thought at once, humming again – 'A Cockeyed Optimist' this time – and began to make the tea, tapping out the rhythm on the caddy with a teaspoon, wondering whether she might allow herself a ginger biscuit: just one. After all, her weight never increased. She remained as tall and slender as she'd been at twenty – her work and self-discipline had kept her fit and supple – and the masses of dark reddish-gold hair were barely touched with grey. It was pinned, as usual, into a mysterious bundle from which screwy tendrils escaped and tortoiseshell hairpins occasionally slipped; her ivory skin was dusted with freckles and her amber-brown eyes were rather shy beneath the feathery brows. As she'd grown older – too old for the roles of Nellie or Ado Annie or Bianca – she'd been cast in small comedy parts and had also had a great success in a television sitcom that had run for several years. Meanwhile, her singing voice had carried her into voice-over jingles for television commercials and now, if she'd wanted to, she could have listened to herself at least three or four times each evening, extolling a particular brand of face-cream or watched herself at the wheel of a popular family car complete with two small children and a delightful mutt-like dog. This last was a very amusing and popular commercial and she'd become a household face – something she'd never quite achieved through those long years on the stage nor, even, with the sitcom – and she was getting used to passers-by doing double-takes and crying, 'Oh, you're that lady in the advert . . .' She longed to be blasé about it, to shrug and smile distantly but, truth to tell, she rather liked the recognition and was quite ready for a little chat, a bit of a chuckle with these friendly admirers. Deep down she felt rather ashamed at the pleasure this gave her but there was no harm and it cheered her up, boosting her ego and warming the heart: reactions not to be sniffed at, especially since Sam . . .

Lizzie seized the biscuit tin: *two* biscuits and a good look at the latest holiday brochure would be an excellent distraction from the long empty hours ahead. Perhaps her friends and her agent had been right when they'd advised that she shouldn't leave London to return to the house in Bristol where she'd grown up with Pidge and Angel. It was simply that London had been so awful without Sam; so lonely and . . . just wrong. She lifted the mug and tasted the hot tea, glancing at the highly coloured brochure advertising the beauty of the West Country.

'Will you be travelling with a party?' the young woman in the travel agent's office had asked earlier that morning.

'No, no. Quite alone.' She tried to make it sound adventurous and gay but the words had a rather pathetic ring and the woman glanced curiously at her.

'I lost my husband three months ago.' The words leaped from her mouth and seemed to lie on the counter where they could both look at them: Lizzie with dismayed surprise and the woman with shocked pity.

'I am *so* sorry.'

The hushed tone and special sympathetic expression had an odd effect on Lizzie; she could feel wild laughter creeping below her diaphragm. Instinctively she breathed in, tightening her stomach muscles, beaming so madly that the woman almost flinched away from her.

'So am I,' she answered brightly, speaking clearly. 'Terribly, terribly sorry.'

The woman's expression grew anxious; she seized some brochures, and pushed them across the counter, muttering unintelligibly, her eyes averted.

Remembering, Lizzie burst into a fit of laughter, nearly choking on her tea: tears streamed from her eyes and she dabbed at them. Could it be that she was crying? Resolutely she took her mug and the booklets and went to sit at the dining-table.

In this big first-floor room, the kitchen had been divided from the living area by the simple means of placing an upright piano in the middle of the floor. Its back, which had a square deal table placed against it, was turned to the sink and cupboards and shelves, hiding the smaller working area very cleverly. On its other side, a long refectory table was set about with assorted battered wooden chairs, one wall was lined with bookshelves, another hung with paintings, and a long sofa, which fitted comfortably into the wide bay window, kept company with three unmatched armchairs and a low carved chest used as a table.

Sitting in the wide-armed carver, pushing an old silk cushion into the small of her back, Lizzie set down her tea, took the brochures from under her arm and opened the biscuit tin. She began to turn the pages. Beyond the window, the plane tree trembled in the light, soft breeze; the June evening was warm and the voices of the children, playing in the square, echoed through the open casement. The room faced west and the pattern of the leaves shifted and changed in the sunlight, flickering over faded linen chair covers. A crimson petal fell soundlessly from one of the roses in a vase on the piano, their scent drifting in the high, airy spaces. Lizzie turned another page.

'Dunster Castle towers above the little village huddled at its gates . . .'

She stared at the picture, frowning, her mind balancing on the edge of a memory: the sandstone castle, glowing rich and warm at sunset, the mosaic of red and grey slate roofs silvered by gentle rain, a peaceful, sheltered garden; the sea breaking on grey stones and shingle, the ache of weary legs on the long walk home from the beach . . . And Angel, restless, brittle, never still.

Lizzie put the brochure aside. She saw a tiny cameo, a sliver of the past: a meeting, charged with tension and excitement, and Angel staring at a woman of her own age whilst she, Lizzie, gazed at the small boy who held the woman's hand.

The telephone bell shivered the memory to pieces and made her jump.

'Hello, dear heart.'

Lizzie smiled with relief to hear her agent's voice and sank into a deep-lapped armchair.

'Hello, Jim. How are things?'

'Things are good. Very good. That holiday you were talking about. You're not going too far away?'

'No, no.' Her eyes strayed to the table, the open brochure, the glossy photographs. 'I thought, maybe, the West Country. On the coast somewhere. Why?'

'Just as long as you're in Manchester on Monday week.'

They talked for a few moments longer, Lizzie replaced the receiver and returned to the table. She stood for a long while, staring down at the picture.

Dunster Castle towers above the little village huddled at its gates.

She slept late the next morning. Half a sleeping tablet had finally released her from an exhausting mental circling, resurrecting memories and sharpening grief, which dogged her into the early hours. Her dreams were curiously vivid.

Pidge and Angel are sitting together at the table, a

bottle of wine between them whilst she sits on the floor beneath the long board with her toys. Angel's feet are bare and fidget constantly, rubbing one upon another or tucking themselves into the long, cotton wrapper that ripples round her legs. Pidge's feet are placed upon the long bar and her shoes, with pointed toes and little heels, are soft, dark blue leather.

'I loved him so much, d'you see?' she is saying. Her voice is full of pain and, more than that, there is a kind of desperate need to be understood, forgiven even. Her narrow feet remain quite still, planted firmly there on the wooden rail, whilst Angel's white, rounded toes, with their brightly painted nails, push at each other restlessly. She murmurs at intervals, in soothing counterpoint to Pidge's recital, comforting her.

'After all, sweetie, he didn't belong to me either. I mean, did he?' Her chair creaks a little as she leans forward. There is a tiny chink of glass, a liquid gurgle. 'To be honest, it's *quite* extraordinary. Rather fun, *I* think . . .'

Pidge's feet come down from the rail, her shoes are eased off and she hitches her chair forward an inch or two: Angel's toes cease to rub together, she crosses her legs, drawing the wrapper about her knees, and sits back comfortably. With the voices murmuring above her head, listening to bursts of smothered laughter and the occasional exclamation, the child continues her game; setting the scene that her toys enact on the soft silky rug, with the refectory table like a roof, the broad end-leg as a wall, sheltering and enclosing them.

Lizzie pushed back the quilt and sat on the edge of the bed. The dream, like yesterday's, left her feeling edgy. Had she sat so, beneath the table, whilst Angel and Pidge talked? Had she wakened in the dressing-room one evening, alone and frightened, and run to find her mother? She was not a stranger to dreams but these had been touched by an almost hallucinatory quality. Her behaviour of late might have given rise to a slight anxiety if she could only bring herself to care. She'd posted a nice little cut of steak in the letter-box outside the butcher's shop, gone off with someone else's trolley in the supermarket, forgotten the car and, leaving it behind in the car-park, walked home from the library. Small things of no great moment, taken separately, yet the dreams seemed part of the same pattern.

'Perhaps I'm having a nervous breakdown.'

Lizzie spoke the words aloud, tilted her head as if waiting for a response, and pattered away to the bathroom for a shower. Talking to herself made her feel less alone and, more importantly, kept anxieties in proportion. It was much more difficult to take herself seriously when she spoke out – rather loudly and very clearly – as if to an audience. She grinned brightly at herself in the glass above the basin as she cleaned her face, slapped on moisturizer and plunged the horseshoe-shaped pins into her hair.

She began to hum: 'I'm Gonna Wash That Man Right Outta My Hair'.

Still with *South Pacific*, then. Well, that was fine, lots of good numbers to carry her through the day. She remembered the little tap routine that had accompanied that particular song and tried it out, her leather-soled slippers clapping softly on the lino, thinking back to her first lessons in the basement room with the painted floor at the dance studio.

Shuffle *hop* step tap ball change. Shuffle *hop* step tap ball change. Shuffle *hop* step, shuf*fle* step, shuffle *step*, shuffle ball *change*.

She could hear, inside her head, the dancing

mistress shouting the steps above the clatter of tap shoes, accentuating the beat; her body could remember the rhythm, arms swinging loosely, head up. She couldn't have been more than seven or eight. How she'd loved the music, the movement, the disciplining of the body; the *barre* that had been fixed to the wall in the attic room forty years ago was still there where Lizzie had once performed her daily exercises, her little routine: *pliés*, *battements*, *port de bras*, watching herself in the glass on the opposite wall. She still did a regular work-out.

'But not this morning,' she muttered as she dressed quickly, pulling on jeans and a black T-shirt.

An appointment with the hairdresser hurried her down the stairs for coffee and some toast. The brochure was lying where she'd left it but she glanced away from it, humming to herself again, concentrating on what Jim had told her about the possibility of work with a touring company in the autumn. Could she cope with the arduous routine, the travelling, the same performance night after night?

'Just what you need, heart,' he'd said reassuringly. He was very kind, very professional and insisted that his extravagant speech and flamboyant behaviour were simply by-products of a lifetime working with actors. Lizzie adored him.

'I feel a bit wobbly,' she told him before she'd left London. 'I need a break. I'm going to Bristol.'

'Back to the Birdcage?' That's what the tall, narrow house had been dubbed back in the early sixties once the agency had learned that three women lived in it, one of them called Pidgeon.

Standing in the kitchen, drinking black coffee, waiting for the toaster to fling its contents on to the floor, Lizzie thinks of Angel's delight at the joke and how she pleads for them to change the address officially.

'It's all very well for you,' retorts Pidge, 'but how would you like your letters to be addressed to "Miss Pidgeon, The Birdcage"? Have a heart.'

Instead, Angel finds a pretty, gilt birdcage – from some prop room? – complete with two brightly painted, little wooden birds perched on a trapeze. Shortly afterwards an even smaller chick, made of soft yellow material, is added.

'That's you,' says Angel to Lizzie. 'See? You're a swinging chick. How do you like that?'

The birdcage hangs above the piano in the sitting-room for years. It becomes a symbol, an in-joke.

'That's us,' Angel tells visitors. 'Three little birds in a gilded cage. Well, one chick and two old boilers . . .' she adds – and waits for the inevitable denial, the compliments.

The birdcage is such a part of their lives together that it is impossible to imagine either Pidge or Angel getting rid of it. When Angel dies of complications following the onset of pneumonia, Pidge lives on alone until she, too, dies after a series of strokes. She leaves the house with all its contents to Lizzie.

'I can't sell it,' Lizzie tells Sam. 'I just can't. Not yet, anyway.'

'No need,' he answers easily. 'It will be useful as a little bolt-hole.'

'That's about right,' she agrees. 'I always bolt back to it. Between productions, after your disastrous love affairs. I always finished up in the Birdcage with Angel and Pidge.'

'That's not quite what I had in mind,' he says, putting an arm round her, knowing how hard she is taking Pidge's death. He makes a face, rolling his eyes, guying a saucy leer, hoping to make her smile, holding her closer. 'More of a love nest, perhaps, than a birdcage?' and she laughs at his feeble joke, winding her arms about him.

Ten years ago since Pidge died, thought Lizzie, swallowing her toast with difficulty. And less than two years ago Sam and I were here together. And now?

She began to clear the breakfast things, the action distracting her from such thoughts, concentrating instead on the missing birdcage. It would be good to see it again; to hang it up as a gesture of the past. She decided that as soon as she was home again she would have a thorough search for it.

All the while, as she collected her keys, hunted for her bag, the photograph seemed to cry continually for her attention. Reluctantly, almost fearfully, she paused to look at it again. 'The Yarn Market is octagonal and dates from the fifteenth century . . .'

Lizzie bent closer to look at the smaller, inset picture. Another fragment, just like the scene in the shop, slid clearly into her mind.

The Yarn Market. She remembers running in through the doorless entrance calling to Angel, who stands on the cobbles outside in the sunshine, and leaning through the big window spaces.

'Look at me? Can you see me?'

'I can see you, sweetie, I can see you.' But Angel is looking up the High Street, her eyes darting from shop doorways to peer at the occupants of a car; distracted, preoccupied, always on the watch.

Lizzie feels the slubby crispness of her yellow and white gingham frock, bare feet in sandshoes, and her long plait, thick as Angel's wrist, knocking against her back as she jumps along beside her mother down the sunken, narrow, cobbled pavement. They pause beside the hotel, with its big medieval porch, before crossing the road to the Yarn Market. It is cool and dark beneath the slated roof and she dances, singing breathlessly to herself, a small, bright flame of colour among the shadows, whilst Angel waits, watching and watching. But for whom?

This question occupied Lizzie as she walked into the town: as she chatted to the friendly girl who blow-dried her hair; as she did her shopping; all the while she was trying to pin the memory down, to capture it. If she could remember which year it had been, then other things might fall into place; but why should Angel, of all people, decide to take a holiday in a tiny town on Exmoor? Angel liked bustle, unexpected outings to restaurants or pubs, friends dropping by for impromptu drinks: she became restive and bored after ten minutes up on Brandon Hill. Nor did she consider it necessary for Lizzie to be taken on holiday except during the summer of that one year. That Dunster year.

Back at home, Lizzie kicked off her shoes, put away the shopping and collected the ingredients for her lunch. Mostly she couldn't be bothered to eat formally – it seemed such an effort for just one person – but today she felt a need to prepare something almost as a rite to the shades of Pidge and Angel rather than for herself. Just now, here in the Birdcage, she felt that they were very close to her: Angel, eyes closed, stretched along the sofa in the window, with Pidge sewing nearby, arguing across the table or perhaps pottering in the kitchen. Pidge was responsible for most of the cooking, although Angel liked to experiment – either disastrously or brilliantly. 'I am never commonplace,' she'd say grandly, shovelling her mistakes into a newspaper whilst Pidge, resigned, began to make an omelette. 'I don't do things by halves.' Because of going down to the theatre each evening, mealtimes were movable feasts and Pidge remained flexible at all times.

Now, as Lizzie set the table, she felt as if she were making them an offering, a simple little puja: smoked salmon with chunks of lemon, rings of tomato in a vinaigrette with herbs, thin slices of cucumber in mayonnaise, and new brown bread. She chose the dishes with care: round, white bone-china for the salmon; oval, blue earthenware for the tomatoes; a yellow bowl for the cucumber. Oddly, the palette of colour and texture worked. Lizzie felt that Pidge and Angel would have approved. Unable to afford the best, each of them had made a point of buying and using things that caught her attention and appealed to her own particular taste.

Pleased with her puja, Lizzie poured herself a glass of chilled Sancerre and sat down.

'I know I shouldn't be eating this because it's for you,' she said aloud so as to placate the shades of Pidge and Angel. 'It's not a real puja but it's the best I can do.'

The little meal was delicious. Afterwards, she cut herself some cheese and made coffee, strong and black. Sitting quietly, she stared out across the room, through the branches of the plane tree out-side the window, to the rooftops and the sky beyond, listening to other things beside the city's sounds.

Later, she climbed the steep stairs to the attic room. Once her own special eyrie, now it was full of those things that had been put aside for later use – 'It might come in,' Pidge had been fond of saying – as well as the items which, out of sentimental attach-ment they'd simply been unable to throw away. It was years since Lizzie had used this room and it was here she hoped to find the birdcage. Which one of them would have decided that the joke was too stale to want to keep it hanging above the piano?

Perhaps after Angel died, Pidge had found it too painful a reminder.

Lizzie moved slowly between cardboard boxes, bulging bin-liners and small pieces of furniture. Old books, with broken spines and ragged leaves, were stacked on the small bookcase she'd used as a child, whilst a chair with a broken leg held a faded tapestry stool in its lap. There was no sign of the birdcage. It was too big to be stored in the boxes that were marked clearly with felt-tip pen; too bulky for the bin-liners, weighty with their burden of old curtains and blankets, which she moved carefully aside in case they'd been piled on top of it. She peered into a tea-chest, which was packed with sheet music and theatre programmes, and stared for a moment at the cardboard box bearing the legend 'LIZZIE'S TOYS'. To distract herself from the mixed emotions that this evoked, she turned aside and glanced along the shelf at the books. Amongst these battered copies were several Reprint Society editions. Elizabeth Bowen's *The Heat of the Day*, two Rumer Goddens, Maugham's *Theatre* and an Iris Murdoch.

Lizzie leafed through the Bowen and then picked up *Theatre.* She remembered that Angel had given it to Pidge as a birthday present and, still feeling their shades close at hand, she decided to take the book down to read later. She looked about her, frowning: the birdcage was nowhere to be seen and she was acutely disappointed. It was foolish and irrational but she'd cherished the hope that she would discover it here amongst these artefacts of the past but suspected now that it must have been thrown away. Angel's rooms, which Lizzie now used, had no cupboard large enough to conceal it and Pidge's quarters, cleared out and redecorated, were let to a young woman taking a post-graduate course at the university.

Lizzie went into the sitting-room and lay full-length on the sofa. She felt deeply hurt that the birdcage had been disposed of without her consent.

'After all,' she said aloud, crossly, as if to admonish the accompanying shades, 'I was part of it too.'

She can imagine it quite clearly. The two little wooden birds have been so delicately painted that it seems that the feathers, blue and green and yellow, must stir; that at any moment the wings might be stretched for flight. Angel, professional as always in the setting of a scene, places a tiny bowl of seed on the floor of the cage and hangs a round mirror beside the trapeze. Pidge refuses to let her put a second bowl of water beside the seed.

'It'll get stale and smell,' she says firmly, 'or get knocked over when people peer in.'

Angel grumbles, her artistic sensibilities affronted, but Pidge won't budge. There is only just room on the swing for the yellow chick, probably an Easter toy from a cardboard egg. She leans rakishly, her bright orange feet wound about with wire so as to attach her to the wooden bar, her fluffy wings poised as if she fears that she might tumble from her precarious perch.

How Lizzie loves them: to begin with, tall though she is, she has to stand on the piano stool so as to see them properly. Angel is the bird whose head is thrown back, beak parted in joyous song: Pidge has her head on one side, as if listening. Lizzie is thrilled to be a part of this little tableau: the chick, safe within the confines of the cage, not quite ready for flight.

Lizzie stirred. Now that she was back in Bristol, her earlier instinct – to block the past, to hum and dance away from those dreams and memories – was beginning to change very gradually into an acceptance: even into curiosity. The mad conception that, somehow, Pidge and Angel were here in the Birdcage with her was beginning to be a comfort rather than a threat.

'Crazy!' she announced to anyone who might be listening. 'Potty. Nuts. Doolally.'

She hitched herself a little higher on the sofa, found that she was still clutching *Theatre*, and, holding it by its spine, shook the book gently so as to dislodge the dust. The pages clapped lightly together and a card slipped from between its sheets and fell to the floor. Lizzie picked it up and looked at it. Even in black and white the Yarn Market was instantly recognizable. The castle's towers and battlements rose from behind the trees on Castle Hill and across the street from the Yarn Market stood the Luttrell Arms with its high medieval porch.

Shocked and disbelieving, Lizzie stared at the postcard. Its appearance at this moment, hedged about with mystery and coincidence as if it were some sign or portent, knocked her off balance and it was some time before she could bring herself to turn it over, so hopeful was she that it should contain some kind of message for her. The ink was faded but Angel's writing was clear enough.

Darling Pidge,
So here we are and the cottage is sweet.
Lovely weather but it's rather a trek to the
beach for poor little Lizzie's legs. Dunster is
the most gorgeous village but – you will be
relieved to know! – not a sign of F. I haven't
given up hope, though!
Love from us both. Angel xx

There was no date, only the word 'Tuesday' scrawled across the top of the card and the postmark was blurred. Lizzie reread the message anxiously, as though by further study the words might give up some secret; the answer to her question: why the holiday in Dunster? The first lines were innocent enough; it was only the words 'not a sign of F.' that held the clue to the mystery.

Lizzie lay down again, holding the card, closing her eyes, remembering. Gently, as in that Looking-Glass world of backstage, with its silently collapsing walls and revolving staircases, her memory began to open, layer upon layer, before her inward eye. It was a long while before she stirred, rousing slowly to the sounds of evening outside the window, aware of the coolness of the shadowy room. She shivered a little, reaching a long arm for Angel's yellow silk shawl, her eyes still dreamy and unfocused.

It was strange that a part of her life once so vital could be so completely written over, hidden beneath the palimpset of subsequent experiences. F was for Felix: oh, how could she have forgotten someone she loved so much? The smell of him was in her nostrils, the feel of him beneath her fingertips which clutched the postcard. For years he was a part of their lives here in the Birdcage; joking with Pidge, bringing presents for the small Lizzie, going down to the theatre with Angel. He'd arrive at the Birdcage on Sunday evenings; Pidge would be thinking about supper whilst listening to the Palm Court Hotel orchestra on the radio. Nothing could have persuaded Lizzie to go to bed until after she'd seen him and very often she was allowed to stay up late as a special treat.

'Hello, my birds,' he'd say, holding out a bottle to Pidge, fielding Lizzie with his other arm, looking across at Angel with that tiny heart-stopping wink. 'How's life in the cage?'

Perhaps, after all, it was Felix and not Angel's

agent who had named it so? For years – or so it seemed – that one Sunday in the month was the high spot of her small existence. Lizzie frowned, drawing the shawl about her, still holding the postcard. There could be no doubt that F stood for Felix – but what had Felix Hamilton, her mother's lover, to do with Dunster? She sat up, feeling about her with her toes for her shoes. Placing the card on the table beside the brochure, she went into the kitchen to pour herself a drink and, sitting down with it at the table, she stared at the postcard as if by sheer willpower she could wrench an answer from its picture of Dunster and the faded inky message.

Closing her eyes, Lizzie groped towards the words that defined Felix: the smell of his tweed coat; the feel of his long brown fingers holding her hand; the queer sensation of an emotional stability. Crazy! For years she hadn't given him a thought whilst now, for some reason, the memories had come crowding back, green and fresh, and filling her with an unsettled longing; a need to see him again. It wasn't so odd that, back in Bristol, she should feel the presence of Pidge and Angel – even her sudden passion to find the birdcage was not unreasonable – but this desire to seek Felix out, talk to him and tie up loose ends, was extraordinary. But why Dunster?

Lizzie opened her eyes; the question continued to puzzle her. The postcard lay face upwards and, as she looked at it, suddenly the tiny cameo, that sliver of the past, slid back into her mind: Angel staring at the woman in the grocer's shop whilst she and the little boy gazed at one another. She recalled the atmosphere of tension, communicated by the sudden tightening of Angel's hand on hers and the expression of resentment on the woman's face. Her memory made another connection: Felix explaining why he couldn't be her daddy, telling her about his son with the odd name who lived in the country.

Gasping with a kind of triumphant relief Lizzie leaned back in her chair, the pieces of the puzzle clicking neatly into place. It seemed clear, now, that Angel had gone to Dunster hoping to see Felix and almost certainly against Pidge's advice: . . . *You'll be relieved to know! – not a sign of F. I haven't given up hope, though!* It was the kind of mad plan that would have appealed to Angel. Perhaps Felix had been on holiday from the office for a while with no excuse to visit Bristol: perhaps his passion had been cooling off a little. Had Angel hoped that, by appearing on his home ground, she might force his hand? Lizzie longed to know what had happened between Felix and Angel; why had he stopped coming to the Birdcage? Frustration seized her. Why, when it was too late, did she feel this passion to unearth the past? She picked up the postcard with its faded message. Were they still there, in Dunster somewhere, Felix and his son – and that woman with the bitter, resentful face?

It suddenly occurred to her that Felix, like Angel and Pidge, might be dead. In remembering the young Felix she'd forgotten that he would have grown old too. Only then did she realize how much she'd been counting on finding him again; of talking to him once more. An unexpected and inexplicable sense of despair galvanized her into action. She reached for her mobile and, peering at the page in the brochure, dialled a number.

'Hello,' she said, swallowing in a suddenly dry throat. 'I expect it's hopeless but I suppose you don't have any rooms empty at the moment? I'd like to come down to Dunster for a few days next week . . . Oh, really? Four nights? . . . No, no, not too soon at all. Monday night to Thursday night. Fine . . .'

She gave the details required by the receptionist, replaced the receiver and sat quite still; the room was full of early evening sunshine, dappled with the pattern of plane leaves, peaceful and full of memories. She half expected to see Angel come yawning from her afternoon sleep, waving to Lizzie with her crayons at the table, calling to Pidge clattering about in the kitchen.

'I need you, sweetie. Could you just hear me in that bit in Act Three? It's the scene with Orlando . . .' And Pidge, quickly drying her hands, taking the script, reading the part in a quiet, colourless voice, whilst Angel lay full-length on the sofa with her eyes closed, responding to the cues.

'I'm sure you realize,' Lizzie said aloud to them, 'that this is a wild-goose chase. Utterly crazy . . .' but her voice trembled with anticipation and she was filled with a new sense of purpose. She must decide what clothes she'd need, find the map, telephone Jim to let him know where she'd be; if she managed an early start on Monday morning she could be in Dunster in plenty of time for lunch.

In Dunster: at these words a thrill passed through her frame. With her head full of plans and hopes Lizzie rose from the table and, pausing only to pick up the postcard, hurried away to her bedroom.

**READ THE COMPLETE BOOK –
COMING IN AUGUST FROM BANTAM PRESS**